_VAC

D0921558

JAN – I – 2021

"Smith is a real find, an elegant st   imagination that's unsettling, paranoid, gruesomely funny at times, and startlingly original. He's written one of the scariest sex scenes I've ever read, but he can even make vacuuming your own house seem scary."—T.E.D. Klein, author of _Providence after Dark and Other Writings_

"In his compelling sophomore collection, Clint Smith dives deep into his characters' psyches, unearthing the histories, the mysteries driving them toward horrors visceral and cosmic. His stories make reference to the work of John Cheever, of George Orwell, and his fiction displays the same attention to style, to grace and elegance of expression, which distinguishes the writing of those writers. In Smith's work, carefully rendered portraits of daily existence open into the weird and terrifying. There are images of body horror in these pages that would not be out of place in the early films of David Cronenberg, and there are evocations of vistas immense as any in the work of Machen and Klein. With these stories, Smith solidifies and extends the gains made in his first collection, and leaves us eager for another."—John Langan, author of _Sefira and Other Betrayals_

"Smith's affect is a pendulum that swings from the classical and the mannered into his own vision of contemporary darkness; a darkness that conceals all sorts of hazards. _The Skeleton Melodies_ is a splendid collection brimming with viscerally elegant horrors."—Laird Barron, author of _Worse Angels_

"Clint Smith's engaging stories have the verve and energy of classic pulp horror, and the character depth and attention to detail that one finds in literary fiction. Very enjoyable work!"—Dan Chaon, author of _Ill Will_

"Clint Smith is a wordsmith of the weird beyond compare, a writer of fierce intelligence and originality well-versed in both contemporary and classic Horror. He uses this knowledge to fashion tales of carefully-wrought brilliance, and the end result is a shadow-stricken oeuvre that is impossible to forget."—CM Muller, author of _Hidden Folk_

"_The Skeleton Melodies_ evokes the hauntingly familiar subverted into nightmare delirium. No other writer pokes at the carcass of our mundane world to expose something malignant quivering inside quite as skillfully as Smith. Drug addicts, the apartment renter down the hall, kids poring over a stash of adult mags and worse; the resurrected flesh of old love, feral _homo indomitus,_ or even deranged cultists, these stories offer glimpses of damaged souls confronted with the impossible. While too much weird horror seems content with concluding predictably like a baleful hand thrust from that nightmare space between bed and floor, clutching vulnerable ankles in the dead of night, Smith's latest presents those talons as only the beginning. *The Skeleton Melodies* suggests these are terrors destined to deteriorate into an existential dread that may very well have no end."—Christopher Slatsky, author of *The Immeasurable Corpse of Nature*

"Witches, werewolves, and Frankenstein's Bride: Clint Smith refashions pulp motifs from the bones of the American Midwest, transposing familiar melodies to a minor key. Disorienting and devastating."—Daniel Mills, author of *Revenants* and *Moriah*

"With Clint Smith's first collection *Ghouljaw and Other Stories*, a new exciting voice emerged on the horror scene. From bizarre body horror to tales of creeping dread, it was evident that Clint was a dedicated student of the horror story. And now with Clint's new collection *The Skeleton Melodies*, he has returned as a master of the form, showing himself to one of the most important writers working today."

"Clint Smith is a master of the literature of delirium. His tales unnerve you and inconvenience you. He takes what you thought you were familiar with, like your body or your day to day life, and renders them new and strange. In an ever more uncertain reality that we find ourselves in, Clint Smith's work is almost prophetic. Let *The Skeleton Melodies* be your guidebook for these unreal times."

"Clint Smith has returned with his sophomore collection *The Skeleton Melodies*, and let me say, it is an absolute masterpiece of modern horror. These are not your amusingly spooky horror tales that you may be familiar with, these are an attack. These are a rotting human limb thrown into a dinner party. These are belladonna served in the birthday cake. Clint Smith understands that horror should never be safe. Read *The Skeleton Melodies* with caution."—Scott Dwyer, *Plutonian Press*

"With unflinching clarity and an unwavering voice, Clint Smith diagrams the locked doors, dark passages, and thin veils that separate our meager world from the myriad darknesses beneath. Haunted and harrowed, *The Skeleton Melodies* is a richly detailed anatomy of the horrors—human and otherwise—lurking just below that skin, as well as a postmortem of their ravages."—Gordon B. White, author of *As Summer's Mask Slips and Other Disruptions*

The Skeleton Melodies

The Skeleton Melodies

A Collection By

Clint Smith

Hippocampus Press

New York

Copyright © 2020 by Hippocampus Press
Works by Clint Smith © 2020 by Clint Smith
"The Profane Articulation of Truth" © 2020 by Adam Golaski.

Published by Hippocampus Press
P.O. Box 641, New York, NY 10156.
www.hippocampuspress.com

No part of this work may be reproduced in any form or by any means without the written permission of the publisher.

Cover art and design by Daniel V. Sauer, dansauerdesign.com
Hippocampus Press logo designed by Anastasia Damianakos.

First Edition
1 3 5 7 9 8 6 4 2
ISBN 978-1-61498-286-9

For Jackson and Everly: Children of the Night . . .

Contents

Introduction:
The Profane Articulation of Truth

Ms. V. was right to worry about me. She asked me, whispered her question while I waited for the rest of the class to finish an exam, "Adam, are you on drugs?" I was amused. "No," —and I told the truth. I looked down on my pot-smoking, beer-swilling peers. Maybe organized sports were lamer? Tobacco and caffeine—okay. Did that make me a hypocrite? Ms. V., the youngest teacher at St. Vincent Martyr High School—in her late twenties?—no one was kind to her. I swiped her copy of *L'Etranger* (the dark blue, 1989 Vintage International edition) from her desk—but returned it the next day. I did not apologize. Nor did she ask me to: "You read this?" she asked. "Yes"—and with great pleasure, though I did not tell her so. Henceforth, I was her favorite. She asked if I would stay after class—"I'll write you a note." She asked me why my classmates never read the assignments. How endearingly pathetic. I said, "No one cares."

My girlfriend, Mary-Anna Apple, did not like Ms. V.—Ms. V. was too earnest, looked too fantastic in a pencil skirt. I was a sophomore. Mary-Anna was a junior. I certainly didn't argue with her.

I wrote a short story called "This Is How I Was, A Killer"; it's about Adam, a high school student who decides to murder his parents, and about his girlfriend, Carolyn, who encourages him. On the eve of Christmas Eve he poisons cookie icing. In a wheelbarrow, and one at a time, he brings his parents' bodies to the reservoir, rows to the middle, weights the bodies with cinder blocks, and dumps them. On Christmas Eve the temperature plummets and the reservoir freezes hard—on Christmas Day,

9

Adam and Carolyn walk out onto the ice together and Adam in narrator mode says, "The sky was huge, like they say it is in Montana, or some one of those states," and Adam declares, "I am happy." He's happy why? Because he murdered his parents? No. He's happy because he did what Carolyn told him to do and she is with him and he believes that confirms her pleasure.

Some curious classmate must've asked about what I wrote and I must've loaned it; I'm not sure the mechanism of distribution, but distributed it was, a pile of loose-leaf pages—ultimately into the hands of parents *who didn't think it was funny*.

Had this happened after April 1999, the repercussions might've been severe; but it was '92. Ms. V. was summoned to the main office where she spoke on my behalf. She convinced a guidance counselor, the principal (a nun!), and the aforementioned humorless parents that I was a healthy, normal boy, who'd written a short story in the tradition of the American gothic, as practiced by Edgar Allan Poe and Flannery O'Conner—"He is in fact," she said, "my best pupil." My locker was searched and I was exonerated.

Mary-Anna wanted to murder *somebody*.

The reason Satan eternally noshes Judas, Brutus, and Cassius (and not, say, Caligula) is they *are* and they *represent* betrayers. Like Satan itself, they went against Christ. Or, for us nonbelievers, they hated who they were and pretended to be *other*. A friend. Popular. Good.

Many of Smith's *Melodies* are about school or school-like regret. Bungled sex, bungled romance. The failure to be who you are when it matters most or the moment you realize that what you thought was true is not. What masks we wear. That is to say, our youthful betrayals and the guilt that trails those betrayals—thirty pieces of silver. Smith writes those moments with embarrassing honesty.

I'm reluctant to point out stories in Smith's collection that epitomize that honesty—you'll find them, you'll "know what I mean"—but: "Lisa's Pieces," "By Goats Be Guided," "Her

Laugh," "Fiending Apophenia," and "Haunt Me Still"—and not just those stories. But, if you read collections out of order, a disgraceful behavior I do not mean to encourage, you might start with any of those. If, instead, you read *Melodies* as ordered, you'll appreciate how Smith bookends his collection with such stories. In "Haunt Me Still," the narrator "staggered backward… from the profane articulation of truth…." That phrase, *the profane articulation of truth*—horror as heart-felt soul-search come too late.

Smith writes realism-horror. What happens that's supernatural (or *may be* supernatural—it isn't always clear) happens in the world. Possibly in the Midwest, someplace drearily, wonderfully American-ordinary. By the railroad tracks, on a school bus near corn fields, at a rented beach house during Discovery Channel's *Shark Week*, in abandoned middle and high schools. Horror as all the guilt you rightfully carry.

As I read Smith's *Melodies*, I thought about Mary-Anna and Ms. V.—high school. There will always be teenagers who want to kill for no other reason than it's a thing to do. Mary-Anna was cosmopolitan and, as my classmates would've said, "wicked smaht." She showed me everything. She graduated and attended a lesser Ivy. We were ostensibly still together but by then I bored her and she terrified me; her departure for Rhode Island was a relief. Ms. V. did not teach at St. Vincent Martyr High School after my sophomore year. If you ask my fellow alums, they won't remember her.

What happened to Ms. V.? Are the memories *The Skeleton Melodies* conjured good memories? Yes. And no.

—ADAM GOLASKI

The Skeleton Melodies

"Even in the darkness, I know where to find them, and they in their turn can find me."

—JOHN CONNOLLY, *Every Dead Thing*

"He looked past the others . . . into the remembered darkness."

—T. E. D. KLEIN, *The Ceremonies*

"A further objection presents itself. To say that we descend in order to lose our way, or in order to have before us the perpetual possibility of losing our way, implies that our lives aboveground are simple, orderly, and calm. This is certainly not the case. Although ours is a relatively quiet town, we suffer disease, disappointment, and death as all men and women do, and if we choose to descend into our passageways and wander the branching paths, who dares to say what passion draws us into our dark?"

—STEVEN MILLHAUSER, "Beneath the Cellars of Our Town"

Lisa's Pieces

"Science, like love, has her little surprises."
—Dr. Pretorius, *Bride of Frankenstein* (1935)

*Astral kaleidoscope . . . orbits stitch themselves into silver sutures . . .
constellations animate . . . streaks of stars shift into a luminous bruise
. . . tonguelessness . . . an eye of eons . . . an I of eons . . .*

*

Life of the party, thought Lew. Colin's still the life of the party.

Lew watched his old friend from across the gymnasium for a
few minutes before snagging Colin's attention. The crowd shifted erratically, clusters coalescing with clusters. Sure, maybe a
twenty-year class reunion was supposed to be a big deal; but
some of his former classmates were acting as if it were the Os-
cars. He'd never made the effort to connect with these people.
No wonder people drifted by, some occasionally giving a nod, a
consoling smile. Rumors, he thought. Word's gotten around
that a deadbeat's in their midst.

Colin—firmly established as a respected and well-known
physician in the state and throughout the Midwest—began
breaking from the human horseshoe. It was impossible to hear
what he was saying under the thump of mid-'90s hip-hop, but
he was clearly conducting a mea culpa for cutting out.

Colin looked practically the same, his features sustained.
Older, more mature, sure—his skin in sequence with his age.
He'd taken to slicking back his black hair. And while Colin (so
far as Lew knew) had never played a sport in his life, he maintained the sinewy build of a swimmer or rower—the aesthete of
the elite.

17

Lew clenched his jaw as Colin approached, his old friend leaning in toward the side of his face. "Tonight, if for nothing else, I thank you for saving me from these hideous people," Colin said, lifting his drink, a solo cheers.

Lew didn't really know what to expect after receiving Colin's invitation. (Lew had, no surprise, never received a formal invitation from the reunion committee.) Pings from Colin's unexpected emails from months before still resonated: neutral ground . . . developments during her consultations . . . answers. Lisa.

Colin glanced over the crowd while Lew stared at the side of the other man's pale face. His straight black hair glistened, the inky strands plucked by light. The physician said, "You know, you'll want to look as if you're having a good time in case this evening turns sour. Can I get you a drink?"

"Nah," said Lew, "rather keep my skull clear. Besides, I didn't come here to stage some sort of alibi." Now he grinned, trying to play along for whoever may be observing. "You gave me your word—"

Colin raised a palm, a bloodless blade of a thing. "And I promise you nothing has changed."

With their eyes locked, Lew considered ordering a drink for the simple utility of smashing a highball glass against the side of Colin's model-smooth face.

Lew shook his head, scanning the crowd. He caught sight of someone familiar. For a long sequence, a memory gained traction and clarity. "You see that gal over there?" Lew jutted his chin, indicating the woman across the gymnasium who was in the middle of a happy chat with several classmates.

Colin cocked his head. Bored. "Perhaps."

"Katie Montgomery," said Lew, pivoting so that both men were standing shoulder to shoulder as they observed the woman. Lew: "She got knocked up our junior year."

Colin pouted a lower lip before giving an aha inhale. "Oh, yes. She looks elegant."

"Yeah," said Lew, trying his best to allow an ironic tone to rise above a catchy, twenty-year-old track from Dr. Dre. "Yeah, I remember the whole thing. Pretty big deal in town. People weren't used to that sort of thing." Lew gazed at Katie. A wedding ring twinkled—her husband, presumably, stood just behind her, smiling, giving her some polite distance as she held her phone for the semicircle audience, their smiling faces illuminated by that blue halo. Maybe photos of kids, family. Something she was proud of. Lew took a step closer to Colin, their bodies flush. "I remember the day word started spreading through school. By lunchtime she had no chance of keeping it quiet." Lew noticed Colin pause with his drink just below his lips. "We were in botany, I think—no, physics." He gave a sad, tight exhale through his nose, a regrettable spasm, the first bar of a chuckle. "Of course I ended up failing that class." Lew tilted. "Do you remember what you said to her?"

Colin blinked and proceeded to take a smooth pull from his glass before producing a broad smile, taking in the room. "I'm certain I don't know what you're talking about."

Lew didn't believe him nor doubt him—Dr. Colin Clevenger was a portrait of self-righteousness, but his self-centeredness would likely result in vast forgetfulness. "You turned around in your seat," said Lew, "and whispered, 'You know, if you're really preoccupied by this whole fetus issue, there are plenty of amazing medical markets eager to harvest organs.'"

Music droned. Colin eventually said, "For someone who can't seem to establish a consistent pattern in their own life, you certainly have evolved a striking memory."

Lew opened his mouth just as a tall figure cut in between them—quite literally pressing himself between the two. Lew blinked and took a step back, recognizing the man immediately, which was no small thing considering how poorly he'd aged.

William Prather took a hefty slug from his beer before wiping his lower lip with a crooked thumb, shifting his wild eyes to Lew for a moment. Prather said, "You kids getting along?"

"Certainly," said Colin, cheerful.

Odd: Prather had graduated a few years ahead of them. Lew's smile played the requisitely genial part, as was his tone when he said, "What the hell are you doing here, Billy? This is for the class of '96."

As though he'd been answering the question all evening, Prather said, "Invitation said people could bring a date. So I'm Colin's date, right, pal?"

Colin raised an eyebrow and gave a weary inhale—apparently an old joke at this point.

Lew assessed Prather: the older fellow towered over them. Billy Prather had been a basketball star, a genius in the classroom. Scholarships to one of the state's universities where he'd gone on to secure a professorship. He now looked like a seamy, dead-hour fixture at a truck stop: long, greasy-gray hair accented his grayish complexion, like jaundice gone sooty. His eyes were set above dark, sagging scallops. There was an unusual, layered odor about the man—aftershave masking hearty body odor, the BO cloaking something astringent.

"You know, Colin," said Prather, "now that our old pal's here, we should probably get going."

Colin flicked a wrist, the silver flash of a watchband. He pursed his lips and nodded once, leaning closer to Prather and quickly murmuring something. Then, over to Lew, he said, "I hope we can start anew tonight, Lewis."

Music pulsed. Lew took a deep breath and said, "I just want to know where she is, Colin . . . I just want to know where you took her body."

Colin and Prather ticked a look at each other before the physician turned and reinserted himself to the crowd, performing miniature goodbye speeches.

And then Prather's meaty mitt was on Lew's shoulder. "What do you say we go ahead and make our exit?" Prather drained his beer and, as they passed, placed it on a table occupied by chat-chirping classmates. Prather said, "Party's dead anyway."

*

Lew—after being guided by Prather through a dark cafeteria—pushed through a nondescript side door near a modest loading dock. "Well," said Prather with what was clearly meant to be a light-hearted tone, "our old boy hasn't changed much." The door closed behind them, returning cricket-trill peace to the night. A variety of flying insects made either kamikaze dives or graceful orbits around a nearby sodium vapor light.

"How many of us really do change, though?" Lew said.

With a pitying expression, the tall professor-cum-collaborator gave Lew a grave appraisal. "How true." Prather's hands shot out and grabbed Lew by the collar, swinging him around against the brick wall. Prather's sharp nose nearly brushed Lew's forehead. "Don't—like much that transpired over the past few years—take this personal."

Prather began ungently patting down Lew's body, scouring under his arms, between his legs, stopping short when his hand landed on the object tucked into the waistband along Lew's lower back. Prather smiled, a lecherous thing he'd likely used during lecture-hall climaxes at the university before being fired three years earlier (Lew'd tried to research Colin and his associate as best he could before tonight's rendezvous). "It's safe to say you have some reticence in trusting us." Prather withdrew a stun-gun from Lew's waistband, which he tested, the brilliant blue spark chattering between silver nodes. His smile stretched even further. "Exquisite."

Lew clenched his teeth, feebly trying to arrange a combination of movements that might result in overtaking the enormous man. *Got to go for . . .*

As if picking up on it, Prather suddenly dropped to a squat. "Let's see what other goodies you have here." Prather slid his hands around Lew's calves, making no scene about removing the diver's knife strapped to his lower leg. Prather stood, a weapon in each hand. "You can keep the sheath," said Prather.

Despite himself, Lew shook his head and tried to smirk. *How could I have thought it would be this easy?* "I'll pass," he said. "I'll just find something else to kill Colin with."

"You may renege after we demonstrate what we are capable of," said Prather.

Lew sniffed. "I know what you two are capable of."

Prather scoured Lew's face for a moment before stowing the stun-gun in his own back pocket, which remained rigidly dangling by his thigh. After developing a moment of dramatic silence, Prather took a pace backward and slowly slid his hand into his jacket pocket. Lew girded himself for the violent act that was about to end his life. Instead of withdrawing a weapon, Prather pulled out a slim, liquid-filled glass vial, a little larger than a track-and-field baton. Within the clear liquid was an object—black, slightly curved. Prather, still grinning, offered the tube to Lew. "Go ahead," he said. "Colin said you may require some reassurance."

After a pause, Lew carefully accepted the device, twitching a frown as he examined it. The black segment appeared to be made of carbonized bone; but before Lew could speak, thin filaments emerged from one end of the slender thing, delicate fibers extending lazily from where the marrow would be. To Lew it called to mind the soft, appendage tissue of a cephalopodic nautiloid.

"Crude, I know; but I constructed it from my own material." Prather unceremoniously tugged up his dress shirt, displaying a torso that was crisscrossed with incisions in varying, tinted stages of healing, all bearing a network of thick sutures. Among other failings, Lew was no scientist or philosopher, but he put the pieces together. "Just as God created woman from Adam's rib, I too have created life from my own earthly toolkit."

Lew stared at the thing in the cylinder, its purple, fragile-looking fibers drifting in the fluid. The long, black rib bone clinked against glass in the slim space. "Ever occur to you that you may have taken the Old Testament too literally?"

"On many occasions, my boy," said Prather. "But there are useful riddles in that heathen playbook. I have made several attempts—with little success, it pains me to admit—to reattach these newly animated specimens."

Walking now, Prather escorted Lew to the far side of the primary parking lot where a black Suburban idled with its parking lights on. Colin was in the passenger seat, his downturned face underlit by the glow of his cell phone. Lew's attention then turned to the large, single-axle trailer attached to the SUV's hitch. The wood-slatted trailer was walled by low, crosshatched railings. Nodding toward the trailer, Lew said, "Planning on doing some yard work?"

"Perhaps just some pruning." He flicked the knife like a conductor's baton. "Won't you kindly get your ass in the vehicle?"

Prather shut the door and Colin rolled down the passenger window, accepting the two weapons with no surprise or apprehension. Prather mumbled something that Lew didn't catch before the man rounded to the driver's side and got in, immediately twisting on the headlights and notching the SUV into gear. Lew glanced to his side. A large, tactical-style duffel bag lay on the seat next to him.

"It's a shame you couldn't have been more trusting of our efforts this evening," said Colin. "Or over the past several years, for that matter."

"I wouldn't trust you under any circumstances." Lew adjusted in his seat. "I've grown to think of you two charlatans as the pair of snakes on the caduceus."

Prather laughed. *"Be ye therefore wise as serpents and harmless as doves."*

"Stop it, William," said Colin. Though he sounded exhausted, there were also threads of heat. "You're not helping anything." Prather cleared his throat and returned his eyes to the road.

"Couldn't you have found someone else to experiment on?" said Lew.

Colin shook his head—a point had been missed. "Of *course*. But you still seem to disregard *your* part in all this."

"*My* part?" Lew leaned forward, eyes fixed on the side of Colin's face. "The last phone call I received from Lisa, she was hysterical—you remember? The night you tried to—"

"A misunderstanding," he said evenly. "She was my patient."

"You're fucking lying," said Lew. "She said you'd tricked her into some sort of radical treatment—promised her some new therapy that might help. Instead you tried drugging her and—"

"At worst . . . a misinterpretation."

Lew sat back slowly, idly looking out the window. Outside, contemporary housing additions eventually spread further apart, allowing for the emergence of fields and dark farms. And now each turn, each passing batch of crooked woods, whittled for Lew a sharper certainty of their destination.

Colin took a deep breath and casually twisted around to face Lew. "She was very sick, Lewis."

"Yes, *doctor*—cancer means fucking *sick*."

"We don't know if it was cancer that killed her."

Lew barked a laugh. "You . . . are . . . deranged, Colin."

Prather interrupted with disinterested intonation: "Signs of cancer didn't begin manifesting until you abandoned her."

Colin raised his voice. *"Please keep driving."*

It was dawning on Lew now; he brought his fingers to his temple, blinked as the pieces shifted. This was not some negotiation where he would, somehow, turn the tables on these two. "You think I made her sick?"

"We *know* you did," said Colin. "Your . . . withdrawal from the relationship was a catalyst in a chain of events, what we have determined to be an ontological disruption that led to physiological deterioration."

"Jesus, you sound so crazy."

Prather cut in again. "What then of the specimen?"

"Just because you have a squid stuffed into a black piece of bone isn't proof you've performed some miracle. It could be a trick." Lew swept his hand wide. "This could all be tricks."

Colin turned back to face the windshield. After a few beats he said, "Please look in the bag." The SUV bounced over a rough patch. By silent accommodation, Prather turned on the interior lights.

The duffel bag. Lew felt his heart tick up a bit, his hands hovering over the black fabric. "Go ahead," said Prather, "take a peek."

Lew unzipped the bag. Glass glinted, liquid sloshed. A canister, similar to the one containing the rib-squid. But this one was longer. Shadows inside the bag prevented a full reveal, though Lew didn't need much light. He recognized the delicate contours. Faint and fiber-thin lines of blue veins coursed just beneath the waxen skin.

Lisa's slender left arm—severed cleanly at the shoulder—drifted in the clear embalming liquid. How many mornings had that arm been stretched over his chest as they lay lazily coiled in bed?

The ring was still there, sparkling in the weak light. When Colin and Prather had violated her grave—an unsolved exhumation the very evening of the burial, a mystery that made statewide headlines—they'd been sure to keep her ring. Lew was surprised her family allowed her to be buried with it. He couldn't have thanked them. He was not welcome at the funeral.

Looking at the ring now, a thin strip of him was grateful to the pair of grave-robbers for this gesture of preservation.

Lew took a sharp swipe at his eyes to eliminate the blur, his attention snapping toward Colin.

Doctor Colin Clevenger—Lew's childhood chum, teenage foil, adulthood tormentor—was angled around, dark eyes locked with Lew, a sleek gun now aimed at his chest.

Then something dawned on Lew—something he'd just tuned in to: a gentle sloshing sound coming from the rear of the vehicle. He twisted partway to see the dark mounds. Four more duffel bags, along with unidentifiable equipment.

They were getting close.

"You have many questions, all of which I'm willing to answer." Lew's chest rose and fell as he gazed at the slender limb. "We are going to bring her back," said Colin. "You are the missing instrument."

*

A gray, mottled punch of light emerges in pitch, lending some sense of dimension, direction. The perturbating glow swells as decades shift, deteriorate and coalesce into mere seconds . . .

*

Deacon's Creek High School—the old one of our characters' era, not the new one, the one that had been nonchalantly abandoned by the township when contracts were finalized for a more contemporary facility—had been scheduled to be razed decades earlier. Now it resided behind a high, chain-link screen braided with ivy and weeds.

With the cloud-webbed moon as some fixed lantern in the distance—blackening dilapidated details—the school was cut into sharp relief; and with the pointed faux-cupola (intended, we suppose, perhaps even in desperation, to venerate some bygone era of education) along with the sloping, ragged-open maw where the roof had collapsed directly over the gymnasium, the illusion was that of an upturned face, the night mercifully hiding its neglected decay.

They used an old service trail skirting the school.

Walls of corn flashed by in the SUV's headlights—green-and-black, slash-shadows of the switchblade stalks.

Prather got out of the vehicle and approached a wide gate with a rusted padlock. A NO TRESPASSING sign hung crooked. Again, Lew's mental query was picked up by Colin, who had now turned away from his former friend. "We have done a fair amount of work here," said Colin, "but have been more discreet than bringing in an actual vehicle."

If there is going to be any peace for Lisa, Lew reminded himself, *I need to see this thing through.*

Colin: "It is foreign for me to discuss, but I hope you realize that Lisa loved you tremendously."

Lew glanced at Colin's gun: "I could do without your demented wisdoms."

Up ahead, Prather raised a pair of bolt cutters and snapped through a lock.

"Lisa was extraordinarily ill when she came to me," said Colin. "Desperate, she'd confessed." He chuckled. "I wasn't sure I was to take that as a compliment." Lew was half listening, half tinkering. "Lisa explained that she'd discovered the cancer after one of her subsequent visits to her doctor. This would have been in the wake of your original loss, yes?"

Lew kept his eyes straight ahead, watching Prather, who appeared nearly done.

"Humans, in their couplings, try to play god too, in so many ways. Yet they tend to view their little experiments as tragedies instead of pragmatic progress. People like you should be commended for dabbling in both creation and confronting the truths of death."

Lew was not looking at Colin. "At what point are you going to apologize for fucking up and accidentally killing her?"

Colin blurted a small laugh. "I'm not responsible for ending her cycle."

"Desecrating her grave?"

"A minor triviality," said Colin. "Having no success in galvanizing life as a whole, we attempted to revitalize segments. Even a genius like Prather sometimes needs to work in baby steps."

On cue, Prather returned to the driver's side. He pulled the SUV into the overgrown courtyard directly in front of the dead school. Colin shifted, exiting the vehicle and opening the side door for Lew. "Come now, old friend. There is one final piece."

The main entrance to the former Deacon's Creek High School was (like the windows and dormers above) boarded up by wide planks of plywood. A nearby section had been (by these two, presumably, or perhaps kids) camouflaged with a separate section of plywood—a knobless dummydoor set on rudimentary hinges. Colin clicked on a flashlight.

Prather was now at the rear of the Suburban, occupying himself with some head-down task at the trailer.

Inside the school, the floor was strewn with assorted debris—some clearly left by trespassers, some a result of the old facility crumbling by degrees. Here and there, sconces (glass broken, of course) hung askew.

"Obviously they've yet to auction and scrap the salvageable items," said Colin. "This whole place is scheduled for demolition next spring, which is to say that some philistine contractors from town will simply backhoe the hell out of it until it's all unrecognizable rubble." With his flashlight trained before him, he beckoned Lew to follow. "Our first breakthrough occurred when Prather and I noticed Lisa looking at a picture of you on her cell phone in the exam room before an evaluation. As I've alluded, her coming to me was more of a last-ditch effort than genuine assistance. This way." Colin motioned with the dust-blurred beam of the flashlight toward a stairwell leading to the upper level. Plaster and glass crunched underfoot as the two ascended.

"Either way, she was in bad shape when she'd initially approached us. The idea, she'd said, was to get better, so that when you came back from your 'altruistic' tour to Michigan, you'd finally be willing to support and care for her."

Lew nearly staggered, slowing enough for Colin to pause as well. "What?" blurted Colin with a mocking laugh. "You didn't think that Lisa was going to keep all details locked away in some vault known only to you two?" Colin made a single *tsk* sound (*How unfortunate!*) with his tongue. "I'm sure you'll configure a variety of ways to make yourself appear innocent; but the fact is that you abandoned her so that you could—how did she put it— go play Don Quixote."

Lew licked his lips. "It wasn't like that. I had no money, I—"

"Yes, yes, we know—no money to support a family. But it was just a miscarriage, Lewis. Many people have experienced them. Many common couples have survived worse.

"No, it wasn't the abandonment that crushed her. It was the dalliances on these meagerly funded trips—these . . . what were they called? . . . Habitat for Humanity trips—that extinguished her hope for you—for *the two* of you."

A sick quiver seized Lew—that Lisa's last assumption of him was that he'd been unfaithful.

Lew could rush him right now, he realized, shove him over the top rail of the stairwell.

"Come now," said Colin, "this is simple reciprocity. After all, aren't the secrets she shared with you twenty years ago what informed you of my true nature?"

Colin's *true nature*. Even the phrase had never occurred to Lew back then. It had been simpler, more innocent than that. Colin had been his friend. His only friend.

It was a mundane, mid-teen scenario. Still, it served as the fulcrum of their divergent, brotherly bifurcation. There had been five of them: Lew (clumsy), Colin (clever), Lisa (sophisticated), Monica (the infidel), and Heather (the mouse). They'd been friends since elementary school, insulating one another as they progressed through the unforgiving social strata of middle school and high school—the four of them a pentagram of pubescent protection. Though Colin and Lisa were the only two who'd developed a romantic relationship.

One summer Saturday night, the plan had been to see a movie, but as the day drew nearer to evening, one member after another began dropping out: Monica had been invited to a party somewhere, Heather's parents thought the movie would be too intense, and Colin had made some excuse about some distracting tasks that required his undivided attention. "Mom and Dad are having dinner at the club," Colin had said. "I have to hold the castle down while they're gone." Lew had tried coaxing to come along, but it was a dead end. Colin listed a number of chores, including ministering to his family's Golden Retriever, which had peculiarly fallen ill. "No worries, pal—I can occupy my time. Have fun . . . take care of Lisa for me."

And so they met at the theater—*Jurassic Park*—and it wasn't until Lisa sat down next to him that Lew felt the first pulse of guilt. Nothing happened. The two teens, surrounded by high walls of stuttering shadows, simply sat and enjoyed the film, both facing the same glowing panel, surrounded by high walls of blackness. Patches of dark depth interrupted by blooming hues of gray and blue—two innocent kids floating through space.

But nothing was the same. Lisa began growing sullen when Colin was present. As it happened, their little group grew apart after that initial drift. Eventually, Lisa just started showing up at Lew's locker after school.

At the top of the stairwell, Colin's voice shook Lew. "Did you know that, after Lisa found out that I wasn't interested in seeing the silly movie, she'd convinced the other girls to cancel?"

"A lie," said Lew. "Lisa wasn't like that."

"Oh, I assure you she was a lot of ways."

"She said you were a pervert . . . that you were sick," said Lew. "She told me about the things you wanted to do to her back then—the things you made her do to *you*."

Colin scoffed. "Nothing more than adolescent experimentation."

Lew shook his head. "You're wrong. You took things too far." *You still do.*

The two stepped onto the second-floor landing, walking over doors that had been pulled off their hinges. Things were, somehow, not as bad up here. As if cognitively catching that, Colin said, "It appears that even the vandals in Deacon's Creek merely had a first-floor aptitude. Or they're scared of *monsters*." He laughed, his shadow long on the wall. "What we discovered during Lisa's treatments was a particular response to the idea of *place*. We eventually surmised that there was a connection between a trinity of locus, physicality, and—more bafflingly—an abstract component: you may call it love, but we've made other determinations." Colin stared at Lew. "Do you remember Lisa's locker number from your senior year?"

Of course he did. They'd conjured mediocre dreams there—solved insipid, small-town problems—sketched an escape plan. "Not sure," said Lew.

"Well, you're going to need to think fast because we—*you*—don't have much time." Colin offered Lew the flashlight with one hand while the other bobbed the gun.

Lew swiped the light from Colin's hand. The two started down the hall, Lew in the lead, both rounding a corner and veering to the left. For a split instant, Lew was struck with a flashback overlay—a vision of the past double-exposed over the ruined, locker-lined walls. The lockers had, twenty years before, been a verdant green. Now: faded, crawling with puffy patches of rust. Lew was already breathing heavily, but began hissing through his nose as his heart knocked into higher gear.

The locks had been disabled, but a shiny padlock rested over the dirty dial on this one. Colin rattled off the combination. *Cute,* thought Lew—*he's set it to Lisa's old combo from high school.* Lew clutched hold of the imposing device, requisitely spinning in the dial and tugging down. The door yawned open.

Another liquid-filled cylinder. Lew sagged to a knee, the unsteady flashlight beam falling over Lisa's severed head, her dark hair nested at the base of her throat. Her eyes and lips were closed.

Lew's first reflex was to reach out and cradle her. Instead, Lew clenched his fists, shuddered, preparing to reel around, preparing for the flash of gunfire.

And then Lisa opened her eyes.

*

The trailer Prather had been hauling—with its high sides of chain-link barriers—was now arranged like a giant operating table. The wooden boards had been coated with some liquid substance and gleamed in the Suburban's headlights (Prather had disconnected and repositioned the SUV); coils of cables and looped wires poured from beneath the vehicle's open hood, as though the engine had been disemboweled. Four more cylinders stood on the wood-slatted trailer, containing the remaining pieces of Lisa.

Lew cradled the cylinder containing Lisa's head as if it were an infant.

"You see," Colin continued—he'd been rambling as they wound their way down from the second story of the school, "we understood then that the last remaining receptor had to be you. It is this idea of . . . love, I suppose you'd term it, that provided Lisa with something to cling to. Locus, of course, is significant, which—well, you see here, explains our somewhat rudimentary set-up."

As Lew and Colin approached, Prather donned a pair of long-cuffed welding gloves and began unscrewing the tops of the cylinders. Lew watched as the two men worked monosyllabically, Prather and Colin arranging Lisa's body parts on the bed of the trailer. Lew watched as Prather, with clinical disconnection, eased Lisa's liquid-slick torso into position along with the rest of her limbs, Dr. Clevenger swiftly applying some thick, dark substance to the exposed interior of each amputation. The smell of ammonia was very strong. Colin looked up quickly, supplying Lew with a *forgive-me* pout.

"Meat glue," he said, hefting the can of viscous gel. "Well, a variation of my own making. At its base is the enzyme transglutaminase, which fosters the formation of isopeptide bonds between amines and acyl groups along protein chains."

Colin set down the container and stalked over, slowly extending his arms. *Visiting hours are over . . . time to hand her over.* Lew, after several slices of time, passed the cylinder into Colin's arms, who accepted it with godfather gentility. He actually smiled and looked directly at Lew. *We have so much to be proud of.*

Colin returned to the trailer-bed. The two collaborators swiftly finalized the arrangement. Colin then spun and went to the back of the vehicle, retrieving a white bundle and returning to the body, wrapping the pale cadaver with a brilliantly white sheet, afterwards turning to address Lew. "We're not savages." Colin connected a pair of silver clamps near the base of her neck. Thin wires were webbed over Lisa's body. "We would not allow such a sacred evening to culminate in profanity."

Prather stood by the front of the vehicle, its hood propped open and a network of wires clamped to chain-link sides of the trailer.

Colin scanned his open-air operating room, glanced at Lew, then addressed Prather. "Begin," said the doctor.

Prather nodded, opening the driver's side door and reaching in; he twisted the key and the engine roared to life. Sparks flew across the trailer, dying down as Colin began calibrating several small generator-like devices.

Lisa's corpse writhed, but after several moments remained still.

Colin took several paces backward and called to Prather. "A little more now, William."

The professor revved the engine, a guttural hum. "Enough." Prather obeyed and the engine idled.

Without taking his gaze away from the trailer-operating-table, but moving closer to Lew, Colin said, "On the day of our breakthrough, I asked her to tell some of her cherished memories. She began discussing school, the days you had together before college. This place—the town, the land—was special to her.

"Most of our methods are, of course, unpalatable for conventional sensibilities. We finally became saturated with the arcane, the dismissed." Colin looked over at Lew. "Mystics, occultists, have asserted some sort of vital energy that conventional science has never recognized—like Mesmer's animal magnetism. Or Reich's orgone energy—Prather and I began re-evaluating bions in living matter. When bions begin to degenerate, the result is what Reich called T-bacilli—what he proffered as a cause for cancer."

Colin stopped, silently considering something. "I'm not explaining this because I want to play pedagogue," he said. There was something new—something old—in Colin's aspect. "I'm providing these details out of respect, because I know you understand them. We were friends once. That is significant no matter what has occurred in the interim."

Lisa's body shuddered, rattling the wooden slats. Colin

checked his watch, withdrew a slim, black case from his coat, and moved to the trailer. "Stop!" he called out, and Prather cut the engine, rushing around to meet Colin, who quickly unzipped the case and took out two large syringes, passing one to Prather.

Without speaking, the men simultaneously inserted the syringes—Prather directly into the center of Lisa's chest, Colin sliding the needle in the lower scallop of an eye socket.

Finished, both men edged away as though the corpse were venomous. There was no dramatic thrashing, no violent gasping. Lisa simply, slowly sat up.

The white, tangle-swaddled sheet clung to her skin. Her long hair hung down, cleaved on either side of her marble-embalmed face.

Lew attempted to take a step forward, but Colin halted his momentum by calling out, *"Lisa . . . Lisa Motley."* Lisa's body appeared to register the words, but instead of turning to face Colin, she slowly twisted her head in the opposite direction. Toward Lew.

Lisa, on jittery limbs, stepped down from the trailer, the wires pulling free from the flesh. Details, now, were swift and striking. Lew noticed a few drops of liquid hanging at the tips of her wet hair. The sheet hung on her in uneven swaths—a ghastly statue, a vein-rivered Venus from some lurid Louvre.

"Step toward her, Lewis," Colin said.

Lew imagined embracing her again, trying to do whatever it took—even if it meant acquiescing to this pair of psychopaths—to bring her *back*. He wanted her to know he was here, for her to dumbly mumble his name . . . he wanted to say he was sorry. For violating their compact.

Again Colin spoke, this time shouting, *"Step toward her, Lewis—you need to be in closer proximity!"*

Lew took her in—*her cataract-hazed eyes . . . skin textured like some lake-dredged organism*—and took a step back. "No."

Colin, at first looked hurt. "Do it now, Lewis."

Colin murmured something and then Prather was moving,

rounding the back of the trailer with a no-bullshit sort of limping efficiency.

Lew shifted one way, reset, saw the huge syringe in the tall man's hand. As Prather closed in, Lew clenched tighter on the bulky padlock from Lisa's locker. After the initial shock of seeing her preserved head in that rusty compartment, he'd thought that Colin would make him drop the heavy device. Instead, Lew had smuggled it into his pocket. Now he slid his middle finger through the metal shackle and palmed the casing. And then as Prather rose up in front of him, syringe slashing up over his shoulder, Lew parry-ducked, thrusting his fist toward Prather's lower abdomen, wildly aiming the metal shackle—like a single-fingered brass knuckle—for the patch of scarred skin containing the webbing of sutures.

The punch paid off more than Lew had expected. His hand tore into the man with a meaty-moist gasp. Lew twisted, stuck up to his forearm just under the man's ribs.

Prather didn't scream, merely looked down at the situation with a disgusted sort of interest. But his calculus came quickly, his eyes went wide and fixed on Lew. Teeth clenched, Lew lifted his boot, placed it on Prather's hip and kicked back, his arm tearing free along with a spill of dark, Nyquil-colored fluid.

Prather staggered but remained on his feet, continuing to scowl down at his midsection as if it were a particularly perplexing puzzle. Lew was cautious to keep the tall man's body between himself and Colin, who had the gun out, half raised in their direction.

Prather was beginning to snap out of it, face rising to concentrate on Lew, who—spotting the gun in the shoulder holster inside the tall man's jacket—now rushed forward with a growl, shoving the man backward toward the trailer, swiping the gun from Prather's holster just as Lew thrust him against the trailer bed. A charged clacking came from the chains and wooden slats—Prather's body contorted, began to steam. Miniature, silver-blue lighting strikes emerged, snapping and forking around his body. Professor Prather had become a child's plasma globe without its glass casing.

Colin took one haphazard shot at Lew, grazing him along the bicep.

A silver device resembling a stainless steel EpiPen emerged in Colin's hand. Lisa's sheet-coiled arms began to rise, as if anticipating an embrace. With Lisa's arms open, Colin didn't hesitate, stabbing the silver syringe into her sternum. Lisa lost no momentum as she leaned into the doctor, one hand grabbing Colin by the throat, the other clutching hold of the front of his belt, swiftly lifting him off the ground. Lew watched Colin's reaction, his expression reflecting a last-second miscalculation: *this wasn't supposed to happen.*

Lisa whirled—a flash of pale flesh and ghostly shroud—and flung Colin into the back of the trailer. Slender forks of electricity greedily latched themselves onto Colin's body as he crumpled to the wooden slats. Colin's howls were eclipsed by buzzing tides of electric clacking. Eventually, screaming ceased all together.

Lew looked at Lisa, who was staring at him, arms limp at her sides. Her sheet hung on her frame with a discordant elegance. Lew began walking toward her, unable to shake the notion that he would have one day walked toward her as she was wearing a white gown. With a movement both lithe and lumbering, Lisa started toward Lew.

An even more distant and disconnected sound began to swell in a portion of his mind pleading just to sink into full, physiological shock. With echo-subtle detachment, Lew conjured a short segment of Pachelbel's Canon in D, the burrowing anthem of a bride's entrance.

Though Colin's trick of fusing her limbs was remarkable, the amputation wounds around her arms and neck were visible, lividly pronounced.

From time to time, a discharge of electricity erupted from the trailer, creating a strobe effect. Closer now, Lew saw that Lisa's teeth were blackened. Her lips twitched in what may have been an effort to smile. In sync with his drumming heart, a diaphanous, double-exposed overlay pulsed over Lisa like a phantomic membrane: beat—*corpse*—beat—*breathtaking bride*. Colin's silver EpiPen device, still stuck in her sternum, doubled as a stand-in bouquet.

She was there in front of him now, film-fogged eyes locked on him. Sparks showered down behind her like an electric weeping willow.

"I . . . love you . . . Lisa," he said, finger stiff against the trigger. He raised his hands, one going to caress her cheek, the other raising with the gun.

With viper-strike swiftness, Lisa's arm shot out—black-nailed hand clasping Lew securely around the throat.

Her expression remained fixed, passive. Lew's eyes were wince-slitted as he slowly raised the weapon to her chest; but as he did so, Lisa lifted him off the ground with renewed strength.

Lew gasped feebly. The world blurred and his heart began to settle, one of the beats held and he saw Lisa as she *should* be. Lew lowered the gun, eyelids fluttering. Lisa, somehow, conjured up one more thrust, inching him higher.

In some movie, maybe, Lew had attached himself to the cliché that people saw stars before they blacked out, before they suffocated. As blackness, like an uneven frame of charcoal vapor, closed in on the fringes of his vision, Lew blinked up at the mercury pulses of stars between the ragged patches of clouds. The stars detached from their pinprick positions and began swirling, spiraling—flecks of silver caught in a coaxing wind. Even as darkness overtook him, the sailing stars remained, grew brilliant. Lew fumbled consciousness and he dropped the gun. Dropped everything. This senseless tug-of-war was over.

Lew stopped fighting and let go.

Let Lisa take control . . .

*

The soundless respiration of the black vacuum . . . In the darkness, I take his hand, which is no hand at all, and we become the black fabric between stars, connected in a hazy chain that stretches into infinite nothing, and rest easy in this empty expanse . . . because we belong dead.

The Undertow,
and They That Dwell Therein

Gwen struggled from slumber—her eyelids fluttering, finally parting to take in the early morning murk, the bleed edging the curtains and touching the sand-colored walls. *A hotel room,* she told herself. *Tennessee,* she refined as she bobbed to the surface of lucidity.

Still not summoning the urge to budge, she took visual inventory: Abbi, her small, cotton-clad form breathing gently, her dark hair spilled on the pillow; and over on the pull-out bed, the larger, haphazard sprawl of her twelve-year-old son, the boy's snore nearly blending with the phlegmy din of the room's A/C unit. That snore had a signature, yet another inherited trait from his father that delicately irritated Gwen.

With a sigh, she reached for her cell to check the time. She'd slept too long. A tiring drive in the van had preceded sleep, and a lengthy drive still loomed ahead.

The sloshing sound of a flushing toilet came from the bathroom. Gwen twisted up on one elbow, her mother's bed in unusual disarray (the woman despised even casual disorder). *Strange for her to be up so early,* thought Gwen.

Gwen found the remote and clicked on the TV. Both kids were stirring, stretching now. Allowing them to ease into coherency, she began organizing today's clothing, preparing requests from Abbi, and generally acting as glue for her diminutive crew. Motherly, staid labor.

"Mommy," said Abbi, the usual sing-songy whine, "I want my milk."

Gwen was actually in the process of replenishing it. "Give me a sec, hon."

Charlie, firing up his tablet, said, "Are we going to the pool?"

Gwen screwed on the cap to Abbi's milk. "I don't know if we're going to have time, bud. We really need to get back on the road if we're going to make it to the rental on time."

"I want my chocolate milk," said Abbi, flipping open a coloring book.

"I heard," said Gwen. "A 'please' would be nice."

"Can I *please* have my chocolate milk?"

"But we barely got to swim last night," said Charlie.

To her son Gwen said, "I know; but we've got a deadline."

Charlie scowled, looking past his mother. "What's *that?*"

Gwen followed her son's eyeline to the television—a news report about the rash of shark attacks along the Carolina coast, what media outlets were increasingly calling "interactions." The anchor explained that in one of the most recent interactions near Oak Island, a fourteen-year-old boy had been bitten in shallow water, the injury so severe that he'd subsequently lost his arm. Several photos and an amateur video (segments of the gruesome rescue scene blurred) accompanied the anchor's bloodless delivery of facts from the attack.

Gwen was busy reading the red crawler at the bottom of the screen when Abbi said, "What happened to that boy?"

Bearing in mind their beach-based destination, Gwen readied a pre-emptive reply, but Charlie cut in. "A kid got his arm bit off by a shark."

Gwen shot her son a stale glance, which he returned with the expressive equivalent of pre-adolescent indifference. *What? What'd I do?*

The little girl's tone was a verbal cringe. "A *shark?*"

Gwen stabbed at the remote, landing on something kid-friendly. "Yes, honey; but that happened far, far away from where we're going."

"Yeah," said Charlie, perhaps in a half-hearted attempt to compensate for his lack of tact. Gwen thought better of it, noting his affinity to sound like a know-it-all. "But that happened like way east of here . . . northeast of where we'll be." He was again gazing at his tablet, no doubt searching for supplements to the story online—photos of shark attacks, how to survive one. It was Charlie's way, perhaps one of the more redeemable qualities passed from his father: compulsively, though selfishly, seeking to exhaustion, no matter what—or *who*—was left behind. Without glancing up from his screen, he said, "We're going to a safe beach, right, Mom?" Was there an attempted note of condescension there? If so, Gwen ignored it; she was about to speak when the bathroom door yawned open.

The older woman who shambled into the room was not her mother—at least not in the aspect with which she'd become accustomed throughout her life. No, the woman who emerged from the hotel bathroom was still in her pajamas, an old-fashioned nightgown thing the woman refused to update, while her hair (dyed dark as she'd never deign the gray to infiltrate her dignity) hung in clumsy clumps, still damp, evidently from a shower. In her hand was a wad of tissue, which she raised to her face, scrubbed and untouched by the escutcheon of cosmetics. It was clear the older woman was fighting against emotion, the guise collapsing as her face twisted with a grief Gwen had not witnessed even last spring at the funeral.

"I had," said Kathy, "I had a dream about Dad." The older woman stanched a sob with the wad of tissue.

Gwen crossed the room, arms outstretched, preparing to offer an embrace—a physical form of consolation that she'd offered her mother many times over the past few months. "Oh, Mom," and when she hugged the woman, there was an unusual lack of rigidity, replaced by an almost helpless deflation to her posture. The kids had gone quiet, likely due to the rawness of the woman's visage paired with the unusual show of vulnerability.

With the small woman wrapped in her arms, Gwen said,

"I'm sorry, Mom." The woman was sobbing lightly, sniffing a preamble of composure.

So low that only her daughter could hear, Kathy said, "It was *awful*, Gwendolyn."

Abbi said, "Are you okay, Gramma?"

Perhaps as a cue that this had been too demonstrative, Kathy gently broke away from her daughter, giving a few final *gather-myself-together* gesticulations before exhaling, regarding the children with a smile. "Grandma is just fine," she said, her grin discordant with whatever she struggled with beneath the surface. "Just tired."

*

While Kathy pulled herself together, Gwen pulled the kids together, explaining to them that Grandma had just had a bad dream. "What about?" said Charlie. Gwen said she didn't know and he should not ask.

Later, the older woman came forth from the bathroom resplendent: hair, makeup, wardrobe. She had her cell phone in hand and said to Gwen, "I'm going to step out and call Mom." Unable to travel long distances at her advanced age, Gwen's recently widowed grandmother—her mom's mom—had requested a phone call each morning.

Gwen almost asked if she needed a key to get back in, but her mother—in a show of mild mind-reading—flashed a keycard. "Tell Grandma I said hi," said Gwen.

After the door closed, the kids resumed their needy pleas.

"When are we going to breakfast?" said Charlie.

Abbi chimed in. "I want breakfast *too*."

Gwen exhaled. "We'll all go together to breakfast after Grandma gets back, but I need to run and get some ice." She had already placed the kids' clean clothes at the foot of the bed. "You can both help me by getting dressed." Achieving no response from her children—Charlie still absorbed in his tablet and Abbi humming softly, head hanging over a coloring book—

Gwen lifted the remote and thumbed off the television. The removal of inane noise got their attention. "Listen—I'm going down the hall to get some ice. I need you both to stop what you're doing and get dressed so we can head downstairs, understand?"

Though threaded with lassitude, the kids mumbled assents.

"This door is going to be locked, but me and Grandma have keys. I'm going to be gone like ninety seconds, okay?"

Giggling, Abbi began counting, "One . . . two . . . three . . ."

Gwen narrowed a look at her daughter and quirked her lips—peeved but far from forfeiting her sense of humor. "I'll be right back, guys."

She pulled the door closed behind her, glancing down the hall. At one end was a tall window, the figure down there, her mother, she assumed—a silhouette made indistinguishable by the brilliant backdrop of morning light. Gwen turned the opposite direction.

Tiles of ice clunked into the bucket, and Gwen snatched one, popped it into her mouth, and closed her eyes, leaning against the machine. Coping with the kids, even in this single-mom gig, was easier than the days of frigid tension between her and Sean. Sure: the accountability was exhausting, but she'd gotten used to the rhythms of responsibility associated with unilateral parenting over the past five years.

And most times, she thought, as pathetic as the outcome had been, it had not been the result of some torrid affair. No real betrayal. (Not as it had been with her own parents—her mother acquiring the title of a jilted wife after more than two decades of marriage.) It was just out of the inelegant and ill-shaped accretion that was their relationship and eventual marriage: they'd successfully collaborated on two children, while also collaborating on whittling down their alliance to one sharp point: Sean had simply grown weary of . . . well, everything: being a husband, being a mortgage-toiler, being a father. It was the birth of Abbi, Gwen was certain, that had put the finishing touches on it all.

In her most selfish introspections, Gwen thought that Sean's decision had really been a crude blessing: their father lived a distant existence, making the business of being a parent completely independent. Sometimes she thought the lack of mutuality made her sharper. Other times—like now, with the ice bucket accidentally spilling over as she absentmindedly depressed the dispenser—she thought she was tidily growing frayed.

Cradling the ice bucket by her hip, Gwen was about twenty paces from the room when she heard the screaming. A child's screams. *Abbi.* Gwen trotted to a sprint, key card in hand; and as she neared the room, the backlit figure at the end of the hall was moving toward her, limp-lurching. Gwen realized, getting to the door, that the figure was not her mother at all, rather something masculine yet featureless, his movements stilted, disjointed. A long arm was raised, beckoning.

Sob-choked cries—*"Mama!"*—continued.

Gwen ignored the man at the end of the hall, dropping the ice bucket and fumbling with the key card, her face inches from the door. "I'm coming, honey, I'm coming!" Finally the keypad clicked green and Gwen pushed through.

The TV was back on (Charlie's doing, of course), blaring news of the shark attacks; but most immediate was the paintbrush-bristle smear of blood swiped across bedsheets, the crimson stroke leading to her screaming daughter.

*

"Perfect storm" had become the darling catchphrase for media agencies covering the shark attacks along the Atlantic coast. And though some of the news outlets used it as a segue to statistics, others went into detail as to why the rash of attacks had emerged, everything from drought along the Carolinas, which apparently affected water salinity, all the way to wind-shifts, producing aquatic treats for sharks in the form of mullet, menhaden, and herring.

It was on Gwen's mind, was all. Abbi had asked about it

again, after Gwen had cleaned her up, wiping blood from her nose and chin. "Are we going to have a shark attack, Mommy?"

She'd answered immediately: no. As a mother, she responded to put her child at ease; but as a cogent adult, she recognized the likelihood to be outrageous. Merely musing on the possibility compelled a memory from college: a story she'd had to read for a literature class—that famous story by O'Connor, the one where the family takes a trip and just happens, by some fictive improbability, to cross paths with a murderer mentioned to the audience in the tale's opening paragraph. It was a coincidence Gwen had difficulty accepting then, and—though she was fond of the suspension of disbelief—it was a difficult conceit to fully entertain now.

Sure: suspension of disbelief.

They continued south along I-65. She glanced at the rearview mirror, snatching a peek at the kids, both quiet, engrossed in a movie on the overhead screen.

And of course there were two stories from kids. Listening to Charlie, she'd heard the excuse that they were just jumping from bed to bed, and when he'd turned his back, his sister had fallen. Abbi conversely put in that Charlie had decided to take a pillow and slap her in mid-jump, causing her to fall, grazing the nightstand between the beds.

By the time Gwen had thrust herself into the room, she saw Abbi was on the floor, her tiny fingers clamped over her nose, rills of blood seeping from between her knuckles. Charlie was babbling, breathlessly trying to explain. *"Quiet!"* Gwen had shouted. *"Get back!"* Charlie shrank away, still murmuring a weak defense.

With Abbi's mouth, chin, and forearm slicked with blood, it initially looked worse than it actually was; the little girl's hysterics had likely encouraged blood flow. Gwen's mom had entered the room several seconds later, asking what had happened, but infusing every move with an air of judgmental distaste Gwen incessantly recognized but had never gotten used to.

Once settled down, Gwen checked to see if anything was broken. Nothing, just a banged-up nose. And as angry as she was with her son, she knew well that Abbi could coax her older brother into ill-advised gambits.

They were nearly out of Tennessee when Kathy, low enough to keep it between the two of them, said, "Goodness, I'm sorry about this morning."

Without raising her voice Gwen said, "Mom, you have nothing to be sorry about."

As strange as it would be to articulate, she was deeply delighted by that brief breakdown, as though that glimmer of defenselessness might signal an endearing shift between the two of them. "You've been through a lot." In that interceding silence, Gwen had two choices: pry or change the subject. She decided to rely on her mom. And after a span of seconds, more came.

"Dad was in a field," said the older woman, her face turned away from Gwen. "And it was winter. Everything was just"—she put her hands in front of her as though trying to grip something—"frigid. I don't know. It was as if the atmosphere had a . . ." She trailed off, allowing for the rough, redundant hum of Interstate beneath the vehicle.

Gwen prompted, "Had a what, Mom?"

Kathy winced. "I don't know—as if the atmosphere had a . . . flavor. As if all I could taste was *gray*."

"Mom," said Gwen. She flicked a glance in the rearview at the kids. Abbi had her eyes locked on the screen, but Charlie suddenly looked back at the movie. *Eavesdropping*. Gwen dipped her voice a tick. "You don't have to talk about this, I just wanted to make sure you were okay."

Kathy looked over then, giving her daughter a frail, dismissive smile. "Oh, I'm fine." Whatever the dream had been about, Gwen realized, it had been enough to make her mother lock herself in the bathroom for an hour. "It's just," she shook her head, "I can't get that residue off my mind.

"I felt I was back in Illinois and I was a little girl. I *was* a little girl, my body was mine when I was young, but my mind was my own." The older woman was referring to a large property in Paris, Illinois. Gwen had only seen the tract of land from the road, driving by on a trip once at her mother's request. The gray-gabled place looked as though it was on the verge of collapse. Distant cousins had been the ones in charge of maintaining the place, custodians of sorts. So crouched and fractured was the farmhouse's appearance that Gwen's mother had suddenly changed her mind, suggesting lunch and sightseeing in Terre Haute. "Anyway. I saw Dad out there in the field. And he was wearing"—she twitched a frown at this memory—"he was wearing his conductor's uniform." Gwen's grandfather had retired from Amtrak back in the early '80s but still had an affinity for locomotive culture, so much so that (until he'd become too feeble to leave the house) he volunteered at the living history museum several times a year.

As Kathy spoke, the casual tone soon faded, replaced by an uncharacteristically introspective quality—a soliloquy, her voice growing distant with each description. "You know how dreams are: they feel like decades and seconds are just squished together.

"At first I thought there were storm clouds far past the field, but I realized it was the forest, just dark and tall and surrounding me. Anyway, Dad was out there. It was snowing. He was waving and I started running toward him. I could feel old, littered cornstalks snapping.

"But when I got close I slowed down. Dad didn't have his teeth in and his lips were sort of . . . withered and puckered over his gums. He was saying something—I don't know, his voice was like going backward . . . as if the sound of his voice was looping down into his throat." Gwen thought her mom shivered slightly. "He was pointing down at the ground, and I finally understood that he was saying something about shells. And I looked down at the field, at all the snowy dirt and furrows. There were broken seashells everywhere. These . . . delicate little shards.

"Dad kept talking. And it was horrible, that dye job. His face was not young, it was the same as . . . as when he passed. But his hair was just this campy black.

"As he kept talking, his hair started draining color; the dye itself was weeping down over his head and staining his scalp. And then as if he'd just delivered a punchline, he laughed and reached out and grabbed my forearm." Kathy looked over at Gwen. "And that's when I woke up."

"God, Mom." Gwen was contemplating the odd detail of the hemorrhaging dye-job. "I'm sorry. What a terrible thing for your mind to make up." Intuition, *something,* told Gwen that there was more to the dream—details her mother was leaving out, for one reason or another.

Kathy was still staring through the passenger window at the passing hills and trees of Tennessee. She said, "It was just uncomfortable to see him that way. Like some type of . . . *fiend*."

Gwen reached over and gently gripped her mother's hand.

They drove on for miles. Some time passed before Kathy said, "I know he's safe, though. Safe in heaven."

Gwen knew from personal experience: in times of crisis, people needed self-soothing testaments—remnants, in her mother's case, of those unflinching, ecclesiastical fundamentals from childhood.

Before he had succumbed to congestive heart failure last spring, Gwen had known her grandfather to be a kind, simple man. She'd not been particularly close with him, and as she grew older (as they both grew older), she respectfully objected to his cantankerous opinions. His unshy positions toward race and gender were acutely distasteful to Gwen. Still, he was a product of World War II, a soldier, in fact, and she found it difficult to argue with the man—she didn't accept the intransigent things he said, but she let a lot of it go.

Gwen watched the road, slightly repentant as she cynically interpreted pieces of her mother's dream. She saw the looming wall of trees in the forest not as naked limbs but as uncountable clusters of tangled antlers from stags, and wondered if her mom had mistaken the shells for pieces of broken bone. Shards of skulls. And the most darkly impertinent part of Gwen took that a step further, wondering if what the grandfather-projection in the dream was saying was not something about *shells,* but rather something about *hell.*

Suspension of disbelief, she supposed.

*

The rental lived up to the VRBO description of "Beach Shack Chic."

With her mother's urging, Gwen had been granted autonomy on narrowing down a rental on the beach. The deal: if Gwen drove the van, Kathy would cover the cost of the condo. Of all the things on her mind, Gwen felt particularly guilty about that, but it was true: the mileage on the vehicle, the gas. It would even out. Besides, the impetus for the trip had really been her mother's idea—quite nearly a demand.

Of course, the mid-'80s decor matched just about everything Gwen associated with Florida: out-of-date pastel aesthetics, innocuously campy beach-bum trinkets. Beneath the Jimmy Buffet façade, though, there was a sense of everything being scoured and scrubbed. Sand-eaten, as though the Gulf Coast were just one slender, eroding jawbone.

As they drove in from the main road, both Charlie and Abbi began chanting entreaties to see the beach. Charlie cheered and Abbi squealed as the buildings and condos fell away to reveal the wide horizon of water. And seeing it, yes, was like some sort of release. She could sense it in her mother too—an air of fulfillment.

After checking in and unpacking, they together agreed on a short walk to the beach, a reconnaissance mission to get acquainted with the vista they'd be enjoying for the next five days.

It wasn't quite dusk, but the sky was indeed easing toward a twilight tinge. The fine, ivory-colored sand was so powdery

Gwen constantly had to steady herself. That gentle, cushion-like abrasion felt good on her bare feet.

They slowed to a stop where the upper teeth of the tide were eating away at the slope of sand. Abbi squealed as the water rushed over her ankles, nipping at her shins, while Charlie was busy scanning the shore for shells and various treasures. The seething sibilance of waves came now and again. "Stay close," said Gwen, her voice serene.

Gwen stood next to her mother, their sandals dangling by their sides. Gwen's gaze drifted, eyeing the south, thinking of Key West, where she and Sean had honeymooned more than a decade before. She blinked a few times, ultimately looking away, releasing the inverted metaphor that the nadir of the country's terra firma was simultaneously the apex of their happiness.

Kathy said, "Dad would have loved this. This is exactly what he wanted."

Gwen looked over, seeing a small smile on her mother's face, her expression infused with something like atonement. Gwen wrapped her free arm around her mother's shoulders. "I know, Mom."

They stood there like that for a moment before Kathy said, "He's with God, looking down on us." There was the hissing sound of the surf as the older woman lifted her chin, seeming to address the sky. "I'll see him again someday."

Though she did not physically react, there was part of Gwen that bristled: yes, at the innocence of the words themselves, but also at the affectation of magical thinking. She was not necessarily surprised by this, yet found herself needing something else— something more realistically sound than self-centered promises of the afterlife. Despite this, she still sought to soothe her mother.

And it was during moments like this, intimate moments where their wavelengths might have a chance to overlap—as mothers, as daughters, as women—that she felt most susceptible to her mother's credulousness, as though her mother's beliefs were working on her, a sort of fundamental infection. But she knew all too well that, when it came to her stubborn mother, there would be no reciprocity, no hope for philosophical cross-pollination.

Gwen was about to say something when she noticed several people down the beach, grouped close together, gesturing toward the ocean. She frowned, scanning for the source of the group's giddiness. It took a few seconds, but sure enough she spotted them out there.

"Mom, look." Gwen pointed. "Kids, look out there." Charlie and Abbi straightened up and swiveled.

"What?" said Charlie.

Gwen looked at her mother, who appeared perplexed. "Do you see them?" said Gwen.

Kathy squinted. "I'm not sure."

Then Abbi said, "There!"

Then Charlie: "Yeah . . . I see them!"

Gwen slipped away from her mother's side and meandered toward the children. The animals were perhaps half-a-mile from shore, cutting toward the west, making their presence known in graceful breaches, the dolphins' dark bodies smoothly curving out of and back into the water. Gwen looked at the astonished faces of her children, how in awe they were, so far from their Midwest habitat, at this simple scene in nature.

And then she glanced back at her mother, who still stood staring at the dark water, a look of mystification—perhaps even mild mortification—etched on her face.

She was no longer smiling.

*

The kids had a small room to themselves, across the hall from Gwen. Kathy had taken the master suite down the corridor.

Long after she'd tucked the kids in, Gwen woke. Three days in and she was still getting acclimated with this place. She turned over groggily, seeking a more comfortable position. In mid-stretch she noticed a pale light from the hall. Quietly she shuffled out into the hall, edging over to the kids' door. Through the slim opening she saw Charlie, his head propped up on an arm, watching TV. The volume was low. Abbi was breathing peacefully, long gone. Gwen gently cracked open the door. Charlie merely gave her a perfunctory look of acknowledgment before returning his attention to the show, some sort of documentary.

She stepped in a smidge. Squinting against the coruscating light, she whispered, "What are you still doing up?"

Hushed, Charlie said, "Couldn't sleep . . . but there's this cool show on. It's *Shark Week*." Gwen glanced at the digital clock on his nightstand. Not as late as it felt.

She rubbed her upper arms. "You okay?"

Charlie nodded, content. Though his voice was just above a whisper, he spoke with eager, tween enthusiasm. "They've been talking about a bull shark that swam into the Matawan Creek back in 1916 . . . and this last guy was talking about how to deal with sharks in the wild."

The narrator was now speaking over a black-and-white re-enactment: *In 1963, Rodney Fox, a spear fisherman competing off the coast of South Australia, was attacked, the first bite slicing Fox's forearm down to the bone . . . the shark repeatedly dragged the man down as he made several attempts to return to the surface . . . in the end, Fox was eventually pulled into a boat with severe injuries: Rib cage bared, lungs and stomach exposed, arms and legs lacerated to loose-hanging shreds. The material of Fox's wetsuit was said to have been the only thing keeping the man intact . . .*

Gwen leaned on the doorframe. Not for the first time while watching her son, she was heartened by his absorptive sincerity—his desire to *know*. Still, it required tempering.

"Why don't you go ahead and turn this off," said Gwen. "I don't like you watching something so intense before bed."

"Mom," whispered Charlie, "seriously, it's fine."

Gwen exhaled, her own internal negotiator on the clock again. Bending, she reminded herself, was not the same as breaking. "Okay," she said, "ten more minutes. Promise?"

"Promise." And he was back in, re-absorbed.

"I love you," she said.

"Love you too, Mom."

Down the dark hallway, returning to her own bedroom, she angled her head around the corner, seeing a small slit of light beneath her mother's door. From this distance, she thought she heard the TV, a late-night televangelist's intonation.

Gwen steered into her own bedroom, slipping back into bed; but her mind remained restless, vulnerable in that space between lucidity and sleep. And what took advantage in that black aperture was not her own thoughts, but rather the clipped monotone from the documentary in Charlie's room—an insistent narration woven together from her own self-conscience, words working in a way that makes sense during a descent. Emotionless and alien—facts about *sharks* . . . about the relationship between predators and *prey* . . . *why the tacit and revulsive realization that human beings, even today, get consumed—that they become food—comes hard to the Western consciousness, and that the aberrant act of being eaten alive is the paramount horror* . . .

Succumbing to the tide, she slid into a vacuum, where the ambient narration grew discordant and began fading. Floating in the darkness, images forced themselves upon her—sleek-skinned amphibians swirled around her, rending some nearby prey; and as terror instigated suffocation, she was nauseous with the awareness that, once they were finished with the flesh of their current repast, she would be next.

*

Another morning of vacation, another early trek down to the beach. Again they set up along a coveted portion of shore, the children (both sun-screened to near comical Kumadori) with their shovels, pails, and boogie boards, Gwen and her mother with the beach chairs, towels, and various essentials.

Colossal clouds formed a mountain range in the distance, the sun free to swell with its regional brutality. Toward noon, a storm pushed in—a short-lived tantrum during which they sought shelter under their portable canopy. Silver needles pelted the surface of the water, shifting it from blue to agitated green. And as quickly as it had arrived, the storm swept southeast, and in its wake came a collapsing dome of dark mist. Once the storm had passed, the children re-entered the water, resuming their raucous play. A sandbar lay a short distance from shore, and beachgoers reconvened there, idly congregating in clusters on the verge of the great depth that lay beyond.

Gwen watched her children out there in the knee-deep surf, skimming on their boogie boards. Under Charlie's not-too-patient tutelage, Abbi figured out the trick of the board, gliding over the low waves.

Gwen had almost smuggled a bottle of chilled Pinot down in the cooler but reconsidered, not wanting to risk any disparaging remarks from her mother. She looked over: her mom's big glasses taking up a large portion of her face, that face trained on an alabaster-tinted book, *Perseverance through Prayer: Unlocking Inner Peace*. She could not bear close proximity with that stuff—and not because of any lingering pretensions. Rather, she'd been there: her friends shoving every self-help book down her throat in the wake of Sean's exodus and subsequent separation. The books were pretentious to the senses, offensive to reality. She was not so narrow-minded as to dismiss purpose—meaning: she understood the Eat-Pray-Love placebo-calm it may bring to those in turmoil . . . it did for her, for a time—but she was having trouble with the discordance of her mother's experience and age. *Who am I to criticize how someone mourns?*

Gwen said, "Are you going to call Grandma later?"

Kathy's lips moved: "Yes. She's been sleeping an awful lot. I'm concerned I'll wake her. And not having enough sleep simply turns her into a bear."

The kids played amid the lazy chew of the surf. Gwen thought one thing, then amended it, and then—in a hapless desperation for small talk—said, "Is there anyone you're looking forward to seeing when you get back home?"

Kathy slipped in her bookmark, gently closing the book. "It's still too inappropriate to talk about that."

"But it's been so many years since Dad. Have you thought about going out and meeting somebody?"

Kathy's expression was partially lost behind the veneer of large sunglasses. She cocked her head. "That's not my priority right now."

"But this is the time when you should be having fun, traveling."

"What do you think this is?"

Gwen sighed a laugh. "I know, but you get what I mean. I really want you to find some sort of happiness with someone." The kids were calling from the water. Gwen smiled and waved.

The older woman smirked and canted her head toward her daughter. "Just because a woman is in a relationship with a man doesn't mean it solves all your problems." Kathy aimed her face back toward the ocean. "You of all people should know that."

Gwen's smile sank. She opened her mouth, shut it, clenched her teeth. *What the hell, Mom?* It was just supposed to be a simple comment encouraging companionship. *So it was going to be one of those days,* she thought, when kindred connectedness was impossible—each attempt at banter would be met with spiky parental barbs. She missed Grandpa too, and genuinely felt sympathy for her mother at the loss of a parent, the long-ago loss of her marriage; but the woman had slathered herself in this new variety of divine victimization.

The kids were calling again, Abbi speaking excitedly about some accomplishment. Gwen brought her shoulders up off the back of the beach chair and looked at her mother. "Mom, all I'm saying is that life goes on and—"

"For some of you, yes: life goes on, Gwendolyn. But there are others who are a bit more—vigilant—about our passage in life and how we navigate it."

Christ, thought Gwen, *she sounds like one of her self-help books.*

"What's that supposed to mean?"

The old woman smirked, calling up whorls of wrinkles beneath those sunglasses. What was supposed to be the misguided piety of a stubborn matriarch was steadily pissing Gwen off.

"Oh, come on, Gwen. Don't you think a lot of this started when you found out about Charlie?"

Was it even possible that her mother was so miserable with herself—dwelling in her lingering grief—that she would actually rehash a topic from eleven years ago? Gwen's silent astonishment must have acted as consent for the woman to continue.

"I mean, look," said Kathy, setting her book down on a blanket. "You are my daughter and I love you completely; but discovering you were pregnant before you were married didn't necessarily set the proper tone between you and Sean, right? And how it wound up with that man, well . . . it is what it is. And yes, Abbi came along a few years later and everything seemed fine. But things were obviously *not* fine. Not with you and Sean, and certainly not with you and God."

Gwen actually blurted a caustic laugh, more of a unrefined cough. "Are you suggesting that my . . . marital status is"—she shook her head—"is a *consequence* of having Charlie out of wedlock?"

The older woman's forearms stretched placidly over the armrests of the beach chairs, her wrists dangling, her hands hanging like well-tanned talons. "All I'm saying is that if we lived the way we're supposed to live, then perhaps life would lessen its harsher lessons."

And I suppose that includes flagellation and wallowing in sanctimonious self-pity. Her mother had not broached the subject in many years, and Gwen hoped that maybe she'd come to understand the absurdity of such an assertion—the absurdity of supernatural transgression, particularly when it came to bearing children.

And like a dull quiver of electricity, she realized she needed her mother to say something comforting, something tender. Intrinsically, Gwen was starved for something thoughtful—something profound. Her mother remained obstinate. Literally: the woman was sitting stock still, impassive, staring straight ahead at the ocean.

The sound of the crashing surf had interwoven with raucous laughter from a group of high school girls nearby. Pulse suddenly racing with rage, Gwen stood, snagged her flip-flops. "I'm going up to the house for a few minutes. Will you please—"

"Mom!"

Gwen spun toward Charlie's scream. The commotion: panels of bodies were rushing out of the water, some scrambling over each other. Gwen saw Charlie pointing at something in the distance. The dorsal fins—cut black against the water's blue—sliced lazily through the breakers. More screams from down the beach to Gwen's right, but she was shoving through the retreating people, trying to find Abbi.

Charlie began hurtling through the water, Gwen almost shouted for him but staggered when she spotted Abbi's boogie board drifting atop a wave, skidding to a stop along the sand. Her son called again. *"Mom . . . help!"* She twisted up. Charlie was hunched over something dark, his fists rising and dropping in desperate arcs amid eruptions of water.

Abbi was up to her neck, her small face contorted with panic. And there, breaking the surface, the fish—no larger than the size of a child—revealed itself in flashes, sunlight glistening on its mouse-gray exterior as its contours contorted with vicious sinuousness. Gwen scrambled, rushing across the water as others converged on the scene. Charlie now had his fingers hooked under the shark's gills, his free fist coming down to batter the fish's eyes.

The jerking shark let go then, curving like a serpent, retreating in a stream of pink flowing from the lower part of Abbi's body.

Gwen practically crashed into her children, Charlie already hauling up his little sister. "Don't let her look, Mom," said Charlie, his tone eerily composed, and Gwen only gave the wound a quick glance before cupping her daughter's chin with her hands.

Others moved in then as they placed Abbi on the beach, several of them swiftly and coordinately delivering first aid. Gwen saw the oozing, crescent-shaped teethmarks along her daughter's calf, grateful for mere punctures as opposed to the gore of loose-hanging ligaments and exposed bone. Her little girl was in one piece.

Still on her hands and knees, her sobs static but manageable, Gwen felt a hand on her shoulder, and knowing, just from the feel, she reached out for her son. Over the shouting, Gwen heard him say, "She'll be okay, Mom. She'll be all right."

Gwen was ready to release tears of relief but froze as she watched her mother shuffling past them, shoulders slumped, babystepping toward the water. She'd discarded the sunglasses, and now the older woman was grinning—an expression of self-satisfaction, mesmerized by something in the distance. Listing from side to side, the older woman's shins collided with the rolling waves.

Gwen staggered, splaying her hand in the sand as she shouted, *"Mom—stop . . . Mom!"*

Someone shouted, "Get that lady out of there!" but most were occupied by the injured little girl, along with several other incidents that seemed to have occurred farther down the beach.

Clawing at the sand, struggling to gain purchase, Gwen got to her feet, chasing after her mother. She splashed into the tide, losing her footing, falling sideways, saltwater stinging her eyes.

In a final thrust of effort, Gwen drew up on her mother, inadvertently glancing beyond, following the source of the older woman's infatuation.

He was about a hundred yards from shore, deceptively standing in ankle-deep water—a dark, slender, human-shaped protrusion. It was just as her mother had described it: Gwen's grandfather—her mother's dad—dressed in that black, bygone train conductor's uniform. His expression was too distant, but his complexion was gray, so ghastly it was accentuated under the domineering sun. He was beckoning—rigid appendages curled on a pale hand.

The image of her grandfather was skirted below with a wide shadow, as though some small island were buoying him just beneath the surface. Gwen's eyes stung with saltwater.

Gwen shook free of the impossibility of what she was seeing and burst through the water.

Her mother was already sunken to her waist, slowed only by the resistance of the surf. Kathy turned then, a haughty smile—her expression a self-satisfied remark: *I told you so.* She had elbows lifted as she waded farther out, and, looking directly at her daughter, said, "I just knew it, Gwen . . . it's an affirmation of fai—"

Something yanked on her mother, the violent tug causing the old woman's grin to disappear instantly, replaced by dismayed horror—a shock so evident that it appeared the woman's eyes had been loosed from the security of their sockets. Gwen batted at the waves, trying to reach her mother.

But as Kathy began to struggle in earnest, the waves began heaving, rising around her in a ragged circumference, slender fins cutting and coursing in its interior.

Gwen made another effort to throw herself forward, her arm outstretched, but she saw her mother's face: the woman was making a defiant attempt to turn back toward the dark, floating figure. Gwen dove, cleaving beneath the surface. And in that brackish water, diffuse with her daughter's blood, an alchemic lens filmed her eyes—her vision, her entire reality, had become a series of snippets: above, beneath, the deep. She saw her mother being pulled into the tumult of foam, gray forms undulating and thrashing, a variety of hides and a multitude of teeth—thin, needle-like, wide, serrated. A febrile kaleidoscope of black eyes and slick skin. Beneath: flashes of her mother's submergence, snatched away within the sandy mist and the withdrawing respiration the undertow. And then scenes from the deep: the impossibility of seeing the thing imitating her grandfather out in the

water; the y-axis image reflected along the x-axis of the surface—
a triangular inversion of the man's black uniform converted to a
curving cape, billowing in sinuous tendrils to become a behe-
moth congregation of sharks. Ancient, distorted, enormous.
Predators gliding with ponderous ease.

Something clasped hold of Gwen then—sharp points digging
into her shoulders, her throat. And now, as many mouths were
pulling her mother away, just as many hands were drawing
Gwen back to shore.

Gwen's legs hung useless as she was dragged and dropped
onto the sun-seared sand. She coughed up water and got to an
elbow, saw her son gazing toward the distance; she blinked at
the freckles of her daughter's blood dappling the sand, and began clawing at the red stain as though it were a lifeline, a crimson vestige of salvation.

Animalhouse

"There are times when the lines around the human eye seem like shelves of eroded stone and when the staring eye itself strikes us with such a wilderness of animal feeling that we are at a loss."

—John Cheever, "The Country Husband"

The uneven serrations of the house key scrape into the front door's deadbolt like teeth tumbling over bone. He twists the knob. A forearm netted with dark, dried blood rises and shoves the door, which glides open.

When he'd left earlier that morning, Gary Mountjoy had neglected to pull the blinds. Now, near-evening light glows throughout the house, casting sharp shadows, as if someone has done a negligent job of hanging dark blue wallpaper.

His fever is insistent—nearly as assertive as the pulsing pain within his arm. Then there is the matter of the body in the trunk of the car.

Priorities.

*

Nashton was close, about twelve miles away.

It was that twelve miles that separated where he'd grown up—in the fielded outskirts of Nashton—and the suburbs with which he identified with his current existence.

Courtney had left town the day before—to visit her family, she'd said . . . to take some time to think, she'd said—and his wife's abrupt two-or-three day absence presented Gary the perfect opportunity to do some thinking of his own, which is precisely why he decided to dismiss much thinking altogether, opting to call in sick to work and spend Monday daydrunk alone.

Well, not alone. He had Gamble.

The morning's checklist had contained two items, both of which had been enthusiastically crossed off: call in sick to work and drop by the liquor store for a bottle.

As Gary drove further into rural stomping grounds, the radius became more tolerable, more enjoyable. It was during this time of seasonal transition when the leaves were turning, altering from green states to tints of nectar, rust, lemon, uncountable tinges of orange. The roads became more narrow, the trees lining those thoroughfares became more prominent, dense.

An atmosphere insulated with Rorschach stretches of forests and cordoned fields, now set in tall stands of harvest-ready cornstalks.

He'd never been one to denigrate his former stomping grounds—not that he'd ever intentionally reside here again. Nevertheless, he identified with Nashton.

Gary grew up out here in an area that had four vital setpieces in his formative years—forests, farmhouses, fields, and railroad tracks that cut through the center of this place like a sort of carotid landmark—the steel rails a symbol of the bygone days when locomotives brought people here. For a brief period in the mid-nineteenth century, this small community was poised to rival towns in their campaign to become Indiana's state capital. That candle of ambition, though, guttered in light of other community campaigns. It was a matter of not being big enough, not being *rich* enough. *A matter of not being* good *enough.*

Oh, yes, Gary Mountjoy identified with good old Nashton. *Nice try . . . better luck next time.*

As a sentimental exercise, Gary took a detour through the town itself. Ghost town was too much of a cliché, though it did seem as if some sort of campy re-enactment could occur at any moment. Outside the diner were two filthy men smoking, perhaps accosting patrons for a handout. *The railroad's doing,* Gary thought. Back in the old days, there had been stories of railriders, hobos hopping off as the train slowed or stopped at

Nashton's depot. Stories of wayside vagrants creeping through the community, wandering from yard to yard, or casually soliciting folks for a handout or a hitch out of town.

The two men held their beady gazes on Gary's car, their faces containing a mummified sort of dignity.

Toward the southeast, the railway eventually connected with Cincinnati, and on toward the northwest met up with the spiderweb network of Chicago.

The elementary school he'd attended as a kid was still out here, yet had been shut down due to some funding issue that spurred a shift in district lines and transportation. Now, kids who were supposed to attend Nashton Elementary were being fed to the nearby and slightly larger town of New Bethel.

Gary pulled into the front lot of the now lifeless school, appraising the low-lying, one-story structure with its mannequin-composed façade—no boards over the windows, no broken glass, just absent energy. He continued his circuit around to the back of the school, the secluded side screening him from the town proper.

Gary slowed to a stop, Gamble already huffing, panting, drooling, mincing an anticipatory dance in the confines of the backseat, his ID tag jingling against the clip on his collar.

Courtney, when she'd walk Gamble around their subdivision, had consistently used a leash on the animal.

Gary glanced over on the passenger seat—the leash there, more of a perfunctory tool than a necessity. Gamble was clumsily kind, oafishly obedient.

Next to the leash was the brown bag. He'd never taken a day off from work for an illness, let alone as an excuse to get drunk as a means of self-pitying capitulation.

Gary craned his neck, wondering about the possible presence of some security guard or errant maintenance man on the grounds, before slipping the bottle from the bag, paper crackling as he withdrew the pint of bourbon. He gazed at the warm, amber-hued liquid, catching sight of his long, gourd-distorted reflection along the edge of the bottle.

Gary peeled away the plastic ring and twisted the cap, the whiff of distillation filling the space. He again glanced around the deserted back lot before raising the bottle to his lips and taking a small pull. He winced, grateful no other males were present to provide any sort of casual shaming. Gary allowed the liquid to descend, savoring the swift-spreading scorch as it traveled down to his empty stomach. Inhaling, exhaling, Gary immediately followed up with a larger gulp, which was better after the previous primer. He wiped his lower lip with the cuff of his windbreaker. The physical thrill of absorbing the spirits mixed with the deviant awareness that he should be at work right now—being responsible, being a teacher of children. He thought about the marriage counseling, about the guy at Courtney's office. *His career . . . his salary.* Gary took one more sip. It was shaping up to be a beautiful morning.

Gamble was whimpering now, his nails tapping at the window frame.

Gary capped the bottle, took a deep breath, and stepped out of the car. Still mid-morning, the sun slowly adding thin layers of warmth, he went up on tiptoes, stretching his arms, the movement felt as if he were allowing the alcohol into far-reaching cells of muscle fiber. He peeled off his windbreaker and tossed it on the driver's seat, rolling up the sleeves of his flannel.

Gary scanned the parking lot of the elementary school, the adjoining playground with its rusted array of disused and outdated equipment. There was a small baseball field on the far side, now overgrown, weeds and ivy crawling up the chainlink backstop.

Hemming the school in on the west side of the property were the ever-present railroad tracks, which separated the property from the ever-present fields and forest. Up beyond that, set on a small bluff overlooking the tracks, was the house.

When they were students here, Gary and the other kids called the house "Corpse Cottage," though it was evident that, back then, it was inhabited by a family. Prone to typical embellishment—no one had ever died there, no crime (of which Gary was aware) had ever taken place.

Later, when high school boredom compelled teens to countryside excursions, Corpse Cottage became a regular haunt. Of course, by this time the house was clearly abandoned—shingles sloughing off the ragged roof . . . paint peeling in oak-leaf-size portions. As a child, Gary had heard tales that the house had been a hideout for transients and squatters from the railroad. Not for the first time he acknowledged that the house's location—set up on a low-sloping bluff, almost hanging over the tracks—would be ideal for transients searching for a place to seek shelter. Gary stared at the house, its gray exterior covered with a netting of limb and autumn-leaf shadow.

Gamble barked sharply. Gary flinched. "Sorry about that, old boy," he said, opening the back door.

Tongue lolling, the dog spilled out of the car and trotted across the parking lot, panting, pausing to sniff the air, his collar and ID tag jangling as he ran, roaming a curious weave throughout the skeletal playground.

Gary took the opportunity to reach back in through the open window and pluck the bottle off the seat, giving panoramic appraisal. Nothing, of course . . . everything in the schoolyard fringes was tranquil, desolate. He swallowed and looked at the bottle, startled by how little liquid remained.

Carl, their therapist—or marriage counselor or whatever humiliating term was being used at one time or another—had suggested during one of their sessions that adultery was really about anger. This initially baffled Gary. For two reasons really—one, he had no idea what his spoiled-to-the-marrow wife had to be angry about; and two, if he were indeed the source of that anger, then what the fuck had he done precisely?

He shook his head, already feeling the gliding, gut-warming sensation of inebriation. *Need to take a break, pal.* He capped the bottle and nestled it beneath the driver's seat.

Gary glanced toward the playground. No dog. The only

thing moving was a tepidly swaying swing.

He straightened, eyes darting. *"Gamble!"* he shouted, stepping away from the car. Gary cupped his palm to his mouth. *"Gam-ble!"* The word skipped, doubling on itself as the echo drifted across school grounds.

Gary heard him before he saw him. In the distance came the metallic jangle of the dog's ID tag. Gary swiveled in the direction of the baseball diamond. Gamble was nosing around the weed-threaded backstop, tail wagging, inspecting the space where home plate would be.

Gary sighed, half smiling as he looped the leash around his knuckles and started slowly for the baseball field. Keeping his eyes on the dog, he mumbled, "All right, bud, enough fun . . . time to go."

Though Gary hadn't raised his voice, Gamble raised his head—ears erect, the set of his body suddenly rigid. His muzzle pointed directly at Gary, two black eyes staring. He actually chuckled. "Sorry, my man . . . but we'll have plenty of days to run around at the park."

His voice held the intonation of a father speaking to a child. Like most young couples, everything was a "starter"—starter home . . . starter savings account. Starter pet in preparation for a starter family.

They'd never articulated the dynamic, that taking care of a dog was a tacit collaborative barometer for their parental potential as nurturers. But they'd sensed it, particularly when Gamble was a pup. Though, as Gamble aged, he became more of a prop in a two-person play. As time went by, Gary was more and more at a loss as to how the script read.

Closing in on the dog now, Gary considered his limited threshold for the thespian nature of noble husband—his wife had crossed the line. She'd made groveling attempts to apologize, which Gary summarily rejected, only accepting the invitation to counseling as a matter of pre-separation perfunctory. Courtney had sworn it was a one-time mistake—something she regretted and could not account for.

The dog's legs were set sturdily beneath it. It slowly lowered its head, its upper lip curling to show the warning gleam of teeth. A low rumble.

Gary didn't come to a full stop but slowed a bit. "Gamble?" he said, some disbelief at this strange response from the gentle dog. Gary stifled the urge to raise his hands in a plaintive gesture. He just needed to get close enough to attach the leash. Soothing: "You want to stay a while, we'll stay a while—okay?"

Gamble, as if stung by something on the hindquarters, twitched, breaking its stare with its approaching owner and whirling in the opposite direction. The dog froze.

Gary did too. Scowling, he examined the outer stretches of the property, out beyond to where the dog had now trained its attention; but before he could gather any sense about what had happened, Gamble barked once and bolted, taking off toward the railroad tracks.

Gary hissed, "Damn it," and began chasing the dog in a dead sprint.

"Gamble!" Gary called out, the sun warm on his neck and shoulders. Gary reached the tracks, but the precariousness of the large rocks and wooden ties slowed him a bit. He shouted the dog's name again just as the animal veered left into the underbrush, loping up the steep slope toward the house.

It took Gary a few seconds to catch up to where the dog had cleaved through the weeds. Leaves made hashing sounds, wand-thin branches snapped as Gary ungracefully navigated the incline of the small bluff, finally pushing against the bole of some anemic trees to get his footing where the ground leveled off in the refuse-littered back yard. Panting, he almost shouted again, but could hear the dog's rapid barking—it sounded as though it were coming from inside the house. For just a second, Gary thought he heard a reedy whistle.

He frantically scanned the exterior. All details, of course, were worse up close (a lesson he'd learned from his demanding inquiries into Courtney's adulterous dalliance). Three stories' worth of neglect: flaking paint exposed scuffed planks . . . sagging gutters overloaded with dead leaves and debris led to fractured downspouts barely clinging to the side of the house. The grounds were littered with an assortment of age-varied trash. Again, like a stuttery newsreel, Gary thought of the rumors that this place had once been a stopover for train-hopping transients. The crooked railing on the L-shaped porch contained broken or missing spindles, and except for the very high attic dormer, all window glass was missing, each transom broken.

Jogging, Gary rounded the sideyard, trying to determine where the dog had gained access. On the back end of the house was a partly open door. He pressed against the door—some resistance there. Pressing harder, shoving with his upper body and craning his neck to see what was on the other side, he saw that two duffle bags—faded green, the Army fatigue variety—were stacked against the door but had been scooted away, providing a narrow margin of access.

He shoved the door and slid into a narrow corridor, still hearing the dog's barking. *Damn it . . . he's upstairs.*

The smell of engine oil was heavy here, and the idea of oil was a pervasive thing: whereas a tint of sepia tiredness may seem noble in some cases, here it imparted a sense that the nicotine-tinted surfaces were coated in grease. A filmy, hibernating scent of nesting insects.

The sound of movement up on the second story—capering claws clicking on the floor overheard. "Come on, Gamble . . . get your silly ass out here," Gary called out, using the most authoritative tone he could conjure. He began clapping his hands together and whistling as he walked toward the deeper interior of the house, shattered plaster and dead-leaf detritus crunching under his sneakers.

Though the windows were bare, little light seemed to filter into the shadow-curtained house. Just as Gary was about to emerge from the corridor, Gamble abruptly stopped barking.

Gary held his breath involuntarily. After a few seconds of silence he said, "Gamble?" Quiet. Gary strode forward and around the corner.

Just a few feet to the left was a staircase, flanked on one side by a wall and a broken railing on the other.

The dog was standing at the top of the stairs. Gamble's body was crisply profiled with his attention trained on something to the left. (The dog could have been an insignia on one of Puckett's designer shirts, the notion coming as a mental sneer.) Now, Gary's voice was nearly a growl. He placed one foot on a riser and said, "Damn it, *Gam*—"

From the second floor came a string of short whistles, each ending with an unsettling chain of cheery notes. Gamble's growling re-emerged, grinding up to reverberate down the stairwell.

With his hand on the wobbly railing, Gary almost swayed when the whistling ended with a series of sloppy kissing sounds—a male voice, threaded with something unsteady—said, *"Come over here, Gamble . . ."*

Skittering as the dog sprang forward, nails clacking and scraping. Gary followed, pounding up the stairs.

The commotion was to the left, at the end of a long, shadowed hallway. Gary bounded into the passageway. All doors were closed here, allowing for insufficient light through the rectangle tunnel.

Gamble was on top of someone—a struggling figure, one forearm angled over his face.

Gary kicked through garbage and newspapers, getting within reaching distance of Gamble and the person he was attempting to maul. He leaned in and grabbed Gamble by his collar, the band of fabric vibrating against the dog's growl-rattling throat. As Gary was struggling to peel the dog away, he caught a better glimpse of the feeble-framed, rag-clad figure.

Just then one of the man's arms shot out, thin fingers clutching the dog's collar.

Gary assumed the man was simply trying to gain leverage to get to his feet, but the pull was strange. Gary slid an arm under the dog's neck, trying to get between the two, almost immediately feeling the slick sting of teeth in the flesh of his forearm, Gamble's snapping jaws snagging on skin. Gary cried out, heaving backward, and in one tug-of-war lunge tore the dog loose. He landed hard on his hip—Gamble still growling, still flailing—and skidded back into the hallway and into the light, not far from the stairway corridor. Still holding the dog in a sort of feeble bear-hug, Gary got his legs to the staircase, looking over only once: a mistake that forced him to falter.

The man was sliding on all fours. As he emerged into a weak shaft of light, Gary first noticed that the guy's skin was pallid, waxy-gray, a tint associated with wasting disease. His fever-rheumy eyes glittering in deep-set sockets ringed dark, as if he'd been rubbing his eyes with coal-dusted fingers. Nearly bald, a few oily strands, resembling limp silk from a sick cornhusk, clung to his pate.

The man's cracked lips were smile-stretched, the grin showcasing a rotted cavern of mouth. Gary's attention was arrested by this detail: his front teeth, the incisors, were missing, but on either side of the gap the canines were shockingly long and sharp.

Gary's terror-pause at seeing the man had been too much. Like most revelations, the ability to immediately rectify his errors came far too late. The sick man edged forward, his long, filth-grimed fingers grabbing the dog by the collar. The smell coming from the man was something from a flesh-fouled trench. Gary tried to scream as he watched the man, almost playfully, open his lip-cracked mouth—the missing incisors making everything blacker there—the long, sharp canines—and watched the man's jaws close on the dog's throat, petals of blood blossoming on fur.

Gamble yelped—a sharp, helpless sound that renewed Gary's strength and he hoisted.

The dog's collar snapped in the sick man's hand as Gary fell backward, Gamble in his arms, both tumbling down the stairs.

They hit the floor hard, but Gary hefted the dog to his chest and broke into a shuffling run toward the door.

They spilled into the yard. Gary sucked in the late morning air, staggering, rounding the house on his way to the bluff and the tracks.

The sound of laughing. Gary twisted, his eyes tracing the laughter to a second-story window. The sick man was standing there, smiling, chin smudged with blood. Those teeth—the missing incisors . . . the pronounced, rot-tinted canines.

Gary winced—from the weight of the animal, from exhaustion—as the man lifted his hand, the dog's collar dangling there, Gamble's silver ID tag catching sunlight—a jolly ornament. The man's expression bore a taunting sort of intent.

Gary turned, doing his best to manage the steep hill and the thick undergrowth along the bluff, sliding the final six feet down the slope. He glanced down at the blood-matted fur along Gamble's neck, crimson glistening in the sunlight. Then the railroad tracks were underfoot, racing over the ties and thick stones.

The run across the baseball field was a mishmash of panting and nonsensical encouragements: *Hold on, old boy . . . few more . . . car . . . get you patched up . . .*

And then they were there—Gary sweating, breathing taxed. He gently laid Gamble in the shadow of the car, trying to keep the dog comfortable. The dog's respiration had gone wheezy. Gary reached over, suddenly seized at the sight of blood trailing from his own arm. In the struggle Gary had been nipped by Gamble—*no—not right.* Gary whirled around, clawing at the back door of the car to retrieve a bottle of water; he uncapped it and poured the liquid over his forearm. Clearing away the blood validated the worst—the puncture wound now clear, literally in his flesh: a ragged bite . . . two distinct canine punctures with a gap between.

His mouth was dry. It hadn't been Gamble. His eyes darted around, lighting on playground equipment, acres of harvest-ready fields. The ruined house up on the bluff above the train tracks. He sank down to one knee, pouring the remaining water over Gamble's neck. Useless. A wide pool of blood had gathered under the dog's upper body. Breathing had stopped.

A barbed ripple of pain pulsed along his forearm. The water bottle in his hand was empty—*the bottle*. Gary yanked at the passenger-side door of the car, retrieving the bottle of bourbon from beneath the seat. He was clueless whether it would help, but he fumbled the cap off and poured the liquid over the wound—an electrifying sting forked along his ulna.

Gritting his teeth, he dropped the empty glass bottle, swiped an old T-shirt from the trunk, and wrapped it around his arm, falling on his backside against the side of the car and sliding down to a seated crouch.

Thoughts—*call a sheriff . . . call an ambulance*—fluttered in the weak breeze of his mind. The one that stood out was Courtney—how was he going to tell her what had happened.

Losing the dog. Eyelids shuddering, Gary tried to focus on the rotting house in the distance, his attention eventually falling to the playground equipment as his vision began to blur, beads of sweat glistening on his brow. And as he slid sideways, his eyes closed, accepting the tightly scoping darkness on the fringes of his vision, Gary Mountjoy heard the hush and hiss of the breeze in the trees, the wailing sound of a distant train threaded in the wind.

*

We've explained already—it was a pretty unexceptional entrance.

*

It was very near dark now.

He was thirsty—the need for water was demanding. He'd have to get the shovel soon.

As Gary shambled through the house he noticed that his vision was pretty good, adjusting to the dimness with crisp swiftness.

The bleeding had stopped, a smear of dark, resin-like liquid crusted over the wound; but, for the moment, Gary could not allow himself to focus on the teeth marks, what they meant. *Human teeth*. He was worried about infection. Unbidden, the word *further* spasmed through his mind. *Better be worried about further infection, my friend*.

Earlier, back at the school, he'd woken disoriented, sprawled on the asphalt. The first wave of flies had mingled around Gamble, and Gary batted them away. He ripped open several garbage bags, spreading out a piecemeal tarp in the trunk, gently lowering the dog into the space. With his hand lifted to the trunk's lid, Gary paused for a moment, reverentially considering the animal. No matter what he would tell Courtney, this physical thing that had linked them was now gone.

Now he teetered toward the bathroom, taking a swipe at the light and instantly regretting it. The figure reflected in the bathroom mirror was a double-exposed version of Gary Mountjoy— tall, lean, but the exterior had frayed. Gaunt—his skin was ashen, if not downright gray, and was pulled tightly over his eye sockets, cheekbones. Facial stubble had grown to several-days'-worth, and his damp bangs hung in a coarse curtain over his brow.

His eyes skittered to his forearm, but before he could remove the knotted portion of the T-shirt, he wondered at the coarse, whisker-thick hairs coating his muscle-corded forearms. He brought his dark-nailed fingers up and unwound the piece of blood-crusted fabric. That was when Gary noticed his fingernails, rimmed with dark tints, as if stained with mulberry juice. And they'd elongated as well, converging to sharp points.

The bite marks were livid, each puncture haloed by a dark network of tendril-like bruises; and though the punctures had ceased bleeding, the dots where his skin had been broken now looked to be surfaced by a thin layer of tissue, as if the wound itself had sunken a few centimeters deeper into his arm. *A hematoma tattoo*. Gary barked a laugh aloud, his lips drawing back.

Again he caught sight of himself in the mirror. Teeth: his upper and lower canines had lengthened, like slender tusks, curving toward each other.

Gary reached over and swiped off the light, pitching back into the hallway in a half-crouch.

Gamble. He had to do something. *Priorities, pal. A good suburban soldier had priorities*.

He grabbed an old comforter from the closet, opened the garage door, and backed the car in.

He had the decency to wait for the sun to disappear.

*

Burying the dog was a series of stuttery, strobe-light stills. In the woods out back, Gary eventually discarded the shovel, digging Gamble's grave with long-nailed hands. The growls grew louder as the pit got deeper.

*

Back in the house, he was coated in a fine film of dirt. He felt as though his fever were beginning to abate, but the pockets of ache remained, particularly along his sternum and spine. His ears popped, as if from a pressure change, just before he felt another shift as something popped along his jawline. Breathing heavily, Gary clenched his teeth and found they didn't line up quite right.

He tried to rise to full height and failed, discovering that remaining hunkered over slightly elicited less postural pain.

Keys. Gary staggered into the garage, fell into the driver's seat, and jammed the car keys into the ignition with a jittery-clawed hand.

Of course, during the months of obsessive questioning—of both his wife's infidelity and his own self-worth—Gary had discovered where Ryan Puckett lived, had even driven by the house once or twice, juxtaposing his life with that of the guy compromising his wife, a self-flagellating exercise that did everything to confirm the young man's vulgar display of income.

Gary would just go over and talk to this fellow. This guy had fucked his wife, apparently. Having a civil, man-to-man discussion was not out of the question. After all, Gary wasn't a total animal.

*

He parked the car down the street from Ryan Puckett's house.

He had no plan, didn't even begin thinking about what he'd do until he was out of the car and shuffling up the sidewalk. A gray Lexus sat in the driveway, its engine still ticking as it settled from some recent outing.

Gary scanned the front of the house—the meticulously manicured lawn, fussy landscaping, precious accent lighting warming the unblemished structure. Gary had a flash of regret, wishing that when he'd been in college studying to be a common parochial teacher, he would have known he'd never be able to afford such an opulent property. Which also reminded him that he would certainly be calling in sick again tomorrow.

Mustering what dignity he could—his filthy flannel shirt smudged with soil—Gary skulked up the driveway. Stepping into the light of the front porch threw Gary's slouched shadow against white brick—the silhouette resembled something like an upright hyena . . . the sharp nails flexing, as if each were competing for his attention.

Through cloudy glass, light shone in a distant room. Thoughts fluttered into his mind like the agitated bats: *Courtney's in there—she's lied about going to visit her family—her car's in the garage—they're in there right now—in the bedroom—in the dark—in her . . .*

A gray, hairy, knob-knuckled hand extended toward the doorbell, a black claw touching the amber button.

A sing-songy tune sounded from within, the cheerful melody triggering a wave of pain, this one coursing across his ribs, sending him reeling. With a pain-lashed squint, Gary sneered and threw his shoulder against the door, producing a brilliant *crack,* a noise he enjoyed. This time—*in her*—heaving heavily, Gary backed up a few paces before throwing his entire weight into the act: hinges splinter-ripped away from the frame, the force of his momentum causing him to follow through, spilling onto the entryway's laminate floor.

A scream was just beginning to die away, and Gary glimpsed a figure—female—retreating toward the inner light of the house. His molars fused, he clawed at the hardwood and broken glass as he hunkered down and pursued.

He made one rushing leap, stretching out through midair, and took a swipe at her, missing her leg by an inch before landing on his side. Gary scrambled to his feet, rounding the corner of the great room at the same moment that Ryan Puckett— mouth ajar, eyes bugged, chest hitching—stopped short by the arm of the couch.

A very large TV was playing some evening game show. Gary could smell the savory scents of dinner, synthetic air freshener— the "normal" aromas accenting just how bad he smelled: fever-soured, mangy, dense. He didn't belong here, which was even more reason for him to stay.

Still stooped, Gary managed to raise up a bit, feeling cords and connective tissues yawn, joints pop. Felt good. He flexed and wriggled his claw-bayonetted fingers, showed Puckett a double row of deadly teeth and took a step toward.

Puckett's mouth was working to say something, but all he could manage was a sort of preface to a question—*"Whu . . . whua . . . wha . . ."*

He tried to make an evasive move but collided with the end table. A lamp pitched over, light and shadows swirling as it hit the floor.

Gary clutched Puckett by the nape of the neck, nails snagging on his dress shirt, and shoved him over the couch. Gary rounded the side of the couch and loomed over Puckett, who now, with an outstretched hand, was working on a word: *Guh-Guh.* Gary raised a claw and took a swipe at the raised hand, the long nails connecting with flesh, leaving a four-lined laceration along the man's hand. The financial advisor cried out.

Gary didn't hesitate—his claw-splayed hand shot down toward Puckett's chest, grinding him into the thick carpet while the other hand rose over his head in a contracting, nail-hooked fist and prepared to come down somewhere along his face to mar the—somehow even in terror—magazine-handsome features.

Only then did it occur to him that the screaming had continued this entire time. Over on the far side of the room next to the fireplace. Gary spared a glance and paused.

He saw the woman's face first, thin fingers drawn over her open mouth as she whimpered in short bursts. A blonde, willowy, faked-tanned thing. Not Courtney.

On some rational plane, Gary registered that Courtney had mentioned this during one of his domestic inquisitions—Puckett had a wife; it's just that Gary never devoted much care to the detail. But now, a rabid-ruthless thought emerged: *how would you like it if it happened to your wife, Puckett? Fair's fair, friend . . .*

Kids. Two of them. A boy and a girl. Both huddled at the waist of their shrieking mother, who clearly intended to place her body in between the children and the hyena-shaped thing in the living room.

The little girl's face was slicked with tears. The boy's expression was nearly impassive—something idling in the gears of terror, anger, and awe. The game show continued its inane banter as a soundtrack to the wife's shriektrack.

There were a pair of patio doors on the opposite side of the room. The glass there—Gary, with the lamplight distorting the shadow angles in the room, caught sight of his reflection. His upper body had taken on a hunched slope, his arms, which terminated in those black talons, appeared too long for his body. The angles of his face, particularly his nose and jaw, were out of proportion. His gray skin was barely visible under patches of excessive hair.

Gary shivered, his lemon-formaldehyde eyes skimming the room. The abrupt, preparatory movement caused the room to go quiet, the whimpering and crying ceasing for a moment. All those glittering, helpless eyes were set on the tall thing in the center of the room. From within his aching ribcage, Gary produced a guttural noise that slowly climbed to a long, grating growl. He raised his face and let loose a wall-quaking scream.

He stopped and looked down at Puckett, who had been an inch away, his bleeding hand still extended as a pathetic sort of defense. The woman had pulled the kids in tighter behind her, almost sitting on them now. Gary's upper lip twitched back from his sharp teeth, as he reached down and grasped the overturned table lamp, flinging it across the room and into the massive television. A thousand sparklers ignited and faded, the room dimmed to darkness.

Gary's chest rose and fell in furious bursts as he twisted and lumbered out of the family room, out of the home. He left them, crying together in the dark.

*

The car was nearly impossible to drive. Not because Gary was incapable—he still felt as though most, *most,* of his faculties remained intact—but because his body wasn't fitting right, his knees awkwardly raised on either side of the steering wheel . . . his curved spine—which continued to give the occasional achy *pop*—felt uncomfortable against the seat. He dismissed the seat belt, entertaining himself with the notion that it was no better than a leash. *Human leash,* he mused. *Leash. Collar. ID tag.* The transient standing in the window, standing there holding the dog collar with a lunatic triumph, the silver disc of the ID tag catching some of the sunlight.

Gary swerved a bit as a nagging revelation gained clarity.

In his mind, he summoned the scene from earlier—the man

standing at the window with the dog collar raised; but now his imagination tightened in on the ID tag itself, the silver disc containing the engraving of Gary's phone number . . . their home address. *Courtney.*

There was still a portion of Gary that recognized what was going on. He was sick, an illness incrementally braising his brain. When he tried to articulate a cogent narrative for what had happened and what he needed to do, his left-brain impulses folded over themselves, replaced by a smoldering sensation that everything was being transformed into a sort of fuel. His ribcage connected to his spinal cord like piston headers feeding some deep, growling combustion.

No matter what, there was no returning from tonight. Puckett had, of course, recognized him. He could drive until he ran out of gas. He'd been driving for a while as it was, and he was now back on narrow, country roads—but then what? The flickering portion of his rational mind followed that the deterioration would continue.

Maybe she was telling the truth. Maybe it was a mistake—a one-time thing with Puckett. Maybe she was sorry. *Maybe.*

Thinking about the two of them together again conjured up a new image: of mauling them, of tearing them down to puzzle-size pieces.

A violent surge of pain swept through him, his body contorted and he lost control of the car, which swerved once before careening to the left, carving two deep furrows in the soil before canting into a deep ditch and jouncing up, colliding with an anemic tree.

With steam hissing from the hood, Gary waited for the pain to die down. He should have worn a seat belt. Again, a yipping, jackal laughter.

But when that settled, Gary was still left with one of his last, cogent thoughts—Courtney. *If the feral man has the ID tag, he could find us.* Gary automatically corrected himself. *He could find* her.

Gary sneered and lashed out, kicking at the glass of the passenger-side window, which shattered. Gary crawled out of the car, his flannel shirt catching on some of the broken glass and shredding the material. Gary clawed at it, ripping the shirt away from his deformed—newformed—body.

He came down on all fours and began loping across field-lined countryside. Nashton was only a few miles away.

*

Gary used his sprinting momentum to crash through the front door of the house—the decrepit panel exploding in a burst of tinder splinters.

The staircase corridor was up ahead. He could smell him up there. Gary rounded the corner, placing his long forearms on the risers. The feral was standing up at the top, a black shape etched in deeper darkness. The figure emitted a warning sort of mewl, but Gary was already pounding up the stairs.

He burst through the threshold, colliding with the feral, the two spilling into the hallway. Gary got his claws up under the man's armpits and thrust him against the wall, plaster cracking behind the feral, who was snarling, taking swipes with his own claws.

Gary shifted, flinging the man to the floor, his body skidding into an open area between the rooms. It took him a moment, but the feral got to a crouching, defensive position. Gary was slung low, his back curved high. As he rose with his forelimbs spread, the feral man dodged, simultaneously slashing at Gary's midsection. Gary yowled, his claws going to the searing laceration beneath his ribs.

Instead of following up, the feral attempted to make a retreat, scrambling for the hallway and the stairwell. But Gary pivoted, leaping, smashing down against him, squashing his body to the floor. Something jingled in the feral's back pocket. Tamping down his squirming body with one claw-splayed hand, Gary picked at the back pocket of the filthy jeans, withdrawing Gamble's red collar, the silver disc of the ID tag.

The feral man was trying to twist around. When he tried speaking his voice was a husky rasp: "Hunters," said the feral, "hunters . . ."

Gary thought there might be a fraternal sort of plea in his tone, the consideration followed by a surge of fury as Gary opened his mouth and brought his face down to the nape of the feral's neck, his long canines piercing flesh and muscle. A high-pitched yelp tore out of the feral man. Jaw still set, Gary pressed down and pulled his face away, ripping a belt of trapezium tissue with him. Gary spit it out, sneered, and went to work again.

*

Sometime later, Gary staggered to the broken, second-floor window, clutching the dog collar in his gore-streaked claw.

The window gave directly on to a wide portion of roof that looked over the scrub-covered gully and the railroad tracks. Gary, his side still searing from the wound, gingerly gripped the sill and crawled out on to the shingled overhang.

He found a comfortable spot with his back against the siding. Light from the moon, which came in patches, occasionally touching the tangled-lattice treetops.

When he'd caught his breath he looked down at the object in his blood-glistening hand: the collar and ID tag. Gary rubbed the silver disc with what used to be his thumb. Gamble's name. His address. *Their* address. Relief—like disturbed black water stilling in a deep well—settled in him. Relief—as he imagined the feral inspired to track him down, to search him out and find the house . . . to find Courtney—braided itself with regret—regret for not having done more . . . as a husband, as a teacher.

Gary clutched the leash and tag and eased the back of his vulpine head against the house.

Time glided sideways with the phantom-cowled clouds. He shot up suddenly, fully conscious, ears perked to the eerie echo of the train whistle. He scanned the horizon. In the distance, a single light—like a phantom lantern gliding through knotted vines—stuttered behind the stands of trees lining the gullied tracks.

His yellow eyes traced the tracks north, those lines stitching through stretches of flat farmland in northern Indiana, cutting through affluent suburbs before terminating in an industrial region just outside Chicago. She was up there with her family. Maybe Courtney was really sincere about the things she'd said—about the desire to make things right. Gary still thinks he should have taken a bite out of Puckett.

He looked down at the yard, his eyes gauging the distance between the house and the tracks. He stood as best he could in his newly accustomed hyena posture and started huffing in both anticipation and an aching call to mobilization.

Staggering at first, he began trotting across the flimsy roof, gaining momentum. He growled, baring sharp teeth as he reached the edge and sprang, arcing over the yard, descending toward the gully-shouldered tracks.

As he fell Gary caught a glimpse of the moon, unobscured now as the coal-smoke clouds had drifted away. He kept his animal eyes trained on it—sneering at that bone-colored disc even as he hit the tracks, his brindle-furred body collapsing in a heap, the train's whistle banshee blaring, the locomotive's quaking light rushing on, eclipsing the moon.

Fingers Laced, as Though in Prayer

Excerpt, *Deacon's Creek Crier:* Wednesday, October 8, 1980:

> *... survivors were discovered by law enforcement a mile and a half from the scene at the former Marlin Meadows elementary school, inoperative and pending demolition since early 1979. Shortly upon release from a local hospital, several children, ranging in age from eleven to fourteen years old, were determined to have incurred minor physical injuries. Grief counselors have been assigned to the middle school for the remainder of the week ...*

*

"Face forward, Mr. Laker, and be *quiet,*" said Ms. Welch, the bus driver, addressing the boy by way of the rearview reflection in the wide, overhead mirror. The bus made its way between the high, sprawling rows of straw-colored corn, jouncing the remaining student-passengers as it rolled over the narrow backroad's ragged asphalt.

Unseasonal heat had lingered into early October, swelling in the afternoon, the severe sunlight accentuating the cornfields' already withered appearance. Susy Hendricks was unsure which was more oppressive: the untimely temperatures or the overbearing stare of Ms. Welch.

Susy, by chance, sat toward the front of the bus, the front four bench seats ahead of her having been dedicated by Ms. Welch to those with discipline issues, a sort of onboard, miniature detention. Only one student currently occupied a seat in the isolated area: Rick Laker, who now slouched on the other side of the aisle, back pressed against the window.

Due to both how the daily route was executed and how the

students were arranged throughout the bus, Susy, an eighth-grader, found herself alone during the early-morning loading and late-afternoon drop-off circuits. Essentially, she was one of the first ones on and one of the last ones off. Her fore-seat assignment didn't bother her—it provided a breathable barrier between herself and the younger sixth- and seventh-graders who composed majority of the passenger population. Secretly, this appealed to her desire for solitude among her middle-school counterparts, most of whom were younger than her. And she didn't get the sense that Ms. Welch had any interest in revising the seating chart. Probably no interest in revising anything, thought Susy, pondering the woman's thick, antique-looking glasses, that unruly, almost mannish cap of curly hair. And that flannel shirt—*In this heat? How old was Ms. Welch anyway? Mom and Dad's age . . . Grandma's age?*

Susy's spot on the bus gave her an opportunity to observe the day-to-day drama unfold, which had, for the most part, ceased to interest her these past few years. She'd be in high school this time next year, after all, and this would be her last year on this particular passage with this particular bus driver.

And again: up ahead and to the left, roughly on her eleven o'clock position, was Rick Laker, who had, since elementary school days, always been a presence—what Susy's father had repeatedly called "likable trouble."

Ms. Welch, for as long as Susy could recall, had been known as *Welch the Witch*. Susy had no idea when Ms. Welch had been verbally vandalized by the nickname. Though it was Rick Laker who had at some point—in that donkey-ornery voice—provided an acidic extension: *Welch the Witch . . . the Bus-Drivin' Bitch*. Susy'd never referred to the woman this way, though she typically snickered along with its accuracy.

Susy'd lost track of what Rick had gotten in trouble for this time; but she did know that his careless posture—his back against the window, legs stretched out, scuffed-up Converse hanging over the lip of the bench seat—was like bawl-out bait for the bus driver. *Just a matter of time*. Susy put down her paperback and stared out the window to her right, burrowing further into the solace of daydream isolation.

The corn was brittle-looking, as if it had all been tea-steeped and left to dry. The faded-gold color suddenly reminded Susy of the tint of her mother's hair, which had shifted slightly over the past year. Dyeing it, she knew, tones passed through a number of phases, rarely allowing those newly emerging threads of gray to remain too awful long. (The thought of that quiet cosmetic adjustment caused a quiver of elusive unpleasantness—the notion like some nightbug fluttering near a lantern before zipping back into the blackness.) On the other hand, there was her balding father. Her teachers often talked about figures of speech, and now her metaphor did a sort of hopscotch, extending itself as Susy looked past the fields at the bordering screen of trees, the leaves clinging in burnt-orange, shattered-lattice patches; and it blended with the notion of her father's receding hairline (which even he teased about with some self-deprecation). And once more the pastoral comparison, no matter how playful, triggered flickers of mild melancholy.

"*Hey.*" Susy's absentminded aspect remained steadfast as the insistent voice came again. "*Hey,* Hendricks." Susy's head slowly swiveled as she glanced across the aisle, up and over to where Rick Laker was leaning forward; as a form of acknowledgment, she raised her eyebrows slightly. "Did you pick your topic for Schanker?" He was talking about the research paper for their history class, a paper that was due by the end of the week.

Susy nodded. "Finished it."

Rick's face puckered, either disgust or disbelief. "No way." The bus rolled roughly. "Prove it."

She exhaled. Not in the mood either to mollify the boy or to prolong the unavoidable, she unzipped her backpack, retrieving the five stapled pages she'd typed the night before. She held the title page in front of her—an Ace in a tedious card game.

He squinted at the cover page, lips silently moving as he

read, a sour smile spreading. "What the hell is a Johnstown Flood?"

Ms. Welch's voice peeled from the front. "Mr. Laker—I won't repeat myself: face forward and be quiet!"

The kids in the back of the bus carried on as usual, unfazed by the daily Rick Laker reprimand. Rick cast a glare toward the front and began slowly scooting back on the seat, but said to Susy, "Let me see it."

Susy automatically shook her head; and instead of saying, *AbsolutelyNoWay,* her face flinched the semblance. She glanced at Ms. Welch: those large, ever-present eyes (somewhat distorted behind thick eyeglass lenses) reflected in the overhead mirror alternated from the road ahead to inspecting the interaction.

Rick again hissed, "Come on, Hendricks—let me see it."

Susy ignored this one and was opening her backpack when Rick, grinning, shot forward, his long arm curving and tearing the essay out of her hand. He recoiled, pressing his back to the window, returning to his insolent position, smug with what was certain to be a short-lived conquest. From the front: Ms. Welch: *"I've had enough of your antics today, Mr. Laker . . ."*

Susy's eyes were wide, her mouth set as she watched Rick mockingly begin to crease and inspect the stapled pages. The boy's entire demeanor was a smirk. "You know," he said to Susy, "maybe I'll just hold on to—"

"Mr. Laker!"

The glass behind Rick Laker's head and shoulders exploded into the bus's interior; and except for flinching and wincing at the percussion and its brief shower of broken glass, Susy's attention remained bolted to the boy, watching what transpired in those two to three seconds with excruciating clarity.

A dark shape had crashed against the side of the bus, the window shattering and the dividing bar fracturing as two long, limb-like things thrust through the shards. In a single, fluid movement, the dark shape's arms had wrapped themselves around Rick's upper body and neck; and for a gaspy, split-instant—before the glittering glass had even settled to the floor—he and Susy shared the precise expression: queasy disbelief.

It tugged Rick through the shattered frame, the toe of the boy's sneaker briefly clipping the window's metal casing before both slipped down from sight.

Ms. Welch stopped the bus so suddenly that Susy's head was thrown into the weakly padded seat in front of her, the impact creating a wink of stars before things became clear again. For a few seconds, all Susy could do was stare at the broken window, trying to grasp what had just happened, contemplating the slender trickles of blood tracing the toothy shards fringing the sill.

*

Excerpt, *Deacon's Creek Crier:* Friday, September 22, 2000:

As part of our ongoing series, Remembrances, *we revisit the bus tragedy of 1980, known locally as the Marlin Meadows incident, one of the more unfortunate anecdotes in town history. Approaching the twenty-year mark, we recently spoke with several individuals present that day, among them Susan Hendricks . . .*

*

A wasp-wing whir hummed into Susy's awareness, the drone finally transforming into overlapping babble. She could hear that some kids in the back were already mildly hysterical, some crying and some preparing to do so; she gripped the back of the seats on either side of her and hauled herself up. Giving a cursory scan of the bus, she saw that most of the kids back there appeared to have been equally stunned by the violent commotion followed by the violent deceleration. Susy spun, looking toward the front.

Ms. Welch hadn't shifted from her seated position, her stocky frame still hunched over the steering wheel; but the woman was leaning left, her face near the driver's-side glass. Susy noticed the woman's jowl pulsing, saw that her mouth was moving. And then Susy followed the aim of the woman's fixation—connected with what the bus driver was staring at.

There was an enormous tree just off the ditch, close to the road between the asphalt and the spreading wall of stalks. Its huge, overarching limbs created an umbrella of heavy shade. Something was standing there, cleaved against the trunk, nearly blending in with the barked bole and wide swath of shadow it cast. It was tall, and for a moment Susy mistook it for something connected to the tree itself. Susy craned her neck forward, her brow furrowing as she used all her attentive energy to absorb details: its dark, mahogany-streaked body was composed of sinewy braids, and its corded arms hung at its sides: appendages that ended in vine-like lengths. Susy was seized by the comparison to veiny brace roots at the base of cornstalks. It had thin shreds of what appeared to be black, tissue-like fibers clinging to it, as though it had dragged itself through a soot-dusted patch of cobwebs, the gossamer lengths drifting delicately in the breeze. Then there was its face.

Initially, Susy was reminded of the pale, corrugated exterior of a beehive, but the longer (merely a stretch of seconds) she stared, the more she understood that it was not paper-like ribbing, but rather the entwined, horizontally woven flesh of human fingers. Susy watched those fingers gently unclasp and contract. Years afterward, she would think about that listless, respiration-like movement and associate it with the fragile flexing of a resting butterfly's wings.

Susy ticked her eyeline from the fingerface thing to the bus driver. The woman had unbuckled her seatbelt and risen, a knee on her seat; Susy watched the woman's mouth working, heard a hissing string of whispers. Then Ms. Welch's voice swelled with emphasis—punctuating something Susy couldn't catch—and the thing outside simultaneously shivered, the ten folded fingers that formed its face unlacing in a fleshy net, an arachnid-legged splay opening wide in what looked like a howl. Susy caught the glint of ivory barbs within that cavity before the thing crouched, slinking away from the tree, retreating into the pale-yellow curtain of cornstalks. Murmurs rose from the rear, and Susy looked in that direction. The kids still hadn't moved and were pivoting, dazed, waiting. Susy's eyes went back to the broken window that had framed the thing just a few yards from the bus. They hadn't seen it, she realized. *The tree is in the way . . . they didn't see.*

When she toggled her attention back to the front of the bus, Ms. Welch's unblinking eyes were fixed directly on Susy.

Several things were exchanged in that short stretch: the acknowledgment that what stood in that field was real; that—perhaps for not much longer—they were the only two people on the bus aware of its presence; and that Susy Hendricks wasn't going to say a single word.

Susy then noticed, beneath the confusion, the low-level crackle coming from the front of the bus. CB microphone in hand, Ms. Welch was stooping over the front seat, alternating her gaze between the side window and her passengers. "Forty-three to base," she said, only to have the chewing sound of interference return to the handpiece. Susy heard a familiar ferocity when the bus driver repeated the call. *"Forty-three to base!"* Ms. Welch tried something on the receiver, which merely produced a further chain of static. She stared for a moment at the microphone in her hand before lowering it, gently resettling it on the cradle. Ms. Welch eventually took a few steps into the aisle and now stood at the front of the bus like a reverend, the bench seats her makeshift pews. "We've had an accident, children." She paused, angling her eyes down to Susy.

Susy Hendricks—eighth-grader, above-average in nothing of any common importance—would not, at this point in her life, have used the word self-control to describe her stillness then, her *silence,* though she would have likely used the word discipline. It was discipline that kept her mouth shut—discipline that prevented her from screaming, *Something out there in the field took Rick—ripped him right through the window—some monster killed him and it's still out there . . .*

But she said nothing. The unspoken threat within Ms.

Welch's expression was tangible; and when the bus driver seemed satisfied that Susy would cooperate, only then did the woman begin blinking, starting and stopping with small bursts of breath before finally producing words. "Now, children, we've had an accident. But I need you all to remain seated, I need you all to stay calm, and I need you to be absolutely quiet while we begin exiting the bus."

Despite this request, a sobbing girl said, "What happened to the window?"

Ms. Welch hesitated, blinking a glance at Susy. "We hit . . . we hit a tree just over there—too close to the road . . . just a little accident . . ." Ms. Welch unbuttoned and removed her flannel shirt, revealing a sweat-stained tank-top beneath. She moved to the broken window, snapped the flannel like a tablecloth, and draped the shirt over the damaged sill, partially obscuring the seat.

From the back, one of the boys said, "Where's Rick?"

When Ms. Welch spoke, some of that drill-sergeant impatience had returned. "Children, I want you all to gather your belongings, do you understand?" The response of tepid murmurs was evidently not good enough. Ms. Welch raised both hands, as if fending off something wide and brute-like. Susy realized that Ms. Welch was good at that: not creating calm but rather squashing the emergence of protest. *Do you understand, children?* The kids bristled and began doing as they'd been told. "We will find Rick very soon, but for now we are going to exit the bus." Ms. Welch ambled down the aisle as she made her way toward the rear of the bus. Once there, she wrenched the handle to the emergency door and shoved it open. Susy heard Ms. Welch give one of the bigger boys, Eric Hiatt (Susy's only eighth-grade counterpart currently aboard), instructions to lower the children from the bus as she released them seat by seat. "Keep them in single file," she said to Eric, who nodded, hopping down from the bus.

Susy watched Ms. Welch return to the front to gather several items: a small metal toolbox, a first-aid kit, a slim fire extinguisher. Still bustling, Ms. Welch glanced at Susy. "Get your things pulled together, young lady."

Susy batted her eyes, the good-student part of her instinctively complying. It was also the good-student part of her that said, "Can I help you carry something?"

Ms. Welch inspected her for a beat, the familiar expression of skepticism; but it broke. "I, um . . . here." Ms. Welch extended the small fire extinguisher. "Keep that safe now, Susy."

The bus driver had not addressed her by her first name in quite some time. "Yes, ma'am."

Susy and Ms. Welch were the last ones to descend from the rear of the bus, and though there was a fair amount of idle tension, the children had followed orders, remaining in an uneasy single file on the edge of the weed-furred ditch.

Huffing, Ms. Welch hefted the first-aid kit and toolbox, scanned her surroundings before speaking. "All right, boys and girls . . . we're going to take a little walk . . ."

Almost immediately, questions began—*To where? . . . How long? . . . Can't you call for help? . . . What're we gonna do about Rick?* "There is an elementary school not far from here—it's a safe place to stay while we wait for help."

As Ms. Welch set out, Susy didn't budge; the bus driver looked back at her. Susy squinted, as much from the slanting sun as from her disbelief. Ms. Welch shuffled to a stop, spinning to look at the unmoving girl. The older woman opened her mouth to say something but faltered; she again addressed the group. "Children, I understand you're shook up, but the rest of you are going to be just fine. We'll find Rick. To tell the truth, I expect he's run off . . . horsing around at this inappropriate time."

To tell the truth. Susy watched the woman bat her eyes, appraising the ground. "You all . . . you all are my responsibility and my priority. No one is going to get hurt, okay? You need to stay with me so I can keep you safe."

The response was subtle, but Susy noticed that the crying had ceased. Though Susy knew better, the kids apparently believed. Ms. Welch nodded stiffly and turned, heading south down the road, instructing the children to follow her along the side of the bus opposite the broken window—opposite, known only to Susy and Ms. Welch, where the creature had dragged Rick off into the field. Still, Susy glanced over, seeing something shift within the stalks, seeing something just across the ditch under the tree; a glimmer of white caught the light, and as the kids began marching along the slim road, she saw that it was Rick's blood-streaked sneaker. Nearby, the damaged pages of Susy's essay were being scattered by the wind, drifting across the ditch and haphazardly gliding into the field, the chafing sound of dry paper merging with the shushing abrasion radiating from the stalks' withered ribbons.

*

Before they were too far from the bus, it occurred to Susy that Ms. Welch was leading them into some sort of trap. She was more wary of the bus driver than ever, but alert enough to try and stay near the woman. *Watch her,* came a guiding voice. *Listen*. Though the mechanics were too sophisticated for Susy to articulate, she caught a mental glimpse of something profound: that in order to maintain their own safety, people were willing to withhold disobedience—people were willing to subscribe to lies.

Ms. Welch moved swiftly, quite a few paces ahead of her charges. Susy took several vibrant strides to sidle up next to the bus driver. The girl twisted at the waist, squint-eyed scanning the line of kids and the fields. As they drew away from the bus, several things occurred to her, not the least of which being the notion that each of them would end up like Rick.

She gave a quick glance at the side of the bus driver's sweat-slicked face—the woman was mumble-whispering to herself in tight little wheezes. Susy was aware of the weight of the miniature fire extinguisher in her hand. She licked her lips and pulled the pin; she squeezed the trigger, aiming the burst of white powder at the cracked asphalt, marking a line with a point to create a crude arrow indicating the direction which they were walking. Ms. Welch, obviously startled by the sound, faltered for moment; but her frown faded, giving a curt nod of approval. After a dozen yards she said, "Clever little thing, ain't you?" They walked for some time in silence. Now and again Susy thought she heard something (some*things*?) moving in the fields on either side of the road. Eventually Ms. Welch spoke. "Susy's a pretty name."

Uncertain, Susy said, "Thank you."

"I almost named my daughter Susan. Is your full name Susan?"

"No." She'd been asked the question before by other prying adults.

"Are you—" Ms. Welch didn't slow but swiveled her head toward the fields behind and ahead. "Are you . . . named after someone in your family?"

Susy hesitated. "My mom named me after a character in a movie."

"Oh?" the woman smirked. "Who's that then?"

"The actress's name is Audrey Hepburn . . . but I can't remember the movie."

Ms. Welch appeared to ponder this for a minute. To herself she murmured, "Susy . . . Susy," and then she smiled, snapped her fingers once, and when she spoke an edge had disappeared from her voice. "Susy Hendrix—*Wait Until Dark*."

Susy nodded. "Yeah. I mean yes."

Ms. Welch was still smiling, thinking back, perhaps. "Clever," she said.

The guiding voice came again: *Keep her steady.* Susy ventured, "What is your daughter's name?"

Susy watched Ms. Welch's smile flicker and fade, and soon her expression returned to its accustomed severity. The bus driver lifted her chin, a reflection flaring in the thick lenses of her glasses. Squinting, as though the declining sun had asked the question instead of a fourteen-year-old girl, the woman said, "Elizabeth." They walked. "Her name was Elizabeth."

*

Excerpt, *Deacon's Creek Crier:* Friday, September 22, 2000:

". . . and it was just a horrendous confluence of events," says Hendricks, president of the Deacon's Creek Civic League. "And, yes, in the months and years that followed there was a lot of speculation and discussion about the woman's personal life and mental state at the time of the accident. Honestly, I'm sympathetic to this aspect of often insatiable public scrutiny," she says. "My own personal life has not necessarily remained unscathed these past few years." Hendricks refers to the highly publicized custody battle between her and her ex-husband, former Louisville City Council member Mark Chambers, who was indicted for bribery and extortion in 1998. Chambers is currently serving a forty-month sentence in a federal detention facility in New York. "No matter what was allegedly uncovered about the woman, the important thing people need to remember is that common gossip often distorts the facts, which ultimately changes the truth." . . . Citing several inconsistencies in the children's stories, damage to the bus itself, and location of the deceased, investigators could never accurately determine and align the actual sequence of the collision, though the most widely accepted report was that the driver had become distracted and made a negligent maneuver, resulting in her swerving into a tree . . .

*

"This heat," said Ms. Welch in wheeze-speak. "I remember autumn when I was a little girl." Something had shifted in her demeanor as they drew farther and farther from the bus, and she now produced the rarity of an unguarded smile, making her appear momentarily younger. "I grew up not far from here"—she waved at a vague place in the distance—"over in Gallaudet. We walked to school back then—the town . . . it was small enough. I remember." She shook her head. "I remember, sometimes on those afternoons, it would rain real light, just enough to make everything . . . glisten. I'd be carrying my books on the way home, just gazing over everything—the sky, after the rain, was like this, oh, tumble of slate-colored glasswool . . . and when the sun would finally poke out, it would ignite the trees . . . honey-glows and burgundies . . . the fields were just murals of gold ribbons . . . and everything smelled clammy and rusty . . . and down under the bridge along the creek those rocks were just glazed with that rain-slick membrane . . ."

No longer doubting it, Susy was certain Ms. Welch was disturbed. Or in shock. Or that the current state of shock had just accentuated her derangement. Susy, too, momentarily wondered if it was she who was in shock—that Rick truly had been thrown from the bus. The creature: a creation solely of Susy's mental making. She turned, surveying the line of kids, their shadows trailing like shaded caps along the road. Far behind them, Susy saw the fingerface thing: it remained within the field, concealing itself as it skulked and wove through the stalks. She held her breath and faced forward. When she exhaled, she was afraid it would rattle loose a scream—a scream for the kids to run: to run away from this woman who had co-witnessed a monster murder a boy and now ordered a bunch of middle-schoolers to march like good soldiers to a "safe" place.

For the first time during this ordeal, Susy had a need for her parents: to ask her dad how to do the right thing—to ask her mom how to do the *smart* thing. Susy's lower lip began to tremble, so she bit down on it briefly before taking a deep breath. "Ms. Welch," Susy whispered, checking to make sure the others couldn't hear, "what is that thing that took Rick?"

Ms. Welch shot a look at Susy. It took quite some time for the woman to respond. "It is . . . a mistake." They'd been walking for twenty minutes, Ms. Welch's face beaded with sweat, her breathing labored. "It is . . . also . . . my fault."

Susy had continued making the intermittent arrow with the fire extinguisher, but now cradled the red cylinder, not wanting noise to distract the woman. "I don't like telling the whole story. But I can say that, when I was a little girl, in those years right after the Depression, my family attended a church—my family, on my daddy's side, for generations, had been members of a church. And it"—she gave an impatient wave—"looked and sounded and behaved like any other Baptist church. But it wasn't. At least not down deep. And my daddy's line was down deep." She went quiet, and Susy thought the woman had gone into some sort of trance. "There were elders who met outside of Sunday services. Several nights a week, my mother and father would meet with the others; and when I was old enough, I started going to the meetings too. We studied old books and hymns that had been in the church since . . . well, a long, long time ago. We prayed, and there were psalms that could . . . make things *happen*." From her back pocket she withdrew a handkerchief, which she used to mop her forehead. "I eventually fell away from the church—ran away, to be honest—but I'd pilfered some of those psalm-books—some of the older ones. Had them hidden away. Hadn't looked at those filthy pages in years. My husband never even saw them. Never said a word to no one." She cast a look over her shoulder before quietly continuing. "Though it's one of them prayers that's keeping those things away now. But it's a brittle barrier. Won't last long."

Susy verbally nudged: "Things?"

"Yes. I suspect there're more than one of them." With some visible caution, the woman went on. "This time of year is very difficult for me. Last night I got to dwelling on my daughter . . ." Susy looked over at the woman: the corners of Ms. Welch' eyes were damp—tears, perspiration, she couldn't tell. "My daughter . . . passed away some years ago."

Hesitating for only a moment, Susy said, "I'm sorry."

Ms. Welch did not seem angry, but she flicked the back of her hand and made a dismissive noise. "She was . . . something like me, I suppose . . . never could quite reconcile her lot in life." That hung for a span before she spoke again. "Like I said, last night . . . well, my mind—as it's wont to do—drifted to a rather poisonous place . . . and I dug out one of those old prayer books. They were frail, just falling to pieces; but I found the one

I was looking for . . . the prayer I was hoping would—"

Susy watched the woman, who now glanced at Susy, perhaps trying to choose her words carefully. "I was searching for a prayer, a powerful one—one that would bring me . . . well, peace."

Susy considered that for a while as they walked, pondering what sort of peace the woman had been looking for that would conjure up that sort of creature. The peace, she figured, was the peace of no longer living. "Why did it attack us out here?"

The woman was already nodding. "All them prayers work a little differently for different people." Ms. Welch pointed at the sprawl of fields in the east, over toward where the corn bordered the woods. "Used to be a little church chapel over yonder, burned down when I was a kid—not one of the churches linked with my daddy's family, but still. Maybe that has something to do with it too."

Susy: "Why Rick?"

Ms. Welch's expression was briefly pained, as though she had stepped on a tack. "I thought . . . the way I'd said the words, what was in my heart—I thought I'd receive . . . instant deliverance while I was alone last night." She shook her head, flinging beads of sweat from her curly hair. "I don't understand why it happened this way."

One of the kids called out from the line. "When are we going to get to the school?"

Ms. Welch did not stop walking but adjusted her glasses and called over her shoulder, "Not much farther, children."

Again, Susy had the urge to turn and scream at the kids—to run for their lives. She heard murmurs, exchanges of impatience. For the sake of harmonious cohesion, Susy wondered how much longer she'd have to operate like an accomplice—how much longer she'd play the part of witch's assistant.

*

Excerpt, *Deacon's Creek Crier:* Friday, September 22, 2000:
  . . . the Franklin Township transportation department had never

received a complaint about Rachel Welch in all her fifteen years of service. Two minor reprimands were reported in her personnel file; Welch took a brief leave of absence in the winter of 1977. Rath County court records reflect an unstable private life. Welch's ex-husband, David M. Welch, had been briefly incarcerated in 1947 for armed robbery; he later accrued several misdemeanors in both Rath and Colfax counties. The couple had one child, Elizabeth E. Welch, who was born in 1951. Rachel Welch (née Sommerville) and David Welch were married in 1952. In 1966, the Department of Children and Family Services responded to accusations submitted by Rachel Welch, submitting a number of allegations against her husband including varieties of abuse toward both herself and their daughter. The two were separated for a number of years before filing for divorce in 1970. Their daughter, Elizabeth, who was then a resident of Michigan, committed suicide in October 1976 at the age of twenty-five . . .

*

The now-vacant Marlin Meadows Elementary School had remained relatively untouched by the errant forces of nature and vandalism. Some of the windows had been boarded over, while others reflected the weakening sunlight. The entire structure was surrounded by a chain-link fence, and the fence was capped with an elongated Slinky of barbed wire.

Susy kept pace with Ms. Welch while the others followed into what had once been the school's parking lot. Susy watched Ms. Welch nervously survey the fields and hillish barrier of woods beyond. We don't have much time, Susy sensed. *Welch's words aren't going to work for much longer.*

"All right, everyone," said Ms. Welch, "I need you to huddle in close here and stay put." The weary kids fell out of line and clustered up. "Susy, you too."

Susy acted as if she hadn't heard and trailed behind Ms. Welch; she watched the bus driver select a segment of fencing on a seam lining the chained and locked gate; hunching over, she dropped the rust-scabbed toolbox on the ground and flipped open the lid. Monitoring the woman's movements, Susy peeked over the woman's shoulder. Rifling through tools, Ms. Welch's hand suddenly froze, hovering over something. Fingers slightly tremoring, from the toolbox Ms. Welch withdrew a slim glass bottle with a difficult-to-read label, brown liquid sloshing inside. Susy thought the woman moved with an odd hesitancy, like someone discovering a forgotten and rotten mystery at the bottom of a fridge. The moment passed and Ms. Welch swept up the bottle, flinging it far into the tall grass. She turned, saw Susy. For the second time that day, the two signed a speechless contract, though this time there was no fever-eyed threat in Ms. Welch's features, only, thought Susy, a sort of shame. Susy's eyelids fluttered and she looked away, appraising the fields, the lifeless school.

From the toolbox, Ms. Welch withdrew a pair of metal snips, which she immediately began using on the interlocking-wire seam. After a few minutes, Ms. Welch had cut enough to peel back a right-angled, waist-high wedge of the fence. Her breathing labored, the bus driver began ushering the children in through the opening. Once all the others had made it through, Ms. Welch clasped a hand to Susy's elbow, directing the girl through space before sliding the toolbox forward and, on her hands and knees, awkwardly crawling through the opening. Ms. Welch did not pause to catch her breath, but rather went to work with a spool of wire from the toolbox, using pliers and the metal coil to bind the fence's seam. The woman's hair clung to her temples in slender, curvy worms. "Get . . . those kids . . . inside, you hear?"

Susy cast a glance, first at the gawking group, then at the school. Susy opened her mouth to say something, but Ms. Welch grimaced. "Damn it, young lady—*go on!*"

Susy's legs were moving then. On the near side of the building, just off the boarded-over main entrance, was a short set of concrete steps leading up to a nondescript service door. Depressions along the overgrowth indicated recent foot-traffic. Not slowing, she jogged up the steps, reached out, and tried the door handle, which twisted freely as hinges yawned into darkness.

An elbowed corridor was revealed. As she sized up the interior, it took Susy a moment to find her voice. "Guys," she said, "come this way." The group was unconvinced, and hesitated; but it was Eric—the other eighth-grader who'd helped lower the kids from the rear of the bus—who made the first strides forward. As he passed through the threshold, he slid Susy a half-second look that contained contents tricky for her to immediately translate: admiration, distaste—the knowledge of possible deception. The others followed Eric inside.

For a moment, Susy watched Ms. Welch, the woman frantically re-rigging the fence before reluctantly falling in line with the last kid entering the school.

It was dim for a portion of the corridor, some leaves and debris coving the hall, but the trek was brief, and tall windows set high in the lobby provided plenty of light. *What light is left,* thought Susy. Plaster and deconstruction fallout covered the floor. In this space, the students unwound from their amoeba-like proximity, their small conversations echoing under the tall ceiling. The group had stirred up dust; specks swam in the slanted spokes of sunlight. Susy noted that Eric, elbows on his knees, had taken a seat on one of the steps along the open stairwell. The boy eyed her for a moment before impassively averting her gaze.

On impulse, Susy swallowed and, trying to intone some hope, said, "Hey . . . we made it." She'd wanted to sound triumphant, but her voice rang soft, self-soothing.

"Why did she bring us here?" said one of the kids.

Susy blinked, looking at the group, looking at the walls, the shadowed hallways that gave into dark recesses. "It's like she said: we're her responsibility . . . she wants to keep us safe."

Several other kids spoke, essentially expressing the same suspicion. Attempting to summon more confidence, Susy said: "I'm going to check on Ms. Welch . . . see if she needs any help." This time, no one responded.

She surveyed the room one last time before turning, leaving, backtracking through the corridor and pushing through the rickety door. She skidded to a stop on the top step, slapping a hand to her mouth to stifle a scream. A water balloon of nausea ruptured in her stomach.

Susy counted five of them: three were on the boundary of the property, lingering in the shade-laden cushion where the fields met the woods; another—as though it were getting acclimated to the practice of using its legs—was simply slinking across the weeded lot; and then there was the one that was against the fence, directly opposite Ms. Welch.

The two were parallel to each other, though the creature stood a few feet taller. Clinging in generous patches here and there, the black doilies of cobwebs responded to the weak breeze. Ms. Welch stood with her arms at her sides, fists clenched; Susy could hear the woman whispering, praying. Susy managed one move down the concrete steps before clasping the handrail and going rigid.

From only a dozen paces now, Susy could clearly see the thing's face: those interlaced human fingers, splayed wide and wiggling; and if those appendages were fingers, then the exposed palms were lined with thorny, sand-shark teeth. Its long limbs were raised—its hands: those brace roots braided through the chain-link grate.

And then Susy heard music. A numb segment transpired before she understood that the sound was being emitted by the finger-funnel of all five of the creatures' faces: unpleasant, record-scratchy, fervid gospel hymns that had been dissected and discordantly resewn—those faces acting as fleshy phonograph horns channeling an overlapping, whining transmission.

Susy was prepared to pivot, flee, finally tell the others the truth—to panic out an escape plan; but Ms. Welch, almost emotionless, turned around and peered at Susy. The woman spoke, her voice uncharacteristically calm, serene. "You need to go back in there with those kids, sweetheart, and lock that door." When

Susy did not abandon her visual paralysis, Ms. Welch moved away from the fence, hobbling over to the girl, raising her voice but maintaining an unusual tranquility. She approached Susy on the concrete steps. "I said you need to get back in there with the rest of them."

After a time, Susy simply bobbed her head but continued standing still. Near enough now, Ms. Welch reached out with both hands and, grasping Susy's shoulders, shook the girl twice, the motion rattling loose a line of moisture resting on the brim of her lower eyelids.

As Ms. Welch gave Susy a not-unkind shove toward the door, she said, "Keep them safe, Susy—you tell them I'm going to get help." A string of seconds passed before Susy nodded. Ms. Welch responded by doing the same. The bus driver turned and limped back toward the fence while the creatures converged on the other side.

Susy smothered the urge for a parting word, and just before the girl retreated into the shadows of the service-door corridor, Ms. Welch called over her shoulder, "And Susy"—the girl turned, vaguely glimpsing the harsh blush of onrushing dusk— "don't let those kids outside, you hear me? Don't let them see."

*

Excerpt, *Deacon's Creek Crier:* Wednesday, December 17, 1980:
   . . . first responders arriving on the scene discovered Welch on the property's exterior, near the fence's perimeter along the front of the building. Investigators believe the woman attempted to climb the fence and became tangled in the upper barrier of barbed wire; the injuries she'd incurred included significant lacerations to her throat and trauma to her torso. Though noting a number of inconsistencies with the investigators' findings, the coroner determined cause of death to be massive blood loss . . . toxicology reports revealed the presence of a number of prescription drugs along with trace amounts of . . .

*

Excerpt, *Deacon's Creek Crier:* Friday, September 22, 2000:

". . . *and for months after the accident, people around town would say things like 'Our thoughts and prayers are with you.' But, to tell the truth,*" says Hendricks, "*I'm not sure that helped [Rick Laker's] family find solace in the loss of their child; and I'd be disingenuous if I didn't acknowledge some regret in not being able to offer more assistance with [the State Police] investigation. I wish I could have helped provide answers to those questions; but the truth is that I just couldn't recall certain things that transpired . . . even now, in the wake of horrific tragedies, people offer the 'thoughts-and-prayers' sentiment, but I wonder if people actually comprehend what their thoughts and prayers might actually produce . . .*"

*

Susy pulled the service door closed, returning to the school's lobby and to the growing anxiety of her younger peers. She did as Ms. Welch had instructed, which was to nurture the narrative that the bus driver was leaving to seek help. But Susy went on to venture an addition, independently adding her own insulative embellishment, fabricating the promise that everything—that *everyone*—was going to be just fine.

By Goats Be Guided

Martin Colegrove flinched when his mother drove over the pothole, the impact jarring the car as the tire snagged over the cavity's ragged lip. October—the countryside a cluster of rusts, burgundies, cinnamons. Most of the fields were filled with soon-to-be-harvested stalks, creating wheat-tinted walls as his mother casually coursed along the cattail-spiked ditches lining the narrow backroads. After a moment, Martin returned his gaze to the passing countryside, eager to resume his daydream, savoring the novel notion that the straight-lined roads and squared-off tracks of farmland represented panels and frames in a pastoral comic book—the borders of his own boring story here in Sycamore Mill.

Martin mumbled, "Derek said it was about two miles down on Carriage." Earlier that day on the school bus, Derek Kirby had scrawled out turn-by-turn directions to his house.

His mother sighed. "Oh sure . . . Carriage Lane." His mom's comment made it sound as though she were talking to herself. Still he looked over at her, sensing that doing so might cough up a clarifying comment. She glanced sidelong at her son and cleared her throat. "It was just a popular place out here in the country"—she fidgeted her fingers at the passing fields and wavy walls of trees—"for high school kids with too much time on their hands." This was punctuated by a prim, almost embarrassed, *I've-already-said-too-much* nod.

Too much time on their hands. Martin got the picture, and the picture was . . . disturbing.

He'd only really started noticing girls over the past few years—in earnest now that he was roughly eight weeks into his freshmen year—and with passing the polished female upperclassmen in the hallways (most of whom were big-haired and made more attractive by overuse of cosmetics—their appearance sort of reminding Martin of the women on TV who were upset with President Clinton), he'd found it difficult not to daydream, and so had only just begun tinkering with the distant idea that his mom, too, had once been a *girl*. Possibly a pretty one. Mostly it was intolerable to conjure images of his mom as a younger woman. A younger *anything*. And now he suspected his mom had just taken a personal trip, however fleeting, down some intimate memory lane.

Martin returned to the window, to the flipping panels of predictability.

After several miles in which a physical ellipsis of silence had settled, the station wagon slowed at the end of an overgrown gravel drive. A large house was crouched up there—a vague gray structure cocooned within a weave-work of trees.

Martin's mother pulled in, slowly jouncing over ruts as he scanned the front yard, the cornfield, the wide belt of woods surrounding the brindle-colored lawn. He was peering out when he saw the figure standing in the woods. Martin, after a second, recognized Derek Kirby, his pale, expressionless face almost floating in contrast to the dark interior of the woods.

Leaning toward the window, Martin thought he saw a thin *gotcha*-grin on Derek's face, just before the older boy was concealed by overlapping tree trunks.

"You okay, kiddo?" said Martin's mother.

After a moment Martin said, "Yeah, sure, fine." He sat back and looked at the house—a two-story Victorian thing—a squarish structure that had once been white (maybe) but was now dishwater gray. Martin would have guessed it abandoned. "Just thought I saw something in the woods."

"Like an animal?"

"Yeah," Martin's brow twitched. "Maybe."

The station wagon slowed to a stop next to the front porch and, as if on cue, a woman stepped out. Martin assumed this was

Derek's mother. He unfastened his seatbelt, craning his neck to look out the back window, saw Derek strolling up the driveway, and shoved open the passenger door, slipping out of the car.

"Hey," Martin said to Derek.

After a few beats Derek said, "You guys have trouble finding the house?" He was taller than Martin, and angled his eyes down when speaking. A thick flannel shirt, his jeans fashionably shredded across the knees.

"No," Martin shrugged. *Something cool.* "No sweat, man."

The women, though strangers to each other, were chatting and laughing. Derek said, "Come on," bopping Martin on the shoulder and gesturing toward the woods. "I want to show you something." Martin began edging away from the station wagon to follow Derek.

"Martin," his mom called, "it's getting chilly out . . . don't run off without a jacket."

Jesus, Martin thought, *does she think this is some sort of play date?* Martin rounded the car and approached the driver's-side window, where his mother handed him his hooded sweatshirt. "Thanks," Martin mumbled, reluctantly slipping into the hoodie.

Martin's mom said, "I'll be back in a couple of hours—about six, okay? I'm just going to go into town to run some errands."

Martin began jogging, catching up with Derek, pulling up alongside the older boy on the wooded trail. "Where're we going?" said Martin.

"It's a secret," Derek said, glancing over his shoulder, combing his scraggly, beginner's goatee with his long fingers.

The path opened up into a small, leaf-strewn clearing situated above the embankment of a creek.

"Well, there it is." Derek put his hands on his hips.

It took Martin a moment to notice what Derek was referring to—a lean-to fort, camouflaged with a dark tarp, branches, and other underbrush debris. Martin grinned, curious, and approached the structure, crouching in for a closer look. "Cool."

Derek picked up a fallen branch, about the size of Martin's

wrist, and broke it over his knee. "I started a new hideout sort of thing." With one piece of the splintered stick, Derek pointed to a crudely dug hole, a shovel sticking out of a large mound of dirt. "I was going to put boards over the top, turn it into an underground clubhouse." Martin nodded, returning his attention to the lean-to. Inside was a crate of junk, a couple of flashlights, a crumpled pack of cigarettes, a bundle of faded baseball cards. He paused on a bunched-up sleeping bag in the corner. "You camp out here?" he asked.

Derek snorted. "Nah," he said. "That's for me and my girl-friend." The older boy reached down and swept up the crumpled pack of cigarettes, fingering one from the pack. He fished a lighter from his pocket and swiftly lit one, exhaling a stream of blue-gray smoke. Martin tried not to gawk at this fascinating routine and instead occupied himself with the crudely dug, dirt-walled pit.

*

A month before.

Because of how the route was arranged—and because of his family's distant proximity to the school—Martin was one of the first kids on the bus, one of the last kids to leave. But on this morning Martin hadn't been the first passenger. A strange-looking guy sitting in the back of the bus. New kid.

The high school boys were a library of (what Martin suspect-ed were defective) facts about sex. Martin eavesdropped a lot—the boasting and bragging, hearing about what to do to a girl's body. Repelled and intrigued, most times Martin convinced himself that he had heard enough to skip what his father had frequently referred to as "The Talk." Martin had deftly avoided that particular chat with his father for several years now; and his father, on a few occasions, had said things like, "Son, it's about time we had that discussion," or "Martin, we should sit down and have a serious chat—a man-to-man conversation." Merciful-ly, his father was a busy man of moderate civic importance in town, whose presence at formal dinnertime meetings conveniently supplied frequent absences at home.

One afternoon in early September—the school bus on the way home: Martin had been sitting alone, as usual, losing himself in one of his comic books. He caught movement at his shoulder.

The new kid was lowering himself over the seat, staring intently at Martin's comic. Martin froze, steadying himself for whatever upper-classman ridicule was about to ensue.

"You like comics?" said the guy.

Martin nodded. "Yeah," cleared his throat. "Spend most of my allowance on them."

Instead of laughing, the guy raised his eyebrows and shook his head. "Shit, man, I hear you." He swung around and settled in next to Martin. "So—you got any other comics on you?"

Martin began rifling through his backpack, producing several glossy comics. The older boy smirked as Martin handed over the slender stack of books.

"I'm Derek."

The older boy offered his pale hand. Martin shook it, said his name.

"Nice to know you, dude. You got nice taste."

Martin waited for a cruel punchline, but finally said, "Thanks."

He was a tall guy—*gangly*, Martin thought. He had black, stringy hair that dangled down over his eyebrows, an uneven tuft of hair on his chin. Though Derek carried himself with the ease of one of the popular kids, he looked gaunt, geeky. Martin was struck with the image—a punk-rock version of Ichabod Crane.

They became friendly—an affinity for illustrators like Frazetta, Mike Zeck, Frank Miller, the duo of Eastman and Laird.

"I have a fucking library of comics," said Derek, though during the intervening weeks he never produced a single issue to share. One afternoon Derek said, "You should come over and hang out at my house sometime." Martin said he'd ask his mom for permission. One day Derek gave him directions.

*

"So," Derek said, smoothly exhaling a ragged, dragon's tail of smoke, "you want to check out the rest of the place?" Derek finished his cigarette, butting it out against the bole of an oak.

Martin was still considering the things that Derek and his girlfriend had been doing out here. "Sure." The boys departed, walking past the lean-to and the partially dug bunker.

Martin followed Derek along a path, which curved and meandered around the property, eventually opening in the back yard. Derek snorted, gesturing toward something. "Take a look at this." Martin saw an old well, which looked like everything else around here: crudely constructed and prepared to fall apart. Derek strolled over to the well, propping his hands on the lip of the opening. Martin approached, half expecting to find a brick-lined tunnel leading into blackness. He leaned in and instead saw clumps of grass-bristled soil less than three feet down. He looked at Derek, who was smiling and nodding, as if agreeing with what he read in Martin's expression. "Weird, huh?"

Martin grinned, "Yeah."

Derek removed his hands from the mouth of the well. He looked around as though scrabbling for another anecdote, eventually extending a finger. "Found a dead fox out that way when I first started exploring—just bones and fur." Martin nodded. "Most all of this stuff was like this when we bought the place."

Martin wondered about the *we*. "What's your dad do?"

Derek shook his head and glanced over his shoulder at the house. "Dad split when I was a kid. Just been me and her." Derek jutted his head toward the house.

Martin noted a rusty swing set on the far side of the yard, two of the seats were missing, a few solitary chains hanging from the overhead rail. Shadows were creeping long across the weedy, untended expanse.

The boys entered the house through a back patio, what Martin would have described as a sun room; but the windows were warped and shower-curtain filmy, letting in little light. The space was cluttered with boxes Martin assumed were left over from their move here. Everything smelled stale, skunky. There was a coffee table in the middle of the room, with an ashtray crowded with crumpled cigarette butts, most of which were smudged with crimson lipstick. Some of the butts didn't look like cigarette filters at all, more like brownish stubs of tar-blotched paper.

The porch led directly into the kitchen. Derek's mom was sitting at the table. The radio was on, what sounded like classic rock, and she was studying a calculator, along with what appeared to be a stack of bills.

"Hey," Derek said, greeting his mom without slowing stride. "We're going to hang out upstairs for a while."

The boys had almost made it to a stairway corridor when Derek's mom said, "Wait a second," and eased back from whatever she was working on. She smiled. "Aren't you going to properly introduce your friend?"

Derek shuffle-turned and exhaled, clearly weary with this formality. Plattering his hand: "This is Martin—Martin, this is Gloria. Can we go now?"

Derek's mother ignored the question, her slender hand shooting out. "Martin, it's a pleasure to meet you. Please call me Gloria."

Martin took hold of her hand, doing his best to avoid eye contact. Her parted-in-the-middle hair, long and straight and shiny. Her eyes were black-coffee bores. Her face, her skin—the color of nutmeg—was startlingly youthful. Not like a mom. *How young is she?* A wood-beaded bracelet clanked around her wrist as they shook hands; and then, releasing his fingers, she crossed her arms over her chest, cocking her head. "So, Martin, tell me about yourself."

Martin rummaged through his mind, finding nothing she'd find remotely interesting. Her posture was loose, her smile disarming. He did not know the word bohemian, but an image of a swaying hippie flashed through his mind as he stalled on her inquisitive expression.

But before Martin could answer, Derek spoke. "Enough with the interrogation."

Still smiling, Gloria Kirby glanced sideways at Derek. "I'm completely harmless, Derek. What's wrong with getting to know your friends?"

Derek rolled his eyes. "All right," said the older boy. "We're all friends now. Martin, let's go."

Martin followed Derek to the narrow opening of the upstairs corridor.

"It was nice to meet you, Martin," she said, resuming her work with the calculator.

"Nice to meet you too"—Martin almost said, "*Mrs.* Kirby," but quickly checked himself—"Ms. Kirby."

For the next forty-five minutes the boys hung out in Derek's room, both poring over Derek's impressive collection of comic books. Martin had taken a seat on the floor at the foot of Derek's bed, swiftly losing himself in the books. The older boy, whose interest was perhaps rekindled by Martin's enthusiasm, leaned back against his bed and began flipping through the comics. From time to time, each boy would point something out to the other—an inventive illustration, a deliciously lurid villain, a vibrantly inked set of panels.

Eventually Derek, sighing, flung his comic on the floor and said, "Hey." Martin, because of the older boy's tone, tore his attention from the comic and peered at his grinning friend. The next thing Derek said was as casual as if he were asking Martin's favorite food. "You like skin mags?"

Despite himself, Martin did his best to appear at ease with the question. "Sure," he managed. In his fourteen years, the nearest thing Martin had ever seen to a "skin mag" was of the topless, tribal women in the *National Geographic* magazines on the coffee table at the barber shop. Martin cleared his throat. "Yeah, man."

Derek's eyes narrowed slightly, clearly weighing something. Then his expression changed. "Hang on a sec." Derek rose, stepped around the scattered comic books, and locked the bedroom door. Martin watched Derek walk to the closet, crouching down and leaning into the shadowed space. Unable to see around his friend, Martin heard sliding and shifting, and after some maneuvering Derek squirmed back out of the closet, cradling a large shoebox. With Derek having stepped out of the way, Martin could see a dark space in the back corner of the closet where a wall panel had been removed to create a cubbyhole.

He placed the box on the floor in front of Martin and slowly lifted the lid.

A blond woman—who was cupping one of her bare breasts with one hand, while the other hand snaked down between her legs—stared up at Martin with an open-mouthed, almost sleepy expression. The title of the glossy magazine read *High Society*. Martin glanced up at his still-smirking friend, who then reached into the box, the gesture somehow granting Martin permission to do the same. After a stretch of hesitation, Martin lifted one of the magazines. Heart drumming, he opened the pages of something called *Club*, his mind instantly swaying as he scanned the photos—segments of flesh he'd only ever guessed at. After a few minutes he dropped the issue and grabbed the next magazine in the shoebox, this one called *Hustler*.

The women in this magazine were placed in erotic scenarios that appeared comically absurd to Martin—a nurse having sex with a patient, a housewife screwing the plumber, French maids kissing each other or rubbing themselves with feather dusters.

"So what do you think?" asked Derek, who was up on the bed, reclining against the headboard.

"Unbelievable."

Derek snorted, "Yeah," and the bedroom fell into a long stretch of companionable silence.

For Martin, with every flip of the page, with every sexual spectacle, another forbidden question was being answered. From time to time the women's faces would blur and blend with some pretty, brittle girl from at school—a vague, hair-spray-plumed stranger. At one point he shifted his sitting position to bring his knees up closer to his body, trying to eliminate the embarrassing possibility that Derek might notice.

A phone rang somewhere in the house. Martin half folded the magazine, sat forward, and glanced up and over at Derek, who was leafing through an issue of *Penthouse.*

He heard Ms. Kirby's muffled voice coming from the kitchen below. After about a minute came a note of finality followed by the unceremonious sound of Derek's mom hollering upstairs. "Boys," came Ms. Kirby's voice. The stiffness in Martin's jeans immediately receded.

Derek raised his voice evenly. "Yeah?"

"Martin's mom will be here in about fifteen minutes."

"All right, we'll be down in a minute."

Derek rolled off the bed and began gathering up the magazines, re-lidding the pornbox and crossing to the closet, where he set the box back in the secret niche and replaced the small panel of wood.

Standing, Martin glanced around the floor at the scattered comic books, which—before the revelation of the "skin mags"—had seemed to contain infinite imaginative possibilities. He picked up one of the comics he'd been particularly impressed with: an issue of Todd McFarlane's *Spawn.* "Hey," Martin waved the comic book in the air, "can I borrow this?"

Derek didn't even look over; he shrugged. "Sure, whatever. But bring it back to me on the bus tomorrow."

"Sure," Martin grinned. "No problem."

*

Friday evening, a week later.

On the night of an impromptu sleepover, Martin and Derek ran through the woods for an hour or so, killing time in the seemingly endless warren of paths, their voices echoing into the tangled netting of black boughs. At one point Derek broke away and disappeared. Calling out for Derek, Martin wandered back to the campsite. He was walking by the lean-to when Derek, screaming, jumped out of the dirt pit like some ghoulish Jack-in-the box. Both boys laughed at this, Derek slightly more than Martin.

The setting sun sent spokes of light through the interlaced branches of oaks and elms, the orange tints dimming to crimson on the sky's fringes.

Derek's mother was in the kitchen cooking dinner when the boys—chuckle-panting and chilled from the dusky air—entered through the back porch.

"Just in time, gentlemen," she said, lifting a crookedly shaped hamburger patty from a hissing skillet. The radio was on in the kitchen and Martin could hear the TV over in the living room; he noticed some lighted candles here and there, as if Ms. Kirby were getting ready for some sort of party. Derek stepped over to a wooden cutting board and helped himself to a segment of sliced orange. Martin noticed that Ms. Kirby's long hair was fastened in the back with a set of chopsticks. "You two get cleaned up," she said, smoothly moving along the stove.

"Do you want to take a shower before dinner, Martin?" said Derek's mom.

"Uh," he glanced at Derek, who made a pinched face, the expression suggesting he'd didn't have to if he didn't want to. "No . . . ..I'm okay, I'll just wash my hands."

Ms. Kirby smiled, resumed her cooking.

As the boys settled down at the table, Ms. Kirby slid two paper plates with two hamburgers in front of each boy.

To Derek she said, "Since I cooked, how about you clean. Deal?"

Derek was already nodding, apparently familiar with the routine. "Sure. Deal."

"Is there anything else you boys need?" There wasn't. They thanked her and began eating. "I'm going to hop in the shower,

Derek," her voice echoed in the dark rectangle of corridor leading upstairs.

"Sure thing," Derek said through a mouthful of meat and bread.

After dinner the boys headed upstairs. Rounding the corner on the second floor, passing by Ms. Kirby's bedroom, Martin could hear the sound of the shower—a needle-hiss noise seeping through the margin of her partially opened door.

Derek flipped on the light in his room, stepped over a heap of discarded clothes, and crossed to the closet, leaning in and removing the false panel. Derek came around with the shoebox, hiked his chin, and said, "You might want to close that," meaning the bedroom door. Martin crossed to the door, closed it, twisted the lock.

And once again, the recently ritualized routine: Martin sitting on the floor, legs crossed, leaning back against the foot of the bed, poring over the pictures: their eyes half-lidded, their faces frozen in mid-moan. Martin regarded the older girls at school differently now. *All secrets known.* Derek sat on his bed, propped up against a pillow like an overworked businessman relaxing with his pipe and newspaper. Now and again (and not for the first time) Martin had the urge to mock the absurdity of some of these scenarios, wanting to point this out to Derek; but he wondered if his host might take offense and, as a consequence, shut the box indefinitely.

Martin—as he'd been rehearsing to do so for days—was preparing to ask Derek if he could borrow one of the magazines when several knocks sounded on the bedroom door.

Martin flinched, slapping shut the magazine on his lap and fixing his eyes on Derek.

Derek looked up but appeared unfazed. "Yeah?"

"Did you do the dishes?"

"Fuck," Derek murmured, then raised his voice to say, "No."

A steady stretch of silence. Then: "I thought we had a deal."

"Yeah." Silence. "Yeah, we did—we do."

Martin waited for the creak of the hardwood indicating Ms. Kirby's retreat, but it was quiet for a long time. "Derek—"

"I'll get it in a minute," his voice grew louder.

"—if you're going to have friends over—"

"I just forgot, it's no big deal."

"—I expect a little help with this . . . The plan was—"

"I SAID I'D GET IT IN A MINUTE, GLORIA."

Nothing for a few beats, then came the creaking of hardwood and fading footsteps.

"Jesus," Derek exhaled. "Stay here." He flung a *Playboy* on the floor. "I'll be right back." He strode to the door, then stopped, his hand clutching the knob. "If you're going to keep *those* out," he said, gesturing at the scattered magazines, "I'd lock this door."

Then Derek slipped into the dark hallway, pulling the door shut behind him. Martin got up and quickly locked it.

He sat on the edge of Derek's bed, waiting to hear angry voices—waiting to hear Derek verbally getting his ass chewed out. But nothing happened. Martin's mind drifted to what sort of punishment his own father might dispense in that sort of situation.

He listened. Now came something like low-level conversation, the distant sounds of clanking dishes, of chairs legs yelping on the linoleum.

No longer interested in the mags, Martin scanned Derek's bedroom—the peeling wallpaper, the rusty blotch on the ceiling. Simply glancing at these things gave Martin a flinch of homesickness, a hunger for his simple comic books, his own bedroom.

He was toying with the notion of turning on the old TV on the dresser when his attention snagged on the closet, the door standing halfway open. Martin blinked at the dark rectangle of false wall in the back. But now he squinted harder, seeing something else—something in the shadowed corner on the *opposite* side of the closet.

Eyes fixed on the spot, Martin moved to the closet, crouching down and leaning in. The other side of the space had a similar section of wall, bowed out, flimsy. There was a black, pencil-scratch fissure there. *Another cubbyhole.* Experimentally, he gave the panel a try. The rickety rectangle of false wall popped out of the coving, a few well-placed nails squeaking from their grooves—a dark interior. With his upper body blocking the light, Martin had trouble seeing into the narrow niche. He slid his hand into the opening, fingers fishing blindly along what felt like splintery, dust-covered studs. His knuckles brushed something: a paper-wrapped package that he slowly withdrew. It was about the size of a large mailing envelope. Martin licked his lips; sounds of dishes being stacked, cabinet doors opening and closing continued from the kitchen just beneath the floorboards. He leaned back into the light and stood, pausing before pulling back the paper lip and peeking in.

The envelope housed a slim stack of magazines—*Witchcraft.* Martin slid one from within.

Seated cross-legged before a red backdrop was a nude woman, hands pressed together, offering a prayer to an inverted crucifix. Her head was concealed beneath a large, taxidermied goat head: thick, corkscrew-spiral horns curling back behind its whiskery, donkey-like ears. The goat's long, frayed beard tapered down to the woman's pale sternum.

Three other magazines were in the stack, all with similar gimmicks—naked women worshipping coiled snakes, variations of cloaked, goat-headed priests—*Death Cults. Orgies. The Law of the Lash.*

There existed the same silliness as the staged, almost comedic porn from Derek's other magazines, but there was something different in these vignettes—something, for Martin, more penetrating.

He then noticed a weight, a hump at the bottom of the envelope.

The envelope contained a rubber-banded stack of Polaroids, about the thickness of an eight-track tape.

The girl in the picture was cupping her bare breasts. And

though her face was out of frame, Martin assumed it must be Derek's girlfriend. He deftly tried to unloop the rubber band, but it snapped apart in his fingers, dropping to the floor. Ignoring it, he quickly flipped to the next shot—this one taken from the side. The girl was on her knees, back arched—the photo all pale torso, curvy hips, rear end. The poor quality of the photos, along with the harsh, flash-bulb glare against her skin, bothered Martin almost more than the clumsily choreographed pornography. Nothing staged here.

A more lurid one came next—the model's fingers forked down. The picture had caught part of the model's clavicle and chin, a partially opened mouth, a dark scarf of hair hanging over her arm.

Martin fanned the photos out in front of him. Though none of the shots exposed her full face, Martin thought, *Same girl, same girl. Same* woman. But then he stalled on one of the last photos, scrutinizing it, understanding the figure in the photos was not a young girl at all.

Three rapid knocks on the bedroom door. Martin flinched. He did his best to rearrange the Polaroids, but in his frantic attempt he fumbled the stack of photos, a few skidding to the floor. He clawed at the pictures, sweeping them up and sliding them back into the envelope.

Raps again, this time with more emphasis. "What's the hold-up, man?" said Derek. "Come on, open up."

"Just a sec," Martin said, voice strained. He crouched back into the closet, returning the envelope to the crevice, doing his best to realign the nails along the seam of the false wall.

Then he was up, striding across the room and unlocking the door.

Derek's white face swam up out of the darkened hallway. "The hell?" he said, re-entering the bedroom. "You jerking off in here or what?"

After a moment: "Yeah," he forced a laugh. "Did you get in trouble?"

"Nah," he said, closing and relocking the door behind him. "She just gets fucking loony sometimes, you know?"

Martin did not. "Yeah," he snorted. "Sure."

Derek appeared as if he were about to reclaim his spot on the bed. But then he bristled and froze in the middle of the room. He was staring at the floor.

Martin followed Derek's gaze, down to the limp length of broken rubber band—a gag parasite.

Martin's already jack-hammering heart sped up to a rapid tattoo—it thudded in his throat and ears, threatened to drown out Derek's voice.

Derek muttered, "Why . . ." but the older boy's voice broke off. A frown wrinkled his brow, as if confronted with a nearly graspable riddle. Then the expression changed, his face growing slack. Derek's gaze went from the floor to the closet before settling on Martin.

Clueless as possible, Martin said, "What?"

Derek crouched down and snatched up the rubber band, retraining his eyes on Martin. Derek's face was a sneering question mark. "Where'd this come from?"

Tell him the truth—I was curious and I was just snooping around. I'm sorry. It was none of my business. He conjured an intrigued expression and reached out. "What is it? Looks like trash."

Derek pulled back. He flicked another touch-and-go glance at Martin, offering no response as he stepped toward the closet, peering in. Again Derek scowled. "Did you . . . ?"

Martin was running out of time, running out of gestures to sustain his play-acting. "Hey, man," he said. "I'm going to grab something from my bag downstairs. I'll be right back."

Derek said nothing as Martin unlocked the door, rattle-twisted the handle, and stepped into the corridor.

Martin maneuvered through the hall, toward the rectangle of light coming up from the steep staircase leading down into the kitchen, his heartbeat in sync with the thudding of his sneakered feet on the hardwood. His duffel bag was in the kitchen, where he'd left it earlier that evening. There was also a phone down there.

Martin closed in on the threshold of the narrow corridor and, moving too fast, nearly collided with the partially clothed Ms. Kirby.

She was wearing a silk robe. "Oh," she said, laughing and clutching some of the shiny fabric near her chest. "You frightened me, Martin." She tucked a shower-damp ribbon of black hair behind her ear as she stepped around the boy.

Resuming some task at the cupboard, she said, "Is there something you needed, Martin?" The bathrobe was dark blue, its design something Martin associated with exotic garb he'd seen in movies. *Kimono*—the word rushed through his mind amidst a chatter of other thoughts. The garment was belted around the pear-shaped curves of her hips and hung loosely over her shoulders. The material shimmered fluidly under the harsh fluorescent light in the kitchen. The hem of the short robe came down well above her knees.

When Martin didn't answer, Gloria turned, eventually smiling and raising an eyebrow. "Martin?"

He breathed, "Oh—yeah," his eyes darting to the dark green phone on the wall. "I was wondering if I could use the phone."

The woman gently shut the cupboard and slowly pivoted. She blinked a number of times. "The phone?"

Martin cleared his throat. "Yeah"—his voice reedy, frail— "yes. I just forgot to tell my mom something."

Something twitched under her pleasant expression—a subtle spasm that momentarily dulled her attractive features. She placed her lacquer-nailed fingers on the counter next to the cutting board. "Is something wrong?" The folds on her loose-hanging kimono had opened slightly. Martin's midsection twisted as he snatched an inadvertent peek at the soft line of her exposed collarbone, the Y-fold opened to expose a milky slit.

Martin refocused—the wall-mounted phone. "No—nothing's wrong." He coaxed a composed smile.

A frown flitted over her face and disappeared. "Sure, Martin," she said, adjusting the partially open fold on her chest. "As long as everything's okay." She turned toward the sink. "I want Derek's friends to be comfortable in this home."

Swallowing, Martin took a few paces and lifted the receiver from the cradle. He was able to dial three numbers when he heard a door burst open upstairs—the sound followed by several long-striding stomps. A voice roared down through the stairwell. *"Gloria?"* Martin froze with the receiver raised next to his cheek.

Ms. Kirby's wet-threaded hair jostled as she jerked her face toward the stairs. "What's the matter?"

"Is Martin down there?" The voice reverberated as it echoed down through the passage.

Ms. Kirby gave Martin a smooth, up-and-down scan, her dark eyes narrowed on him. "Yes, he is."

Silence for what seemed like a hundred heartbeats. Finally Derek's voice came again. "Martin?" he said. If Derek had been attempting to sound calm and inviting, it didn't work. To Martin, the voice no longer sounded like Derek but someone older. For a nauseating moment Martin imagined it sounded like his own father's voice. "Martin, I need you to come back up here for a minute."

Phone still raised at chin-level, Martin's lips had gone numb and were parted in a dumb expression. He was holding his breath. His paralyzed silence served as his response, provoking another call from upstairs.

"Gloria?" The voice still sounded older—a distorted version of Derek. "Don't let Martin leave."

For a moment, Ms. Kirby and Martin were staring at each other in unblinking unity. And in that moment Martin thought he saw something uncoil in the dark, glittering pinpoints of Ms. Kirby's eyes—something like comprehension. And maybe panic.

Ms. Kirby slid her hand off the cutting board at precisely the same moment as Martin dropped the phone and dashed toward the patio door, flinging open the screen and launching himself off the porch steps.

It was deep night now. The October-chilled air filled his lungs, stinging in quick gasps as he broke into a sprint across the yard. He rounded the side of the house, intent on getting to the driveway. Then came the whine and bang of the patio door, followed by the brief pounding of feet on the porch.

He gambled a glance over his shoulder. A tall, slim shape emerged from the side of the house—a swift-loping, long-limbed silhouette. As Martin crossed the front yard, the porch light came on and Ms. Kirby opened the front door.

Martin darted across the gravel driveway, suddenly catching sight of the tunnel-path that led into the forest. He pumped his fists, racing along the leaf-littered trail.

Martin was sickly certain that if he stayed on the path, Derek would catch up with him. He angled left into the underbrush, weaving through the black-stilted trees, swatting at the low-hanging branches.

His frantic thoughts came like hitching gasps. He had the fleeting idea that if he could just make it through the small belt of trees—if he could find the creek and follow it out of the woods—he would emerge in the cornfield over by Carriage Road—follow Carriage Road back to the main road, back to familiar streets. He was already pasting together an explanation to his parents—*Derek and I . . . I don't know . . . I just wanted to come home . . .*

The forest rushed up and around Martin as he pitched forward into the large hole. Derek's half-finished bunker. The hide-and-seek pit. He collided against the bottom of the earth-chilled ditch, the wind thrusting out of him in a wheezy punch. Martin tried to turn over, his fingers dragging damp dirt and tendrils of exposed roots.

Wincing, clenching his teeth, he rolled over, fighting the urge to vomit, blinking grit from his eyes, spitting dirt. Through squint-slitted eyes, Martin looked up out of the hole, expecting Derek to appear at the edge. But instead—and with the exception of his pain-stitched breathing—he heard only crickets and night-stillness.

Far off, back toward the house, a single, sexless scream unsutured the silence. There came then the snapping of twigs and underbrush, the rustle of dead leaves.

As the footsteps drew closer, Martin caught sight of the bone-colored rind of moon, partially visible through the branch-knotted canopy overhead.

A pale face, appearing gray in the dim moonlight, slowly bloomed over the dirt-ragged rim of the crudely dug hole. Awful truths crawled their way into his mind—the final frame on the last page of his imaginary comic. With the black backdrop of forest behind it, the marble-gaunt face gave the illusion of disembodiment—a skull balloon floating in the gloom. The skull spoke. "Martin." It was the voice again—not Derek's as he remembered it. Fatigued. Torn at the corners. His father's voice. "Come back up to the house," it said. "Gloria wants to see us."

The figure knelt and extended what may have been an extremity. Though his cheeks were slick, Martin was no longer crying. He sniffled, swiped at his eyes, and dragged himself up to a crouch. Martin Colegrove reached out and took hold of the long thing, what felt like a sinewy, hoof-ended limb.

The Pecking Order

Meg had decided to enter the funeral home through an unassuming side door rather than the central entrance. The place appeared to have once been an actual home: a wide, Colonial-style Georgian that, at some point, had imitational elements grafted on to it so as to aesthetically accommodate its utility as a place of ceremonial mourning. Verdigris covered an elaborate birdfeeder that had collected some dead-leaf-steeped rainwater. A high school social studies teacher, Megan Settles was sensitive to these architectural incongruities and perhaps, on any other occasion, may have taken a moment to enjoy some of the more subtle features.

The parking lot up front was not quite full. Still, Meg, not certain of how her presence would be received among Calvin Mize's relatives, wanted to scout the situation inconspicuously.

Her classes having finished the week before, Meg was used to these subsequent weekends being filled with visitation to graduation parties. She tried to do her best to honor the RSVPs, but had in fact skipped several in order to make the nearly two-hour drive here to Glasgow. Meg eyed her phone. Along the way, cell service had continued to deteriorate to the point of uselessness; but, as a precaution (partially prescribed by her father, who still called to check in every other day or so), she had utilized the navigation device attached to her console. She thumbed off the contraption before turning off the engine.

Meg inventoried her small purse, just to confirm the essentials, not the least being the silver flashdrive, and stepped out into the leaf-shade. Clouds drifted languidly, a movement as stagnant as the humidity. The day they'd conducted the showing for her mom it was nonstop rain, the sky a dome paletted by alternating grays that spilled needles all afternoon. That had been six years ago—six this autumn, to be precise. She tried to run in the morning, before work, meticulously logging time, distance, speed. Healing, on the other hand, had proven trickier to track.

Meg draped her purse strap across her chest (a habit of mugger deterrence she and many of her female classmates had adopted in college in a self-defense class near her dorm) and crossed the sidelot, her flats muted over strikingly fresh asphalt. If things got tense, she reminded herself, she would quietly find a relative and hand over the flashdrive, explaining that it had been Calvin's.

Shortly following the final incident—not long after she'd been notified of Calvin's dismissal from school—Meg's English-teacher colleague, Ms. Beatty, delivered the device. The older woman said something about providing evidence, if it came to that. "Most of the stuff he wrote in class was too disturbing to share," she'd said, handing over the flashdrive. "Sad, really. The whole thing."

"Yes," said Meg, accustomed to the woman's scandalmonger-ing. "It really is."

"From what I hear," she continued, "what with that mother and father of his, he really didn't have a chance."

"Yes," she repeated, twisting the nondescript flashdrive in her fingers as if it were covered in Braille.

Now she mounted the stairs of the funeral home, her pulse in sync with her dutiful pace.

Meg quietly opened the door, giving up the oppressive air and trading genuine humidity for artificial air-conditioning. The light was dim here, several lamps fanned out feeble light. The décor was as it should be in its funereal, alabaster-and-taupe pre-dictability. The consolatory soundtrack of harp and piano plinked in the background, and as Meg stepped further into the space she noticed the two elderly women propped up on a couch.

She hadn't been aware of them at first, their ivory-and-floral-print dresses so closely matching the catchpenny patterns (that's something her mom would have said of those garish prints: *catchpenny*) of the outdated couch and wallpaper which functioned as their background.

"Oh," said Meg, trying to sound less startled than she truly was. "Good morning." Neither woman responded. Just stared. One was strikingly rotund, while the other was sharp and twiggish. The way they were arranged reminded Meg of a raft and a rusty anchor.

"Do you know where—?" she was about to ask about the Mize funeral when one of the women, the willowy one, raised a thin index finger, gesturing toward a corridor. The extended hand reminded her of a pickled chicken foot. She was not proud of the disparaging comparison, but still. Nerves, she thought. Laughing at inappropriate times. That sort of thing. She hadn't initially felt culpable for what happened at school, yet guilt worked like an unexpected bruise, one you catch in the mirror—surprised to see it, but unsure of how it had set in so deeply. Her parents had instilled in her this base sense of right and wrong (social mores, came her father's voice); but Meg felt as though she were doing this more for her than anyone else. Sure, the conceit—the *excuse*—was to hand over Calvin's meager flashdrive, offer her condolences, and make the two-hour drive back home.

"Thank you, ladies," she said, giving a meek nod as she started through, and with an almost panicky impulse, followed by saying, "I'm sorry."

The women almost immediately resumed a murmured banter as Meg distanced herself from the room, catching the word *teacher* from one of them as she turned the corner.

Sconces lit the way; and as she neared what felt like the central lobby of the building, the imitation Schubert rattling from the outdated PA gave way to a messy discordance as it blended with rap music burring from one of the adolescent attendee's portable speaker.

Teenagers, most of them clad in casual clothes—Meg spotted

several Insane Clown Posse T-shirts—milled around the lobby, the majority with their heads crooked down, inspecting their phones. She wondered how many were friends (she hoped most) and how many were family. The orderly, teacherly part of her wondered, too, if there was a funeral director allowing this sort of informal congregation. She spotted someone she assumed to be the funeral director: a sharp-featured, suited man standing with his hands clasped officially in front of him. Meg smoothed the sundress against her stomach and skirted the margin of the room; she observed an easled placard, indicating the room dedicated to the Calvin Mize "celebration."

Opposed to the lobby, things were more sedate in here. The room contained several rows of chairs (nearly all unoccupied) while the bouquet-crowned casket glistened on the far side. The casket was closed, of course. According to more reliable reports, there was no other option, really. Hands clasped in front of her, Meg made her way around the chairs, approaching the casket.

A photo shrine (hastily assembled, it appeared) had been set up, mostly older pictures of Calvin. Family picnics, a few birthday parties. Uncles, grandmothers. In one shot, Calvin was sitting on the lap of a man who, she estimated, might be his estranged father. As she scanned the collage a thought twitched. She turned and regarded the viewing room and the lobby beyond. She wouldn't have noticed it at first, perhaps; but not counting the teenagers loitering in the lobby, there seemed to be a notable lack of men. Sure, perhaps what she'd guessed to be a grandpa or older cousin here and there, but now that she truly scrutinized the evident oddity it was conspicuous: *where are all the adult men?*

"You must be Miss Settles," came a voice from behind Meg.

She twisted and saw a young woman approaching, hand out to shake. "I'm Haleigh—Haleigh Dowdle," she said, her voice bright, cutting through the calm climate. As Meg took hold of Haleigh's hand the woman added, "My grandma"—*grammah*—"said she seen you walk in. I'm Calvin's aunt . . . Roxy's sister."

The name Roxy was a matchflare in Meg's mind; she had, on several occasions, met with Roxanne Mize (a generally clueless woman) at various parent-teacher-counselor conferences throughout the past year, each meeting growing more erratic and unproductive as the argument between mother and son became more pronounced. The sessions ostensibly devoted to learning and behavioral strategies disintegrated as Calvin's demeanor became more corrosive while his mother's histrionics grew more poignant. Roxanne had hectically canceled the last meeting—the one shortly before Calvin's final, violent breakdown at the school.

Meg nodded at the name. "Oh yes, of course." Meg glanced around the room but did not catch sight of Calvin's mother. Obviously comprehending this, Haleigh said, "Roxy had to go out for a bit and catch her breath." She lowered her voice, crinkling her nose. "This has been such an ordeal."

Meg nodded. "I can't imagine." She could, in fact, imagine: the need to run, the need to flee this sort of ritualized orchestration. Meg had promised herself that she would not make this excursion about herself—would not come here to confront some sort of intangible closure. She needed to come here because Calvin Mize had endured, by her accumulated experience over the course of the previous school year, a fundamentally shitty life. He'd been neglected by a group of adults who'd called themselves family and had missed signs (read: ignored) that may have helped him. His mental deterioration had been viewed as rambunctiousness, and when that assignation wasn't quite clinical enough, it was attention-deficit or bi-polar—anything to fog the fact that there were grown-ups culpable for his instability. By the time he reached high school, the various maladies attached to the young man had been paired with a cocktail of medications that (Meg's opinion only) mitotically altered his perception, further propelling the boy out into a dark region of vulnerability. As a pupil, he'd never been wholly pleasant with her, though he'd never asserted his obstinacy as far as she suspected he'd wanted to. It was only on the last day—when the school authorities were dragging him, literally kicking and screaming, down the hall—that Meg realized his faculties had irrevocably fractured long before, and had only been held together by a weak, cyclic adhesive of attending school and evening counseling sessions.

Yes: she was still mourning her own mother, but, as best she could, she'd consciously avoided making *this* about her. Calvin needed someone of some normal significance to vouch for him. And regardless of their purported sincerity, Megan Settles was bitter about the insufficiency of *words*.

This was about presence. Not platitudes.

Haleigh slid her hands along her thin arms as though rubbing away a shiver. Judging by the neglected, dark brown roots of the woman's stringy hair, it appeared as if she were recovering from an experiment with some ultra-blonde coloring months earlier. "Calvin had lots of nice things to say about you," she said. Meg took this for what it was worth: kind, simple small talk to fill the tense silence.

"That's very kind of you to say."

"He was always talking about the stuff you was teaching him about the government and local history stuff. And he sure liked writing in that other class of his."

The mention of his English class brought to mind the flash-drive in her purse, which Meg went for but paused—perhaps not the right time. *Wait for Roxy, the mother.* She considered the casket.

Again, evidently adept at tuning in to a line of thought, Haleigh said, "Obviously, we had no other choice but to do a closed-casket." The comment, to Meg's ear, was a tad blunt considering the reverent climate. Still, she checked herself, lowering her brow a bit. Appallingly, Haleigh continued. "It's just that the state of his body would have been too"—she raised her knob-knuckled fingers—"shocking for everyone."

There had been vague social-media rumors that accompanied the earliest announcements online. An overdose. He'd shot himself. He'd slit his wrists. He'd hanged himself. Though trusting none of these, Meg had come across one unusual claim on Twitter that Calvin had been involved in some sort of explosion—a homemade pipebomb, went one narrative.

As much as Meg wanted to know, this neither seemed the time nor the place to discuss the grisly state of the body.

"I see," she said, averting eye contact. "I understand."

After a moment Haleigh said, "Are you coming to the funeral?"

As loud as the woman was talking, Meg wondered if Haleigh had had a few drinks (or something more potent—*methamphetamine?*) before the showing. Meg now realized that Haleigh was older than she'd first assumed. Maybe they were the same age. From time to time Calvin's aunt made a stilted, flitting gesture with her forearms—a sort of involuntary twitch that accompanied her voice, which was growing into a squawk. She explained how, after the incident at school, Calvin had come to live with his mother here in Glasgow. How Roxy thought it might be good for him to be closer to his father, even though Roxy, during several previous conferences, had claimed that the dad was the abusive root (not her phrase) of Calvin's instability.

Shifting the conversation, Meg finally went to her purse. "I wanted to leave this with you," she said, producing the flashdrive. "He'd forgotten this in his English class. His teacher found it plugged into one of the computers." In the two months that Meg had been in possession of the small device, she had not, though tempted, read any of Calvin's entries, going only so far as to open the location window, discovering a number of folders, each labeled with a date; and within the folder, hundreds of documents with oblique, often unsettling titles. Actually reading these docs, she felt, would be like prying into someone's diary. Perhaps even worse. "His teacher said Calvin loved writing on his own—daily journals were his favorite. She said he wrote a lot about his family."

Haleigh's head was canted slightly, as though attempting to catch the aberrant melody of an off-tune music box. As if physically prodded, Haleigh twitched and smiled. "How thoughtful."

She raised a hand to accept the flashdrive but froze.

A commotion now—several gasps—from the lobby. At first, Meg thought it was just the clusters of teens goofing around. She frowned then, hearing genuine, fear-fed screams. She caught momentary sight of the man she'd believed to be the funeral home manager—the pale, sharp-featured man she'd spotted skulking near the crowd—as he fled with visitors in a panicked exodus.

Haleigh was working her way forward now but didn't make it far as the tall, bearded man toting a shotgun strode into the parlor.

A distant part of Meg attempted to summon the training imparted to her students in an active-shooter situation. She had nothing.

Spotting Haleigh, the man said, "Tell me where they're going to do it."

"What in the hell are you doing here, Jasper?"

Meg had backed away, shifting closer to the wall, slipping the flashdrive in her purse and clasping hold of the pepper spray.

"Goddamn it, Haleigh, you know there ain't time for that. Where are they?"

Haleigh put her hands on her hips and actually giggled, her composure suddenly that of a petulant child. "I don't know what you're talking about."

The big man racked the shotgun's slide. "Haleigh," he said calmly though quaking, "you tell me where—"

A moist-corded hissing emerged from the small woman. Her arms shot out above her head, fingers curved like talons, as she rushed forward, her stringy hair lifting off her shoulders. She was banshee-babbling something now; the only word Meg caught was what she thought was, *"Eurynomos!"*

Calmly, almost listlessly, the big man leveled the shotgun's barrel on the woman and fired.

The concussion was incredible, causing Meg to collapse, instinctively pulling a chair up against the front of her body, simultaneously keeping her wide eyes on Haleigh. The blast had caught her in the upper portion of the chest, scarving her neck and head with large pellets—what Meg's mind wanted to call *birdshot,* though the severity of the wounds called for something larger—the impact causing her to pirouette, a patch of scalp flopping out as her body crumpled to the carpet.

A thin film of blue smoke hung in the soured air. The man—*Haleigh had called him Jasper*—dug around in the front pocket of his denim overalls and fished out another shell, sliding it into the chamber. His attention remained intent on Haleigh's body, as if she might suddenly thrust herself off the floor and lunge at him. A profuse pool of dark fluid was now expanding from her head wound. Jasper seemed to consider something before slowly walking forward, giving the body a wide, apparently cautious berth.

Behind the overturned chair, Meg was quaking, understanding, now that he was distracted, that this was her chance—this was her chance to run.

Her mom had likely been like this. She didn't think her mom had been given the opportunity to run, to flee. She'd been caught off guard—that was the consensus. She wanted to believe that if she could have, she would have run and not tried to talk her way out of it.

Jasper was visually inspecting the casket, mumbling curses. Finally he grunted and turned, striding toward the wide threshold of the viewing room.

Meg lurched up, a little off balance. Her fantasy was moving faster than her faculties, and she thrust out the pepper spray; but before she could get a good shot, the man briskly swatted at her arm—an annoyed motion as though batting away a cobweb. Her pepper spray flew away, rolling to a rest against the alabaster baseboard.

"Damn it—don't do that again," said Jasper, scowling, walking toward the door. "Leave me alone, you hear?"

Breath coming quick, she reached out for a chair, and the man swung around. "I said stop." The drawl came out *stawp.* "I'd only hurt you if you tried something stupid."

As if the obvious needed addressing this instant, through clenched teeth Meg said, "You . . . just murdered that woman."

The man hitched in a breath and exhaled. "It ain't," he started, but then looked directly at Meg. "She ain't . . . you wouldn't understand and I ain't got time to explain."

She tightened her grip on the back of the chair, causing a creak. The man's dull eyes caught this and he said, "I swear," the shotgun hanging loosely by his side. "You should just leave." Meg's grip remained on the chair. She was steeling herself for maybe her first and last try as one badass lion-tamer. He said, "Listen. I ain't ever seen you before, but if you came out here today it must mean you cared something for that boy."

Meg tossed the chair aside and pulled out her phone. "I'm calling the police."

He shook his head. "I'm his damn uncle," he said. "That . . . traitor down there, his 'aunt,' was my sister-in-law," said Jasper. "But this is no more Calvin's funeral than that thing down there on the floor is his aunt."

Meg's new strategy: keep the big man talking until law enforcement arrived. "How can you—"

Hitching in a weary breath, Jasper started forward, back toward the casket. Meg didn't have time to react before he raised a dirty boot and kicked the casket, sending it toppling off the raised frame, the lid jarring open and spilling the contents.

Meg almost recoiled but paused. Jasper was now using his boot to kick through the strewn pile of dark dirt, the mound peppered with books, notebooks, drawings. Among this, too, were matted patches of thick-quilled, black-veined feathers. It was as though a small, reeking pocket of a landfill had spilled out here. "You see—this is all that's left of him—all that says something about my nephew."

She hadn't been aware of it, but Meg had shuffled forward a bit.

Jasper made a disgusted sound and turned, again attempting to retreat.

"Wait," Meg blurted. She'd almost caught up with cogency, but not quite yet. "Where is he?" She seemed to have somehow appropriated Jasper's script from only minutes earlier. Nearly to the lobby now, Jasper didn't slow down. Shouting this time, Meg said, *"Wait!"* She didn't care if he was insane—she'd yank information out of him, anything she could get to tell the police if she survived. Jasper slowed, stopped, turned. Meg thought there was more sadness in his expression than rage. "Please. Tell me. Where is Calvin?"

"You must be his teacher," said Jasper, intoning futility. "He talked about you some, couple of the others too. Said you tried to help." His delivery suitable for a eulogy, he continued. I think—I think toward the end, Calvin knew what was happening to him. What *they* had planned for him." Meg narrowed her eyes, her confused expression evidently compelling Jasper to articulate. "The Crèche," he said. "The goddamn Crèche."

A sound emerged. Coarse and dry. Scratching—an unseen creature gnawing at a rotten spot in a wall. Meg looked around for a moment but saw nothing, save for Jasper's attention, which had been retrained on Haleigh's corpse. "They thought he was close to some sort of . . . threshold. What all them was saying was mental deterioration was really getting close to changing the way they do things . . . their rituals."

A few more minutes, thought Meg, surely the cops will be here. She took a stalling stab: "The last time I saw him it was . . . awful."

"Yeah," said Jasper. "You seen it. How close he was to it. Losing his mind meant mental illness for regular people, but it meant something else for *them*."

Meg recalled that day in class a little over a month before. It had been an otherwise unnotable morning, her social studies class moving from one topic to another. She still could not put her finger on what, precisely, had triggered the argument between Calvin and, at first, another classmate. The debate deteriorated into a verbal dispute in which Calvin clearly felt was outnumbered. Seeing this, Meg reined in the dialogue, attempting to re-establish civility.

She believed they'd switched gears, moved on to something healthier; but then Calvin shoved himself away from his desk, swiped a pencil from a peer's desk, and stabbed the male student in the soft webbing of his hand. The stocky kid hollered, recoiling but also throwing out his good hand, connecting with Calvin's face. Meg waded in, trying to get Calvin away from what would surely grow into a mob; but he too was screaming now, thrashing, thick channels of blood freely flowing from his broken nose, coating his face like a glistening, crimson surgical mask. He began wailing something about a nest. About reverse regurgitation. That all this, he'd said, screeching at his classmates, was *premastication*.

Other teachers arrived, mostly male, none appearing eager to move in on the bloodied boy. Still, they sort of cornered him until a school security guard arrived. They all assisted in detaining Calvin, who was sobbing now, too weak to fight. As they dragged him out of the classroom, Meg, feeble as it may have been, opened her mouth to say something, when Calvin bore his unblinking gaze into her. *"You fucking bitch,"* he said, stalactites of spittle and saliva hung from his chin. *"You're fucking doomed . . . I'm going to use your skin as a fucking blanky!"*

The fading of Calvin's screams brought her back to the present, back to the funeral home. Meg hadn't realized it, but she was staring at nothing in particular, and it was Jasper's voice that jostled her from the mesmerizing recollection.

"He told me about that too. They wanted to use him to open something up—like some sort of . . ." Jasper winced, the claw of a hand coming up to trace the length of something imagined in front of him.

Meg: "A conduit?" *What am I saying?* But it was a pedantic reflex—the impulse to bring cohesion. With belly-wringing certainty, Meg now realized that the sound she'd heard a few seconds earlier was coming from Haleigh's body. Movement, now.

The woman's damaged skull was rattling with arrhythmic twitches. Of all the things she could not accept, this took precedence.

"If I was you I'd get the hell out of here," said Jasper, finally moving out of the room, crossing the lobby; and just as he'd shoved open the front door, Meg hustled up, keeping her distance but begging just the same. "Why? Please just tell me why."

It didn't take long for Jasper to consider. "Because . . . if my brother, Augie, Calvin's own father, would allow these folks to do this to his own son, then he wouldn't think twice about letting them get to my own little boys." Meg's respiration slowed a bit. "And if Haleigh has allowed the men to use her property to"—a momentary, molar-clenched stall—"fucking *pervert* their old Eastern Star rituals . . . then it's worse than it used to be." Meg opened her mouth, but Jasper cut her off, explaining as though he owed her a favor. "They needed the body intact, you see—don't ask me why because I don't know what they mean to do with it. It didn't used to be like this—those Eastern Star girls started changing things, started talking about a Tower of Silence . . . and," he winced, clearly trying to recall something, *"ex— car—"* He struggled, but it came: "ex-car-nation."

The kernel of recall broke from its husk. One of the perks of being an educator, particularly at the bizarre high-school level, was the panopticon-like exposure to, and omnivore intake of, a wide spectrum of anecdotes and information. *Excarnation,* the word clinking in her mind like a penny touching the bottom of a porcelain wishing well, something akin to Tibetan sky funerals— *defleshing,* came another term from years before.

"I think . . ." He looked away from Meg, his voice trembling. "I think Calvin knew what was happening to him—what they meant to do to him, and he tried to figure out a way to spoil the plan, I reckon. I think he tried to kill hisself the way he did so they couldn't use his body in one piece." The ephemeral news Meg had read about Calvin tinkering with a homemade explosive gained clarity. People would have simply assumed that the mentally ill teen had just shamelessly taken his own life in grisly grandiosity. "I don't think he was building a bomb to hurt anybody but himself. I think blowing hisself up was the only way to escape and spoil whatever they had in mind for him. And goddamn it if they ain't still trying.

"They're mixing shit from other religions for this . . . experiment—this . . . appeasement. Call themselves The Crèche." He spat directly on the carpet of the lobby and pushed open the door.

"Hold on," Meg said. "Where are you going?"

Jasper licked his lips, his expression shifting more distant. "Now that I know she is partly behind this, then they have to be going to her property, something those fellas ain't never done before." His gaze went deadly then. "Don't try calling the cops. In case you haven't figured out, the funeral director is in on this thing too. The sheriff, if you want to call him that, is just as crooked." Jasper shoved the door open. "Don't try following me neither." He glanced back. "They'll kill you and do unspeakably worse, young lady."

Meg glanced behind her. Haleigh's head was still jerking in small bursts.

And then Jasper was in his truck, grounding the ignition to a chug, his tires yelping over asphalt.

Meg's chest rose and fell, and the sense that something was coming—not help, necessarily, but eclipsing corruption—was gaining gut-instinct gravity. Jasper's warning now mingled in the chambers of reptilian intuition: *you didn't have much time.*

Meg rushed back into the viewing room. Now she was the one giving Haleigh's body a wide berth. Frantically, she found Haleigh's purse hanging over the arm of a chair, rifled through it to isolate her driver's license. Meg, using her own cell phone, snapped a picture of Haleigh's address and, with her eyes still on the twitching corpse, sidestepped out of the room, jogged through the lobby, and was out in the lot. Her heart was drumming as she tore away from the funeral home, simultaneously keying in Haleigh's home address into the navigation device.

Meg slowed at the whine of sirens; and sure enough, rounding a sharp curve was a sheriff's cruiser, followed several seconds later by a blaring ambulance. Within minutes, the cruiser would certainly be in the lot, and the sheriff (perhaps gun drawn) would enter the funeral home. But for the next few minutes it would remain empty, save for the other bodies staged for their own respective ceremonies. And in the viewing room dedicated to Calvin Mize's funeral, what used to be his aunt still lay on the floor, her limbs zigzagged like a neglected marionette. There was still the pecking sound, louder and more insistent in the silent room. With each insistent nudge, Haleigh's head wrenched on its thin neck. Finally, a trapezoid-shard of skull broke away, while more dark fluid flowed with the emergence of a glistening black beak.

*

It took Meg about thirty minutes to find Haleigh's house.

The proximity still felt as if she were on the outskirts of town, but most of the roads either did not match up with what appeared on the display screen or simply did not exist. She'd nearly given up, her resignation aided by her descent from the hormonal high of epinephrine, having almost plateaued on a rational plane, when she nearly collided with Jasper's truck.

It was canted in a ditch next to a skinny, thickly wooded trail that served, according to the warped mailbox, as a driveway. Meg turned around and brought the car up behind Jasper's vehicle.

That vertiginous sense reasserted itself: that she could stop something from happening—that she could save someone. She almost laughed aloud as she thought, *I have no lesson plan . . . but someone will learn a lesson.* A heroine. Meg did not believe she could save lives anymore. She was certain that parents could affect, or infect, their children more than some simple schoolmarm. Miss Settles could not necessarily save these kids. But maybe *Meg* could save *one*.

She gave her purse a quick assessment, pushing past the flashdrive and withdrawing the pepper spray. She thought about the cops. She thought about calling someone else. Her dad? She'd make a call, to someone, just as soon as she confirmed whether this Jasper fellow was either a murderer, an avenging uncle, or a psychotic commingling of both.

She punched in 911, her finger poised over the send button like a trigger as she passed Jasper's truck and stepped on to the overgrown path.

Meg made her way through the sun-spoked tunnel as birds and the hum of insects swayed and folded like the pleats of an all-encompassing curtain. She finally got up to it, coming to a low-lying ranch with faded paint, the face of the house hooded by the rotting upper lip of a bowing, shingle-sloughed porch roof. A number of trucks and a few cars were parked haphazard-ly here. Meg approached cautiously, not quite crouching, but ducking a bit as she wove through the maze of vehicles. Round-ing the front end of a truck, Meg clasped hold of her mouth to stifle a scream, nearly stepping on the body of a woman.

But now she noticed the jawline and the thick cover of stub-ble. The long-haired wig askew.

He'd been shot in the chest, recently—the blood flow from the ragged scattershot evincing as much. She slowly slid her hand away from her mouth. The man was dressed in a long, gar-ish wig lying nearby, all the way down to the dress and campy makeup. He looked as though he were preparing for a commu-nity stage play.

For the second time in her life—for the second time today—she stepped around a corpse. No twitching with this one. Just a big, dead man.

Shouting now from the woods beyond the house. Meg scanned the back, catching echoes of a distant argument. Toward the back of the house she made her way.

The shouting became more intense as she worked her way through a scrawl of a path, the aggressive verbal exchange helping—

hoping, she wished—to provide an audible cover for her approach.

Between the tall bars of dark-barked boles she spotted them: eight or nine men, one of them Jasper, hefting the shotgun as he shouted at one man in particular. She tried to crouch behind the trunk of a sycamore, but she used it for support as she essentially collapsed against it, no longer able to comprehend or utilize physical energy to support what she was seeing.

In the trees up above the circle of men was a crudely constructed pulley—the system serving as a sort of gallows for the noosed body at the end. By the size and shape, Meg understood it to be the corpse of Calvin Mize. Hope—a hope almost as insane as the rationale that had propelled her here—drained out of her like an unforgiving vortex.

But details were obscured, not only because of the damaged state of the body, but by the two teardrop-shaped creatures clinging to it. They were dark, leech-shaped, roughly the size of a child's sleeping bag. Below the body, where a gruesome mound had amassed, were three more creatures, these having more aspects of vultures. No feathers—the flesh of these things were completely black, like a lamination of obsidian latex that caught the gray light of the afternoon. Their heads were the same as vultures: fleshless for the ease of carrion scavenging, the diaphanous quality of their black wings in contrast to the bone-and-beak coarseness of their skeletal heads; and where eyes should be were empty pockets of sunken tissue as though the sockets had been cauterized. These creatures moved—crawled—like bats, using their thumbs at the ends of their wings, which were leathery and semi-translucent. Meg imagined the texture of filthy silk. They used their thumbs to shift and skulk across the leaf-and-gore spattered ground to feed on what had fallen from the suspended body.

Jasper's explanation at the funeral home came back to her now, along with something else—a kernel of recall from when she was a student. She freed the seed from some half-forgotten kernel of learning. The Tibetan Sky Funeral, where bodies were stripped of their flesh to ensure passage of the soul.

Her need to be a hero tempered the living hallucinations—
the impossibilities of what she was seeing.

Meg's nails dragged against bark as she sank even lower behind the trunk of a sycamore, and hearing the name Augie only
secured her assumption that the ringleader was Calvin's father.

Jasper raised the shotgun directly at Augie, who was cos-
tumed in something like gypsy-woman garb. Meg caught the
end of what Jasper was saying as his voice carried across the
clearing: "*. . . your own son.*"

"You know he wasn't my son just as well as any folks around
here," said Augie, appearing irritated by the interruption.

One of the men from the circle, this one dressed in something like a full nightgown and a long black wig, broke away at
Jasper's left, rushing forward. Jasper swiveled, the shotgun buck-
ing as the man jerked back and crumpled, the blast catching him
along the right shoulder. He squirmed, gasping, bringing up his
good arm as an entreaty.

The black vulture-things were already crawling toward him,
the nubs at the ends of their batlike wings stabbing at the leaf-
carpeted floor. It seemed to take a cruel amount of time for the
creatures to drag themselves over and begin taking vicious, poking bites at him. Meg covered her ears at the high-pitched
screams, which did not last long. She tried to pinch hold of
something cogent before she passed out—she kept her eyes on
Jasper, who racked another round into the shotgun's chamber
and aimed at one of the feeding creatures. He shot, a mist of
dark fluid exploding from the thing. Then came a keening
scream from all around, as if tiny versions of the birds were hidden in the black bits of the forest.

Meg stifled a scream to warn Jasper as Augie took two
strides forward, a large knife raised. The blade flashed for a moment before it came down low in Jasper's back. The big man
winced, uncoordinatedly trying to pivot, clearly trying to get his
hands on Augie; but he fell.

Meg looked at her phone, absent of bars, when, in the reflection of her cell screen, she caught movement.

Too late.

The stove length in the man's hand came down across the side of Meg's head, cell phone spilling out of her hand as she went sprawling from her hiding place.

A big, dirty hand was pawing at her neck, getting hold of both the top of her blouse and the purse strap. He began dragging her down the slope.

She was dropped down near Jasper, whose breathing had gone ragged. He appeared to be attempting to pull the knife out of his back with grueling futility.

Meg brought herself up to one arm, hair hanging in her face. The forest see-sawed, dark trees and sky carouseling as she tried to steady herself. The men—their dull eyes staring at her—began chanting something, Augie's voice the loudest as they began shambling forward.

Bite. Thrash. Scratch. She would do anything she could here—anything to fight. To fight as she hoped her mother had.

Meg was away at the university when it happened, her father out of town on business. By all indications, they'd said, it was a random act. Three males at least, said police. They'd forced their way in through the front door. Likely having arrived on foot or dropped off by a separate individual. They'd stolen Mom's car after taking what they wanted from the house, after taking what they wanted from her. Some of the police reports stated that most of the struggle occurred in the kitchen, which was where the body had been found. Though, in some of the interviews with police, she'd picked up on the detail that a kitchen knife contained blood from one of the murderers.

When it became clear that—without either suspects or witnesses in the neighborhood—some of the narrative would remain cruelly unclear, Meg pressed police about her mother's final moments, most of the cops unwilling or reticent to share. There was, however, one detective who after an interview caught Meg in the hall on the way out. Throwing glances over his shoulder, and in a low voice, he said, "She fought those sons-of-bitches like hell, ma'am." She still didn't know whether or not this was true—whether or not to take these words as true fact or intended to be consoling salve.

That's when the words came.

The simplistic mental liniments. Mostly from her family and friends, mostly useless, some from her father trying to console her. Prayers whose sentiments were ostensibly intended for the grieving but ultimately utilized to soothe themselves. Over the past seven years, the words had been useless.

The men, their voices growing louder—the chant containing a familiar word that had before issued from Haleigh's mouth: *Eurynomos*.

One of the men crouched to withdraw the knife roughly from Jasper's back, while another—his quivering, glazed eyes fixed on Meg—absently dragged the woman's wig from his head.

The forest had darkened, the silhouettes of the trees filigreed with mercury striations.

The chanting grew louder, seeming to double over itself from unseen recesses and shadowed folds all around her.

Meg tottered as she shifted, her shaking hand going to her purse for the pepper spray.

She screamed as her fingers met charged heat. She did not pull away, but rather withdrew the painful object.

That's when the words came.

Calvin's flashdrive, visibly glowing with green light, hummed with a seething tangle of words—his voice, she knew, hundreds of thousands of words. Meg looked past the encroaching men, toward the makeshift gallows, to where the smaller vulture creatures had dropped off Calvin's corpse, which smoldered with a verdigris glow.

Only Augie paused as the other men continued to loom closer. Meg raised the flashdrive, Calvin's voice spooling itself with the chanting. The flashdrive burst in Meg's hand as forks of green lightning shot out into the clearing. Like electrified ivy, bolts leaped out in undulating waves, wafting against the men and the creatures, the chanting altering to unrestrained screams as Calvin's words—burying one another in a frantic rush—overwhelmed the clearing. Pulses of green light continued to burst from Meg's hand and from Calvin's corpse, the men howling and collapsing, some of them beginning to smolder. With some of the nearer men, their mouths stretched open in heat-racked howls, their teeth and the whites of their agonized eyes glowing as if under the influence of ultraviolet illumination.

Uncountable thoughts swirled into the clearing. The jagged branches of emerald light began to take on tornadic aspect, kicking up leaves and debris in crooked isthmuses.

Meg tried to get to her feet as she blinked against both pain and fleeting consciousness. Calvin's babbling, disembodied voice—that demented diary indicting a familial tribe that had abused, abandoned, and ultimately betrayed its own child for its own ends—was growing to what she felt was a painful crescendo when the ground on the far side of the clearing quaked.

It was lying low on the ground, nothing more than a large mound covered with fallen leaves, stretching across the fringe of the clearing. As it rose up, debris quaked off the thing. What emerged was an identical though much larger version of the vulture-bat creatures—a black, featherless body, corded with obsidian tendons. Roughly ten yards wide, the thing rose up, its wings flapping with staggered swats, snapping low branches as they scooped in momentum-lending air. The enormous, fleshless skull-beak hissed as the wings bit at the air with great, gaspy flaps.

No longer able to defend herself from the shadow-edged eddy swirling on her periphery, Meg swooned, spilling out on her side not too far from Jasper. Before giving in, she blinked at the sky as the shadow licked up over the clearing, a streak of darkness sweeping across the sky. The wide wings were black and sharp against the gray sailcloth, as the shadow of its unacceptable expanse licked up over Meg, swiping lucidity with it.

*

Morning light was coming earlier these days, and the run would be a brisk one. Her mom had once said you burned more calories when you ran in cold weather. Still, Meg tried to get in a few miles before heading to work. She stepped out onto her front porch, giving a glance up and down the street of her neighborhood. A threadbare featherbed of fog lay over the dark lawns. Somewhere in a nearby tree came the dulcet, melancholy melody of a dove. She stretched, raised a leg, and scrolled through the playlist on her phone. Lavender light misted the dawn sky, slowly heaving at the retreating ceiling of night.

She looked up and down the street. Most of the neighborhood was still asleep. Still, she scrutinized the few vehicles lining the street, wondering (as she had so many times in the past ten months) if there might be a strange truck parked along the curb.

She returned to her playlist.

Nearly a year ago, she'd woken in the clearing, the smoldering bodies of the men and the vulture-things charred to carbonized distortion, the corpses whispering coiling ribbons of smoke. Jasper, though, had remained untouched by the electric flames; his motionless body lay contorted, his face aimed in the direction of his nephew and the broken circle where the attempted ritual had taken place. Calvin's body had fallen and now lay in a heap.

Meg looked at her hand. The flashdrive was gone; all that remained in her numbed hand was a wispy asterisk of soot.

Daylight was receding, a gunmetal corrugation of clouds heralding the onrush of dusk.

In time, Meg got to her feet, postholing her way over and around the scattered bodies. It took her a long time to return to her car, and when she did she crashed in behind the wheel. Her shoulders quaked as she wept for Calvin. She wept for her mother. Eventually she twisted the key in the ignition, turned on the navigation gadget, and tried to find her way back home.

Throughout the course of that remaining summer break, she'd steeled herself for the imminent knock on the door, the impending phone call from some law enforcement agency in

Glasgow. She cobbled together alternate versions of what she'd witnessed, but the only thing that brought solace was telling the truth. Using the right words to tell the right story.

She believed Calvin had done that. Whatever painful things were contained in that journal, his words had transcended abstraction.

One month turned into two. Two turned into six. And before Meg knew it, nearly a year had passed. Over that time, she'd come to think that whatever members of the experimental cult—The Crèche, Jasper had called it—still existed, for the sake of seclusion, would want nothing to do with her. Other times she thought they'd want nothing more than to find her.

Stretching done, she stepped off her front porch and turned north, picking up speed and steadying her pace. On the sidewalk up ahead, beneath the leafy, umbrella shadow of a tree, were a cluster of low-lying black shapes waddling toward the street, a shadowy, shifting hedgework of serpentine silhouettes. Canada geese, Meg realized. They were everywhere at this time of the season. As she drew closer, she considered the featureless silhouettes, their long necks appearing so much like erect snakes rising from some oblong vessels, their serpentine napes undulating as they listlessly padded forward.

Meg changed course, bounding off the sidewalk and cutting across the street, keeping the shadowed congregation of geese in the corner of her eye before refocusing on her run, putting some distance between herself and the large birds.

She was long gone, on the far side of the neighborhood, when one of the grazing geese lifted its wings wide and began hissing, exposing a rigid, pink tongue as its black beak scissored open. The black flesh of its webbed feet slapped over the ground as it rushed forward to one of the nearest members of its gaggle, clamping its beak on the other member's slender neck, thrashing viciously.

In the shadow under the tree, the entire gray-feathered collective—whether out of inherent terror or instinctive glee—sounded a raw, sibilant hiss.

Her Laugh

1

Clay Cooper wasn't crazy. But Chicago fixed him. The screaming fixed him.

In the summer of 2000—after several failed attempts at acquiring the identity of a serious college student, each half-hearted foray concluding in his lapsing back into the status of a dropout—Clay Cooper had made the casual statement that he should move away to go to school, that he should get out of Sycamore Mill and, as he phrased it, "just start over." On more than one occasion, he made this suggestion to his drinking buddies and his mom.

Clay's martyr's gamble backfired. His mother—who had become a sort of doting and indulgent landlord in the years following high school—actually supported the idea, even going so far as to fund a down payment on an apartment; that is, if he were fortunate enough to find a school willing to accept him. Clay's mom, evidently, wanted her twenty-one-year-old son to "start over" too. To Clay's interpretation, variations of the phrase "clean slate" slowly began to translate into the tacit suggestion that he grow up. And despite his distorted perspective, he vaguely suspected that his mom and his dropout buddies were right.

Concerned his reputation might be damaged if he backed away from his bluff, Clay approached a school willing to accept him—conditionally, of course; and in early August he made final plans to head up north. To fend off the notions of both homesickness (*I hate this pathetic town*) and the possibility of missing his friends (*they all hate me anyway*), Clay tried to conceptualize his impending endeavor as having its own loner soundtrack, something in the vein of, say, an AC/DC album—leaving town with a sneer to the tune of "Highway to Hell," and making a prodigal return to the blues-groovy conclusion of "Night Prowler."

These were the things Clay imagined.

He'd read parts of Orwell's *Down and Out in Paris and London* for one of his classes, and he considered his self-imposed expulsion from Sycamore Mill as being a sort of romantic exile, a Byronic exodus. In the end, Clay would discover that Chicago wasn't London or Paris or even New York, for that matter. It wasn't romantic. But it did *fix* Clay.

*

The apartment complex was located several dozen blocks north of the city. And the neighborhood, despite being fringed by some less-than-savory side streets, fell in a district that seemed to have maintained a bygone air of esteem—one-way streets lined with remodeled carriage houses and French Renaissance brownstones. That's not to say the neighborhood was without mediocrity, buildings whose renovated, regal-looking façade belied the shadow-drab shabbiness from within. That was Clay's apartment.

As opposed to the rent, tuition wasn't so cheap, even with the generous monthly check his mom had promised to send. Clay quickly found a job as a dishwasher at an unassuming bistro around the corner from his apartment. The work, for Clay, was nobly menial and lent itself appropriately to his loner's sojourn.

In the mornings he'd taken to buying a newspaper before catching the bus, skimming the pages as a means of avoiding potential contact or conversation. For Clay, this apparent cooperative disregard for politeness and conviviality—elements so pervasive in his bucolic hometown—was one of the more appealing aspects of living in the big and busy city. He hadn't been good at being affable or gregarious in Sycamore Mill anyway, so the funny game of acting indifferent suited Clay just fine; and, initially at least, he appropriated this daily lack of interest to all his neighbors.

All his neighbors. Except one.

2

In November, winter grew teeth and began devouring what was left of autumn. Clay had narrowly passed his classes for the fall semester and went home to Sycamore for two weeks during his Christmas break.

Clay returned to Chicago on a slate-colored, snow-swirled Sunday afternoon. Stomping slush from his boots, he walked into the lobby of his apartment complex and saw a girl, whom he'd never seen before, over by the bank of mailboxes. She was bundled up, but Clay could see the profile of her small, elfish face under a thick wool cap, a few strands of black hair fraying out on the sides of her cheeks. Clay guessed she was close to his age. He went to his mailbox, acting as if she were just another neighbor to be dismissed.

Clay pressed the UP arrow on the elevator, stepping inside and taking a jab at the button for the fifth floor. She turned then, as if cued by the sound of the elevator's sliding doors. Clay leaned forward and caught the door. The girl offered a quick smile as she slipped into the elevator. "Thanks," she said, raising her eyebrows, her nose and cheeks pink; she was sniffing a bit from the cold. Moving to press the already dim-glowing button for the fifth floor, she hesitated, apparently understanding that Clay had already hit the button and simply said, "Oh," before returning to leaf through her mail. The lights overhead flickered as the doors closed and the compartment rattled to ascension. She was standing close to the doors, and despite himself Clay ventured a few curious glances over her shoulder, at the bills she was leafing through, wondering what her story was. But after a few moments, Clay's attention was drawn to the unpolished panels on the elevator doors, where he could see the girl's reflection—her chin tilted down, her face obscured in shadow under the thick wool cap. He thought she was unusually attractive, even in the funhouse-mirror distortion of the tarnished door.

The elevator lurched to a stop, the doors opened, and the girl, still flipping through her mail, stepped off, steering to the left into the corridor. Clay followed and began fishing in his pocket for his door key. The girl—whom Clay now heard humming to herself—had rounded the corner. As he stepped up to his door, he could hear that her humming was now joined by the jangling of keys at the end of the hallway near the stairwell. *She lives on my floor?* He'd never seen her before. And he would have remembered *this* girl. He unlocked the ancient-looking deadbolt and entered his apartment, closing the door and abandoning any personal sense of restraint as he swiftly leaned up against the peephole and squinted. From Clay's angle, and through the bulging scope of the convex eyehole, he merely glimpsed a shape making a mouse-quick slip into the apartment, and the sliver-nictation of the door winking closed behind her. *Lucky me.*

3

During the day, returning from school or heading out to work, Clay frequently ran into a neighbor or two. Most of the people on his floor were elderly, and in the winter months he'd seen very little of them. *Maybe it's cheap for them to live here,* he often wondered. *Maybe they've lived here since it was built.* There was a garbage chute around the corner on his floor, down at the end of the hallway. From time to time Clay would walk by someone taking out a small bag of garbage. Sometimes he'd say hello; more often than not, he'd remain silent.

There was an old black woman who lived on his floor, just down the hall in the direction of the elevators. She lived alone, as far as Clay could tell. Because of her observable independence, and because Clay had acquired a healthy sense of anonymity, he never asked if there was anything she needed, or if there was anything he could do to help. One day when Clay noticed the woman struggling into the lobby with her groceries, he offered to carry her bags for her. Whether out of pride or suspicion about his motives—Clay wondered if it might be a little of both—she rejected his voluntary advances. "Now, now," she said, her smile contorting wrinkles along her cheeks and near her eyes. "I didn't get to be a tough old bird by lettin' boys do all my work for me." Clay bristled at being lumped together with "boys." *Have it your way,* he thought, giving the encounter a mental shrug. *Yeah,* he turned toward the sidewalk, *a tough old bird*.

4

The girl down the hall, Clay was convinced, was some sort of art student. Or a musician, maybe. Or part of some avant-garde acting troupe. She dressed with the trendy eccentricity of a contemporary bohemian, and her demeanor—when he'd see her in the lobby or on the sidewalk—seemed to fluctuate between fussy hostility and friendly contentment. On the weekends Clay could hear her playing her stereo down the hall—usually some sort of techno-melancholy that he found agitating. She played it loud, but none of his elderly neighbors appeared to notice or complain. They, in fact, kept their televisions up near distracting levels, particularly for game shows or the local news.

During those first, late-winter weeks, Clay never saw another person enter or leave the girl's apartment, and guessed she was living alone.

So much about her was intriguingly strange—and that strangeness, for Clay, translated into exoticism, and exoticism into something like tepid obsession.

During the day, sitting on the bus on his way home from school, Clay would begin toying with ways to introduce himself. He'd walk down the snow-slushed sidewalk, wondering if she'd be in the lobby getting her mail. Of course, the climax of these daydreams was the indulgent fantasy of the girl—for whatever reason—inviting Clay into her apartment and, with movie-script convenience, consent to sessions of consensually unobligated sex.

Ordinarily, the lobby was empty when he returned in the late afternoon, and he'd taken to habitually peering in the small glass slit of her mailbox to see if she'd picked up any envelopes for the day. In the elevator, propelled by the possibility of seeing her in the hallway or taking out the trash, Clay often dreamed up possibilities for what the name on those envelopes might be, what *her* name might be—tumbling Ls and Ms over his tongue, aroused by the hiss-syllabic quality of her imaginary appellations. During the day, Clay created seductive vignettes in which he whispered her name. But at night, lying alone in bed, he imagined the girl whispering his.

5

One Saturday night in March, Clay was stretched out on his couch—half-dozing, half-watching a movie, his face paled by the anemic mercury-flicker of television light—when he thought he heard some muffled giggling in the hallway.

Earlier that night, after clocking out from his dishwashing shift at the restaurant, Clay had decided to unwind at a popular pub around the corner from his apartment. He'd sauntered in, slid onto a barstool, and ordered a beer, scanning the smoke-filled tavern, glancing at the clusters of good-looking, loud-laughing twenty-somethings—*mostly college kids,* he thought. *Just like me.* No. *Not like me.* Clay drank his lukewarm beer, alternating between trying to affect a loner's air of mysteriousness and hoping to make eye contact with one of the well-tanned coeds. This little social experiment lasted five beers. Clay finally decided he was tired—tired from work and of not being noticed.

The security attendant in the lobby of his apartment, an old man—who, to Clay, seemed too old to work security and too happy to work a Saturday night—greeted him as he tottered to the elevators, and, as usual, Clay did his best to tolerate the old man's attempts at small talk.

Now, laid out across his couch, Clay's cheap-beer drowse dissipated as he heard the voices coming from the hallway. He blinked a few times, shaking some clarity into his head. He thought he heard *her* voice.

Springing off the couch, Clay bumped his shin on the coffee table—grunting a curse and clenching his teeth—before weaving through the darkness and stumbling into the corridor leading to the door and the peephole. Clay approached on tiptoe—a useless movement that he'd grown accustomed to when peering through his tiny spyglass.

Two people were at the end of the hallway, down by the girl's apartment door: the girl, whose back was against the wall; and a guy, who was standing in front of her, looking as if he were whispering in her ear. In the wide-angle distortion of the peephole, the pair looked like one groping tangle. The girl intermittently gave up a tinny string of stifled shrieks.

The guy was tall and lanky, a slim body type that Clay associated not with toughness—not like the bigger guys at the bar earlier that night—but with a sort of harmless ghoulishness. Dark, mod-looking bangs—which he continually shrugged off his forehead—fell over his brow, obscuring his face. Clay caught only fleeting flashes of paleness between the hanging bangs of the guy's stylishly disheveled hair. The girl continued giggling, swaying against the wall. The guy occasionally buried his pale face between her shoulder and her ear, eliciting vampirish images to Clay, although this victim sounded as if she were enjoying the attack and appeared to be putting up a pretty weak fight.

During all this pawing, the girl's laughter gave way to a series of elated exhalations—the pre-ecstasy sounds of foreplay; or at least a sort of corridor foreplay. Clay held his breath, intently imagining the girl's face changing. With erotic clarity he pictured her expression morphing from mischievous contentment, to lip-biting bliss, to brow-furrowing euphoria—eyes closed, jaw unhinged—as she inched toward the deep end of orgasm. Clay began to feel the images as a dull twinge in his pelvis.

Clay's legs were getting stiff as he stood in front of the peephole; and as he shifted his weight from one foot to the other, he bumped his forehead against the door, producing a soft but tangible thud. Clay winced. When he opened his eyes the couple was still there, the girl still pressed against the wall. But after a few seconds she gave the guy what looked like a playful shove, to which he reacted by straightening up and giving her some space.

Clay listened to the brief chiming of keys and heard the girl hiss something as she dropped them on the floor. Retrieving them, the girl finally brought the jangling tangle to the lock, and the couple shuffled into the apartment.

Everything, save for the whispery background sound of his own television, was quiet now.

Clay, still aroused by images of the girl, pushed himself away from the peephole and began walking back to the living room. He passed the darkened kitchen, catching a glimpse of the trashcan in there. He quickly conjured the pretext to take the trash to the garbage chute down the hall; and while he distantly recognized a lingering compulsion to want to see and hear her, his beer-imbued logic was that maybe taking out the trash— taking one final stroll past her apartment—might shake free this urge for *more* of her.

He slipped on a pair of sandals, covered his lunatic hair with a ballcap, and knotted the half-full bag of garbage. He opened the door and squinted at the bright, fluorescent light in the hall-way—the corridor's normal symmetry seeming almost alien after he had viewed it for so long through the marble-sized bulge of the peephole.

Although he gave the girl's bronze doorplate and peephole a quick glimpse, he didn't slow as he passed by, rather continuing his casual gait to the back hallway, turning left around a crook of wall. The garbage chute was halfway down the hall. Clay opened the lower lip of the thing and dropped his garbage, listening as it skidded against the inside of the shaft before making a glass-clinking landing.

Quiet again.

Clay slipped his hands into his jeans and headed back. As he rounded the corner wall, he slowed as he walked by her apart-ment. The door was almost out of his field of vision when he heard something that made him hesitate—something he first took for a muffled scream but now realized was a low, throaty murmur. Coming to full stop, Clay turned toward the door, staring at it, straining to hear. The sound came again, as if from the inner recesses of the apartment. Giving a cursory glance at the bronze number plate, he took a couple of sly steps toward the door, holding his breath and leaning in, the side of his face and ear nearly touching door.

Clay listened to his pulsing heart for several seconds before a voice suddenly spoke. *"I seeeee youuu,"* a male's voice sang from the other side of the door, just inches of wood dividing Clay's face and the speaker. Clay reeled back as if he'd dipped his face into a thickly spun spiderweb.

And now there was the eruption of laughter on the other side of the door—a guy's laugh and a girl's laugh, *her* laugh—and the unrestrained chuckles echoed into the corridor. Clay stared dumbly at the peephole for a moment before retreating, walking swiftly toward the sanctuary of his apartment, his flipflops making an absurd suck-pop sound as he strode down the hallway.

The crow-caw laughter began to diminish as Clay neared his door. He went for his keys, sliding a hand into the pocket of his jeans. The empty pockets of his jeans. He could picture the keys now, laying on the coffee table in front of the TV, along with his wallet and a spill of loose coins.

Clay, attempting to maintain some dignity, tried the door-knob only once—there was no frantic twisting, no shoving. It was, of course, locked. The laughter had died down now, but there was still the intermittent titter of something—*whispers*. Clay turned and walked over to the elevator, pressing the down arrow. He listened as the yawning cables and gears lifted the compartment to the fifth floor. The doors dinged opened and Clay stepped in, clenching his teeth and stabbing the button for the lobby. He'd have to request an escort from the security guard to unlock his apartment. He could already imagine the old security guard beaming at the prospect of late-night company. *Damn it.*

On the ride down, Clay inspected his own distorted reflection in the warped and tarnished panels of the elevator door. He closed his eyes, trying to chase away the echoic laughter that seemed to have followed him into the tiny compartment.

6

Spring—or at least spring-like weather—overtook Chicago almost overnight.

In the weeks following his mortifying eavesdropping experience, Clay had done his best to avoid the girl, as he was beyond certain she'd designated him a four-star creep. Now he used his peephole *before* leaving his apartment, to make sure she *wasn't* out there. If he happened to pass her in the hall, he'd avert the possibility of eye contact by keeping his gaze trained on yellowed, peeling wallpaper and the antiquated stains in the burgundy carpet. If, coming home from work or returning from school, he'd see her through the foyer windows getting her mail in the lobby, he'd take a short walk around the block. And she was usually gone on his second pass.

One spring evening Clay entered the lobby, tucking his newspaper under his arm and steering toward the bank of mailboxes.

The girl silently came around the corner over by the stairwell. Clay, out of the tail of his eye, was fortunate to register her presence, so he quickly shut his mailbox, giving her a wide berth as he flipped through his mail, reading nothing, and briskly walking toward the poorly lit stairwell. But as he pivoted, doing his best to avoid her face, his attention snagged on something— his eyes did a touch-and-go on her subtly curved abdomen, at the gentle distention of her belly. *Pregnant,* he thought as he sorted through an admixture solution of reverence, disbelief, and curiosity, laced with traces of jealousy and carnal covetousness. "Pregnant," he repeated in a whisper as he clomped up the concrete steps to the fifth floor.

7

Months passed. And as the weeks accumulated and days folded over on themselves, Clay did a reasonable job of ostensibly disregarding the girl as he circulated through the pleasantly monotonous cycles of work and school. He was approaching the end of his spring term and for the first time felt a foreign sense of confidence at having coped with college.

The girl being pregnant, for Clay, somehow affirmed that she had her own life to worry about and therefore couldn't be concerned with some lonely guy down the hall with a questionable preoccupation. Pregnancy somehow indicated that her life was moving. And Clay took this as a cue that he should do the same with his own. And no matter her opinion of Clay, he felt as if he (*the peephole creep*) were off the hook.

She seemed as flightily independent as ever—more so, in a way. When Clay would pass her in the lobby, sometimes she'd be humming to herself, her tiny belly plumping by degrees. But, as far as Clay could discern, she was still alone. And aside from the one night he'd been caught by the mystery man at the peephole, Clay had never seen anyone else go in or out of her apartment. And while he wouldn't allow his eye to linger too long, Clay, out of his periphery, thought that maybe—*maybe*—she was trying to make eye contact with him. And in that fuzzy sort of instant-replay, Clay was sure she was grinning at him, gently trying to reel his attention toward her.

8

The summer of 2001 was particularly miserable in the apartment complex, and not for any reason that had to do with the girl or school or his friendlessness. It was hot—in the apartment, on the bus, in the subway. Clay, lying in bed at night with the windows open, listened to car alarms and the horn-honk rhythm of taxis; he listened to the voices inside the apartment, imagining the old building as being a stifling beehive producing only an ambient buzz and sauna-haze streams of steam. Sometimes he coaxed himself to sleep by placing himself on the night-cool sand of the waterfront, gazing out at Lake Michigan, drifting away to the metronomic lapping of black waves curving over the lake shore.

One sweltering afternoon in July, Clay was sitting in the laundry room, waiting for the dryer to finish and reading a newspaper. One headline said: *SUICIDE BOMBER KILLS DOZENS;* and another: *FOOT AND MOUTH OUTBREAK IN U.K.—MILLIONS OF SHEEP, CATTLE KILLED*. He was frowning at the article, fumbling with the word "epizootic," when the girl walked in, toting a laundry basket on her hip. She was wearing gray sweatpants, pink flipflops, and a hooded sweatshirt—the thick material stretching over her breasts and the pregnant hump of her stomach. Her raven-black hair—which had dyed streamers of purple in it—was pulled back in a pony-tail. *A hooded sweatshirt in July?* he wondered distantly.

In a panicked movement, Clay shot his face back down to the newspaper. His heart, thudding in sync with the rhythmic tumble of the dryer, was drumming in his ears. As if through cotton, he heard her say, "Hell-o," drawing out the two sing-song syllables as she passed behind him.

There were a few other people in the laundry room, and Clay fought the urge to swivel and see *whom* she'd spoken to. In the reflection of the dryer window, Clay watched her as she hefted her laundry basket and, humming to herself, began to pluck panties and bras and pajamas from her laundry basket. His eyes eventually returned to his paper, concentrating on the columns of small words until the tumbling stopped.

A few weeks later, Clay was on his way to work and waiting in the hallway for the elevator. When the bell gave a flimsy ding and the doors slid open, he stepped forward, nearly colliding with the girl as she exited the elevator. They both reacted simul-taneously, skidding just short of bumping into each other. She was carrying some sort of wicker crate filled with pink tissue pa-per and what looked like baby-shower gifts; and in that torturously awkward instant, Clay noted a plastic baby doll sticking out of the crate.

"Sorry . . . excuse me," she said.

Clay, eyes aiming at the floor, made a face that was his version of an apology. But as he stepped on the elevator he paused—his mind lurched as if trying to stop his mouth from wandering into a busy intersection. It was too late. "My, um . . ." he said over his shoulder. "My dad . . ."

The girl stopped and turned. "Pardon me?" she said.

Clay cleared his throat and made himself look at her. Her face was soft, pretty and puckish and confident; the way her eyebrows were raised implied sincere curiosity instead of haughty impatience. *Was she being an actress?* The crate was propped up in front of her, on her belly. *Is that hump . . . is her stomach smaller?* Clay's eyes flicked down at the crate, alternating back and forth between her eyes and the eyes of the baby doll—the sort of ubiquitously nondescript toy that was a staple of garage sales and donation centers.

He started again, hoping to sound casual, "My dad used to tell me not to rush onto an elevator, that people should give other people enough space to get off"—*what the hell am I talking about?*—"so that was my fault." He offered a clench-thin smile. "Sorry."

An easy, no-big-deal smirk appeared, her lips arcing up. It was a smile that, in Clay's perception, suggested that both his tepid attempt to interact as well as his pointless anecdote were both acceptable gestures of simply acting decent. "Sure, no problem. See ya." She turned and disappeared around the corner.

Clay stood for another moment, waiting for his mind to retrieve some control, before stepping in and pressing the button to the lobby.

Through the front doors, past the breezeway, the afternoon light had lost its fight with the transitional cobalt tones of evening. The sodium vapor streetlights hadn't turned on yet, their automatic solar-sensors still apparently clinging to the lingering threads of sunset. The elderly lobby security guard was arranging some materials for his shift—a brown bag, a radio, a box of Kleenex—on top of the desk. The old man hobble-turned just as Clay was striding past him. The old man adjusted his glasses and offered Clay a smile, which he returned, taking the uncharacteristic effort to add, "Have a good evening."

"You do the same, young man."

Clay pushed through the front doors. The blue-gray sky, paired with the slightly static feel of the air, made him wonder if a storm was coming. He walked down the sidewalk, unaware of the threadbare smile on his face. He passed under a streetlamp.

The lamp, in the oncoming darkness, clicked on.

9

September.

Clay was several weeks into his second fall semester at the university. On Tuesdays and Thursdays his classes started early, and for the first time since he'd moved to Chicago—even more than that, for the first time in years—Clay was growing confident with the work he was doing in Chicago, with the job he'd moved here to do.

It was a Tuesday morning, Clay's alarm beginning its staccato bleating at the accustomed time, and he began eliminating items on his daily itinerary: coffee, shower, check weather, get dressed, load up backpack, shut down and lock up the apartment.

One of the morning rituals to which he had remained faithful was buying a newspaper to read on the bus. While those inky pages still served as a device with which to disengage and tune out other passengers, Clay now found solace in the comfort of catching up with the city and the world.

As usual, he boarded the bus at the same spot with most of the same people, and as he shuffled on to the normally crowded bus he was surprised to find an open spot on a bench seat along the window. He sat and flipped through his newspaper, occasionally glancing out at the passing strips of blue sky between the slate- and sandstone-colored buildings. Blocks passed, and the bus slowly filled with passengers. Clay looked up again. The sky between the buildings was growing narrower as the bus neared downtown.

After creasing his paper, Clay gripped a bench pole and began to stand, but as he did so a passenger strode by him, bumping into Clay's shoulder and knocking him off balance, almost back down into his seat. Without glancing back, the guy simply continued on, joining others in the short line near the front of the bus. Clay was still leaning over from the jolt. A girl sitting directly across from Clay snickered. She had stringy blond hair and was wearing a pair of headphones—her smile appeared as a sneer to Clay. He scanned a few other faces. No one else seemed to notice. He yanked himself the rest of the way up, adjusted his backpack, and began shuffling toward the front of the bus.

The guy was now a few heads in front of him, his face pointed straight ahead. Clay's pulse began to percolate, to throb along his throat in his ears. The bus slowed and lurched to a stop, the doors folded open and the people poured out. The guy stepped down to the sidewalk and turned south. Clay stepped off the bus, balling his fists as he steered in the same direction.

His plan was simple—*Catch up with this prick on the crosswalk . . . return the favor.* But the guy was moving fast, and keeping up quickly became a task. Clay was only several paces behind the stranger as they neared an intersection where a cluster of people were waiting for the light to turn. Clay judged that this guy was roughly his own age. But now as he glowered at the back of the guy's skull, Clay grew nervous, considering what sort of possible retaliation might occur. *Would the guy ignore me too if I just kept walking?* And that was what infuriated Clay the most—it wasn't the physical contact so much as it was not being acknowledged. The guy had just kept moving as if Clay hadn't—*didn't*—exist.

The light turned green and the crowd stepped forward. Clay made a halfhearted attempt to pass the guy, but the stranger was moving fast again, pulling away. Clenching his teeth, Clay allowed himself to fall back. He was now a block or two out of his way and heading in the wrong direction. *Fuck it,* Clay thought, abandoning his pursuit, watching the guy blend in and disappear with the bustling multitude.

No longer in the mood for school, Clay caught a northbound bus to take him back to his apartment. He'd take the day off. *It's a gorgeous day and people are ugly.* He was thinking of the girl on the bus with the headphones. In the eye of his imagination, her tiny teeth were filed down to haphazard fangs—cannibal's teeth. And when he imagined his own version of the stranger's face, he saw the guy turning slowly on the crosswalk, gleefully revealing a broad, piranha-mouth smile.

It took Clay a long time to get back to his neighborhood.

Walking into the lobby of his apartment, he could already sense a different atmosphere about the place. Being a weekday morning, and even with the significant number of elderly people in the complex, the place seemed—looked, felt, sounded—more subdued than usual. There was a drowsy-feline sort of languor about the place. Clay checked his mailbox. Nothing. He stepped to the elevator and stabbed the UP arrow. After waiting for what seemed too long, Clay gave a to-hell-with-this exhale and walked toward the stairwell.

Four flights later, Clay emerged through the fifth-floor door, strode past the garbage chute, rounded the elbow of wall, and passed the girl's apartment, giving her door—the number plate and the peephole—a quick glance before steering straight ahead and proceeding down the hall toward his own apartment. He noted the TV sounds coming from his elderly neighbors' rooms, a sound he'd grown used to. But even their hard-of-hearing volume seemed more suppressed this morning.

As Clay pulled the key from his pocket he heard something else—a scuttling sound, like a mouse scrabbling along coving. He turned, fidgeting a few glances here and there, he looked and listened. *Whispers?*

Clay swept it away, jamming the key into the lock and twisting. He pocketed the key, slipped off his backpack, and sauntered into the living room, where he crossed to the window, yanked up the shades, and cracked the sill. A warm breeze—a unique mingling of the best qualities of summer and autumn—sighed into Clay's apartment. He took a deep breath and flipped on the television. It would be the network news at this time in the morning.

He was about to head into the kitchen when the sound of a reporter's voice—something unusually unrefined—seized his attention. The reporter was saying something about airplanes. ". . .the plane struck the building . . ."

Standing directly in front of the screen, Clay instantly recognized the dark pair of skyscrapers, one of them hemorrhaging a thick trail of grim-tinted smoke. Over the summer, the newspapers had had several stories about private planes crashing in strange places, or recreational pilots making emergency landings; and in a presumptive flash, that's precisely what Clay believed he was watching now.

He increased the volume. The flustered-sounding reporter was saying something about a possible hijacking ". . . *and then the airplane struck the north tower . . .*"

Even as he listened to the piecemeal details of what was happening, and even if it was a hijacker, Clay had almost automatically assumed that hijackers had stolen a private plane—a small Cessna, or something like that—and had executed the crash among themselves, among a scant number of terrorists. But slowly Clay began to comprehend the certainty that the airplanes had been larger aircraft—passenger planes. *Full of people. Probably some kids.* The reporter was suggesting similar things now.

It wasn't just a few people who were now dead in New York. It was hundreds.

Clay absently took a seat on the coffee table, staring at the dark building with its ugly, smoky tail curling into the blue sky. Prefaced by terms like "alleged" and "uncertain," the reporter continued to repeat the words "hijackers" and "terrorists." The news anchor in the studio was dispensing information about the airplane, confirming that the 767 had been part of a commercial flight from Boston to Los Angeles, and that the hijackers had targeted this particular flight because it had been fueled for a long-distance trip. *They used the fuel for the explosion.* There was no sign of the airplane, as it had imbedded itself deep within the building—the source of the black smoke metastasizing from a smoldering, high-octane core.

Clay licked his lips, which felt numb. He was suddenly aware of the sound of other televisions. Glancing across the room, out the window, Clay could hear the dissonant chatter of overlapping broadcasts coming from his neighbors' apartments. He could still feel the delicate breeze drifting in through the window; the sky was wide and painfully blue.

The aerial shots of the Trade Center continued. And suddenly—just as Clay rose to pick up the phone—another airplane violated the screen, momentarily disappearing behind the other skyscraper. A second later came the explosion, an almost gelatinous, slow-motion swell rupturing horizontally along the side of the building. Glittering shards of glass and steel spilled from the building. Clay thought he heard a collective gasp issue from the neighboring apartments, as if united in the horror of witnessing was happening in New York. Clay's stomach began to wring itself in his midsection as his eyes scoured the screen, acknowledging what he was seeing but not really comprehending it.

Several minutes passed. Both buildings were smoking in earnest now, and the city skyline was streaked with billowing charcoal smoke. And Clay reluctantly imagined the scene inside the buildings—the panic, the tramplings, the suffocation, the furnace-blackened bodies. The reporter now mentioned that people had been seen jumping from the buildings. And that repulsive notion was nearly too much for Clay—the nauseating gratuity of bodies, of pieces of bodies, littering the debris-filled streets. Clay thought about the kids who'd likely been on the plane, the kids in the building. Moms and dads. "Christ," he muttered—a weak sound that simply reaffirmed his being anchored here: breathing, safe, sitting on a coffee table, staring at the TV like some helpless, friendless, useless . . . boy. He thought about the people in his apartment, the city strangers he'd made his tacit adversaries over that past year—even if only inwardly, privately. Clay thought about the guy on the bus. Compunction, and something that was almost shame, began to needle him. He quickly dismissed it.

On wobbling legs Clay stood and took several steps toward the phone, but stopped when he heard a scream.

He punched the mute button on the remote and waited. Again, an echo-softened scream sounding as if it had come from the hallway. He made a few strides for the door, giving a cautioned check through the peephole to discover the hallway empty; even so, Clay opened the door and stuck his head into the corridor. Frowning in concentration, he was prepared to close the door when he heard it again.

Clay heard another scream and knew it was coming from her apartment. And in that last wall-cushioned call for help, he thought he heard his name, *Clay*—maybe even *Clay . . . help*. He rushed forward, down the hall.

Distantly aware of the layered discordance of televisions and radios filling the hallway, Clay slowed as he approached her apartment door, his eyes moving from the bronze number plate to the peephole. He swallowed, extending a loosely clenched fist to knock, then stopped, noticing the vertical black slit of the door jamb. The door was cracked open slightly, almost imperceptibly. *Had it been open when I passed by earlier?* Clay shoved the question aside as another sob-laced wail escaped the inside of the apartment.

He pushed through the door, which opened into a narrow entryway. The apartment was dark inside, and that darkness swallowed Clay as the door creaked shut behind him. He squinted, his eyes adjusting to the darkness in the corridor; he noticed

dim light coming from the room in front of him. The air was stifling and held the perfume of patchouli and something like the
stagnant incense of decaying plants.

"Hello," Clay called out, instantly hating the frailty in his
voice. "Is everything okay?"

"Please," came the girl's voice, sounding as if she were panting. "Please . . . come help me."

Clay, still squinting against darkness, strode forward. He
emerged in a living-room area. The windows on the opposite
side of the room had been covered with some sort of purple, tie-
died wall hanging, which tinted everything a dark shade of lavender. There was an old stereo cabinet, some pieces of furniture,
a patchwork couch.

Clay glanced left, toward the kitchen and beyond to the
shadow-darkened rectangle of the hallway, which—as the layout
was evidently identical to Clay's apartment—surely led to her bedroom. Still frowning, Clay called out again. "Where are you?"

Suddenly part of the girl's face sprang up from over the top
of the couch. Her skin was pale, almost gray in the purple-dim
light of the room; her eyes were shaded beneath with dark scallops. Her thin eyebrows were arched in an expression of pain
and expectation.

"Please, Clay," she said in short bursts, "it's . . . the baby."

Although his mind twitched at the peculiarity of her *knowing*
his name, Clay rounded the side of the patchwork couch.

She was lying on the floor between the couch and a coffee
table, her bare legs splayed in a sit-up position—one slender
hand fanned on the couch cushions, the other braced on the coffee table, which was cluttered with what looked like spools of
yarn and sewing paraphernalia; threads of her dark hair clung to
her fever-damp forehead in stringy clumps. She was wearing a
long white nightshirt, the hem of which was pulled taut across
her knees, canopying her inner thighs in shadow. Wanting to act
and react with the same momentum that propelled him in to her
apartment, Clay crouched on one knee.

"You have to help me . . . I'm going to have the baby."

He thought he could see dark smears along the inside of her thighs, and his eyes darted back up to her deathbed face. "Listen, I—" He licked his lips. The room was so dim. He gave a panicked glance around the apartment, as if uselessly seeking for help. *How does she know my name?* "I don't know what I'm doing . . . I don't want to fuck this up. Let me call for a doctor or someone—"

"No," she hissed. An expression, as if she were going to laugh, skittered across her face and disappeared. "No—it'd be too late. You have to help me, Clay. It has to be *you*."

And again, with the uttering of his name, Clay was moving. Leaning forward, squinting, willing his eyes to adjust to the purple gloom, he now saw something under the hem of her nightshirt, in the shadowy fork between her legs. Something pale. Clay's eyes bounced back and forth between the dark smears on her thighs to the pale shape between her legs. He had been frowning; but now, pausing on her face, his expression went slack.

She was smiling, her tiny teeth glittering in the purple half-light. Whey-faced, her eyes—still feverish, still nested in bruise-colored sockets—had gone from being filled with desperation to almost dancing with feral delight. And behind her tiny teeth, a cackle began to swell.

Clay recoiled, falling back on his palms.

With lurid smoothness, the girl slid her hand off the couch and down between her legs, withdrawing a plastic baby doll. A mock umbilical cord had been knotted around the baby doll's midsection.

Clay—on his ass, his knee-bent position looking as if himself were giving birth—watched the girl's pale hand crawl across the coffee table, and from the loose-spooled clutter of yarn she withdrew a pair of scissors. She was still cackling softly, her unblinking eyes still locked on Clay, as she opened the blades with a clean sounding *shink,* and moved the silvery knives to the baby's fake umbilical cord, severing the fleshy material. The plastic baby doll clomped to the floor.

The girl's giggling stopped suddenly. Clay had been inching back on his palms and heels, but the unexpected silence forced him to stop. The girl was no longer smiling and she seemed to be measuring the space between herself and Clay. Both, sitting in the same position, simply stared at each other for a moment, their chests rising and falling with labored breathing. The girl's lower lip was glistening with saliva.

She began blinking rapidly, eyebrows twitching, as if intently listening to telepathic instructions from some unseen stage manager. And then, as abruptly as the silence had settled, the girl's face quivered and contorted as she raised the scissors over her head.

In one galvanic move, Clay twisted up and was on his feet, scrambling for the shadow-boxed corridor. In the darkness he groped for the doorknob, at the same time hearing the sound of feet pounding the hardwood floor.

Stumbling into the hallway, he bolted straightforward, nearly tripping once and only slowing as he neared his door. He whirled, giving an over-the-shoulder glance as he began fishing through his pocket for his key. For a moment everything was silent. He began walking backwards, then stopped, the pounding of his heart giving the drumming suggestion that he start moving his ass again. But Clay stood still, absently stalled on the elusive notion that he'd missed something. *This can't be right,* he began repeating silently. *This can't be right. This can't be real.*

A queasy ripcord tugged his midsection as he watched the girl—slowly, almost sleepily—emerge from her apartment doorway. Her stare was empty, an unblinking expression resembling someone in a critical stage of shock. With her long, loose-hanging nightshirt looking like a hospital gown, she was a vision of delivery-room misery. But all at once, here, in the fluorescent sterility of the hallway, Clay could see the girl clearly. The dark scallops under her unblinking eyes seemed overdone, and her bloodless complexion seemed grossly vaudevillian—horrifyingly burlesque. He briefly considered how skinny she was—that her belly held no sign of having ever been pregnant.

Her arms hung loosely at her sides. Dangling in one hand was the plastic baby doll. Clay paused on the object before the light caught the silvery glint in her other hand. The scissors. The girl slumped one shoulder against the wall and began sliding, almost gliding, toward Clay.

Clay was still fishing for his key, frantically sifting through loose change, pens, his bus card . . . then it was there, in his fingers.

He pulled the key from his pocket, jittering it around the lock before quieting his mind long enough to slip the jagged teeth into the deadbolt's keyhole. In the instant it took for Clay to push through and slam the door, he had the flashbulb glimpse of the girl raising the scissors, her slender arm hooking over her head in an almost celebratory gesture, her mouth arced up into a rictus. She sneered and rushed forward.

Clay braced his shoulder against the door just as the girl slammed into it. He could hear her, growling, making hissing sounds as through clenched teeth. But this dissipated, and the short-lived silence was replaced by a scratching sound—the sound of wood being gashed and gouged. *The scissors,* he thought; *she's carving up the door with the scissors.* This sound, too, subsided after a minute.

Slowly, gently spreading both palms to either side of the peephole, Clay moved his face, his eye, to the peephole.

She was out there, but was walking backwards now, arms at her sides, in a sort of tiptoe retreat. Her body language— slumped shoulders, underhung chin, scissor blades aimed toward the floor—suggested adolescent defeat or childlike disappointment. Then she stopped moving.

Clay swallowed, held his breath and listened as the silence was lacerated with a single tormented scream, and watched her arm recoil and fling the plastic baby doll, causing Clay to flinch back from the peephole as the toy hit the door. A few seconds later he heard a door slam shut, and when he returned to the marble-sized peephole, the hallway was empty.

Gripping the knob, Clay opened the door a sliver. He was again aware of the faint sound of news coverage on televisions and radios. He glanced over at his mutilated door, scanning the damage. There were long slashes and zigzag scars in the paint-flecked wood. He took one tentative step into the hall, and his sneaker squashed something. Clay took his foot off the plastic baby doll. Reaching down, almost tenderly, he picked up the doll—the toy's long-lashed eyelids bobbing open and bobbing closed.

A door swung open down the corridor. The elderly black woman, his tough-old-bird neighbor, leaned out into the hall-way. With her door open, Clay could hear a TV droning loudly from within her apartment. "You screaming?" she asked, grimacing. "Who's screaming out here?"

Clay slipped the baby doll down and behind him, out of sight. "Yeah," he said, clearing his throat to affect confidence. "I thought I heard that too." For a moment, both craned their necks up and down the hall, as if searching for the source of the scream.

"You been watching this awful news?" she asked, her wrinkled face scrunching up.

"Yeah . . . it's unbelievable." Clay then heard himself ask, "Are you okay?"

The woman twitched a smile, which rapidly faded. "Yes, yes. It's just terrible," she said, raising a withered hand to her cheek. "All those *people*."

Clay glanced askance down the hall, toward the girl's apartment, before returning his attention to his neighbor. "Hey." He hated how thin his voice sounded through the thrumming pulse in his ears. "Let me know if you need anything."

The woman said, "What's that?"

Clay spoke up, his voice filling the hall. "Let me know if there's anything you need." He felt the plastic coldness of the baby doll in his hand. "I'll be right here."

A weak smile fluttered on and off her face. "That's kind of you, young man, that's kind," she said, shuffling back into her apartment and closing the door.

Clay shot another anxious look down the hall, toward the apartment from which he'd just fled. He listened to the sound of televisions and radios from other apartments—breaking-news noises. The occasional scream.

Edging the door closed and locking it, Clay looked out the peephole one last time before returning to his living room, to his own television and to the chaos unfolding before him. He inspected the baby, eventually dropping it to the floor as he watched the skyscrapers collapse into the streets.

10

Clay stayed in school, and in Chicago, until Christmas. And in those three months before breaking his lease and moving back home to Sycamore Mill, he never saw the girl again, only hearing what he thought might be an occasional laugh.

He never told the landlord about what happened. Or the police, for that matter. Clay never told anyone the truth. It did occur to him that he had entered the girl's apartment without permission, no matter how frantic, or how sincere, she'd sounded that day. He did see and speak to his neighbors frequently, particularly in the days following the historic cataclysm in New York City. He had arranged for his deposit money to repair the apartment door.

Most times, Clay is just grateful for escaping whatever happened in that girl's apartment.

After moving back and re-acclimating himself with his native town, Clay ended up finding a job and an apartment on the outskirts of Sycamore Mill. Meanwhile, he discovered that working full-time—for menial pay, menial status, and for the camaraderie that came with doing so—was a satisfying detour, however temporary, while he solemnly debated what the hell he was going to do next.

Sometimes the thing that happened in the girl's apartment seems like an elaborate piece of performance art, and Clay hadn't properly played along with some game. But in the moments after jarring himself awake from the dreams—awakening in his new apartment in the darkest and most silent part of the night—Clay's memory strains, and he struggles to maintain crystallized accuracy in his mind's eye. Sometimes he recalls something else.

There, in her apartment—in those moments of hesitation when the girl was on the floor, cackling, clutching the scissors as he readied himself to run—Clay believes he sees something over in the hallway on the far side of her apartment, someone in the darkened corridor further off toward her bedroom: a tall, slim silhouette, as if cleanly cut from black paper, standing within the corridor—a distinctly darker shadow mingled with other shadows. Sometimes his mind accents this voyeuristic entity with eyes, a ribald grin. Most times, he convinces himself that this is just his memory playing tricks on him. Most times.

Clay kept the baby doll in a shoebox and cushioned it with crunched-up newspaper clippings from September 2001. Once in a while he will pull that box from his closet, sit on the edge of his bed, and inspect the toy, turning it in his hands, examining it for any peculiar clues about where it came from. He watches the baby's eyelids wink open and wink shut, and wonders what she is doing now.

Knot the Noose

I'm on the cliff now—the same remote outcrop Josh and I visited our first week in Negril. The climbing rope has been clumsily wound around my neck. The principal tallthing in the ragged robe (I count three, but there are noises in the nearby forest) is limping toward Josh. This gray-blue, pre-storm ceiling accentuates the shadowed vascularity of the tropical vegetation and the tallthings' lineaments: gray, flaking skin inadequately imitating the texture of leprous, reptilian flesh.

What will surely take you a few minutes to hear is simply a synaptic strike: just a mental spasm, really. A last-ditch panic-plea.

Josh can't scream: a strip of black duct tape is over his mouth; but I can hear those panic-smothered bursts. My mouth, for whatever reason, is not covered, and all I can produce is a stammered series of word-chokes.

Despite your suspicion, this is not a hallucination. More likely (it occurs to me from a distant gut-suspicion) this may be a consequence of some supernatural transgression involving our smuggling-collusion to obtain a sacred strain of Jamaican Landraces. I assure you, the rope is very real. Josh's nosebleed is very real. My feelings for Cassy are real. Consciousness is this lightless cave; I hope you can retrieve the echoes from this blackness in which I now exist . . .

*

Earlier, Josh and I had been by the pool outside the resort. For the past year and a half, our impermanent residence (so we'd been told) had been a run-down condo on the north end of the parish; but the walking-distance resort tolerated our presence, mostly to remain equanimous with our vindictive supervisors. Basically, our bosses' attitudes: *Don't fuck with our boys and we won't fuck with you.* All this meant for us, really, was threadbare protection and a few free drinks.

It had been a typical morning. We phoned a rep from Rendon's ring (Josh's turn this time), submitting our coded update. While Josh was occupied, I made a separate call on the laptop (also private). Requisite for the job, Rendon had always been paranoid; but his behavior had grown jittery in the past few months since our involvement with the obscure variety of Landraces.

A few years before that (before *this,* I suppose), a chance meeting on spring break led to another meeting, then a flight, then an indefinite stay in Negril—your classic *felix culpa.*

"Keep hunting," Rendon says. *Making progress,* I regularly report. *No worries,* Josh repeats.

A pair of things continued to surprise me during my time here in Jamaica: the enduring, clandestine correspondences between Cassy and me; and the fact that Josh had apparently suspected nothing about the relationship between his former fiancée and myself.

Josh and I had grown up together, but had not grown close until college, particularly as the things that suture our culture's flimsy social structure began to slough away. I enjoyed thinking that Josh and I were tough like that: we saw the end of high school coming, and we'd already spent years pre-adjusting to transition.

Which is how we wound up here, acting as proxies as we negotiate movement of a rare strain of Landraces.

Kissed by a tepid hangover, the burrowing music and commotion from the nearby pool had me bobbing in and out of a drowse. I felt a chill-sting against my forearm and shuddered, scowled, sat up rigid.

Josh, reclining next to me on a lounge chair, offered a frosted bottle of beer, its exterior weeping with condensation. "Trick or treat, bitch."

I wiped my forearm and returned my friend's grin. "The hell are you talking about?"

"It's October thirty-first, man." Josh handed me one of his two beers from the walk-up bar.

Time had sluiced—days, months included. *Was it really almost November?* I clinked my bottle against Josh's. "Cheers, man."

Off toward the west, a low-creeping cluster of dark clouds were edging the horizon. I said nothing of it. Storms emerged and disappeared in tantrums, temporarily interrupting our ambient paradise.

"Had a dream last night," said Josh.

"Oh, yeah?" I looked over, waiting for a punchline. "Was it entertaining?"

But Josh wasn't smiling, he was inspecting his beer, running a thumb across the exterior's tears. "I was up in Evanston, at night, out by that big cemetery that skirts the lake." He was talking about Calvary Cemetery, but I didn't interrupt. "I was trying to get through the gate, just running up and down the sidewalk trying to get *in* there. I just—I just remember being desperate to get in. Like, once I was safe inside the gate people could find me, you know?" I did not. "And there were these—*things*—coming out of the lake." He looked out across the pool. I watched him idly scanning the reclining banks of bikini-clad sunbathers, ticking his attention to the nearby forest. "These people were walking out of the water, just clawing up over the rocks. And I knew it was too late. I just gave up . . . just sat down on the sidewalk."

Josh laughed then, a sort of clunk-choke sound. "And then only one of the figures came into the light—that sort of sickish-blue light from the streetlamps" (*mercury-vapor lights,* I wanted to assist). "And it was *you,* man—except"—he chuckled—"you were wearing this ridiculous Dracula outfit, like just fucking . . . campy." He shook his head after taking a drink. "You were soaking wet . . . had those plastic teeth in your mouth and like a"—

with his fingers he made a V gesture on his forehead.

"A widow's peak?"

Josh looked at me, smiling, almost—I thought then—verifying I wasn't wearing garish whitewash makeup. "Yeah." We finished our beers; Josh waved at the bartender over by the cabana. "But you know the worst part?"

I considered this for a second, dread-assuming he might say that one of the other lurching figures was Cassy.

She'd been the one who'd pushed (I suppose the "push" was literal when she'd pressed the buzzer in the downstairs lobby, her crackling voice coming over the speaker), and I'd discovered an enticing equilibrium when I complied, both truly and figuratively, with pushing back. Of course I insisted she come up, assuming something (good) had happened between her and Josh, and that he would be in tow. She was alone.

I grew attached to that like-pole repellence the first night in my apartment over two years ago: the push-pull effect of what we were doing. Of what we were not only *still* doing to Josh, but the manner, though inconsistent, in which we'd continued to carry on our depraved liaisons.

"The worst part?" I said, clearing my throat and submitting the obvious: "That you couldn't see the other people?"

Josh was wincing against the sun, quirking his gaze at the forest. "No. It was that we'd worn those goofy-ass costumes as kids. And I had this feeling like . . . I missed that—like we'd never be able to—"

A flicker of saccharine sentimentality, of a sort of loss, tickled my midsection before I swiped it away. I tolerated the silence a few seconds longer. "Never be able to what?"

He shrugged. House music lightly thumped around us. A sheepish laugh. "Nothing."

Josh was struggling to create a thoughtful moment amid our extended parlay as drug-smuggling intermediaries. I was a little embarrassed for him. Still, I tried to keep things casual, jocular. "Sounds like you've been sneaking too many tokes from Rendon's inventory." Josh stared ahead, said nothing. I recalibrated. "Listen, man. You can't live in the past, it'll only make you—"

"The hell is *that?*"

I frowned, first looking at Josh then tracing his eyeline to some vague place in the forest. "The hell is *what?*"

He inched forward, raising a finger. "*That,* man."

Though I saw nothing, my automatic thought was that we'd not seen it coming—"it" being some unknown confluence where a rival ring would move on us. I slipped my hand into my backpack, just to nudge my thumb against my gun.

And then Josh was on his feet, moving faster than both my mouth and my legs, striding toward the far end of the pool where the property bordered the forest. "*Josh,*" I hissed, "wait." It didn't matter that I left my gun in the bag, all that mattered was that I was following him, not wanting to make a scene. A paltry substitute, I still had a hefty gravity knife clipped to the waistband of my shorts.

He didn't hesitate as he hustled down the grassy slope that leveled off at woods; there was another root-covered slope here, more severe. I called for Josh to slow down, but he never turned. I was very close to catching up when he edged through the ropy verdure.

I looked over my shoulder, appraising how we must appear to the other guests. No one seemed to care. Josh was half obscured by some broad-leaf vegetation; I heard him say, "Here, man—help me . . ."

Half turning, half distracted, I reached out for Josh's hand. Instantly: the slick, bone-grip texture of what I'd clutched sober-seized me. Wide-eyed, I saw that, instead of my friend's hand, I was holding some sort of sinewy claw. Quivering out of my paralysis, I was summoning an expletive when another sharp-nailed limb pistoned of out the foliage, snuffing out everything.

*

I come crashing awake, lying on my side, the tallthings surrounding me like repulsive pillars.

One of them is shoving Josh closer to the cliff.

I scream things—incomprehensible cousins of *No*. The one with its reptile talon on Josh's shoulder jerks a look at me, its iguana waddle of loose flesh under its neck wagging as it cants its head. An obscenely slender appendage extends toward the tape on Josh's mouth, peeling it away.

Josh gasps. "What the fuck is happening, Luke?"

The principal tallthing stares at me: febrile human eyes set in sick-iguana sockets. All I can manage is a croak. I have just enough time to assess the set-up: the climbing rope is knotted around Josh's throat, and I follow its length down to an unspooled coil on the rocky ground, notice it running toward me—its opposite end is connected to my neck.

My opportunity—to speak, to act—has passed. The tallthing shoves Josh off the cliff. My friend's face in that last instant: it's something I can't adequately express. All eyes and sorrow and awareness of onrushing nothing.

With Josh's descent, the rope is zipping across the ground. I have no time. I make two moves that temporarily save me: I wind my forearm around the segment before me and scramble to brace my sneaker against a cluster of rocks.

The slack catches with a taut hum and I'm being dragged, Josh's weight hauling me within a few yards of the cliff's lip. Wincing, I swivel. My hip catches on . . .

I gamble a free hand into my waistband and flick open the gravity knife, swiping the blade over the rope, and in a few seconds the tension is released. Josh's anguished echoes Doppler down and fade, replaced by my own panting. I blink at the cobalt-curds of the sky, maybe drift for a few minutes. I'm conscious of the tallthings lingering, observing with sentinel absence of interest; I adjust the grip on my knife. I'll go for their soft spots as fast as—

I hear the ticking, punctured wheezing and realize it's coming from near my feet, near the cliff. I wrench myself up just in time to see the quaking hand rise over the ledge and latch onto my ankle; the force of the pull is insistent, tremendous. My calves are over the verge when Josh's gray face emerges, rills of blood leaking from his nose, ears, eyes. The blunt shards of his shattered teeth twinkle in the cave of his grimace. He uses my legs to *climb* me. Josh brings a broken hand up, its fingers puckering the front of my T-shirt. And then, with its urging, the weight is simply too much to bear.

The Rive

"Many happy and excellent natures would owe their being to me."
—MARY SHELLEY, *Frankenstein*

"I am a triumph of modern medicine."
—Lou Reed

Facility-granted family visitations typically end in one of two ways: survival and attendant conversion (which is, as we've mentioned, rare, because there's only so much room at the "big kids' table"); or outright rejection followed by on-site harvesting. Either way, the most predominant result is that you are severed from the public. More often than not, severed from homeostatic activity altogether.

It's evening, on the verge of what appears to be a charitably star-filled nightfall, as Mick Pew slowly steers his car off the main road. A snaky, tree-lined drive will, in moments, terminate at the main entrance of Autumn Manor. Even in his current state of heart-racing trepidation, Mick smirks and shakes his head—the names they pick for these places! *I mean, come on* . . . Meadow Passing . . . Sunrise Pointe—they reminded him of those inane appellations companies used to choose for subdivisions, which have now become little more than fortified fraternities—pockets of refuge, haphazard hamlets. Everyone now, whether you like it or not, lives in some variety of gated community.

Here's one of the baffling details: the administrators of these senior-living facilities—an all-star comingling of former medical, military, religious, and civic representatives—continue to maintain the appearance of benign nursing homes. Old-folks homes. Extended care centers. Considering the climate elsewhere in the country, there are no hurdle-hedges of barbed wire, no black-clad security guards zipping by on segways.

It would be swell to describe what you've already observed, but here's a reminder: the façades still possess a tone that, like all these bygone establishments, evokes apartmental pretension and funereal refinement. Lots of soft whites and alabasters and ivories juxtaposed with the classy coarseness of exposed stone. A one-story, immaculate mannequin filled with ambulatory corpses that, despite their own quibbles, should have left the corporeal party years ago. Though he's only heard stories, read tales, Mick has grim images of these gaunt and gray people hunched over chess sets, their bony shoulders knobbed up like resting wings, some scowling at elaborately displayed bridge tables, some sitting with their mausoleum faces angled up, their wattles hanging loose, watching archived episodes of *Lawrence Welk* on the wall-mounted television. *"A one and a two . . ."*

The parking lot here at Autumn Manor Assisted Living Community is packed this evening. Mick decides to forgo an attempt at jockeying for a spot and simply pulls into the grass. *Tailgating at your own funeral.* Mick locks the car, not out of fear but out of habit.

If he were truly being philanthropic he'd leave the keys in the ignition—a gift for some passerby. It might give them a chance to split before it's too late. Mick swoons suddenly and has to rest his splayed hand on the hood of the car for a moment. He thinks he might be sick but recalls the warning about exhibiting any unusual signs of frailty.

Mick is also careful to keep his hands out of his pockets as he approaches the one-story facility, the silvery-brilliant accent lighting creating a haphazard halo around the structure.

Now Mick notices the shapes of figures in the other vehicles—just dark outlines of heads and shoulders. Last-minute jitters. As he walks toward the low-lying carport, he can see that some vehicles contain a single occupant. Others are teeming with entire families. He ignores what might be the muffled whimper of a child—the meek protests of those who are wisely suspicious, who know better than to play along. *Big picture, pal. Keep walking.*

They allow this sort of loitering at most of the facilities. They turn a blind eye. Because if these people have made it this far, it's inevitable that their desperation, curiosity, or—perhaps—love will lead them inside.

Mick has nearly emerged from the parking lot's field of shadows when he hears a car door slam nearby. Footfalls coming quick. Mick keeps walking but slows, twists his upper body and narrows his eyes.

A guy, roughly Mick's own age, is approaching, the palm of one hand fanned high, the other hand pinching what appears to be a pamphlet. His expression reads: *Greetings, friend . . . I'm no threat. I just want to chat.* When the dude opens his mouth he says, "Hey . . . hey, my name's Andy." He's still extending the pamphlet. (Andy's probably not his real name.) "Do you have family in there?"

Mick almost mutters, *None of your fucking business,* but rather shuffles to a stop, and in one clumsy but fluid movement arcs a punch into a bony spot between the guy's nose and cheek. "Andy" flails and falls to the pavement, the pamphlet dropping from his hand with a clatter as a slim box-cutter—or some other kind of shitty little razor, Mick doesn't really stop to inspect it— skitters across the blacktop.

Mick had been half expecting something like this. Protestors. Or people trying to "save" family members from voluntary visit- ations.

Mick's chest rises and falls—as much from the current con- frontation as from the potential one ahead—as he begins to edge away. He stops. "Andy" is ass-scooting backward on those palms that only moments ago were demonstrating peace. Mick clench- es his teeth, steps toward the box-cutter, and kicks it away before hovering over the guy and thrusting out a hand.

Andy, breathing through his nose in steady bursts, eventually reaches out and takes Mick's hand. Mick yanks the guy to his feet and leans in toward him; in a low voice: "Do *you* have family out *there?*" Mick juts his chin toward the packed parking lot.

Andy blinks about a dozen times before supplying an almost imperceptible nod.

This is the first time Mick has ever tried telepathy (still a silly, unproven fiction from old books and movies according to doctors working in the now black-market medical fields and who still possess some integrity), but he hopes the guy understands: *Get back to your family, keep them safe. It won't be much longer.*

Mick Pew backs away and begins walking again, and from a sidelong stride turns and says, "Yeah . . . my old man's in there."

∗

Those assisted living facilities (or ALFs, if you wish to sound like an insider)—retirement homes, senior communities. Whatever you want to call them. That's where this all started. Of course, it wasn't the poor folks dwelling within these facilities (although some of the elderly inhabitants, both original initiates and those who were fortunate enough to attach themselves to the practices in the wake of the first stages of panic—a classic case of right place, right time—did unspeakable things in the name of "senior" rehabilitation); it was the wildly wealthy contingent who had the means to pollute the operation of these places. It was the people who had the political "pull" to pervert their possibilities.

You know these places, maybe how they used to be. On the way home from work you'd catch sight of a construction project, the beginning stages of some stable-shaped buildings: wide, one-story complexes of Tyvec-sheeted plywood. The layout was, from your assumptive experience, similar to an assisted-living establishment—hexagonal quarters and wings wreathing a central tower in the center. In time, garish East Coast accents would be grafted onto the exterior with the hope that it reflected some sort of heritage or nostalgia. Monticello architecturally fused with the aesthetics of a dwarfed lighthouse. *An assisted-living panopticon,* thought Mick.

Mick Pew knows very little about history or social science, at least in the academic perspective. He is very good at very little—was groomed to believe in very little, including himself.

Since his teens Mick has been content working as a butcher and meat-counter clerk at a local grocery store—a once-pervasive, commonly recognized chain that provided identity and a living wage. And "living" for Mick meant a huddled apartment on the outskirts of the city that catered to, and capitalized on, human ferity and maintained a potpourried atmosphere of shellfish mildew and dope smoke—no wife, no kids, no five-figure student loans that some people his age were, just before The Rive, finally paying off.

A habit formed in the waning days of his adolescence, Mick educated himself with abused paperbacks on lunch breaks and during solitary cigarette sessions on the loading dock. Mick absorbed all the words he could and found no need to waste those words on anyone else. The other arm of his education was his vocation as a butcher, and he learned a thing or two about organ arrangement, utility, meticulous fabrication.

For a significant segment in his mid-twenties, Mick—having tacitly deemed his life maximized in the role of deli-counter butcher at the neighborhood grocery store—had become enamored with the history of French butchery, particularly the tales and practices of the *charcutier* and *traiteur* guilds. He mentally devoured all the antique cookbooks he could find, savoring the neglected possibilities of the pig; the ones he enjoyed most had some sort of anecdotal notes pertaining to the Revolution, and how the guillotine and its ensuing, redeveloped social order had opened new job opportunities for once-ignoble butchers and cooks. (Mick had, in recent months, heard stories of the re-emergence of the street-erected guillotine over there in France. He hoped the right people were having the baskets placed below their faces.)

The "living" part of his paltry paycheck also meant that he had nearly no direct "bloodline" family members of any real concern. A couple of aunts in another state. His grandparents on both sides were long gone. He hadn't seen his mom in years, knew she was remarried but hadn't corresponded with her since the more advanced stages of The Rive kicked in (the stockpiling, the disappearances, all that). When the social tapestry began to rend itself unidentifiable, all previous divisions among the vox populi—the arguments of race, economic status, educational standing—vanished with the swiftness of jackal-torn flesh.

Some would say that The Rive happened fast. Breathtaking in its speed and bloodlessness. Well, perhaps not bloodless, but you concede our point.

Mick's father, though, well . . . how had we put it earlier: he'd been at the right place at the right time.

*

In the beginning, the problem was that the elderly were the predominant segment buying into the new healthcare system. Not the young. The system, to extrapolate that antiquated data, could not sustain itself. Originally it was asserted that if people liked their policy, they could keep it. And, after all, this was for the greater good. But like all good things, there was something better behind the affluent façade of on-stage policy.

The policy would be, for a brief time, that panic and pandemonium were in no way part of the plan, but they were indeed planned for (if you're one of the people still fortunate enough to have access to the proper electronic resources, you can research the vagaries and devices of something called the "Shock Doctrine" in your own time). And the tacit understanding that there was—on the federal and state levels—a clandestine plan hidden within a syndicated contingency and obscured from even high-ranking civic officials. (Not even the president, apparently, was aware. No one's heard from him in months.)

The intuition that a subversive and unapologetic emergency

plan had been constructed years, maybe even decades, before pronounced problems only exacerbated the widespread divergence.

It was difficult to trace, but someone—some sparrowfart
blogger or mediocre media personality—had referred to the assisted living communities, the activities of which were becoming
more mysterious and more isolated, as "rehabilitation hives,"
which parlance eventually blended to rehab-hives, later conflating
to The Rive—an ideal title for the ongoing social laceration and
the myriad severance taking place within the retirement homes.

Even politicians—those in the sub-human variety of central
casting—were not safe. When The Rive kicked into high gear,
these men and women—who, by and large, had dedicated themselves to the dichotomous dogma of the two major parties—
were somehow more susceptible when it came to the nature of
the new division. There was no side to fall on, only a gray chasm
cushioned by a sort of unintended oblivion.

Where the fringe entities on both sides had failed, now they
infiltrated. No more snakes eating their tails. This was a more
insidious form of the ouroboros—a new, self-devouring creature
altogether, and it gobbled up the mid-level politicos first.

With the help of a collective group of wealthy doctors,
members of The Rive, i.e., those who had aggressively adopted
the practice of selective subsumption—of physically absorbing or
imbibing the crucial nutrients already genetically instilled in each
subject—flirted with techniques that resulted in a sort of ambulatory equilibrium. The somatic requests (or "reqs") were divided
into three categories or dissective departments: 1) kinesthesics
(muscles, tissues, organs, viscera, etc.); 2) fluid (blood, bile, liq-
uids); and 3) mental imbuement. Mick thought he could guess
at the techniques utilized for the first and second procedures—he
recalled the inventive utilizations employed by eighteenth-
century butchers and couldn't fathom the possibilities when
paired with advanced, restorative medical technology—but the
third category still carried an air of holistic mystery. This was the
most meatless, the most abstract.

The very young were only useful in supplying certain organs (which in some cases—say with eyes and ears—resulted in what Mick could imagine was a grisly, asymmetrical patchwork of carnal augmentation).

Charnel house.

Once, many years ago—before life collapsed—after clocking out from work one night in July, he happened to be walking to his car at the same time as one of the female cashiers, a seasonal employee at home from college, he gathered. He'd encountered her before, had had enough casual-passing proximity to acknowledge her small talk. This was back when Mick might have had a chance at forming a bond with another human being, a woman. As they loiter-strolled across the parking lot, the woman (it doesn't and shouldn't matter, but her name was Monica) asked an innocent question that had segued from something about the nighttime: she'd asked which he thought was scarier, the novel or film version of *Frankenstein*. Mick shrugged, recalling many heinous evenings when his old man was passed out on the couch as Mick, lying on his belly, his small fingers clasped under his chin, watched the late-night Nightmare Theater. Occasionally, throughout the duration of the old black-and-whites, Mick's father—unconscious and alcoholically incapacitated— would mumble something incoherent, something vicious in his dreams. Sometimes his dream-wracked murmurs were syncopated with the sneering grunts of Karloff's monster.

For just a few moments there in the parking lot of the grocery store, their shadows were briefly tethered under the orange glow of the tall pole-lamps. Mick (not reading for pleasure at that point) pulled his car keys from his pocket. "The movie, I guess." His tone was the equivalent of shrug.

"Not me," said the girl, barely taking a breath. "I think the book is scary as hell—the part that creeps me out the most is when Victor admits that he's been collecting things—like just different pieces and stuff—from charnel houses." A space of silence. "My instructor said they kept animal parts there too."

Mick—unequipped with any sort of response that might foster further conversation, let alone flirtations—helplessly nodded his head. "Sounds cool."

Charnel house.

Months later, after the woman had dropped her mediocre summer job as a cashier and returned to the university, Mick pulled a beat-up copy of the book from one of his flimsy shelves, its pages tea-tinted and reeking of smoke. Sure enough, there it was: *"Now I was led to examine the cause and progress of this decay, and forced to spend days and nights in vaults and charnel-houses. My attention was fixed upon every object the most insupportable to the delicacy of the human feelings. I saw how the fine form of man was degraded and wasted; I beheld the corruption of death succeed to the blooming cheek of life; I saw how the worm inherited the wonders of the eye and brain."*

He closed the damn book.

"*I am alone and miserable,*" Mick had read. "*My companion must be of the same species, and have the same defects.*"

*

Obviously, the entire process exceeded the simplistic matching of blood types and procuring vital organs that would "take" in a recipient's system; but the most pronounced place to seek suitable biological pairings would be within the branches of one's own family. Remember that game at birthday parties, when all the kids drew a sucker and checked the stem for a red dot to see who would win the prize? Yeah? Well, it was sort of the case here, except those original members of The Rive—the ones fortunate enough to begin the process within the seclusion of these unassuming facilities—when they'd gone through the trial-and-error phases on single mothers, vagrants, the other unsuspecting segments who panicked in those early days, knew exactly where to find the red dots.

*

Mick slows near the front door of the ALF as an elderly woman emerges in the foyer, striding forward to greet him with TSA automation, producing a slim electric wand from her pocket. She's strikingly old for a security guard, sure, but functions with the efficiency of a spry phys-ed instructor.

As he's witnessed on news clips from TV and what little is left of the Internet, Mick sinks to his knees, raises his hand, and laces his fingers behind his head. Another man is coming through the doors now, clearly some sort of enforcer. No smiles with that one. No greeting. The henchman is supposed to get a go-ahead from this lady so that Mick can get to the front desk. As we said, there is still an abhorrently laughable need to maintain the pointless illusion of a well-meaning, pseudo-medical facility. There's a portion of Mick that sort of understands—this need for adorned normality.

After a minute (she smiles the entire time, silent, her tiny teeth glinting like polished pebbles from an infected creek) the old woman's wand-device beeps, a green light on her screen glows under her face. Her skin reminds Mick of a dimestore witch's mask—gourdish, hooked nose and gray-green, wrinkly folds of latex.

*

Masks.

Halloween.

Back then, that one time when he was eleven, maybe twelve—that age-range when trick-or-treating is questionable. Mick ran out into the neighborhood just before dusk, his mother calling out with a shrill litany of requisite caveats—*stay out of the street . . . don't go inside any of the houses. Be home before dark.* Mick's father, Harrison, had not come home from work. Should've been home already, though. No surprise, really.

Mick's costume was a mix-matched ensemble intended to mimic a picture he'd seen on the cover of an old issue of *Famous Monsters,* the one with Lon Chaney, the ghoul from *London After*

Midnight. Of course, there was no way Mick could pull off the eye-pop trick like Chaney, but he'd daubed his sockets with his mom's black eyeliner and had a set of those sharpened cannibal's teeth. Black cape, small top hat, a toy lantern. Not bad for a kid.

Time sailed, light declined. Mick had been out too long. But he was running with a contingent of neighborhood friends, their laughter shooting into the shadows down the lane, leaves crunching with shifty hisses.

A car approached and slowed on the group of kids. Mick's smile faded with recognition. Mom was driving, of course. Mick shuffled forward, noticed a large figure in the passenger seat. The few pieces of candy that Mick had already consumed now began to sour in his stomach.

Without a goodbye to his friends, Mick tossed his bag of candy onto the back seat and slid in, his mother starting: "I told you . . . I told you . . . before dark." Mick slouched. ". . . never listen . . ."

His father, sitting in the passenger seat, teetered from time to time but continued leering straight ahead. If he'd just come from a costume contest that called for intoxicated insurance agent or gloating ad-salesman getting tanked at an airport lounge, he'd have snagged first place.

There was a run of chain-linked silence before his father mumbled, "Getting too old to play baby games." It came out as a single, slow-slurred word.

Mom cut in: "Your father"—she flitted a glance in the rearview mirror—"I needed to help your father and had to leave the house. I couldn't wait for you—"

They rolled over a rough patch of pavement. In the reflection of the rearview mirror, mother and son momentarily met eyes, Mick's narrowed for an explanation. After exhaling, she said, "After work, your father met some associates at a restaurant."

"A tavern," said Harrison, angling his face over toward his wife, briefly twisting his long, pale face toward the back seat. "We went to a tavern."

Mick had no trouble fitting the clumsy pieces together now. The tavern—probably a place in town that hosted his father and his regular band of business-suit drinkers—had called the house because he'd had too much or been cut off or been kicked out. Mom waited as long as she could before leaving to act as a chauffeur.

"I could have left a note," she said, "But I—I didn't want you to worry."

They were almost home, the car jouncing over the last stretch. Of course, there would be no repercussions for his father. There never were. He always had someone eager to bail him out in the name of corrupted reciprocity. Small-time sheriffs. Low-level lawyers. Connections.

The "baby games" comment was still buzzing in Mick's brain, and his mouth was working too fast. "What was your costume for Halloween, Dad?" His mother didn't slow the car, but the look she shot into the rearview mirror was supposed to function as a sort of brake.

His father—a large, gangly grown-up teetering in the front seat—snorted but continued facing forward. "You're . . . a real . . . *pussy* . . . you know that?"

"Harrison!" his mom shouted, almost steering off the road this time.

Mick kept going. "Did the tavern hand out any sort of treats tonight besides gin?"

Harrison Pew spun, the seatbelt restraining him as his arms uncoiled and began swinging into the back seat. Mick's eyes went wide as he dodged the first sloppy punches and slid down away from his father's manic movements.

At one point—between his mother's screams to stop and his father's uncoordinated flailing—Mick got scratched by one of his father's fingernails, and for an isolated instant he was astounded by how feminine his father's hands were—smooth, long appendages. Not the hands of your typical boozy bully. They're politician hands. Priest fingers. Palms polished by crisp currency.

By the end, Mick's hysterical mother had stopped the car and shoved Harrison back into his seat. Mick was a mess, his ghoulish eyeliner running down his cheeks in jagged black rills.

It wasn't the last fight, only the first. But both father and son transformed into different kinds of creatures that night.

*

Mick is made to execute several rapid procedures before being escorted through the main entrance. Again, in the foyer, he is quickly scanned—both verbally and electronically—and chaperoned through a wide pair of French doors.

He's led into a commons area, a vaulted-ceiling space accented by faux-Doric columns where the stark white walls and marble floors make an echo of every footfall and whisper. The acoustics here accommodate the soft drone of some schmaltzy champagne music that Mick can't readily identify. *The real act of sabotage,* he thinks, *would be to replace this geriatric garden party soundtrack with an Immortal album.*

Clusters of spidery, verdantly lurid ferns here and there. The wide swaths of blank space are occasionally interrupted by a bulky-framed piece of lethargic artwork—*God, oh God,* thinks Mick as he glimpses what he believes is a Thomas Kinkade painting. It's warm in here and, with all the hanging flora, Mick can't help thinking about the opening sequence in *The Big Sleep,* about Marlowe's initial meeting with General Sternwood in the greenhouse. Mick will miss reading books; he will miss books. He swallows hard, passes a hand over his lips.

Over on the far side of the room, a small group of visitors—what appears to be a family: middle-aged father, mother, teenage daughter—speaking with an old, old woman. This has to be the grandmother to the younger girl. And as Mick had feared, the girl looks dizzily apprehensive. Almost hostile. *She knows better.* But the parents appear to be attempting some sort of ulterior exchange as opposed to the straightforward examination process. *A side bet,* Mick thinks. But no, it doesn't work that way. Before being repelled by the thought, Mick has a flash of those naturally attractive elements being carved up, divvied, scattered among the recipients—the green eyes going here . . . the follicles of that long brown hair being stitched and imbedded in the liverspot-blotched scalp of some former socialite.

And here's the fucking kicker: none of them over there—the mom, the dad, the daughter—are old enough to join the club. All three will be harvested in one way or another—eyes, skin, toes, nose, tongue, lungs, spinal fluid, cochlea. Anything goes. The trick has been that there exists a possibility that, after the exam, family can stay.

Damn it. The girl—because of course she's sharp and suspicious—makes a break for the door. There's an awkward struggle before she, along with her loony-eyed mom and dad, are swiftly whisked away by some outdated orderlies down a corridor. A door opens; Mick spies a long, anemically lighted hallway. More goddamn Thomas Kinkade paintings hanging on the wall. The champagne music rushes back in with casual constriction, like a palm soothingly closing over a throat.

Standing stoically over on the far side of the room is Mick's father, Harrison. The man is still taller than Mick. Thinner, too. But with all the stories circulating, he thought his old man would look healthier. His father's complexion, though having lost the jaundice tinge from his lifelong abuse of his liver, is not unlike the marble on which they both stand: gray-veined, bruise-swirled. Most of the geriatric creatures here are dressed absurdly "smart"—the fossilized fashion of postwar formals. Harrison Pew is wearing a simple suit, a bowtie.

There's not a lot of time left, so we'll make this quick: a small fraternity of healthcare providers were infusing certain prescriptions with synthetic agents (what non-privy pedestrians might think of as preservatives). The problem emerged in the method for which the incubated—or nurtured, if you like—substances were to be ingested or absorbed. These rapidly erected assisted living facilities were convenient coveys for which these conversions could transpire.

You're about to see an example of how this next routine goes down: Harrison starts forward, his face convulsing for a moment, twitching itself out of a flex of what appears to be pain before drawing up into a grimace-grin. Teeth: beaver-long, yellow-dull. An echo sneaks up on Mick, something he retained from his second pass of the *Scarlet Letter:* "Thou art the man."

For as long as Mick can remember—the ruined birthday parties as a child . . . the physical altercations as a teen . . . the persistent, ammoniacal aroma of whatever the old man had been drinking . . . the decades-long disappearance . . . the eventual, privately funded placement in Autumn Manor—this man, this skin-grafted skeleton stumbling toward him, has existed as a monster.

There is still a fledgling part of Mick that cannot reconcile this. He doesn't have enough time left if he sincerely tried. But he thinks now that monsters—just as the elite members of The Rive distilled themselves and unnaturally prolonged their lives with the help of their loved ones and the community at large—can be transformed.

Harrison is standing at arm's length in front of Mick.

"Hello, son." The sound of his old man's voice, this old thing's elocution, is something like vellum chafing alleyway brick.

According to his father's clandestine correspondence, which began about eleven months ago, Mick, during this segment, would have to make an initial acknowledgment. *They'll expect a sign of good faith on your part first.* Unable to control the impulse, Mick blinks a glance at the old security woman, standing just off to the side, her tiny teeth framed inside a rotten smile, what might be intended to be casual and grandmotherly but affects the wrinkle grin of a swamp hag. She looks as if she might rush forward and hug Mick any second. Or take a bite out of him. Or jam that high-tech Taser into the small of his back.

Mick looks at Harrison. "Hi, Dad."

And now one of the final, silent signals. During initial admissions, a member of The Rive provides one of two signals: extending one hand (either left or right, doesn't matter) indicates that the family member should be escorted elsewhere, their donation being useless for the purposes of subsumption. However, offering both hands simultaneously is a sign that they may proceed. As we said earlier: in both cases, these desperate folks are never seen again.

Mick's father, already an expert in toxifiying his own body, had, for the preceding months—and after a very delicate and tenuous set of letters meant to be, as Mick figured, a trap in the guise of some father-son rapprochement—secreted instructions to his son on how not only to disguise and ingest the home-brewed poison within his corporeal vessel, but also to delay the effects for more pervasive infection. Not a cure, but corrective corruption.

Mick has, in the past months following his father's step-by-step instructions, become an amateur kitchen chemist. Yes, there would be the requisite screenings (what the facilities were still terming "signing in"), but not before his father could assist in exposing the community with the contents of his son's sabotaged circulatory system.

For months since receiving the first of his father's secretly sent messages, Mick had been gambling with acceptance—not acceptance of the proposal, but acceptance that this was something other than a trick. If it was truth, Mick's father had undergone some sort of holistic transmigration to produce a healed man. Reverse conversion. *What had he consumed to change his philosophy?* Again, Mick wondered about that third surgical category—*mental imbuement.*

> *. . . my apologies certainly ring hollow . . .*
> *. . . dependence distorted my sanity . . .*
> *. . . loved you and your mother very much . . .*
> *. . . more than you can imagine . . .*

. . . depraved . . .
. . . unforgivable . . .
. . . alone now . . .

Wipe out this honeycombed covey? Or decimate a whole district? Didn't matter. All that mattered was that: It. Could. Be. Done.

Harrison, with a jittery, unsteady gesture, reaches out with both hands and embraces his son. Mick doesn't know if he forgot that a hug was part of the script. He didn't think so; and now he wonders if it is another silent sign, if he's being led into a digressive trap. In his gut, he doesn't think so. The hug is too awkward to have been planned.

Doctors did things to you—the words came like slender fingers of mauve light breaking through gray-curdled clouds. *Who'd wrote that? Hemingway?* Mick thinks back for a second. Yeah, he thinks it was Papa. *Doctors did things to you and then it was not your body anymore.*

Again, there's that longing for the books. The books he's read, the books he'll never read. The woman in the parking lot who might have changed his life if he'd known how to interact with normal human beings, knew how to carry on a normal human conversation. He doesn't think he's very smart, but this last stunt may prove to have traction. He and his father collaborating on something . . . smart. *Consider this my first statement in the collective conversation.*

Harrison Pew whispers, "You ready?"

They pull apart. Mick can see that his father is leaking some sort of murky fluid from his tear ducts; he takes a hasty swipe at his cheeks. Mick says, "Yeah—are you ready?"

Harrison stiffens his lower lip, a bit of that arrogant politician re-emerging in the way he carries his upper carriage. "You bet, son." They walk toward the adjacent doors. "I've been ready for years."

The Fall of Tomlinson Hall;
or, The Ballad of the Butcher's Cart

Ostensibly, this story—or more accurately, this account—concerns the fate of the erstwhile Tomlinson Hall. I am not, to be clear, a writer by trade, but rather a simple cook. This exercise consists of merely transforming into narrative what my uncle had secretly recorded in ink. Yet I remain conflicted whether this exercise will result in entertainment for you, catharsis for me, or justice for a pair of young cooks.

I admit that—like my uncle, Smitty (whom I intend to visit later today)—I have served as a line cook at the Columbia Club on Monument Circle. I would enjoy sharing with you tales of the unusual things I've glimpsed there—the disturbing things I've witnessed (whether political, paranormal, or—believe it or not—an unsettling commingling of both) within the Scotch-scented, wood-paneled corridors. Perhaps I will impart those tales another time.

Perhaps. Because it wouldn't be a shocker if I disappeared too.

But I'm already digressing as I'd warned myself not to do.

My function here is a mere omniscient emissary, and I can offer the following as the most accurate illustration of what my uncle experienced.

I know my uncle enjoyed reading, and I've learned a lot about writing just from absorbing his journals (most of which were scrawled on the back of sauce-smeared recipes), and he admired a certain writer whose sentiments are an appropriate starting point, as I believe I am a better hand at "worming out," as it were, a story than either my uncle Smitty or his fellow cook and ill-fated friend. "Perhaps there is no other man alive," wrote that author, "who could narrate to you the following foul and unnatural events."

*

It was almost ten o'clock and the tickets were nearly cleared from the pass on a predictably slow Thursday night. Yet perhaps for this night in 1958, it was not all that unusual: it was the end of January, which called for the typical Midwest bouts of frigid air and windblown snow, the weather alone working to keep reservations low in the Harrison Room.

Over on the grill station, Gills had just finished plating one of the last dinner specials: beef tournedoes topped with artichoke bottoms and béarnaise.

Smitty was already wiping down the sauté station, certain this was the end of the night.

"Have you seen the menu proposal for spring?" said Smitty, using his apron to remove the cast iron grates from the gas range.

Gills kept working. "Yeah. Chef had a copy in the dining room last night, showing it to a few of the members, said he wanted to 'brainstorm' some ideas." Moses "Gills" Gilliam had acquired his nickname through the inevitable surname deterioration so prevalent in the boot-camp fraternity of the kitchen, but also through the rumor that he surreptitiously pilfered a quarter-pint of rum—or "gill," in maritime parlance—from the club's bar each night before clocking out. "It's a decent menu."

One of the dishwashers had a radio playing on the far side of the kitchen, one of Jerry Lee Lewis's popular songs.

Smitty transitioned to rolling up his meager collection of knives into a canvas satchel. He said, "Did you notice that sweetbreads are on the spring menu?"

Gills was shutting off the gas to the grill. "Uh-huh."

Smitty nodded. "Aren't sweetbreads—"

"Brains," said Gills, hefting one of the charbroiler panels. "Really just a small piece of the brain."

Smitty had been a cook for years, since his mid-teens, but he'd never encountered a cook—had never encountered *competition*—like Gills, and had grown fond of the ritual of working with the young man from Crispus Attucks High School. "So what's Chef going to use then, beef?"

Gills was clearly intent on getting his station cleaned; but his tone remained composed, tutelary. "Veal."

Smitty smirked. "Brains . . . kidneys . . . livers—I don't know why people eat that trash."

A grin appeared on Gills's face. "Ain't you ever had *foie gras?*"

Smitty had heard of it—something that had to do with force-feeding ducks or geese to fatten or swell their livers. "Nope."

"Man," said Gills, again shaking his head, "you're missing out." A long stretch of clatter from the dish pit. Eventually Gills said, "Besides, that 'trash' you're talking about is a delicacy."

"I know that," said Smitty with a stitch of defensiveness.

"And if you say the word *delicacy* around those bigwigs they'll devour it, no questions asked, just for the sake of saying they did it."

Smitty made a click from the side of his mouth. "What a shame—brains and livers are probably all those poor Republicans can afford."

Gills looked over at his fellow cook, a broad smile stretching across his face. The two young men began laughing, the light-hearted sound mingling with the music coming from the static-lashed radio—a Buddy Holly tune—"*. . . That'll be the day . . .*"

*

The club's policy: cooks and dishwashers were prohibited from using restrooms to avoid commingling with esteemed members. After all, moneyed politicians likely wouldn't want to piss next to a sauce-and-blood-spattered cook. It was just another way to maintain that quiet divide between prosperous and proletarian.

That's why Smitty used a stall. The last one, to be precise—more discreet that way. Smitty finished and was zipping up when he saw it, on the left side of the ceramic tank cover, barely noticeable under the shadow between the lid and the cistern. A small piece of red ribbon.

Smitty had heard stories of toilet tanks—the water within being stale but nevertheless potable—being used as caches for clandestine treasures. It was a game—a sort of private scavenger hunt for drunks. Smitty wondered if that was the case here, and could only guess what these aging playboys would be hiding in here. He reached out and pinched the piece of fabric, experimentally pulling on the ribbon. From inside the tank came a metallic clink. Still holding the ribbon, Smitty cautiously lifted the lid.

From within the cistern Smitty withdrew the ribbon, which was attached to a brass key. He ran his thumb over the base of the key, squinting at a design there: a red circle etched with one horizontal and one vertical line, creating quadrants.

Smitty's first thought was to slip the key back into the tank and get the hell out of here. That would be responsible, mature. That being said, Smitty slipped the key into the pocket of his wool pea coat and quietly exited the bathroom.

On his way to the rear corridor, he spotted Gills gliding out of the darkened Harrison Room bar and caught up with him near the back dock. "Hey, man," said Smitty, "I want to show you something."

With a smirk Gills said, "If it's how to be a pathetic cook, you already showed me that." Smitty produced the brass key. Perhaps waiting for some sort of punch line, Gills said, "So what?"

"Found it in the men's restroom, in the toilet tank in the back stall."

Gills winced, angling his face away. "You say you found that thing in the toilet?"

"Not the bowl, dumbass, in the tank."

Gills said, "Man, you know you're not supposed to be using the members' facilities."

Smitty canted his head. "And you know you're not supposed to be sneaking around the Harrison Room bar after hours."

Gills's expression became momentarily deadly, the aroma of rum evident at this close proximity. Eventually he blinked, slowly lifting his hand to inspect the key.

Smitty eagerly pointed out the design, the crudely scrawled quadrants cutting through the center of the red circle. He said, "You ever seen that design before."

Gills was quiet for several long moments as he examined the key. Finally he said, "Yeah, I have."

"Where?"

"Downstairs."

"Like down in the members-only area?" Again, Smitty had the flash of some seedy fraternal ritual—cloaks, paddles, prostitutes.

"No," said Gills. "Down in the storage cellar."

Smitty squinted, trying to conceive where this symbol was located. "Where?"

Initially, Gills appeared to ignore the question as he continued examining the key. He offered it back to Smitty, warily eyeing the small device. "On a doorknob." Smitty had never noticed another door. "It's at the back along the brick wall, behind one of the racks where they keep the old Champagne." Gills began slipping on his knit cap ahead of the cold walk to the bus stop. "You probably wouldn't notice it anyway. It's been painted over to match the bricks."

Smitty twisted the key between his fingers. "Show me."

Gills chuckled. "No way, man. I'm clocked out and I've got tomorrow off. I'm going home. If you're so interested, go find it yourself."

Smitty stepped in front of his friend. "Come on. Go down there with me." He brought the key up between them. "I just want to see if it works."

Gills was still shaking his head and made an attempt to side-step the other cook. "I told you, I'm not trying to get in trouble tonight."

"Yeah, but after all the trouble you and me have been in around here," said Smitty, "wouldn't it be nice to have some dirt on this place for leverage?"

Gills had nearly made it to the back dock but paused. He turned slowly, stared at Smitty, and exhaled. "Leverage," Gills said flatly.

Smitty smirked. "Leverage."

*

In the end, it was Smitty who inserted the key.

As both of the seasoned cooks had been groomed by the pi-rate-ship resourcefulness of the kitchen industry, the pair man-aged to enter the storage cellar with inconspicuous ease.

A bare, pull-chain bulb hung from the ceiling. Gills had been correct: there was a door down here painted to match the brick, partially concealed by a wooden rack. And sure enough the sym-bol on the key, that dark red circle sectioned into four portions by a vertical and horizontal slash, matched the worn design on the doorknob.

Smitty looked at Gills. "Well," he whispered, "do you want to do the honors or shall I?"

Gills cocked his head. "Your idea, your show. I'm just look-ing inside, that's it, then I'm gone."

Unaware that he was holding his breath, Smitty lifted the brass key and placed it in the lock, the teeth coarsely chattering as it tumbled into place.

As the door yawned open, a curtain of cave-cool air billowed through the threshold, the cellar light falling on a set of narrow, stone-and-mortar stairs that descended into darkness.

Gills had already shuffled backward. Smitty slowed his friend's retreat by producing a lighter. "Man, don't tell me you're going to turn back now."

Gills responded by petulantly producing his own lighter. With the blade of one hand, he made a wide sweep toward the opening—the mock-gesture of a subservient doorman. "After you, sir."

Smitty bowed his head with equal vaudevillian exaggeration. "Much obliged."

Both cooks were quiet for a moment before Smitty entered the corridor, the glow from their lighters dancing on the stone walls. After about thirty feet the stairs leveled off into a passageway.

"Can't believe I'm following your dumb ass," said Gills.

"You can turn around anytime you want."

Gills hissed a laugh. "Man, both of us are risking our jobs. Plus now, this might be trespassing."

Smitty said, "Actually, you've got more to lose than I do."

Gills actually chuckled. "What do you mean?"

"Drop the act," Smitty said without heat. "You know Chef is considering promoting you to chef de cuisine."

Gills was quiet for a few seconds. "Man, there's no way I'd get promoted before you."

Smitty frowned, still shuffling forward with the bouquet of flickering light. "Please. You know more about food than I'll ever learn. Chef knows that." Smitty's lighter was getting too hot, and he let his thumb off the lever.

Gills gave Smitty a hard look. "It ain't got nothing to do with skills, man." Silence for several moments. "Even in the kitchen."

Smitty opened his mouth to protest but thought better of it. He now realized what Gills was talking about and clenched his teeth. Now Gills took his thumb of the lever. Darkness. Smitty said, "You know I think that's the most crooked racket there is."

Gills exhaled. "Don't matter what you think. What are you— what am *I*—going to do about it?"

"I'll tell you what I'd do first," said Smitty, who was preparing to spark his lighter. "I'd march up to those bigots and—"

Gills cut him off. "Shut up, man—check it out."

In the dark, Smitty's vision had adjusted. A faint, amber-orange light flickered in the distance.

The young men made their way to the mouth of the passage. It perpendicularly terminated at a T, and a wider tunnel with an arched ceiling stretched in two directions, to the left and the right. The light here, though dim, was produced by a guttering glow within wall-mounted sconces, a seething sound making it apparent that natural gas was fueling the shadow-shifting illumination.

Despite himself, Smitty gave an astonished laugh. "What the hell?" Both took several steps into this wider tunnel. The masonry down here was impressive—stone blocks and limestone columns—and every ten feet or so the walls gave into unlit, barrel-shaped recesses. Smitty noticed something else: on the wall next to the cellar tunnel were a set of chalk marks—a crude pair of double zeroes.

Smitty glanced at Gills. "What do you think this is?"

Gills was quiet as he looked toward the ceiling, scrutinizing the tunnel, casting his gaze to the left and to the right. "I have no idea," he said, turning to inspect the direction from which they'd entered. "But if we just came north from the cellar, up above us is Monument Circle, or at least really close."

Both cooks were silent as they continued studying the poorly lit space. Gills pointed left. "So that tunnel would run under Market Street east, and the other one west."

Smitty stepped a few more paces into the tunnel and stopped, training his attention to the concrete floor. "I'll be damned."

Stretching out in opposite directions were a pair of slim rails, the type used for a light train car or trolley.

To confirm this, Gills said, "I know, look up." Above them were a corresponding collection of wires and cables. "Just like on an interurban."

Smitty shook his head. "It doesn't make any sense."

"Well," said Gills, scratching his chin, "this all might have been a stock vault."

"For what?"

"I don't know. Sometimes I see farmers coming into the city market. Maybe they use it to store food."

"Food?" Frowning, Smitty said, "Storing food a quarter of a mile away?"

Gills cocked his head. "Man, I'm just guessing."

And with that, both young men angled their attention in the opposite direction, toward the west. Smitty: "So what's your guess about where that track goes?"

From behind them, a ragged cough echo-swirled through the tunnel. Both young men spun around, wide-eyed.

Smitty looked at the arch-shaped recess he'd noticed earlier and jogged toward it to seek cover.

"Man," said Gills, "what are you doing?"

Smitty waved for Gills to join him in the shadowed space. Gills hustled over to join his friend. Inside the small alcove, Smitty saw that there was a hallway running parallel to the main tunnel, connecting each stone cubbyhole. The metallic whine of wheels sounded on the railway.

Both young men pressed their backs against the wall as the front end of a small-scale trolley appeared on the tracks outside the alcove. The tram—painted black, the gas lights playing over its glistening exterior—was moving slowly but smoothly over the tracks; the vehicle came to a stop near the corridor that led to the Columbia Club's cellar. A figure shifted up in the front car, as if inspecting something. Smitty thought of the weird chalk marks scrawled on the side of the wall.

Smitty's heart was thrumming at what he thought was full capacity until he noticed the cart hitched to the rear of the trolley—a flatbed of wooden slats. A thick blanket covered a mound of oddly angled shapes there. Smitty counted six pairs of feet—some with worn shoes or boots, some without—poking out from under the fabric.

The black trolley began moving again, and the protruding feet, jostling slightly, gave the impression of waving goodbye on behalf of their supine owners as the black tram disappeared over the low slope on the west end of the tunnel.

Many silent minutes passed before Smitty and Gills budged or spoke. "Like I said," whispered Smitty, licking his lips, trying to get his pulse under control. "What's your guess about where *that* track goes?"

After a while Smitty shifted his attention in the opposite direction—to the east, where the small black tram had come from. Gills said, "You're going to ask me to follow you that way, aren't you?"

*

They headed east, staying out of the main tunnel and out of sight, remaining in the narrow aisle that connected the barrel-shaped alcoves. Eventually their momentum slowed when they came upon brighter light and coarse voices.

Crouched down behind a stack of wine crates, they could see movement in some of the spaces up ahead, but the commotion was difficult to define because of the corner of a stone wall. Finally the commotion ceased and Gills began to move forward. Smitty grabbed his friend's coat. "Wait, man," he whispered, "they got to be coming back."

"I know," said Gills. "That's why I want to see now."

Smitty clenched his teeth, let go of Gills's coat, and followed him out of the alcove.

They shuffled along the wall, nearing the corner. Just then an arm sprang out near the floor, filthy fingers weakly scrabbling at the concrete and dirt.

The young men recoiled; but Gills said, "Wait." Now Smitty saw that the hand was moving with such frailty that it was an unmistakable signal for help. They ambled forward and turned the corner.

A man, dressed in tattered, grim-smeared clothes, was lying

on the floor just outside a large stone stall. Smitty was about to kneel when he noticed the other men, none of whom were moving: several figures stretched out on benches, a few slumped in the corner, all wearing the threadbare clothing of vagrants. The smell was very strong here, a mix of alcohol, sweat, and the pungent aroma of rotting produce.

Both young men knelt beside him, his eyes bobbing open and shut; his chapped lips feebly worked to form words. "Gave—us—a drink . . ."

"Who did?" said Gills.

"Same—guy—who told us . . . it was warm down here." Smitty thought about the frigid January night, and how easy it would be to lure a desperate person indoors.

The man's eyes closed, but Gills gently clutched the guy's shoulders. "Where did they bring you?" Gills had to shake him again to open his eyes.

The homeless man seized a final moment of consciousness and looked directly at Gills. "Tomlinson Hall . . . said they'd give us a warm place to sleep, something to eat. But . . . that ain't where . . . they taking us."

Smitty said, "Where?"

The man mumbled, "Square . . . 22." His head lolled and his upper body sagged in Gills's arms. Both young men checked for a pulse. Nothing. Smitty was certain no pulse would be found on the other motionless forms either. Smitty looked at Gills, whose expression held a mixture of hopelessness and fury.

Smitty and Gills were distracted and did not notice the tall, lantern-jawed man standing on the far side of the room. Smitty was the first to register movement as the big man, holding some type of long baton, rushed forward.

"Gills!" was all Smitty could manage as the cop-shaped man, clad in an all-black jumpsuit, brought the baton down across Gills's back, who cried out and toppled over the dead vagrant.

Smitty staggered backward and fell against the wall, the collision rattling his satchel of rolled-up kitchen knives. He unfastened the clasp and dumped the knives, grabbing one and running forward.

The tall man was yanking at Gills's collar when Smitty swung his arm in a haymaker slash at the man; but the man's baton came around quicker and it connected with Smitty's temple. He reeled, colliding with one of the flickering sconces and sending it into a stack of wine crates, which toppled over as he crumpled to the floor.

The tall man was shouting something now, hovering over Smitty. But just as the man raised the baton Smitty saw the flash of silver and watched Gills plunge one of the other spilled knives into the guy's upper arm.

Howling, the man whirled on Gills, who instantly threw his fist into the guy's face. The two then tangled in a vicious struggle.

Smitty was struggling to his feet, now noticing the flames licking up within the stone stall.

Gills, who had his fists raised as he hitched in breaths, had landed enough punches that the tall man was down on one knee. Smitty ambled forward and clutched Gills's coat. "Come on, man—"

The tall man, lit from behind by the glow of the growing fire, lurched to his feet. In his hand was a revolver, which he unsteadily attempted to train on the pair of trespassers.

Gills looked over at Smitty, giving his friend a terrible message in that glance a split-instant pulling his arm free from the cook's grip and sprinting forward.

"Don't!" Smitty cried out, watching Gills barrel into the tall man and hearing the peal of a gunshot. Still, Gills had rushed into the man with enough momentum that it sent both of them crashing into the fire-consumed stall. Smitty scrambled forward, seeing that his friend continued fighting with furious, churning movements. He heard another gunshot; then everything—save for the spreading flames, which were now creeping into the crate-lined corridor near the stairwell—became still.

The snaky shadow-light of spreading flames danced on Smitty's face as he clasped a palm over his mouth, turned, and ran.

*

Tomlinson Hall burned beyond repair on a Thursday night in January 1958. People who witnessed the event said that, due to the frigid night, the overrun from the fire hoses transformed Market Street into a lake of ice. They demolished what was left of the scorched structure the following summer.

The last things you need to know from uncle Smitty's notes: Square 22 was a small parcel of land on the westside of Indy, originally used as a "lunatic" asylum back in the nineteenth century. Later, the state purchased 160 acres three miles from the city, constructing numerous facilities that would later be called Central State Hospital, or as former patient Albert Thayer termed it, the "Indiana Crazy House." And beneath the grounds of the bygone asylum lies a dark warren of service tunnels that spans five miles.

Though my uncle Smitty survived the night, he never returned to work and disappeared a few weeks later. According to my father, my uncle was last seen boarding a bus bound for the west side of the city. I like to believe he confronted those involved—on the medical side, at least—in that perverse practice of body snatching.

I'm going out there later today, to the west side, to the Medical History Museum. I don't ask questions on the tours; I just examine the specimens and wonder if one of them is my uncle. Sure, they say the brains in those whiskey-tinted jars are corporeal gifts—contributions to science; but I think about the things my uncle recorded and remain skeptical.

And I'll let you speculate about the cellar in the Columbia Club, and of any culinary *quid pro quo* that may have occurred in those sordid spaces beneath Tomlinson Hall. As Gills said, people will eat anything if you tell them it's a delicacy.

Fiending Apophenia

"Everything is a cipher and of everything he is the theme."
—VLADIMIR NABOKOV, "Signs and Symbols"

A fisherman and his friend found a torso floating in the White River over the weekend. There was more—to the story, that is.

With the television murmuring on one end of the bedroom and my wife's blow dryer droning in the bathroom, I only caught snatches of the report before gathering my things and leaving for work this morning. My daughter was still asleep, snoozing in almost imperceptible waves.

The fisherman, who didn't want to be identified, said the head and arms appeared to have been "hacked" away, while the legs below the knees appeared to be cleanly "severed." Detectives will certainly identify the remains, perhaps match them to a missing person. There will be some assumptive association with gang activity, drugs.

I leaned in the bathroom and told my wife goodbye, *I love you.* She mouthed it back in the mirror.

Before heading out, I peeked in on my daughter one last time. Three years old, she's a small shape among stuffed animals roughly the same size as her. I draw the door closed on my child's chamber, as though this insufficient gesture may prove a means of protection.

So. The torso. It occupies my mind on the drive to work. And while I continue to consider ways to frame my eventual resignation—how I need to convince my wife not of the need but of the necessity to abandon my current career—I am also thinking about the inferences of that grisly little starter courtesy of the anonymous fisherman. *The head and arms appeared to have been hacked away.* Then a number, like a whisper—like the rasp of rough hands shuffling playing cards—emerges: 283.

I roll down the window a bit. Fresh air though it is, for April it's almost frigid. I think about this torso's family hearing about the news on television—a male, it will be. A son. A dad—that a child might hear about her father's pieces found floating in a polluted river on the west side of the city.

It's often easy, suppression; but conscious disconnection is feeble and finite. Whatever we attempt to bury eventually bobs to the surface.

283.

Though there are times when dissociation is so severe that now becomes then—so severe that I flinch. *We* flinch. And fade.

My bearing braids with another as *me* shifts to *he*. And then the other turned as the figure rapped on the passenger-side window just a few inches away from his face.

Sitting here on the far side of the gas station parking lot, Wes, a bit dizzy, had not noticed the girl approach and could not account for the details of his daydream. The Kyuss cassette, *Blues for the Red Sun,* was still playing on the stereo. Must have been about three-quarters of the way through. Wes had to squint and shift a bit to see the figure standing outside the car. The morning sun glowed behind her, casting her features into silhouetted obscurity. Her corona of hair looked like a tangled halo—auburn threads on the bulb of some wildflower. Wes thought he discerned a smile. He turned down the stereo's volume a touch and began cranking at the window. A tide of cool, autumn air spilled in.

"You don't have to turn that down," said the girl, flipping a hand at the stereo. "I dig that shit."

Wes smirked, still wincing against the sun. He kept the volume where it was. "Everything all right?"

The girl leaned in a little, resting her knobby elbows on the door's window frame. She was wearing an airbrushed T-shirt—*I Rocked Panama City, '94*—that looked as though it had been grazed by buckshot. "Oh, yeah—everything's fine." She slid a thin-wristed hand in front of him. "I'm Valerie." Wes noted the tiny tattoo on the webbing of her hand, three tiny dots in the shape of a triangle. Wes clasped the pale thing in front of him and gave his name. In a low voice, the girl said, "I'm just wondering who's got the dank."

Startled, Wes glanced around. Despite the gas station's anonymous squalidness, and despite being parked out of view, he marveled at his lazy stupidity. Valerie giggled. Her lip bore a dainty split. "No, silly. I can just smell it, is all." She lowered her voice further—*just between you and me:* "I can smell decent Jane a mile away."

Wes adjusted his posture and ran a few fingers through his bangs. "Oh." This stuff was . . . unusual that way. He and Todd hadn't even smoked the whole jay. The batch, wherever it had come from, had—the word thudded clumsily into Wes's mind—*personality*. He assessed the gas station's lot. Todd had parked them on the far side, near the back of the building, while he went up front to use the payphone. He'd been gone what seemed like too long. Wes turned the radio off now, a fork of spine-stinging paranoia coursing through him.

He opened his mouth to submit a lie when she cut him off. Rolling her eyes, she said, "I ain't a narc or nothin'."

Wes distractedly appraised the girl. She was still grinning; and now he noticed that her smile was not as inviting as he'd initially thought. Rather, her irregular teeth were quite small, like pieces of broken shell washed ashore; on the molared fringes they held notes of either overwhelming neglect or outright rot. Still, something about the lineaments of her face were disturbingly attractive, a sort of primal, serviceable beauty.

He swiveled in his seat. "Where'd you come from?"

Without hesitation, Valerie flitted fingers toward the two-story motel adjacent to the gas station. "Staying there for a few days with a couple of friends," she said. A giggle: "Road trip . . . just us girls."

Wes peered over at the low-lying building before returning to Valerie and giving her his full consideration. The skin on her arms was so pale that he could see a fine network of veins. Her cut-off jeans did little to hide the spotty cloudcover of bruises visible on her thighs. Wes exhaled, pawing at a pocket for his pack of smokes.

"You going on a trip too?" said Valerie.

Having forgotten what Todd had stowed in the back, he followed her eyeline and little head-nod, craning his neck behind him.

A bundle of fishing poles was angled across the back seat of the Cutlass, sunlight shining on the lines as though threads of delicate silk. "Oh. No. My buddy just picked me up—wants me to go fishing with him when we get back home."

"Somewhere nearby?"

He lighted his cigarette and shook his head. "No. Out east. Back toward Indy."

"That where you're from?"

In his current state, Wes thought he could stand one or two more questions. "Not really. Just outside the city, though." He gambled a final detail may help stifle the junkie's interrogation. "I go to school over in Terre Haute. My friend's just giving me a ride home for the weekend."

"You both go to college there?"

Wes shook his head, almost ashamed to answer. "No. Just me."

"So," she rested her forehead on the door frame, "if you're a college guy you must be pretty smart" (Wes barked a genuine laugh at the absurdity of the statement), "so you'll understand what I mean when I say I need to score some dope but don't have any cash to pay for it. Just looking to barter."

Wes's grin wore off—sobered by the notion of a local sheriff rolling in. He said, "I don't know what you're talking about."

She made a noise with her tongue and snorted. *Bullshit.* She pulled a matted length of hair back over her ear, her loose-hanging shirt pouting open to expose the pale upper portion of clavicle, the sweat-stained strap of her bra. "You look like a bright guy," she smirked. "And you ain't in a hurry?"

Wes shrugged. "Sort of."

"Bet we could work out some sort of trade."

Wes thought about the hive of that hotel in the distance. What sort of trades—what sort of seedy exchanges—were taking place this instant? He snickered, stretched. "Even if I was interested," he'd almost said, *I'm not even sure you'd like it,* which was the truth, as the effects of what Todd had shared were not particularly pleasant. "And besides," he looked out over the lot, "it's not my shit."

Only just then did he notice her thin wrists dangling casually into the car, hovering directly over his jeans. Wes gave a second's thought to where such a transaction might take place. He shifted and coughed. "Look, it's not my dope." Valerie's expression did not change—a schoolgirl being told a parable. "I'm just along for the ride."

She withdrew her arms a bit, resting her forehead against the upper portion of the door frame. "Oh." Though deflated, she still appeared ready to haggle. "Me too." She took in a breath to say something else, perhaps to update her proposal, when Todd rounded the front corner of the gas station.

Not slowing his sloppy stride, Todd said, "Hey, Wes. Did you make a buddy?"

Before Wes could answer, Valerie stood erect. Perky. Her voice a spoke of sunlight. "Hi."

Clutching a soda, Todd's lopsided grin widened as he shuffled toward his car. And just like that, Wes Bridges no longer existed. Valerie slid away from the window.

*

Wes's mind slid away as well.

After it appeared that Todd and Valerie had worked out some sort of arrangement—with Todd rifling around the trunk for a minute before the pair disappeared around the back side of the gas station—Wes settled in, savoring the last few tracks of the Kyuss album as he descended from Todd's dope, or whoever's dope he'd bought it from. *A bizarre high, this thing,* thought Wes.

Wes wondered too about the phone call Todd had placed to Bernie: a response to the pager's message of 283—the only real reason they'd stopped here in this dump in the first place.

He'd met Todd Carson a few years before when they were still in high school, before Wes moved from Indianapolis to Terre Haute to attend college—a flimsy venture in which his skepticism and lack of commitment were metastasizing. An hour or so earlier, Todd had parked out in front of the dorm, and once Wes was in the passenger seat of his friend's nearly two-decades-old beast of a vehicle—a 1977 black Olds Cutlass, released the same year Wes was born and looking in similar condition to when it rolled off the line—the pair took off, the car's tires barking over the parking lot's blacktop.

It had been Todd who'd introduced Wes to Bernie at a party two summers before. Bernie Pryor was, in the grand scheme of things, not a notable drug dealer. Not like his (oft-discussed but rarely seen) supplier, Zoot, whose apt moniker was a nod to his resemblance to the saxophone-playing Muppet: shaggy hair, shades, low-hanging bucket hat (though Wes had never seen the dealer with any sort of instrument aside from weighing scales). But Bernie was indeed an alpha dealer on the south side, supplying low-level folks with plenty of product.

Wes couldn't help but think about that hotel, and kept craning his neck to examine it. Earlier, he'd been so distracted by Valerie that he hadn't noticed the actual state of the place. He now fully took in the state of that broken motel.

It was abandoned. Most of the windows, he saw now, had been crashed out, giving the effect of dark recesses in some sort of depraved concrete hive. Gray-green shrubs lining the front looked like lacy mold crawling up around the hem of the paint-flecked edifice.

Eventually, Wes stepped out of the vehicle and stretched. He thought about another cigarette, but his lungs weren't up to it. Amazing, that junkie's recklessness, attracted to the aroma of pot smoke. *Like a yellow jacket.* He now wondered if the weed was indeed laced. Once again Wes stared at the hotel. He shivered, strolled around to the rear of the gas station, and cautiously scanned the back lot.

The sky had gone from flawless to flirting with overcast at some point, gray overhead punctuating the gray on the ground. Not much back here: a rust-sloughed dumpster. The lid was closed, but spills of various substances had dried, or were drying, on the concrete surrounding it. Here, the lot sloped down a small hill toward an overgrown, brindle-pricked preamble to woods. Debris decorated the weed-quilled ground.

Wes was about to call out when he caught a noise. He turned and squinted down the hill. There was a thousand-gallon propane tank down there, and he could now see Todd, eyes closed, mouth ajar in a sort of dumb delight. Valerie was down lower, slightly obscured by the propane tank, working on him with rocking, rhythmic motions. But Wes winced now with new curiosity, as Valerie, oddly, had donned what looked like a soot-smeared cloak. A *vesture*—the term came unbidden, the retained remnant from some droning, has-been World History lecturer. Wes gave Todd's euphoric expression one last glance before turning and walking away.

But he didn't make it far. Not past the dumpster. A determined, almost gulpy sound came from within. Wes's heart was already tacking rapidly as he slowed, paused, stared—something moving inside there. After nearly a full minute of listening, breathing with feeble hesitation, Wes pinched the filthy lid and raised it up a bit, allowing a plank of light to infiltrate the interior.

The spider was roughly the diameter of a semi-truck tire. With the introduction of light, the animal recoiled slightly. Wes had certainly damaged his brain a bit since falling in with his small band of hoods, but not enough to wholly deplete description. It very much resembled what his grandfather had called a jumping spider, its legs and torso covered with fine needles of hair, its obsidian, doorknob-sized eyes glistening. Not once did it occur to Wes that he was hallucinating. This strange strain of dope had done something to him—girded him, scraped away flecks of perception. He took in the large spider with instinctive acceptance: a reptilian intuition piercing the membrane of conventional sensibility. It was as though a creature like this, outrageous as it was, had been waiting here, in a place like this. The dregs of the morning's drug-infused sensation dovetailed with a sobering realization: it was Wes who had never compelled himself to look under the cover of this filthy dumpster, of *any* dumpster, and he accepted the impossibility of what he was seeing with an adrenaline-sustaining fidelity.

Just as he was about to lower the lid, Wes's eyes adjusted. He'd been so empirically seized by this revelation that he'd ignored the thing on which the spider crouched. Its furry legs were draped over the body of man. His dark clothes, making him difficult to see at first, accentuated the paleness of his translucent flesh. The spider wriggled its black legs, clutching the corpse tighter, the movement reminding Wes of the fingers of a poker player, covetously clutching chips.

Just then the corpse's opaque eyes rolled over in their sunken sockets, locking on Wes. They stared at each other for a long moment before the figure serenely raised a hand, gesturing for Wes to lower the lid. The movement was completely calm, coldly composed, his expression going from vacant to weakly imploring. *Please, friend . . . close the lid . . . turn off the daylight . . . leave me be.* Wes, his thumb quaking on the rim of the lid, slowly settled the top back down, returning the interior to its quilted darkness.

*

Todd wasn't much longer before returning to the car. No sign of Valerie.

"Damn, brother," said Todd, adjusting his belt as he passed

the front of the car and falling in behind the wheel. "You missed out. Said she's got a friend if you change your mind."

Wes's skull was set against the headrest, his elbow against the passenger door as he appraised the dumpster.

Todd switched cassette tapes, popping in Sepultura's *Chaos A.D.* They were well into the first track when he said, "Hey, man—did you hear what I said?"

Wes ignored that and said, "What did Bernie say?"

Todd's face pinched with incomprehension. "Huh?"

"The pages, man," Wes pointed down at Todd's hip where he carried his beeper. "The whole reason for us stopping here was to use the phone. What the hell did he want?"

Todd ran a palm from back to front of his crewcut hair, as if to make himself presentable. He put the car in gear and steered out of the lot, the route back out to the main road giving Wes one last glance at the hotel. Up on the second floor was a figure. Nude. Gray flesh in a column of light. She stood there between the two drapes, shoulders hunched slightly. He turned away, regarding the side of Todd's face.

Earlier that morning, not long after they'd fled the campus perimeter and headed east on I-70, Todd had begun receiving a familiar, three-digit code in his pager: 283—Bernie's convenient, alphanumeric stand-in for "BUD": the dealer's simplistic and private invitation to partake in new product. It was usually just the five of them: Wes, Todd, Bernie, Dusty, and Scoli. Usually it was just a one-time communiqué; but not long after the initial pager message, Bernie had repeated the code. *283 . . . 283 . . . 283 . . .*

There was something unsettling about the insistent repetition; so much so that Wes had urged Todd to pull over and use a pay phone.

"What did Bernie want?" Wes repeated.

Todd adjusted his seatbelt. "He just wants to hang out. I told him I'd driven out to rescue you from college. He just wants to burn a few jays with us. Maybe have a party tonight. But I told him that you and me were going fishing."

It took half a minute for Wes to respond. "Maybe later on that. Let's check in with Bernie first."

Once on the Interstate, picking up where they'd left off, heading east back toward Indy, Todd, sulking about the delay in his plans to go fishing, lit up a puny joint. Wes declined and for the most part remained silent, watching unappealing picture pages slide by under a gray sky resembling an inverted undercurrent. *Overcurrent,* his mind mumbled dumbly. *Overcurrent . . . undercurrent.* He tried easing into the heavy-metal static, grasping the rigid reality of the music as it stitched itself into the hiss of his mind.

What he'd seen back there was real. The searing intuition that these things were always there—*here*—and that no one was looking properly lay over him like a lead vest. The dope was working on him again. No. Not quite right: They were working on each other.

Todd was drumming his nicotine-stained fingers on the steering wheel. For the remainder of the drive Wes interacted at a minimum, and as much as possible averted his eyes from his friend—and he reminded himself of just that: that Todd, of all the members of their gray-matter-abused crew, was what he would consider a true ally, right down to playing getaway driver from a college town where he was certain he'd irresponsibly burned his latest bridge.

His reluctance to interact with Todd during the drive home had nothing to do with loyalty or affection; it was just that Wes had trouble looking at the face shared by the rotting body back in the gas station's dumpster.

*

Bernie Pryor's house was situated on the outskirts of a suburban fringe of the city, where the seams of factory pockets faded into vacant, flea-marketed strip malls and shit-beaten bars. It was an old house, doubtless a farmhouse when this area was still undeveloped, quite a number of overgrown acres set up away from the road, a maud of mature trees obscuring clear view.

Todd's Cutlass rolled up the gravel drive slowly, thick chips of stones pinging and popping. Bernie often commented that he enjoyed the noise. "Cheap security system," was his repeated remark. While Bernie was no kingpin, he was indeed a notable dealer on the south side. He didn't work anymore, and the house was really owned by his older brother (mortgage paid by his older brother too), but after their folks had died (a custody-related murder-suicide following an argument at a pay lake), his brother had taken off. He existed, according to Bernie, solely through the infrequent letter and even more infrequent phone call. Through pinched snorts and coughs following an incredible toke, Bernie had once said, "He's my mortgage ghost." Wes had thought the concept genuinely funny.

Closing in, Wes noted Dusty's car. And if Dusty was here, Scoli was too. Being Bernie's subordinates, Dusty and Scoli still had to work most days. Transient day labor. Various construction jobs. Always construction. Tax free, Wes assumed. Dusty and Scoli were Bernie's two-legged attack dogs. Dusty was the hammer, Scoli the nail. Scoli's real name was Corey, but had acquired the moniker early on as his severe, and worsening, scoliosis manifested, acutely affecting his lumbar. He still wore a brace (what Wes knew to be something called a Charleston brace, though Scoli had never referred to it so clinically) and walked with a lurching limp.

Wes said, "Bernie say anything about the other guys being here?"

Todd bowed his lower lip, his lids stoner slits. "Nah, man. Just said for us to come hang out."

Todd hooked the Cutlass on around the back by the garage, which served as more of a body shop for Bernie. One of the wide doors was up, showcasing the front end of Bernie's 1970 Plymouth Roadrunner, gray light glinting off the purple air-grabber hood. The machine hadn't run in a long time, and Wes had only heard it growl to life once, but the hotrod was a sort of trophy for the local drug dealer and a talking point for his clientele.

As Todd twisted off the engine, Wes again thought about the repeated code on Todd's pager. *283 . . . 283.* "Well," Todd said with a weary, workman's intonation, "let's go burn some rope."

It felt like a long time before Wes's hand clutched the door handle, though he was ambulant in due time. He had pulled up alongside Todd, who was hitching up his baggy jeans, when a scuttling sound came from the garage; and from the stacks and folds of shadows emerged Scoli, limping his way out of the cluttered gloom. His crooked teeth were ringed within a crooked smile. *Everything about Scoli,* thought Wes, *is crooked.*

"Well, well," said Scoli. A cigarette was clamped between skinny fingers at the end of a hooked wrist. "Look who it is. Been missing you fellas." He shuffled closer. "What took you so long?"

"Nothing, man," said Todd, "just a mellow drive."

Scoli gave Todd a half-hug and Wes a low slap on the palm. "Been a while," said Scoli, eyeing Wes from brow to britches.

"Yeah," Wes said. "Has been."

Scoli nodded, his inane grin unwavering. "Let's go." Wes pulled up the rear as the three young men mounted the sagging stairs, leading in to a sort of greenhouse porch that fed into the kitchen.

The kitchen was a catastrophe but serviceable—a place that, perhaps once in its prime a dozen decades before, had provided many a decent meal. Now it was simply a feeding area. Cypress Hill was pulsing from another room, the music commingling with the senseless dialogue of some trashy daytime talk show.

Dusty was over by the sink, tinkering with something in the basin. "It's about time, bitches," he said. His broad back swiveled around and he smiled, wiping his hands on a gray towel. Dusty's head was shaved on the sides, leaving only a greasy skullcap of short red hair. He smacked a hand with Todd and gave him a shoulder-slapping half-hug, repeating the greeting with Wes. He was still clutching Wes's hand as the bigger guy appraised him. "You look different," said Dusty. Now Wes couldn't tell the difference between a smirk and a sneer. "College turn you queer or something?"

Scoli giggled on his way to the fridge, where he began scanning the contents. Todd, evidently magnetized by the prospect of munchies, followed.

"Fuck off, man," said Wes, half laughing as he wriggled out of his grip.

After a mild staredown Dusty shouted, "*Bernie* . . . our boys are here."

Over on the far side of the kitchen, cordoned off by a hanging panel of fabric that held the hallmarks of an old, meal-stained tablecloth, was a hallway (from previous visits, Wes knew this to be a seldom-used passageway to the upstairs and attic). The cloth parted and Bernie slid through. His smile was warmly welcoming—a father reeling in his kids for the weekend.

"I was hoping you fellas would show up," said Bernie. He had long, rusty hair that hung down on his chest in straight, thin-stranded planks. Though a mutt to the marrow, Bernie, in his build and intense demeanor, reminded Wes of a Native American warrior. Bernie was the alpha here—on the south side and in this broken kitchen. A tribal leader of working-class tokers. He slapped Todd on the back as he passed, approaching Wes and delivering a fraternal hug. "How's the fucking schooling going, bookworm?"

Dusty, who'd strolled over to lean against the wall adjacent to the living room, chuckled. "You got the *worm* part right."

Wes pitched a look at Dusty before turning back to Bernie. "Not really for me." Wes rested his rearend against the kitchen table. "Thinking about dropping out."

"Oh, yeah?" said Bernie. He hopped up on the counter by the sink, his scuffed boots dangling off the filthy floor. "Why's that?"

"I just don't"—he scratched the side of his face, ruffled his hair while he waited for the right words—"it's just that I'm not sure that sort of—institution—would be good fit." Wes was hoping Bernie would switch gears, dissipate the hanging silence; but he simply stared at Wes, his expression urging elaboration. With stilted explanations, Wes discussed the status of his classes—the culture with which he'd have to assimilate, the unlikely enterprise of pursuing a respectable career. *I don't have the mind of an educator,* is what he could not quite articulate. Bernie smiled, tipped his head. *Go on, man.* "It's like," Wes struggled, "to be a teacher, I just can't see myself standing there in front of a bunch of kids—kids like we used to be—lecturing the same fucking concepts year after year, over and over again, reading from the same goddamn textbook. Everything identical," he waved a hand, "just a different iteration."

Dusty, his face pinched with mild disgust, said, "*It-er*-what?"

"No, no, Dusty," said Bernie. "I know what he means."

Laughing, Wes said, "I was going to skip class indefinitely before Todd called last night to say he was coming to pick me up."

There was a brief pause before he said, "So it was Todd's idea to come get you?"

Wes: "Yeah. Said he was driving out to 'rescue' me."

"That's right," said Todd through a mouthful of food; he and Scoli had settled on something, perhaps unspoiled, which they were noisily snacking on. "We're going fishin'."

Bernie nodded at that. Silent percolation. He leveled his gaze on Wes. "So what took you so long?"

Wes gave a weak twitch of the shoulder. "What do you mean—like, to *get* here?"

"Of course, Wes," he said. "When I talked to Todd he said you were at some gas station in Cloverdale. What took you so long?"

Wes exchanged a quick glance with Todd. *Time to take the lead here, playboy.*

Todd squished some food in his mouth and squashed a smile. "Got caught up with some skeez."

Bernie evidently didn't hear this and to Wes said, "Did you get my pages?"

"Yeah. Sure."

Bernie shook his head. "No, Wes—did you *get* my pages?"

He thought about Todd's reaction to the alphanumeric code—*283. BUD.* Their small crew's call to collectively get stoned. But the insistent repetition hadn't sat right with Wes. Something waiting right behind it. A message hiding on the other side of the message. And as Wes nearly grasped what Bernie was implying, the dealer spoke. "Twenty-eight-point-three, Wesley." He wobbled a palm in a give-or-take gesture. "Roughly the gram equivalent of an ounce." Now he crossed his arms—mock tutelage: "Which is precisely how much got lifted from my garage sometime last night." Wes fought the urge to tick an eye over at Todd, who he peripherally noticed had stopped eating and was watching Bernie. "See, it's a minor amount, compared to what I've got on hand," he continued. "But this isn't any ordinary rope." Wes still hadn't dared a glance at Todd. "Zoot has gotten himself into something . . . unique." With a magician's flourish, Bernie produced a pin-joint from behind one of the lengths of hair curled over his ear and lighted it. He took a hit and extended it to Wes.

Wes cleared his throat. "No, man. I'm good." The incessant, almost jeering cadence of rap music felt synced with his heartbeat: his pulse a V forking up from his clavicle. "I'm gonna take it easy for a bit."

Bernie hesitated, then arced his arm toward Dusty, who ambled over to accept. Through expelled smoke Bernie said, "You're going to take it easy because you've already smoked too much of my shit or because you know what its capable of?"

Wes sadly aligned the tiles of this narrative: *Todd's mysterious supply of not-normal dope.* Still, his impulse was to feign cluelessness. "I don't—"

"An ounce is really nothing; but someone breaking into the garage to snatch it?" He still hadn't looked over at Todd, who was frozen with the fridge door open. "No one—not even these two," he gave an uninterested wave at his two enforcers, "knew about the panel at the back of the garage." Bernie, step by step, explained all the alarms he had around the property, but there was a camouflaged panel—"about the size of a pizza box"—at the back of the structure by the slab. "More of an escape hatch than anything else. And no one would even notice it if they didn't know precisely what they were looking for." Bernie had been hiding this special strain of smoke in the trunk of the car. He said, "The Roadrunner is just a big fucking safe, really."

Music thumped. Bernie was about to continue when Todd started, "Bernie, man, if you think that I—"

To Wes, Bernie said, "Zoot warned me about selling this stuff to just anybody." He flexed the muscles along his jawline. "Said he'd gotten it from some guys down south. He even delivered it, pounds of it, in ceramic pots covered with some fucked-up symbols and shit. Cost me an arm and a leg . . . which is exactly what I'm thinking of taking from the guys who stole it from me."

The coward's hemisphere of Wes's mind jumped on the pluralized designation of "guys." He almost blurted out that he had nothing to do with it.

Bernie said, "But at this point I'm more pissed that someone I know—someone I trusted—figured out how to steal from a friend."

Bernie slid himself off the counter, landing on the linoleum with no apparent sound, and paced over to face Wes. "And there have been other things that have been stolen, little things, sure; but it's still friends stealing from friends."

Fiends stealing from fiends, thought Wes. "I know," Bernie said, "you had nothing to do with it just as much as you know exactly what I'm talking about when it comes to apophenia—that's what Zoot called this shit." Wes looked over at Todd now, whose face had gone white. The plodding of Dusty's boots sounded on the floor as he crossed the kitchen behind Bernie. Wes was on his feet now too but stood still. "There's a bigger picture here, and I know you know that. These guys may not be able to see it, but *we* do. I picked up on it as soon as I saw you standing here, high as hell—you're practically humming with it, man. But this"—he wagged a finger—"this is about payment. And while you've been gone trying to be a scholar, there's been no one around to keep Todd on his leash."

And with that, Dusty rose up in front of Todd and slashed a meaty punch into the side of his face. Scoli, snickering as he did so, crawled up behind Todd to restrain his arms.

Wes flinched as Todd staggered, but Scoli held him up, his withered wrists hooked under his armpits, as Dusty drove a fist into his stomach. Scoli laughed, *"Arm and a leg . . . arm and a leg."*

Bernie, unblinking, didn't budge. Wes took a deep breath. "Whatever you saw today," Bernie went on, "—and I can tell you've seen something—know that these things are *real*. They're not some lysergic delusion. This shit's not some sort of intrinsic illusion or hippie hallucination." Wes had never heard Bernie speak this way, use this sort of language. *"They"*—he placed his palm on Wes's shoulder—"are not coming for us, you see. *We* are slowly steering toward *them*. And then all will be as it was."

All the while Dusty had been hissing an interrogation; he cracked a vicious slap across Todd's face, his head rocking to the side.

Wes sprang forward, shoving past Bernie and striding toward Dusty. He made it about four steps before the bigger guy wheeled and stabbed a fist into Wes's sternum. The world flashed a chromatic negative for an instant, only returning to normal when Wes hit the floor. Dusty loomed for a moment, warning Wes not to try it again, before returning to Todd.

Wes was wincing, gulping. With the side of his face against the filthy floor, he could see to the far end of the kitchen, to the partitioned corridor from which Bernie had originally emerged. There was the discernible outline of a figure in there, gray light cutting its outline sharply and blacking out detail. *Something with a scarecrow's posture propped on insectile stilts.* The too-tall thing remained hidden, only shifting to peek at the commotion in the kitchen.

Wes curled his body, his eyeline toggling back to Bernie. He noticed now, as the dealer neared, that he had levitated an inch off the floor. He rose up over Wes, tenderly helping him to his feet.

Getting an elbow up on the counter, Wes gave a quick swipe at his face with his forearm. Todd, never acknowledging guilt, had forfeited what little fight he had. Still hitching in a string of broken breaths, Wes watched as Scoli gripped ahold of Todd's wrist, bringing his hand up to his mouth. Scoli's long rodent teeth clamped over Todd's left pinkie finger. Todd howled in the strand of seconds before Dusty tamped the cry with another slap. After a minute of thrashing, Scoli pulled his mouth away from Todd's hand, which now bore a ragged wound where his finger had been. Blood coursed down over Todd's wrist, as though his forearm had transformed into a candle, the taper weeping crimson wax that plinked over the linoleum. Wes swooned as he watched Scoli spit the digit onto the floor, but Bernie propped him up.

"Smoking apophenia aligns us in a depthless spectrum, Wesley," he said. "Some tune in quicker than others, I've come to understand these past few weeks. Imagine, sitting in your car during your daily circuit home from work—the same thing day after day. What is it you said?—identical but a different iteration. What if you just pulled over on the shoulder of the road, left the engine running—aberration from the routine . . . alignment by deviance—and stalked off into the woods. Imagine the ferocious horrors you'd witness hiding in plain sight. This isn't about catching the ancients off guard. It's about letting our own guard down. *They* are watching us . . . and waiting for us to *see* them."

Now Dusty and Scoli were wrenching Todd to his feet, and

as they began hauling him across the kitchen, Wes thrust himself off the counter, but it was Bernie who placed a restraining hand on his chest. As the trio passed, Todd, a smile flickering, angled his face up to Wes. "Maybe . . . we can go fishing . . . some other time, Wes."

Wes blinked.

With their arms looped under Todd's armpits, neither Dusty or Scoli slowed as they passed through the threshold and around the corner into the rap-filled pandemonium cacophony of the shadowed living room.

Bernie now used the restraining hand as a guide to the back door. "You know the gas station down the street. You can use the pay phone to find a ride."

Wes still clenched his chest from where Dusty had battering-rammed his ribcage. As he shuffled out into the gray, afternoon light, he peered down at Bernie's feet. No longer hovering.

"Stay in school, Wes. Become a teacher. Years from now our children—*my* children—will need someone like you to guide them, someone who's good at seeing the texture of iteration. But don't ever fucking think about coming back here." Bernie closed the rotting door, and in the quaking glass Wes caught his reflection, from which he eventually recoiled.

He started down the drive, the sound of gravel grinding underfoot doing little to cover the screams he heard peeling from within the house. Only distance seemed to help.

*

It's nearing night as I shuffle out of the pub, the music sealing to a murmur as the door glides shut behind me. The air had cooled and the weak band of trees are doing a poor job of hiding the receding yet discernible lavender light.

I should have been home hours ago. Told my wife I wouldn't be long—just meeting a few people from work. Other teachers. Other teachers who'd left the pub hours before. The gravel lot was touched by neon from the front of the pub. As I started for my car, I again pulled my cell to check and see if my wife had texted. Nothing lately. She was probably dozing or, I very much hoped, cuddling with our little girl.

I never smoked after that day at Bernie's, opting rather to quell that self-induced controlled burn of my mental vista. Often I become so absorbed in these disconnected recollections that I somehow begin to see that young man as a negation of myself. As though that young man were something I'd concocted. I understand this is just a mechanism of anesthetizing culpability, along with adopting conventions and a career in which I'm supposed to change the way young people view the world . . . widening their consciences to a better way—so that I may protect their hope, and so that they may better understand the gossamer nature of truth. I sometimes wish I had just settled for petty thievery instead of making lying my craft—deceiving my students about their potential to change this place . . . about the value of life, humanity, friendship.

I think about that young man—wonder how much of him remains in me, how much unconscious effort I exert to mask what's really beneath the membrane of these liminal layers.

When I completed college and returned home, I tried writing stories where my central character would confront his phantom double. I sketched these (unsuccessful) stories in the vein of Dostoevsky's *Notes from Underground* (which I'd fallen in love with in lieu of the heavy-handed *Fight Club*). My protag would conjure internal aberrations, manufacture selfish set-pieces, self-indulgent tableaus. But what I did not have the courage or capability to convey was that these things were indeed *real*. Not ghosts, not some cabal's calling. The gargoyles and beasts are *here* right *now*. It's just that the sequence of our meeting requires calibration.

Memory, I've come to understand, is as similar and inextricable as skin. Just as I am as inextricably sutured with that kid named . . .

"Wes!" I flinch, twisting toward the shout. *"Wesley Bridges!"*

At the far end of the lot, just outside the perimeter of neon light, is a car: three figures posted in different positions around a vehicle. I am less startled by the shout and presence of the three men than by the revelation that the car is a 1977 Cutlass Supreme. In the frail light, the black paint job looks almost liquid, as if it had recently emerged from a lake of ink.

The three figures slip and slink away from the car, their arms and hands beckoning me over. I can probably make it to my car, act as if I don't hear them, don't see them. *Coward.* At some point I become ambulatory and cross the lot, gravel crunching underfoot. I wish I'd have left earlier in time to tuck my daughter in to bed.

They are pale, the hue something subterranean. They've changed a little, Bernie the least. He's still affecting the feral shaman look. Dusty, grinning, has layered fat on his bulk of muscle; his face is underlit by the blue glow of a cell phone. Scoli's frame has headed in the opposite direction: wilted, wiry, every angle of his body warped. Their eyes are wet and electric— the only element about them untarnished by time.

"We thought that was you," says Bernie, sounding genuinely pleased. "Saw you sitting in there by yourself a while ago."

I glance over my shoulder, back at the bar. "Yeah." My laugh is unsuitable. "Long day."

"Shit," says Dusty, "I hear that."

Scoli chimes in, his voice weasel-slurred. "Haven't seen you around town in like fucking forever."

After a segment of silence Bernie says, "What have you been doing with yourself?"

"Um . . ." Some night animal screeches in the woods. "Well, I teach now."

Both Dusty and Scoli snicker. Scoli says, "You're a fucking *teacher?*" He lights a smoke and expels a ragged cloud. "Man, they'll let anybody teach these stupid fucking kids nowadays." The pair guffaw, but Bernie remains thoughtful, his forearm draped across the top of the car. He stares at me—his gaze and expression are as good as words: *I told you so*.

I smile, let my head bob a few times. *Funny, fellas*. Maybe they're right. "Yeah, well, they certainly have lowered their standards," I say.

"Aw," says Scoli, then snaps: "Hey—I know something that will cheer you up." He slaps the trunk of the car. "You want to see an old friend?"

I could shift and sprint toward my car. But I am certain they would just follow me. Follow me home. The notion makes me instantly ill.

Dusty is next to me then, wrapping an arm around my shoulder. Old pals. His body is ripe with an oily odor. "Come on, bud. Got somebody here that wants to see you."

We take a few paces toward the car—the same car that had picked me up in front of my dorm over a decade before. Bernie remains poised by the driver's-side door. The consummate captain. After the dramatic pause, Dusty sweeps open the passenger-side door, the interior light casting merciless illumination on the thing in the back seat.

It's Todd, of course, blinking at the harsh emergence of light and peering around as though uncertain of his surroundings. I have to place a palm against the roof of the car as I process what I am seeing.

He is huddled in the corner of the back seat, his skin a shade of gray-blue. A rill of blood extending from his nose has dried over his upper lip. One eye socket is scalloped with a greenish bruise. But his disoriented movements are inhibited by the thick layer of webbing crisscrossing his torso like a straitjacket made of filthy silk. The spiderweb filaments glitter—spooled around his body like a wretched vest, clinging to the upholstery in clots. His forearms are exposed, though, and waver in front of him. I see the hand missing the pinkie finger has not healed well; the ragged wound glistens with what appears to be infected dampness. The odor of stagnation is very strong. Todd steadies himself, growing calm as he apparently comprehends my presence. The eye that's not blackened widens. "Wes . . . shit, Wes . . . what's up, man?"

I am breathing shallowly through my nostrils, my tongue fused to the roof of my mouth.

Scoli, giddy, says, "Aren't you going to say hello to your old buddy, Wesley?"

"Don't you mean 'Professor Wesley'?" says Dusty, and the two of them bray.

As though suddenly stung by something unseen, Todd's body spasms, tendons on his throat go taut, his mouth yawns open in pain, fangs of saliva stretch between his cracked lips. I notice he's missing many teeth. But the moment finally passes, and a fragile smile settles on his ruined face. "Wes . . . Wes . . ." he says.

Bracing myself, I lean down as much as I can bear. I swallow then say, "Yeah, buddy. It's me."

Another wince, but he fights through it to say: "We . . . should go . . . fishing . . . some time," he licks his lips, "just you and me. Nobody else."

I clamp my teeth, close my eyes. "Yeah." I tilt my head away for a second, appraising the faces of the three ghouls (three men in a tub from some perverse nursery rhyme yet to be penned) before refocusing on Todd one last time. "I'd really enjoy that, man."

Bernie's voice is as black and slick as the Cutlass's paint job. "Time to go, fellas. Reunion's over." He gives me a lingering look, and something he'd said a long time ago rolls through my mind like foul fog. *My children will need someone like you.*

Todd's too wrung-out to keep his head up. Scoli squirms into the back seat alongside the cocooned thing while Dusty sinks down in the shotgun spot. The car roars to life, as does its stereo. Before Dusty slams the door, Bernie casts a glance and, under the thrash metal distortion, mouths, "See you around." Then everything goes black behind tinted windows. The car tears out of the lot, flinging wings of gravel.

As though painted on, a uniform numbness covers me. My legs get moving and I start toward my car, fishing out my cell phone to text my wife that I am finally on the way home.

The crunching of rocks ceases as I freeze, gazing across the lot toward the back of the property. Toward the dumpster there. There is nothing unusual about it, just a nondescript disposal device. I slip my phone back in my pocket and pivot, slowly skirting the front of the pub and stalking my way around back. I have come to understand that there is no avoiding what has already arrived. These doomed dots already lie scattered. We just have to connect them.

I pass through canted columns of dirty light; high grass creeps up around the receptacle. There comes a nocturnal overture from the starved woods. Music from the bar buzzes with a cicada cadence as I reach for the lid, hesitate, and fling it back.

Dark contours of shifting shadows snake away from the weak light. In my current state, I no longer have use for describing the reprehensible horrors with which I've become acquainted—the egregious creatures that are, sadly, coming to claim us all.

There is a heaving hunger in these bottomless apertures between who we were and who we *will* be, a quickening that allows the veil to subside momentarily—for revelation, for revulsion, I do not know—before the tide retakes the light.

Amid the tumult of ever-folding and refolding spines and hides within the jigsaw shadows, my hesitation and scrutiny of this subsistent snag appears to elicit a contraction of the things there in the dark. But one form does not retreat—rather, it gains substance: ashen, delicate lineaments contrasting the coarse, stygian insulation. It opens its eyes. It rises, floating up from the variations of overlapping blackness.

I cower only for a moment as Valerie ascends, clawing at the clinging tendrils of animated shadows, rising out of the dumpster until she is before me, above me. As though brandishing awful, wondrous wings, she spreads wide her rotten robe, sweeps open that dark cloak to reveal her bare body, her pale torso marbled with soot. Her features have gone unaffected by the passing of over a dozen years. Valerie's expression suggests welcome. Acceptance.

I clasp a palm over my eyes, the tips of my fingers gripping my temples for a moment before I focus, calibrate, crawl up into her embrace and, with a reverence that I've anticipated, we sink down together.

Details That Would Otherwise Be Lost to Shadow

A rational reader would certainly prefer I begin at some accommodating sequence, but I'm afraid I must start here: standing at a second-story window in a room, in a house that is not my residence, looking through the glass at my own home across the street.

What I see is my husband getting out of his sedan, a smile apparent even from this distance: the trace of some joke as he rounds the rear of the car to help our daughter from her car seat. They pick up whatever riddle they're sharing, but I'm less interested in this interaction than I am with the woman who emerges from the passenger seat, unnaturally rising out of the vehicle.

Yes: she is a stranger, but the similarities seize me—same build, proportions, same hair color and length; conversely, it's the contrasts that freeze me. Her complexion is gray, her hair scrambled, fresh from a nap on an asylum's padded mat. She's wearing a tattered sundress that may have once possessed a floral pattern, as though from this distance the petals' edges have smeared. She moves with a stilted gait that calls to mind a brittle assembly of bones—a ballerina in a production that mocks human movement.

And as my daughter trots up the drive, the woman—this other woman whom Ben has brought home for some reason—reaches out toward Brooke in what may have been an otherwise affectionate gesture but is rather something more aggressive: that hand of hers extending, uncoordinatedly taking a slow-motion swipe at my little girl's trailing hair—those flexed fingers appearing like a talon compromised by rigor-mortis coordination.

I still imagine that scene with a passive clarity of focus: Ben, briefly placing his hand on the small of the woman's back—so sensitive as to be obscene. The thing I am watching in helpless petrification. A dull, though familiar, ache pulsing along my right leg wakes me and I am moving, running out of this house that is not my own. In which I am a prowler.

I'll come back to this. Promise.

*

We'd moved to Olmstead Estates seven months earlier. This after a grueling period of attempting to negotiate alternatives. Essentially, Ben's company provided several choices, all involving relocation, and the outskirts-of-Detroit option was the most feasible and, for a number of reasons, the most appealing. Ben's income increased, but so did his daily commute.

Nine years before this, Ben and I, having not been married long, were living a twenty-somethings existence in Chicago. Back then, Ben worked downtown, and our respective lines of work had afforded us, and continue to afford us (though more so, now, on Ben's end), numerous comforts for which neither of us has ever apologized. If either of us were typical, we'd not have suited each other so well. We are, I suppose, conscientiously cutthroat, though having a daughter altered our lukewarm ruthlessness.

Back then, we were both profiting by catering to the affluent whims of those living in the suburbs to the north and west of the city.

My routine in those days was almost shamefully selfish. I'd wake before Ben, slip into my running gear, and be on the sidewalks and streets by 4 A.M., sneaking in three or four miles and make it back in time to trade places with Ben, sliding into the shower just as he was drying off.

After Ben was out the door, I'd fire up the computer and get ready for what lay ahead: most days were occupied by coordinating site-visitations with clients, colleagues, or real estate agents who'd scheduled interior stagings for a shoot. Lunches were breezy things, usually conducted with a cell in one hand. Meetings and responsibilities would typically recede around early evening, when Ben and I would reconvene at the apartment, split a bottle of wine, and laugh until we grew drowsy; then we'd begin the work-week routine again. Embracing our lassitude. We were frivolous with time, not with each other.

But I'm a long way from Chicago, and on some days—like the day I'm presently disclosing—I'm a long way from that ambitious interior designer with a niche startup sipping wine in a brownstone on the fringe of Lincoln Park.

*

Before I get us back to that second-story window in the Motley House, let me draw your attention to our current subdivision of Olmstead Estates: a long-established residential area, totally idiosyncratic in my experiences. Built in the late 1970s and developed into the early '80s, Olmstead Estates began as a secluded tract of land within a heavily wooded stretch, the neighborhood proper completely invisible to nearby thoroughfares and the Interstate, with a single, sinuous road acting as the subdivision's sole entrance and exit.

Any 101 urban planning class will illustrate the functions of boundaries. Essentially, boundaries lend themselves to the identity of a neighborhood: too flimsy or permeable, a neighborhood will not maintain its character; too rigid and energetic transactions will grow limited, and so too will the personality of that particular environment. Boundaries have a certain "charge" in people's minds because of our recognition of zones and gateways (often tacitly so).

I do the neighborhood and its opulent homes a disservice by my description, as it is a coveted swath of real estate.

Ben and I had taken great care to acclimate and ingratiate ourselves with the neighbors along our street—not that the fall and impending winter allowed us much time for front-yard small talk. Still, we've made friends. But the house across the street:

that is different. I'd grown puzzled by it, the Motley House, immediately after we'd moved in.

I'd taken to calling it the "Motley" House due to the schizophrenic selections made by the designer. Part of this had to do with mere composition: caught at a particular perspective, portions of the house bore peculiar tilts, the roof—with its dissonant imbrication of shingles—appearing at a visually unappealing pitch. Still, more had to do with sheer aesthetics. As I'd mentioned, many of the homes were constructed nearly forty years ago; and while there are indeed touches that signal that period, others are sheer anomalies. Take for instance the second story: a board-and-batten scheme along the facing and dormer windows, while the sides of the house are all brick and windowless. Now toggle to the lower level, where wide swaths possess Tudor-style exposed planking, while other segments are composed of cut cobblestone with thick spaces of mortar. A baywindow bump-out skirted with brick, capped with discordant tiles. To describe the effect concisely, it is as though four or five capable craftsmen had lent inimitable elements and could only compromise by installing their own portion, no matter how incongruous.

I'd only seen snatches of activity over there. Lights shone in the windows infrequently. The driveway remained unshoveled throughout the winter—not a single tire track or bootprint over the course of those seemingly relentless storms. I'd only mentioned my curiosity about the place to Ben on a few occasions. Anyway, as it is my discipline and my craft, conjuring images of a floor plan, and how the interior décor was composed in such a strange schematic became a tepid obsession.

Then, in early April—after an arduous release from winter's frigid grip—a FOR SALE sign appeared in the front yard of the Motley House.

This, I thought, would serve as a conceit to meet the occupants and, perhaps, sneak a peek at the interior. And so I assembled bits and pieces of discarded plans, consolidating them into one. I'd simply approach the house under the guise of curiosity: *"I saw the sign in your front yard and wanted to say hello before you left the neighborhood . . . so sad to see you go"*—something like that. I didn't need a bullet-proof scheme, just a crutch to make it to the door.

And so there we were: a spring morning.

I'd kissed Ben goodbye just before dawn and had dropped off Brooke at school a few hours later. Truth be told, it would be an ideal time to update the website or catch up with former colleagues, test the waters for new clientele. But the creative atrophy I'd allowed to settle in over the past nine years had become (though lingering insolence would have prohibited my using the word) debilitating.

It was still early, before 10 A.M., when I walked outside and began a pre-run stretch (never *not* a painful affair), watching the house in narrow glances as I had for the past seven months. And so I started toward the house, cutting across the street at an angle to their drive, a crumbling mess. With spring here, green stipels and unknown growth were beginning to whisker their way through uncountable cracks (I made a mental note to contact the HOA).

Adopting the gait of a friendly neighbor (which I was, I suppose), I made my way along the walk that collared the front of the house, casually inspecting the front windows, which were curtained.

Three concrete risers lifted me to a glass storm door protecting a sturdy-looking and rather elaborate front door (painted a hideous tint of what may have once been hunter green). I pulled open the storm door and, after a blink-steeling pause, knocked on the front door, noting a digital real-estate lockbox secured over doorknob.

On the final knock, I froze with my knuckles in midair. Each one of my raps was repeated in a series of staggered echoes. Initially, I thought someone was toying with me, imitating the sound on the other side of the door; but when I knocked again, the sound certainly existed but was distant, as though I were knocking against a barrier that opened into something cavernous. I held my breath before giving the door three punctuated knocks; and again, from the other side, the sounds fell away in mimicked echo.

This time I pulled away, gently closing the glass storm door as I cautiously stepped off the risers, appraising the mismatched face of the house. The scale math didn't add up. Had I missed something? What sort of interior layout would produce that unsettling, rib-vault reverberation?

And there was something of a challenge in this now—my cluelessness about the inside. I felt less shy about piquing my need to understand, to *see*, and I started off toward the side of the house.

I reset, addressing the house from the ruined driveway, passing the garage on my way around back. A tall, wood-plank fence totally hid the back yard from view. I proceeded into the rear of the property not unlike the sociable neighbor I was (or was portraying myself to be). I thought about the antigodlin contours of the Motley House itself—how it had been expertly pieced together to evoke unison. It bothered me: that discordant chorus of harmonious intent. The builders may have fooled some, but not me.

Though the fence was tall, I could see the tree-shrouded second-story levels of two or three adjacent homes—no doubt the back yard's condition was no secret to these folks. And it wasn't all that outrageous, just unkempt and uncared for. Trees hung low, their barky torsos covered in verdigris-colored lichen. The dull grass was uncut and hunched, tinkling with dew in these early morning hours.

I crossed through the tall grass and made my way to a rickety patio, an old layer of paint scabby across its warped planks.

The wide, sliding-glass panels provided a reflection of myself as I crossed the elevated patio deck; reflected too was my vaguely hitching stride, something, even after all this time, I was still unaccustomed to witnessing with some objectivity. I had to avert my eyes as I moved closer to the glass.

With the awareness that someone might be eyeing this inter-action, and still embracing the affectionate semblance of amiable neighbor, I approached the sliding glass doors and called out while striking my knuckles on the surface. "Hello? Anyone home?"

Nothing budged behind the vertical blinds. No cathedral echo issued from within. Still, I gave it another try, this time pairing the knocks with "I just wanted to introduce myself . . . I'm your neighbor from across the street."

Morning sounds. Birds in the trees.

Disappointed but not done, I swiveled from the sliding glass doors, canting my head as I noticed an enormous shrub growing directly against the backside of the house, something unusual about how it hugged the brick. It reminded me of a prodigious, kelp-covered starfish cleaving to a hull that was this home.

Staring, I noticed the shrub was obscuring a shape against the house itself, a dark rectangle—I caught the dull gleam of something. A knob. Suspicion confirmed: a door. I flexed back a few limbs, getting a clearer shot.

The door was dark, blending in with the dark nervous system of the shrub's interior. I could imagine this leading to a garage or mudroom, but the layout was wrong—I'd passed by the gar-age on the other side of the house. Biting my lower lip, I reached out, fully expecting any sort of test to result in a solidly locked door; so when the knob twisted and the door creaked open a few inches, I pulled a small inhale of shock.

With the shrub acting as concealment (my unkempt accom-plice), only shards of sunlight punctured the dim space. Awk-wardly, I hunch-pressed myself between the shrub and the side of the house.

I could see a narrow corridor, the walking space carpeted with a traffic-worn, burnt-orange pattern populated with lan-tern-like swirls, a style I associated with the mid-'70s. Again I gave an innocence-tinged call. "Anyone home?" Silence, even from the morning birds.

To answer your question: yes, of course it occurred to me that this was grossly illegal; and I was aware that entering a home under these circumstances amounted to simple trespassing or criminal mischief (though intent obviously dictates either criterion). But the clueless concern of a good-natured neighbor certainly wouldn't qualify for these charges, would they? And sure, I'd considered the possibility of an alarm; yet, like many of the exterior's non-contemporary features, no up-to-date blips or bleeps sounded from within. Besides, my intent was driven by two things: the bloodless need to *know* and the designer's-eye desire to assess the *persona* of its occupants. My career had been about telling stories not with words, but rather with *things*.

I stepped over the threshold, the door hanging open behind me, allowing in a wedge of sunlight.

My pacing increased as my eyes slowly adjusted to the corridor's dimness; the passage eventually terminated, opening to my left, to a kitchen.

Meager morning light filtered through the crepe-like drapes, providing a diffuse hue, fabricating the illusion that a frail mist permeated the house.

The layout, no surprise, was an amalgamation of schemes: touches of split-level step-downs, stylish, load-bearing dividers separating rooms. There was a large, inglenooked fireplace in the living room composed of mini-boulders, lending a cave-like quality to the space. And though the architectural skeleton was clearly from a bygone era, the residents had done a deft job of creating a refined living space.

In my early twenties, one of the design teams at the university had researched the Japanese discipline of *wabi-sabi* and *shibumi*: the restrained principles of home and interior design. While the last component reflects taste in its conscious reservation, the other two elements concentrate on how the aesthetic elements—organic and inorganic—are gripped in time itself. Understated austerity and reduction of excessive visible distractions are chief foci of *wabi-sabi,* which literally translates to "rust," refers to design elements that have been age-worn, achieving a serenity in their distinction from the new.

As I wandered the first floor (not delving into any of the nearby darkened hallways, mind you), I called up this ethos and how well (and, again, incongruently) it applied to the *feel* of the Motley House.

These alterations are often rushed—people, in other words, temporarily change habits in order to provide the guise of good taste. That said, as bizarre as some of the spatial choices had been, there was something cohesively comforting in how the disparate elements transitioned so seamlessly from room to room: a sensible respiration for how the first-floor spaces were so elegantly sutured together. There seemed to be something, here, in the ritualistic aesthetic—an enduring, holistic ethos.

I gradually gravitated to the front-door vestibule, assessing the surrounding space, contemplating what sort of depth and impediments could have created that eerie echo. Biting my lower lip, I lifted a knuckled fist and knocked on the door—*one, two, three*. Silence.

Then movement, from the margin of my vision, swivel-snagged my attention.

A shadow at the top of the stairway—only catching its sudden, receding slide down—the second-floor wall. The erratic rhythm of my heart—though refreshing and calling to mind many a long-distance run—flooded my ears with static. I took the stairs two at a time, using the railing to haul myself up. Pain forked up my lower leg with each exertion.

And then I crested the landing, listening for a few seconds, trying to hook to any sound. Nothing. If this was indeed some sort of game, I would have to wait for my partner (or adversary) to make the next move.

The second floor teed to the left and right, the doors in either direction all closed, except for one, its opening framing a rectangle of inviting, morning light. Warily, I peered into the room.

A generous space, dedicated as a large den or study. Wide windows with slender muntins overlooked the neighborhood. Sleek bookshelves lined the far walls. A small sofa, a reading chair, an ottoman. A potted fishtail palm stood near the window, and I approached just as much to get a better view as to see if the thing was an imitation. I ran my thumb over one of the wide, silky leaves, confirming verdant life.

The panes provided a generous snapshot of our tree-lush subdivision with which I, and perhaps Ben too, was still growing accustomed.

Contrary to what some may assume, with windows it's not the provision of light-wells to which people are attracted, but rather the access to meaningful views. Office workers, for instance, feel a need for refreshing vistas that open to lives, and often worlds, other than their own.

A few intruding tree limbs cross-cut the view, and it clicked then that perhaps these were the culprits of the shadow I'd seen tickling the wall—a play of the slowly ascending morning sunlight.

The view favored our spacious house across the street, and I felt a pang of guilt for some of the things I'd said to Ben about it—about the neighborhood, the tectonics of relocation in general. In truth, he really had no choice. Well, not true: it could have been so much worse. I pulled away, appraising the room.

It was a tidy, balanced space. Too often in my line of work I'd forfeited meaning for creating a pretentious *mise en scène* for prospective buyers or staging for clients who were too easily seduced by artificiality. The truth is that one must strike a balanced point of view: equilibrium between the perception of the inhabitant and the POV of those who enter. While there are standards, too often clients are clueless about their own needs and unaware of how much (to their detriment) they want to impress strangers (or people who will never actually witness their living space); and though I admit to practicing some of these methods, interior designers are all too willing to exploit the anxieties of clients who have no direction about the expressive process of reflecting *meaning*.

I approached the desk, aimed at an angle to the window. Just to get a feel for the space, I gently pulled the chair away, hesitated, then descended into the seat. A small stack of clean stationery was placed in the middle of the desk, the sheets curled with creamy contours. A tray containing gleaming ink pens was nearby; I picked one up and with a smirk imagined myself to be on the brink of some brilliant declaration. I was once assigned to a physical therapist who, aside from the merit of our daily routines, was an intrusively insufferable woman. Still, she infrequently suggested that, as a healing exercise, I write down some of my resentments—not just with my physical state, but with the fears I'd been unwilling to articulate—to place what's inside, by whatever means, on the outside. I estimated her at the time to be rather presumptuous, and my terse responses during PT clearly reflected this subscription.

With melodramatic flair, I scrawled, *My name is Tara Keltz, and I was in an accident.* There was something too ordinary in it. Directly beneath my first lines, I started again: *My name is Tara Keltz, and I was nearly killed ten years ago.* Was that too overwrought? Affected? I thought not. Though my leg was almost ruined, it could have been my spine, my neck. My brain. Now I looked down at the words on the paper: the brief skating of the ink pen over paper felt alleviative, as though a small amount of malignant liquid had been leeched.

And though a person can admit that pain is acceptable, often it is difficult to remove oneself from how close one came to the cleft of the worst. The ink followed a path along the paper, just as I'd been following a path that morning a decade before.

It was still in our Chicago days, the years (though not too many years) before Brooke was born. I was faithful to my morning routine: on the sidewalks and streets before daylight to stretch and prep; headphones on; sneakers on concrete.

It was this consistency that I applied to my life and made me an appealing commodity for clients. It was a consistency I'd abandoned and mourned in the preceding years.

I'd been intent on some coincidental lyric in a song—one of those moments when you see something, a color perhaps, or a number on a sign, at the exact same instant a line is spoken. I remember the headlights to my right, slashing across the crosswalk. And then the black impact.

The front end of the vehicle briefly transformed my body into an acute "less-than" sign (or "greater than" sign, depending on a witness's point of view), the collision simultaneously causing my lower leg to get kinked between the car's right corner panel and its wheel well, my shoulder connecting with the poorly patched street as I scraped to a stop against a parked car. I never lost consciousness (until the hospital); and though I was instantly furious, my body would not respond to the rage. It, apparently, was too focused on the pulsing volts of pain radiating from my lower leg.

The car was idling in the intersection, one headlight shattered. I was able to snag an agonized glimpse at the driver: a young man whose face was brushed with sodium-vapor glow from the streetlamp. Sometimes that smooth face crumples with creased contrition before the driver stabs the accelerator. Still, other times my mind's eye plainly sees the dismissive sneer of a young woman—coming home too late from a club, perhaps—as the car's tires yelp on the pavement and the taillights fade.

The major injury was to my tibia. Like most compound fractures, it was hideous to behold. It reminded me of some sort of gory imitation of a tipi: the jagged wooden poles of my bones protruding through the torn fabric of my flesh. Most vividly, at the hospital while they were working on me, I recall the sense of violation: something that had been so intimate a part of my interior had ruptured the exterior, exposed.

Later the same physical therapist I'd mentioned previously echoed similar sentiments from various doctors: that the fibular fracture did not cause irreparable damage to the peroneal nerve, which could have resulted in something more severe than occasional aches and an altered gait.

I stared at the stationery, at the words I'd written. *My name is Tara Keltz, and I was nearly killed ten years ago.* I was about to remove the piece of paper when the sound of a car door being slammed compelled me to the window.

Heart racing, I glided over, out of sight. The driveway here at the Motely House was empty. Relief was brief, though, as I ticked my focus across the street, over to the scene unfolding at my own home.

And you already know this next part: where we began.

Ben was in our driveway. Sliding out from the passenger seat was the pale woman. *Was she in trouble?—had he brought her home from the office?* Ben had his flaws, but I doubted he was dim-witted enough to try to engage in some morning tryst suspecting I was out of the house. Never mind the flawed calculus of my car being in the garage.

She began moving toward the house with those somnambulatory baby steps, as if a storefront mannequin had organically sprouted gray matter.

And then there was Brooke, her little backpack a point of color. Why had he picked Brooke up from school so early in the morning? A new question: was our daughter sick? Then the woman lunged at Brooke—an ungainly rake at her hair.

And then I was moving, too quick to avoid clumsiness. Retracing my steps, I sped down the stairs and through the house, trying to comprehend a rational narrative for what I'd just seen.

I jogged down the side-entrance corridor, the open door urging exit with a glow of illumination. Stepping through the threshold, I was confronted with the barrier of the shrub; I forced my way past its rigid, inhibiting limbs.

Through the gate—across the street—back in my own

driveway. I was sucking in snatches of air as I strode through the garage and into our house.

Not slowing, I passed through the mudroom and rounded the corner that fed into our kitchen. I stood there on the cusp of it, not moving, hearing my racing heart but trying to listen for anything—the sound of this other woman's voice.

What I saw instead was Brooke, perched at our dinette, hovering over some coloring project, her backpack having spilled its first-grade contents. She didn't look up as I, trying to control my panting, stepped in.

"Hi, sweetie," I said tentatively.

"Hi, Mommy."

I waited. "Where's Daddy?"

Brooke remained intent on the colored sheet in front of her. Her tiny shoulders shrugged. "I don't know."

Commotion down the hall, toward the master bedroom. I sliced through the kitchen, stanching the impulse to affectionately stroke my daughter's hair, as I'd witnessed the pale woman do only minutes before. In seconds, I pushed through the partially closed bedroom door. Ben was in the bathroom, pulling off his office attire. He said, "That you, hon?"

Barely moving, barely blinking, I sight-scoured the room for *her*—hiding: erect and discreet behind the bedroom door, maybe, or crouched low on the other side of the dresser, her knees drawn up to her chest like that preserved corpse from Chile—the mummy of the "tattooed lady." I rejected the urge to sink to the floor and check under the bed, salvaging a bit of dignity in doing so.

Nothing. "Yeah," I said, licking my lips.

"Go for a run?"

"I, um—yes. Just got back." And as I was about to ask why he had shown up in the middle of the morning with both Brooke and a strange woman, I saw the clock on the nightstand. *4:30.* An icy sensation, like chilly tendrils spreading under my skin, thrived with my understanding that the slant of light was not at all right for the morning.

Tugging on a T-shirt, Ben came out of bathroom. "I tried calling earlier. Got out a little early . . . thought I'd surprise Brooke"—he began, but stopped, scowling at me—"Geez, hon—what happened to your face?"

One of my hands instinctively rose to my cheek, fingers testing the flesh. Sure enough, a soreness there; I frowned, rounding the foot of the bed in pursuit of the bathroom mirror. Ben hovered nearby as I inspected my reflection. Slender scratch-abrasions were visible from my temple to the lower hinge of my jaw.

Wincing, Ben gently placed his hand on my back. "Did you fall or something?"

I blinked, my eyes joysticking—mentally backtracking and realizing: the shrub at the back of the Motley House, its witch's-broom branches. During my hasty retreat, I'd swatted through the tangle of limbs. My awe elicited a long pause; I finally licked my lips. "No. I—it was a tree branch. Hanging too low. Wasn't paying attention."

He made a light, seething sound between his teeth. "At least you didn't break the skin," he said. "You should slow down, sweetheart." Ben's finger pulled a strand of hair from my forehead and tenderly hung it over my ear. I nearly recoiled at his touch—not because of *him*, but because of *her*. I wanted to know who had emerged from the passenger seat of his car; then I realized that it wasn't just my misunderstanding of time, but that I had more than one thing wrong here, namely the woman and *me*.

In the mirror, I angled my eyeline from my own reflection to Ben's. He was still frowning, still waiting to see if I was all right. My lips drew into a small smile. The question on the tip of my tongue was, *Who was she?* But the words slid off, replaced with something dismissive. Something that kept the more difficult questions at bay.

*

That night in bed, I listened to Ben's steady breathing and stared at the ceiling. To compensate for the lack of street-noise,

Ben and I had taken to running a box fan.

It had been less than an hour since tucking in Brooke (we were still in the phase where she wanted one of us to lie down with her before she fell asleep). Ben was out when I slipped back in and turned off the reading lamp. As my eyes adjusted, my mind—finally freed from the mundane, evening's-end obligations—recounted what had happened.

Bothering me the most, of course, was glimpsing the strange woman and the perplexing passage of time.

Taking a deep breath, I soberly attempted to consider, with scalpel precision, what I'd seen through the second-story window, trying to dissect anything I'd missed. The scene remained the same: the pale woman's ungraceful progression into our house . . . her long fingers at the end of her long arm taking a swipe at my little girl . . .

What have you missed?

And then something else came. Unintentionally, I gasped and sat up. My mind rewound a few more paces—to the desk . . . to the stationery: *My name is Tara Keltz . . .*

Whatever else had happened—my confusion with the woman, my confusion with how the previous day's hours had passed from morning to late afternoon—seemed like absurd figments, their fabrication less important than my neglect of concrete evidence. The mitotic complication that would arise from such invasiveness stimulated a heart-pulsing nausea.

Resting on my elbow, I considered the embarrassing and convoluted excuses I'd have to submit if someone—not the least of whom the homeowner—read the lines on that sheet. I might as well have written, *My name is Tara Keltz, hapless trespasser.*

After a few calculations, I slipped out of bed. A few minutes later I was dressed and silently moving through the house. In the kitchen I retrieved a flashlight, clicking it on and off to confirm life. At the front door, I disarmed the alarm and quietly made my way into the night-chilled air. On the front walkway, I only accumulated a few paces before shuffling to a sneaker-skidding stop.

Across the street: in the second-story window of the Motley House—the window of the study, to be precise—a light was on. My eyeline was then drawn to the driveway over there, to the parked car, a rib-bone of moonlight catching its bumper.

My plan to extricate myself from a foolish intrusion dissipated. Then, up in the second-story window, a shape coalesced, a figure emerged. Tall, slender, the faint, sagging-fern shape of a deranged mane. Absent of details, it was nothing more than a lithe silhouette; but it was intent on me—the rigidity of its presence.

I slowly backed away, retreating into the shadows that my own house had created, reluctant to pull my eyes away from that figure in the window.

I slipped back into my home, re-cued the alarm, and returned to bed.

Uneasy sleep overtook me at some point.

*

I'd spill my guts. With sophistication. Contrition.

I'd just drop by (again) and attempt to introduce myself (again).

As I prepared Brooke for school, I intermittently peered through the blinds, checking on the car in the driveway at the Motley House. Now in the light of day, I could see that it was a dark blue Mercedes, '70s-era, like the house itself. Ben said, "You expecting company?"

I withdrew my fingers from the blinds and sheepishly returned his smile (Ben continues to be disarming). For the sake of simplicity, I thought about being dishonest; but I had no reason to be. Ben had never given me a reason to be. "Just . . . I saw a car parked over at the Motley House."

He finished filling his travel mug with coffee, coils of steam curling from the top. "Yeah, I noticed that."

I brightened a bit. Not that I was fully convinced I was imagining its presence, but to have someone acknowledge something tangible added another layer of affection for him. "You think it's an agent?" he said.

I shrugged, putting the finishing touches on getting Brooke ready for school. "Who knows?" As he was saying goodbye to Brooke, I re-entered the kitchen, wrapped my arms around him, and kissed him. Just like the old days.

*

I waited an hour or so before changing, occasionally slitting the blinds, checking for activity.

And so, mimicking the friendly momentum I'd adopted the day before, I crossed the street to the Motley House; and like the day before, I pulled open the glass storm and gave three tight knocks. This time, though, there was no succession of echoes, no taunting reverberation into penetralia. Instead, there came a curtain-twitch at the window. Considerate of boundaries (at least wanting to imply as much), I took a step back, allowing the glass storm door to close on its own.

The unrushed sound of locks being unfastened sounded before the knob twisted and the door drew open several cautious inches, just wide enough to reveal a small, paunchy old man. I smiled and gave a carefree, sternum-high wave.

Friendly-looking, he widened the aperture of the front door and creaked open the storm door. "Yes?" he said, eyes glittering.

"Good morning, I'm Tara Keltz"—I gestured over my shoulder—"I'm your neighbor." I extended my hand with blithe flair.

His mouth was a small O as he nodded. "Oh, yes—the three of you. Moved in last autumn." His diminutive hand pumped mine several times before letting go.

With that cordial, physical contact, a wash of normality spread over me. I laughed. "Yes—that's right. We've been meaning to introduce ourselves to everyone, but the weather turned nasty so abruptly last fall and didn't let up."

Still smiling, he stared at me as though the winter recap were just delivered to him. He had a full head of white, wiry hair, scrambled as if I'd woken him. According to the wrinkles lining his exterior, I gauged him in his mid-eighties. I'd just then grown self-conscious of the inordinate seconds of silence that had passed. "Well, we just love it here. Such a one-of-a-kind neighborhood," I said. His grin widened—his glittering eyes were now companioned by glittering, nub-yellow teeth. "Have you lived here long?"

The waxy wrinkles wrenched, his friendly features contorting under confusion. "Oh"—he cast a brief glance behind him, at the darkened, shadow-shaded interior—"we've lived here for ages. Since the beginning." I now noticed something oddly neutral about the timbre of his voice—an asexual quality that was simultaneously sonorous and shrill.

My expression implied wonder. "Wow. That's amazing." Risky, but I pushed: "You say 'we,' so you're not alone?"

His hand still holding open the glass storm door, his face whorled with what was clearly a growing bewilderment. "We . . . my family," he said, "all have our own rooms." His stricken expression hung on me a few ticks too long. Something about his features was no longer charming, his shriveled aspect suddenly appearing to me like some sentient, overripe root vegetable. I took a step back.

"I'm sorry," I said, as kind as I could, "what did you say your name was?"

His expression was abruptly cheerful, and he regarded me as if I were an old friend. *"My name is Tara Keltz,"* he said, his voice lilting with a mocking, patty-cake pitch, *"and I was nearly killed ten years ago."* The old man continued grinning as I took another step backwards off the risers.

And then, from behind and above him—from the backdrop of lightlessness—emerged a gray hand. It came out of the darkness slowly, the pale forearm hooked around the side of the door, concealing its owner.

The lissome appendages of the splayed hand searched for a

moment with cave-creature blindness, finally came down on top of the old man's head, where the fingers spasmed, snagging his hair; his teeth clenched and his neck strained in response, jiggling the wattle of his throat. And then the arm was retracting, slowly pulling the old man back into the darkness of the house by his hair, his hand slipping from the storm door. Then, devoid of any violent crescendo, the front door simply, and soundlessly, eased shut.

I pivoted. I pivoted and ran.

*

That night, I lay in bed and waited for Ben to fall asleep.

The evening had unfolded predictably. At some point between Brooke finishing her homework and the commencement of dinner, the Mercedes disappeared from the driveway across the street. I'd then spent the meal mentally committing to returning to the house.

And so here I was once more: stealthily slipping into dark clothes and retrieving the flashlight, disarming the alarm, creeping outside. (Over the course of these past two days, I'd undergone a remarkable makeover as pseudo-intruder.)

The sky was cloudless and clear. Stars shone like quivering mercury, but the moon and its crisp circumference held suspended supremacy. My shadow trailed behind me like a distorted compass needle as I unlatched the back gate and crossed the patio deck.

The large shrub cloaking the door looked darker under the moonlight. I clicked on the flashlight, using my fingers to dull the glow. I pressed myself between the brick and the limbs and clasped hold of the knob. The door gaped open, widening with what sounded like an agonal gasp. I slipped through, sweeping the door shut behind me. As with my initial entrance, the corridor's burnt-orange carpet led me into the interior.

Shadows leaped and receded as I entered the kitchen. Beyond, over in the inviting convolution that was the home's interior, my flashlight compelled dark projections to spring open and fall flat, as though I were walking through a pop-up book, its black pages guided by an incoherent hand.

Again: despite my multiform, self-inflicted failures, my innate impulse remained—visual dissection, interpretation. I didn't need to ask too many questions about these occupants, as the answer to most people's stories lay exposed before us. And so it took some self-control to maintain pace and stay on task.

I arrived at the vestibule adjacent the staircase. The spindles of the banister cast jail-cell shadows, dozens of bars creating a sort of gyroscope.

Fingers, wrapped around one of the spindles, withdrew as I approached; a figure, barely discernible through the vertical shadow-bars of the banister, scuttle-scaled the stairs. "Wait!" I called, gripping the banister and racing up the risers. Panting, cresting the landing, I angled the beam down the empty hallway and, trembling, clicked off the light and tried to calm myself, waiting for my breathing to steady. The house was silent.

In the study, generous moonlight streamed through the wide windows, the powder-blue glow through the muntins creating tiles of light on the carpet. The tree limb outside cut a crooked silhouette.

The once-lush palm next to the window was dead. Anemic leaves were scattered beneath it, skirt-like. Verdant two days before, it stood now like some enormous, withery neuron, its dehydrated dendrites bare and vulnerable. I was conscious of the undercurrent-thrum of my pulse.

Despite my awareness of the wrongness of this whole thing—the palpability that I'd stumbled into something I didn't comprehend—I simply couldn't expedite the imperative: grab the stationery off the desk and get the hell out of the house. I sidestepped the ottoman on my way to the desk. Though I recognized that using the flashlight here near the second-story window to be reckless—though no more negligent than the intrusions I'd already committed—I could not resist but clicking on the light, using my palm to deaden the beam.

The paper was where I'd left it; but my midsection crimped when the dull light touched the surface. The opening line was there—*My name is Tara Keltz*—but added to it was either a childlike or deranged endeavor in ink: black latticework of lines and scribbles, an ivy of invective, the majority forming obscenities in precious cursive. The looping script of *BITCHROT* has lingered with me.

Pursing my lips and clicking off the flashlight, I slid the paper from the desk, folded it, and slipped it in the pocket of my pullover. I made it merely two steps and halted, my entire awareness arrested by the tall, pale woman standing in the doorway.

Though her ghastly pallor had a contrasting effect with the darkness, the shafts of moonlight illuminated her—flesh seeming to radiate a gray-blue hue. She stared at me, her lips bent in a tired simper. Her dark hair hung over her shoulders in ratty panels; she was wearing that forsaken sundress which exposed her shoulders, arms, shins. I recognized it now, a garment I'd given to Goodwill more than a decade before. I could describe her to exhaustion, but—notwithstanding the rot-mottled condition of her flesh—the enterprise would be as mundane as imparting what I'd seen in the mirror each day most of my adult life.

I managed a step toward her and she responded by doing precisely the same (albeit with a hitching stagger); and as I summoned another step, so too did she, until we were standing only several feet from each other within the window-tiled moonlight.

We lined up symmetrically, in height, in the set of our bodies. I ignored the requisite repulsion in encountering such a cadaverous essence. Her purple lips still bore a small smile, and I realized that I (though I had no idea why) was smiling too. A distant recollection asserted itself.

A long time ago, there was a television station that played old movies in the middle of the night. This was before Ben, and the nighttime, used for studying mostly—used for getting a "leg up" on my academic competition—suited me. Flipping stations, procrastinating between chapters, I'd stumbled on a Marx Brothers movie—that mirror scene in one of those black-and-whites where Groucho and one of his brothers amusingly duplicate each other's movements.

Tentatively, I lifted my hand, palm out, in a gesture that was intended to reflect a greeting, or a sort of truce.

Her forearm—as violent as a suddenly unencumbered coil—sprang out, her frigid palm and long fingers cinched my throat.

A wash of acidic sobriety sluiced through me, my momentary reverence and awe disappearing in a synaptic shiver. Her expression had not changed; her cracked lips still bore that simper, her eyes were wide, unblinking—the moonlight reflecting slender sickles in her slick sclera.

Shock-stalled, I was now aware I couldn't breathe. This reshaped the inflectional state of my perception and brought an objective immediacy to what I saw before me: to what I see happening to Tara Keltz.

Tara's eyelids flutter as shadows in the room double and coalesce, overlay and assimilate. As the decayed figure tightens its grip around her throat, Tara staggers, catching herself on the corner of the ottoman. The moonlight is fading; she feels the weight of the flashlight in her hand. Tara lashes out, punches wildly. One of the clenched strikes connects with the woman's chin. Tara summons another, more accurate blow, this one eliciting an audible crunch as it lands squarely against her nose. The icy smile is still there. Even with the rills of blood freely streaming over her philtrum, the smile is still there.

The woman's grip compresses with renewed intent, and Tara understands that she is supposed to close her own eyes now. Through her narrowing awareness, she thinks of Ben and Brooke. She thinks of pain—how it is inflicted in forms of casual cruelty, in manifest forms of wonton physicality. She thinks of the excuses she's made to conceal her own pain in an effort to present herself as superior. Tara Keltz thinks of the aberration of exposed bone—that obscene tibia-tipi draped with the gore of torn flesh.

My leg, thinks Tara. *My shin.*

Tara claws at the last threads of consciousness, shifts her weight, and spears her foot out and down in a vicious kick, her sneaker connecting with the other woman's lower leg.

The howl does not ascend in volume as much as it is just instantly *here*—funneling out from the rotting woman's midsection, echoing down the hall. The house's atmosphere itself, agonized.

The decay-corrupted woman releases her hand and collapses; and though Tara feels like doing the same, she braces herself against the bookcase, wincing as much from the pain as from the sustained keening. The other woman is on the floor, cradling her lower leg, the moonlight catching the glint of blood-streaked bone.

Then Tara is limp-hauling herself across the room; the pale woman removes one hand from her strangely angled shin and takes a swipe at Tara; but she sidesteps it on the way to the hallway.

Tara does not look back as she clicks on the flashlight. The shadows of the staircase risers rush toward her, as though she's running down the wrong way on a malignant escalator. Then she's in the kitchen, and when she sweeps the light over the space she falters. None of the shadows move here, but hang static behind each corner, each shape, disorienting Tara for a moment. The sound of something thumping its way in pursuit gets her going again.

Tara turns the corner to the side-hall corridor. Licking her lips, she runs the length, yanks open the door, and propels herself through the threshold. The screaming ceases and she draws in achy gulps of night-cool air. With the large shrub netting itself around her, the light playing the limbs creates a veiny, incessantly reweaving animation.

Tara leans against the side of the house, begins to slide away but is roughly seized. She whips the flashlight beam down to her ankle, to the shackle of a decay-riddled hand protruding from between the door and the jamb; but the grip is weak, fever-meek. Breath coming in ragged gasps, Tara slowly reaches down and tenderly unfastens those stiff, gray fingers from her ankle. She does not glance within as she gently hinges the cold forearm back through the black breach and solemnly pulls the door closed.

*

That was a long time ago.

And the greatest challenge in those following days was con-cealing the clamp-shaped bruises on the sides of my neck, and I made adroit choices to my clothing, accessories, and with how I styled my hair until the purple striations faded.

We are happy. If you ask Ben, I suppose he would say we were always happy; but I have invested energy and understand-ing to validate that statement.

In the ensuing months following my final entry into the Motley House, I approached my discipline of interior design with a renewed sensibility. I revamped not only the website but the mission of my niche business venture. I run nearly every day, in the early mornings, just as I used to.

I've made friends, colleagues, and progress. Brooke is taller now.

The Motley House goes through its phases. Often it is se-rene, and voicing chit-chat observations proves unnecessary. Still, months go by when a FOR SALE sign shows up in the front yard before abruptly disappearing. I watch the daily postal carriers place items in a mailbox that is apparently empty upon each visit. The lawn is neat and fastidiously maintained.

I've never again seen the dark-blue Mercedes in the driveway, though from time to time I snag a glimpse of a shriveled old man creep through the opened gate to the back yard.

More than anything, I try not to dwell on it.

But as I run by on my morning route, I consider the façade, doing my best to avoid making undue eye contact with the second-story window. There are moments, though, when I fail. Sometimes there is nothing. Yet, frequently, behind the reflective murk there is a figure. On those occasions, she is distinct behind the pane, her grave-gray pallor contrasting with the gloom behind her. Tightening my focus, I see a smaller, darker shape that is her mouth, and I've remembered the residue of that howl, the rugose scales of the ouroboros that is her lips.

Still, she has the meaningful view from her second-story aspect.

It's a perspective they can both accept.

Haunt Me Still

Masses of black-clad mourners were still filing in off Wichita Street, converging and passing through the wrought-iron-fenced entrance to the cemetery, their meandering courses leaving assorted furrows in the snow. I waited in my car, slouching in the driver's seat, trying to gauge the most inconspicuous moment to assimilate and enter.

Or even to enter at all.

Here and there, I recognized a few of the Crooke's Chapel residents. I'd spotted several news vans further down the street; and predictably, considering the circumstances, there was a pronounced police presence from Colfax and outlying counties. The slate-streaked sky above the bevy of bereavers was suitably subdued for the occasion.

For a nondescript community, Crooke's Chapel sprawls—from newly constructed attempts to elicit a sense of contemporariness (apparently in its need to achieve exurb status), staggering its range toward neglected manufacturing tracts cordoned off by meshes of rusty fences—the town takes its time to unfurl over an insulative landscape of underwhelming farmland.

I checked my phone for the time, eventually twisting the key from the ignition, and slipped out into the biting breeze, giving a quick scan up and down the vehicle-lined street before cuffing up the collar of my coat. Snow had been drifting in diaphanous drapes all morning, covering the tops of the waist-high headstones as I fell in line with the other visitors.

The burial site was up on a small rise just outside the skeletal scrim of a tree-covered hill. A green tent had been erected there, obviously for accommodating immediate family and for those who felt compelled to get within close range and visually graze the casket. The tent's crowded, shadow-capped interior stirred with figures.

As I walked, I caught hushed segments of conversation—disassembled snippets that essentially echoed the local news-static: *Deputy Mark Lacefield, thirty-three years old, involved in high-speed pursuit that resulted in fatal crash . . . chase began just after 2 A.M. on Sunday, when Deputy Lacefield joined pursuit of a stolen vehicle that had fled a traffic stop . . . Officer Lacefield was approaching the intersection of Pilcrow and Route 700 West when the suspect lost control, veering into a ditch . . . ice . . . as officers approached, a confrontation ensued . . . gunshots . . . Lacefield struck in the torso and head at close range . . . rushed to Colfax Memorial with grave injuries . . . the suspect of the alleged stolen vehicle was apprehended after a brief footchase . . . Mark Lacefield had joined the Crooke's Chapel Sheriff's Department six years earlier, accumulating numerous awards including rookie of the year . . .*

Variations of this account had been circulating over the course of the previous week.

I was no longer a Crooke's Chapel resident. And yes: I'd watched the news because I wanted to stay abreast of the small-town tragedy. Some of it, I admit, was due to morbid curiosity. Still, my principal interest was the possibility that I might catch sight of a televised image of Nina.

Three days following the locally publicized incident, another televised conference was held at the hospital announcing that deputy Lacefield would not recover from his injuries, and that his family had implemented the process of organ donation.

Organ donation, I thought as I skulked up the slope to Mark's grave. I'd never broken a single bone in my body, let alone incur an injury that would put me in the scope of such a profuse sacrifice.

My dress shoes glistened against the snow as I bypassed the headstones, once again calculating if I had the courage to go through with this. I eyed several baroque mausoleums, hunched like miniature stone-carved mansions in the distance.

Superstitious.

Though it had never brought me any discernible luck, I sensed I'd be better off with some sort of totem. Around my neck I wore a simple silver chain, from which dangled a slender brass key, which felt cold and heavy on my chest.

The burial site was up on the hill, backstaged by a dense copse of trees.

Because of the line of people that was currently passing the tent, it was clear that the burial ceremony itself would commence soon, and visitors were now simply offering condolences. *Couldn't they have taken care of that at the showing?* I thought, not sure why I was irritated with this part of the ritual. The more people the better, I supposed: they would only insulate my need to be indistinct.

Hands deep in my pockets, I stood in line—that crawl . . . the way people were moving in crooked channels on their way up the hill reminded me of corded coils of ivy recoiling to their centrally rooted source. As opposed to my fellow attendees, I was less concerned with the corpse in the coffin than with the woman standing next to it.

The coffin: its glossy exterior nearly completely hidden by bouquets and other offerings. Even as I approached, I had trouble making eye contact with that . . . container, as though its inanimate occupant were diffusing sentinel awareness. I could hold my eyeline no better than the last time I'd seen Mark Lacefield alive—when he'd been shouting at me from across a crowded dining room—more than a decade before. And even when I looked away, I could not dispel the mental conjure of that lid quietly quaking, of a gray hand slipping out from under the lid, black-cuticled fingers squirming, allowing a little illumination into the velvet-lined interior . . . gray light catching the pale flash of flesh . . . livid rims of his empty eye sockets . . .

Mercifully, Nina did happen to look over, her large eyes growing wider when she saw me. She whispered something to her mother, who was already clearly distracted by the bombardment of well-wishers. Nina emerged from the overhanging shadow of the tent and stepped into the gray light. She'd changed very little. Soft features, elflike. "My god, Spencer," she said, and unexpectedly breached what I'd assumed to be a barrier of tact as she strode forward and embraced me. I returned the hug, taking in streamers of her scent. I tried to focus on that, aware that several sets of eyes were on us. Nina pulled back, fingers still clasping my upper arms. "I can't believe you came," she said, her eyes scouring my face.

Nodding, I attempted to sustain eye contact, feeling as though aversion lessened the veracity of her visual appraisal. I had steeled myself for—I don't know what: something else. With Nina engaged with me at this intimate distance, I felt less vulnerable, shielded, lest I renew my role as pariah.

She covered her mouth—mainly, I'd thought, to hide her smile, which may have been inappropriate under the circumstances. "I just can't believe you're here."

I nodded, not smiling, though I wanted to—I wanted to peal laughter at the unanticipated wash of forgiveness I'd felt at that precise moment. Taking in a deep breath, I said, "I don't really know what to say. I know everyone says they're sorry for your loss, but. I don't know." Nina's eyes pinched against the wind. "Mark was such a good guy," I said. "I know he was a wonderful brother."

Nina gave a tight, quavering smile before looking over her shoulder, evidently considering the casket. "He was the best big brother," she said, taking a few prolonged seconds to turn back around. "Thank you for that, Spencer."

And just that quick, I'd reached the end of my devised, contrived script. At any moment up to this point, and not really knowing precisely what I was getting in to, I'd been prepared for an abrupt retreat. But Nina's response had been an ember in that frigid cemetery. I made an unintendedly awkward gesture. "Well, I just wanted to pay respects." I hesitated. "And to say I'm sorry." I inadvertently intoned too much subtext. "Listen, you should get back. You've got a lot of people to see."

Nina again cast a glance over at the tent. "I think Mom has things under control." Mark, I knew, was not married and had never had kids. Aside from his immediate family, there were only a handful of uniformed officers under the shadow of the tent. She tightened the knot of her crossed arms, shaking away a chill. "How have you been?"

"Better than I deserve."

"You still live here in town?"

"No." *This town is an unforgiving, forsaken place.* "I've been up by Gallaudet for a while now." Nina gave a noncommittal bob of her head, making it difficult to know whether she was surprised or not. Didn't matter, really.

I opened my mouth to say something when I noticed a sheriff's deputy approaching from the tent, marching our way, his eyes trained directly on me. His face was instantly familiar, and it only took me another second or two to place it.

Patrick Asher had been in the same class with Mark Lacefield in high school. Best friends. Had run for various class offices together. Had been record-breaking wrestlers. Crooke's Chapel's very own small-town dynamic duo. Sure, Mark and Patrick had been tight in high school. Inseparable; so his presence here made perfect sense. *But goddamn cops together?*

Whereas Mark had been massive and thickly muscled, Patrick had been lanky, sinewy. This updated version of Mark's former right-hand man looked no different—all freckles, knuckles, and muscles, his jaw flexing with a wad of chewing gum. The only thing that had changed about Pat's features was the overbite, which had become more pronounced and imparted the aspect of a know-it-all rodent. And those eyes didn't help: that unnerving, unblinking copgaze. As he closed in, I hastily summoned a cordial chin-jut of acknowledgment along with a weak smile. Neither were returned. The delicate crease along his frown-wrinkled brow distinctly asked, *What the fuck are you doing here?*

He finally dropped the stare, quietly addressing Nina. "Hey,

I think your mom and dad are ready to get started." I glanced past Patrick, over toward the tent, where I saw both the Lacefield matriarch and patriarch, the pair appearing hollow and haggard but speaking to passing mourners with an assertive, composed sort of warmth. It is not for the sake of this story that I admit my envy for that variety of determined decency.

"Sure," she said. "Thanks, Pat."

He gave a curt nod paired with a parting scowl. *You—do not—belong here.*

Nina canted her head and jutted a thumb toward the departing officer. "That was Patrick Asher; he and Mark were on the department together. Do you remember Pat from school?" She appeared to be preparing something further to say when a flutter crossed her features, clearly realizing now. I remained silent, not having to say, *Of course I remember him. He was there with Mark that night at Dillinger's.*

Nina shook her head. "Anyway, I need to get back over to Mom and Dad."

"Yes, of course."

She took in a sharp breath and moved her arms to hug me. I pulled her in. "It really is nice to see you, Spencer."

Not really meaning to blurt it, I whispered, "We should talk sometime."

Nina did not break the embrace, though it took her a moment to respond. "That would be nice."

She pulled away a few degrees. I said, "Maybe coffee."

Though her lower eyelids welled with tears, she surprised me when she smiled. "I'll probably need something stronger after all this." She gave a small swipe at her cheek. "How about Westminster Quarters . . . around six?"

I was familiar with the trendy tavern up on the north side of town. "I'll be there."

She said nothing else as she swiveled and returned to the tent.

Here I recognized another verge, one I could not cross without irreparability, whether good or bad. I felt then an electric twitch of optimism, reminding me that there could be a happy ending in store: that the possibility of healing—for not just me, but perhaps for both of us—existed in this revisit-venture.

I spotted Patrick under the awning, still glaring at me. I blinked, breaking his staredown spell by inadvertently invoking that daydream hex—arousing the impossibility of that casket quaking violently, the bouquets sliding off as that polished lid thudded and began to open . . . then the purple-gray fingers worming out . . . a plank of light widening on the dark interior . . . the gunshot-ruined skull . . . the shadow-scooped sockets that had forfeited their glistening prizes to organ donation . . . What cast condemnation, then, is the mouth: the lip-cracked cavern spilling a croak, *Parasite . . . pariah . . . I hope you're happy, asshole . . .*

I adjusted my coat, wincing against the wind, turning my back on the continued procession, dodging not only the snow-capped headstones but the initiatory sentiments of the minister who'd begun addressing the crowd.

My own transgressions, by many standards, have been minor, and by all accounts, what I'd done to Nina had been sophomorically superficial—as meaningless as an insipid episode of *Dawson's Creek*.

But that's not how ghosts work.

That's not how ghosts are born.

It's not necessarily the degree of our misdeeds, but how we allow the sylphic amalgamation of those infractions to layer our existence. You can bore me with accounts of rural poltergeists tormenting innocent occupants of a home or cold spots in abandoned, turn-of-the-century asylums, but genuine phantoms are *present* this instant, and they chose to be close long ago.

I won't insult your intelligence (whoever you are and whatever that acumen may be) by prattling on with platitudes about ghosts as metaphors, projections of the past, stand-ins for guilt. I will suggest no such thing. Rather, these things produce themselves after a prolonged accumulation of breached and abused liminality. Recording this story is yet another exercise in scratching at the omnipresent layers draped around each of us, and recounting it has been the only thing keeping me from going crazy (but not the kind of crazy you likely want me to be).

I will not admit I love, or *loved,* Nina Lacefield because I am, I admit, afraid of the ramifications. I won't add a simple, thoughtless incantation to the complications I've already caused; though I will say that I've tried, in my pathetic way, to defy these phantoms. They are, I'll say again, everywhere. Right behind both of us this instant. Compelled by confrontation, we claw toward each other, scratching our way through this corporeal cocoon.

As many games as we play to rationalize our behavior, as many stratagems as we mentally assemble to make sense of our impulses, there are just as many phantom fingers at work beneath the surface, orchestrating course-corrective adjustments.

*

It was a weeknight, so Westminster Quarters was pretty dead. The cold didn't help. Between drinks I checked the time on my phone—six forty-five. About a half-hour before, it occurred to me that, having the afternoon to contemplate my presence at the funeral, Nina had begun dwelling on our brief relationship more than a decade before and therefore second-guessed meeting me. I couldn't have blamed her, really. She may have even assumed I was the same person. In many ways I was. Though, in other ways, it was as if the passing of time had whittled away the distractive exterior of this town's small-minded mentalities. What we were left with, I hoped she recognized, was that we could have happily rejected the limitations of this place.

Nina arrived eventually, spotting me as she slid by a cluster of beer-hoisting young men. Her nose and cheeks were pink. I pushed my chair away awkwardly and stood to greet her.

Slipping out of her heavy coat she said, "I'm so sorry I'm

late. Of course, I don't have your number or I would have called."

"Oh, please, there's no need." I took her coat and placed it over the back of one of the chairs.

She shook her head. "Mom and Dad . . ." She began with a note of exasperation, and then, almost murmuring to herself, said, "I think if Mark had been married . . . had a wife, or maybe kids . . . then—" She broke off with a frazzled gesture and a bout of rapid blinking.

We both sat. Her chest rose and fell with an exhale of what I took as relief. She smiled then, her eyes catching sharp barbs of light from the tea candle on the table. "I could really use a drink," she said, sliding a menu closer toward her.

I smiled, tried to laugh—tricky navigating this sensitive scape. "Well, there's certainly a lot to choose from."

Between beverages being ordered and arriving, it was small talk about the bar itself, about how much the town had tried to change itself. After an inceptive sip of our drinks, she settled her disarmingly confrontational energy on me. "It really is amazing to see you," she said. "I mean, to look at you, you haven't really . . . *changed* much," she said, lifting her glass. "It's like having cocktails with Dorian Gray or something."

Hanging my head, I chuckled at that, wishing at that moment that I could remember the details of that old story from school. "About ten years or so."

"Twelve years, if you want to be precise about it," said Nina.

"Yeah. You're right."

"Our ten-year was two years ago this past September. I kept thinking you might show up."

I shook ice in my tumbler and shook my head. "Not really my scene."

"But showing up to a funeral that half the town's attending *is* your scene?"

Adjusting the slant of my shoulders, I said, "That's different," hoping my tone would temporarily fill in the gaps.

Nina—after several thoughtful nods—mercifully released me. "Fair enough." The softer sounds of the bar afforded a transitive moment. Eventually she said, "So tell me something about your life." She scooted her chair closer, resting her forearms on the tabletop. "Tell me something about what you do for a living."

I shifted the bev napkin with my fingertips. "Meadow Bend Realty."

"Real estate, huh?" She appeared simultaneously unsurprised and unimpressed. "I can see that being a good fit for you." She lifted her drink, ice clinking. "What's it like being an agent?"

I leaned in. "Well, I'm not actually an agent, I'm a broker's assistant. I do structural stuff—follow-up phone calls, meeting arrangements." Suddenly I felt self-conscious about the description. I stammered, "But not like a secretary. When agents close I get a portion of the commission."

Nina nodded. "So if you know how the system works, why not just go ahead and get your broker's license?"

I smirked. "I don't know how to answer that." In that intervening period between early and late evening, the pub was still rather mellow, and I recall wishing some nearby chaos would cover my uneasiness. "Never been very good at negotiations. I sort of like working behind the scenes. And besides, I'm comfortable. I have a place on the south side of Gallaudet, used what I know about 'the system' to buy a relative's house after she passed away." Mouth moving faster than my mind, I inwardly winced at the mention of death, at the possible perception of venality; but Nina simply listened. Trying to bring some end-note dignity to the mediocre ambition of obtaining a broker's license, I said, "I don't know . . . maybe someday," placing a full stop on it with a pull from my glass. "So, Miss Lacefield," I said, stealing a glance at her left hand. Owing partly to lonely desperation, but partly to preparation, in all my online rummaging (with social media still in its infancy) I could not definitively ascertain her marital status. She seemed to maintain a staunch barrier of privacy. A reasonable portion of me applauded her. If I were a cynosure of decency, I'm sure people would be trying to track me down too. "Sorry—is it still Lacefield?"

But her expression did not waver. "Yes, it is." She batted her eyes, looked over my head for a moment as though she were attempting to frame something. "But it wasn't for a brief period." I twitched my brow and tilted my head as an encouragement to continue. "I was married for less than a year . . . but"—she did something with her palms, a sort of repulsed push—"that's a whole separate story. But yes: to answer your question, it's still—well, I guess, again—Lacefield."

I wanted to hear more, but not at the risk of overt invasion, and in trying to maintain some normal sort of rhythm I unsubtly said, "Kids?"

Nina responded almost immediately, as though expectant; and the ease in her demeanor—whether girded by practice of otherwise—salvaged our conversation. "No." She listed her head slightly. "We tried. Came close, but . . ." Nina gracefully repositioned her back against the chair, as though resetting, wagering what to say. She looked straight at me as a summative, painful punctuation. "We came close."

I was already nodding, wanting her to stop—for her sake.

We sipped our drinks simultaneously, our exhalations as appropriate as pages turning.

Dipping my head, I took a transitive leap. "All right, Miss Lacefield. What has become your calling?"

"Social work, over in Rath County."

"Social worker," I pondered aloud. "A perfect fit."

She smirked. "Oh, yeah. Why?"

Of all her characteristics at which I marveled, I could not readily summon one that did not sound as though I had been obsessing about her mildly in the long-term since our young-adult breakup, and almost feverishly since seeing her on television. *Because you're the closest thing to decency I've ever known . . . because, for you, helping people is as easy as respiration. Because people are healed in your proximity.*

Saccharine sentiments. Laughably banal.

I shrugged, desperately attempting to maintain the conversation's effortlessness. "I guess because I can see you showing young people how to find their way." I took an unsteady, melodramatic leap. "You're good at helping the helpless."

Nina batted her eyes down to her glass before lifting it and taking a sip. "That's very kind of you to think so." A moment passed as though she were assembling something complicated. Then she blurted a small laugh, maybe to dust away whatever had been accumulating on the tip of her lips. "Sometimes I think I could use just as much help as the kids." Speculating there was a thread of light-heartedness in that, I laughed too, hoping it alleviated the weight of the unspoken. "Besides," she continued, "we haven't seen each other in a dozen years. How do you know I'm not a totally different creature?"

Whatever sense of objectivity I had in high school had gone into atrophy in the interceding years, so I certainly would not have been able to describe it then; but I will say that Nina Lacefield had a truer sense of self than any of our adolescent contemporaries. People—particularly guys I went to school with—chalked this up to Nina having an ingrained puritanical bend. It had nothing to do with the clerical whimsy of religion. (As far as I knew, Nina had never attended any sort of ritualized Sunday morning service, which made the body-burial of her brother only slightly more intriguing.) No: Nina Lacefield's most attractive feature was that she was untouchably, uncannily aware of her *self*, resulting in a duality that seemed to baffle people: on one hand, she was an enchanting cliché (and I've elucidated as much to this point); on the other hand, socially speaking, she was nearly unapproachable—a profile reserved for your more affluent Pollyannas.

Language in general, like Nina herself, was out of my league in high school; but the most appropriate description is that her energy was *numinous*.

That intrinsic brilliance was still there, and whatever changes had taken place in the past twelve years, including the revealed details that she'd endured a short-lived marriage—along with, what: a miscarriage? the loss of a child?—they did not alter my estimation of her.

"I don't know," I casually gestured at the space between us. "This seems pretty easy."

She nodded, drank. Westminster Quarters slowly filled with people. We talked. I listened, but did so dissectively, extracting pieces that would help me assemble the puzzle, discarding more meaningless slivers.

But to keep this up took some vigilance, because while Nina spoke of the present, I slouched back into the past.

*

The Foundry was a large, brick-and-steel facility nestled deep in the backroad woods. It had been in disuse (so we'd been told) since the late '70s, and the elaborate barbed-wire fence boxing in the property spoke of a monied parent company that would per-haps someday discover a plan to make the site more useful. Until then, though—for most teenagers around Crooke's Chapel—the Foundry was generally the surrounding region of woods, snaking sideroads, and secluded coves of graveled turnarounds and recessed deadends. It was simply a province for township kids to get high or get laid on a Friday or Saturday night.

Aside from local lore, I was not overtly familiar with the Foundry. Nothing in my life accommodated such familiarity: I was neither popular nor unpopular, I was associated with neither extremity or in-between of the social spectrum, which is some-times worse where identity is concerned—a kind of communal stagnation.

Antithetically, Nina Lacefield was someone who had all the qualities of an upper-social-caste system but never chose to ex-ploit it. I wish I could come up with a clever way of describing someone who is at once plain and radiant—a sort of unassuming presence that harbors our best qualities and suffers most of our flaws. She was, more than anything, unusually normal.

The digressive anecdote I'll sidestep is actually meeting Nina Lacefield, which is boring and borders on artlessly bland. There might be some substance to it, but recounting it has not assisted my current state. Just understand that in three large leaps I went from saying hello to this genuinely pretty girl in the hall at school, to dating exclusively (gaining some attention and maybe social respect in the process), to convincing her—after an accumulation of fun though altogether ordinary dates—to accompany me to the Foundry one Friday night in the fall of 1991.

Among my more gormless male counterparts, the prevailing narrative (I can still hear those locker-room murmurs, see their smirk-curled lips, crooked teeth) that Nina was a virgin—that when it came to dating; seeking to drop the curtain on the deed, she was a dead-end. *Don't waste your time,* was the common encouragement. Other, more odious though laconic theories was that she was simply an uppity pricktease. Yet for some of my more seasoned classmates of more prominent popularity, there was a more nuanced theory: it wasn't Nina, it was her brother, Mark.

Mark Lacefield was a hero at our school, excelling in both football and baseball, breaking records with ease. I acknowledge that it's a lazy description, but it's painfully apropos: he was our—and *your*—All-American Guy. If Mark had bullying tendencies, then he did a hell of a job hiding them. His reputation was one of wholesomeness. Virtue. That's also not to say that it wasn't past him to get a little rough. Aside from playing on the field, Mark Lacefield had never outright kicked someone's ass; but, I realize now, he had a bearing about him—a way he moved through the halls, his entourage in tow (Patrick Asher not far away)—that lent a sense that he was reluctantly playing a character that flirted with invincibility. It would have been a gift to have Mark acknowledge your existence. So, of course, the tacit, incessant threat of Mark Lacefield protecting his little sister informed the force field radiating off Nina.

That didn't stop me from trying. I'd met Nina right before

homecoming, just when the air was beginning to brisk, the scenery around Crooke's Chapel easing into the burnt-orange bromides of autumn.

Our dates had been easy. More fun than I'd ever had with a girl. And I think it's because I did everything backwards. I realized from the beginning that I had nothing to lose, and was constantly aware of the looming threat from her older brother; but instead of pursuing her like the other girls with whom I'd had interesting though ultimately forgettable encounters—essentially the reciprocally quick, mindless lays—I approached our outings with no preconceived notions of how the course was supposed to be charted.

It did, though—owing to its reputation—take a few months to convince her to venture out to the Foundry. In our time together, and when it came to actual physical interaction, Nina was alarmingly competent in her self-imposed tentativeness.

When I recognized my actual care for her—a base compunction that I often ignored—I realized that what I was attempting was beyond simple teenage conquest. Nina—not the high-school version of her, but an estimated projection of what, *who,* she would someday be—was an endeavor beyond my reach. It was as though she were biding her time to get out of high school and flourish beyond the borders of the Chapel. I felt that by pairing this newfound care for her with a physical initiation—the marriage of the emotionally intricate and the corporeally simplistic— I could bridge . . . I don't know. I didn't know then, precisely, and I don't know now. Something else. Something bucolically transcendent? An emotional eclipse? A convergence of consciousness: confirmation that I held some sort of value, perhaps. That I was worth the risk. I was also just a fucking kid.

In the months that we'd been dating, we'd not really discussed sex, though I was confident a convergence was possible.

We'd already had the conversation about the Foundry itself.

"How many times have you been out here?" she'd asked.

I immediately gave a tight shake of my head. "Never."

We'd found a spot just off one of the old service roads, noticing only a few cars hiding out.

Time passed. The windows fogged, something was said implying how far we'd go. I wanted her to know that I wasn't expecting anything, though I was cautiously prepared. Nina made it clear, in whispered exhalations, that, for this night—for all the previous nights, really—we had taken things far enough. Nina seemed confidently content to linger on the threshold.

The brutal light that bloomed from behind my vehicle was not the requisite red-and-blue flashers of a common patrol car, but rather a single spotlight that filled the interior with astringent illumination, triggering both of us to scramble to regain some semblance of decency, Nina tugging down her bra and shirt, me fumbling with my buckle.

For the sole reason that we could quickly compose ourselves, I was grateful that our amorous session was confined to the front seat.

I'd noticed no headlights approaching. The light had simply appeared.

Nina's silence and rapid breathing filled our space. I rolled down the window to let some cool air drift in. I wanted to comfort her, to let her know that cops chased kids away from the Foundry all the time. A rite of passage. I recall repeating different combinations of low-key assurances—cautious that my tone should not unduly frighten her. Conversely, and perhaps detrimentally, I also understood that this implied a seasoned insouciance: that I'd done this before. I was a little concerned that this revelation would result in an unsavory estimation of me.

Forecasting what would certainly ensue, I arched my hip and squirmed for my wallet, immediately self-conscious of the condom I'd stowed there. (Now was really no time to remind Nina of my ambitions.)

My window already rolled down, I heard a door open and close, gravel began crunching as heavy footfalls neared. In my side mirror I saw the wide, ambling silhouette nearing the car.

There came the squelch of leather from a shifting belt as a flashlight clicked on, the beam steadily swiping over the side of my face. "Evening," said the man. An unsettling, wheezy breathing compelled response.

"Hello."

"License and registration, if you'd be so kind." As I handed over the ID, the flashlight ticked toward my lap, to my wallet. "The whole thing, son." It took me a few seconds to realize he was talking about the entire wallet, and he seized on my hesitation to snatch it out of my hand. I squinted over, catching the gold gleam of a badge. The light flicked to my face. "Registration," he said. As I reached over, I thought I heard a small click as though something were being unfastened near the holster. "Nice and slow, son."

There were several heartbeats where I caught Nina's eye. Her lips were tight, and, with the brilliant spotlight streaming into the car, I could see a throbbing cord on her throat shifting, her pulse racing.

Having given the wallet and registration a cursory inspection, the officer said, "So, aside from the obvious, what brings you out here onto private property this evening?"

Again, I was cautious to tread lightly—for my own reputation as well as Nina's peace of mind. "Just came out here to talk."

The flashlight shifted past me, over to Nina. "Is that true, young lady?"

She angled her face a degree, wincing against the glow. Her voice was faint, but she nodded. "Yes, sir." The light lingered on her face for aa prolonged period.

I cleared my throat, snatching another glimpse of the man: wide, mustached, belly straining the evenness of his button-up shirt. I gambled: "Honest, sir. We're not trying to cause trouble. Mind if we just head out of here?"

The beam was back on me now, so near I had to look away. "You just sit tight." And then he was moving back to his car.

I looked over at Nina. How to dispel her fear without emphasizing that I'd been out to the Foundry dozens of times with a dozen different girls? While I'd heard unfortunate stories of folks getting caught (quite literally with their pants down), I'd never been accosted by a cop, or anyone else for that matter, out here. The smirk I displayed was ironic enough to break the tension. "Don't sweat it, okay? He's probably just going to scare us a bit, give us a warning. We'll be out of here in no time."

She considered me, her expression implying that I, apparently clueless, had missed some fundamental fact. With the quivering undercurrent of a sob, Nina said, "My parents will crucify me if they find out I've been out here." And there was something hanging on that last word, something about the aspect of her wide eyes, a sort of night-prey terror, that I instantly finished shaping her sentiment: *My parents will crucify me if they find out I've been out here . . .* with you.

We were quiet then, which seemed for the best. At some point, the cop was on his way back to my side of the car. Prepared for a severe, verbal warning—at worst a full-fledged ticket for trespassing—the cop said, "Why don't you go ahead and step out of the vehicle, young man."

It took me a second to get my legs going. I slid out of the car, shutting the door behind me. He was taller than I'd estimated. I noted that he had my wallet and registration dangling by his side while he stared straight at me.

In my dual attempt to appear unshakably brave in front of Nina and reasonably contrite before the cop, I had not evaluated the scene—how *off* it all was. The cop had never turned on his reds-and-blues, which really wasn't that big of a deal, but for the fact that his cruiser, though marked, looked like a dinged-up piece of shit. The officer, too, was in a sort of degenerated condition. My heart drummed at the notion that this was a rent-a-cop, some sort of private security guard paid to patrol the property; but my pulse ticked up when a thought occurred to me: that this was no cop at all.

"Mind telling me what you're doing out here?"

Because the answer was evident, I would have blurted a laugh if not for my unease. The goal now was not my reputation, but getting Nina out of here without causing a scene. Or worse. I exhaled and waved my hands, an impatient gesture meant to convey surrender. "Just bored, I guess. Nothing to do in town. Came out here to talk."

The officer, whose name I never caught, was turning my wallet in one hand; the other had the flashlight aimed at my chest, just under my chin. It was hard to discern features. He was wearing a pair of thick-lensed glasses, the shifting light distorting his eyes to black beads. And something about the way the light touched his complexion, his waxy jowls, gave the fleshy impression of something translucent, putrid. The word (not unlike the many lessons I've learned in the interim) would come later, but his entire essence was oleaginous. I had the sense that, if touched, that flesh would be as pliant as swamprot.

He took a step closer to me, his voice low, his breath sour and stagnant. "Folks only come out to the Foundry at night for a few things . . . and all them eventually discover trouble," he said.

I gave a conciliatory dip of my head. "Yes. I understand."

He said nothing, his breath coming in congested waves. He licked his lips then—a thick, uncoiling sound—and as he edged in closer, a subterranean body odor trailed off of him. He gestured with his flashlight past me, toward the interior of the car. Toward Nina. "You want me to show you two some trouble?"

I don't know how long I stood there, silent, too numb even to twitch, though I did finally flinch when he stabbed the light directly into my face. I shook my head. "No," I said, not proud of my timid tone.

His face came to life with a sneer. Uneven teeth, fringed with what looked like necrotic traces of decay, clasped together as he hissed, *"What did you say, son?"*

"No, sir," I stammered, almost shouting—it came across as more of a plea than an outright affirmation. I let out a level breath. "I just want to get my friend home."

The phlegmy sound of the cruiser's engine rattled in the background for a while. Finally he shoved the registration and wallet against my chest, his long nails chipped and filthy. I took my belongings, glaring at him with what little defiance I had to spare.

I sank in behind the wheel. And then the root-like claw of his fingers clamped on my shoulder. The officer said, "You get this pretty little gal home safe, you hear?"

I made a noise of assent as I started the engine and notched the car into drive.

The rearview mirror fringed the reflection as we drove away. Behind us, the cruiser's headlamps backlit the man's bulky, unflinching frame. And even now I am certain what I saw in those last few seconds: the lights growing brilliant in their dented sockets, swelling to a glow of impending, blackout rupture. As we drew away, the overlapping tree trunks, fluidly crisscrossing one another, created a crooked fence, each dark bar pulling jagged slivers of the man from his homogeneous silhouette until the headlights were extinguished and he simply became part of the night.

*

For the first few miles after leaving the Foundry, we were silent; but then Nina began to unwind with warmth, her tone tinged with a sort of exhilaration. We arrived in her driveway, my headlights falling on the immaculate edifice of the Lacefield family's imposing home. I kept forgetting what it was, precisely, her father did for a living. Not for the first time, I calculated that—even if my own parents were back together, having figured out some way to salvage the reciprocally irreparable damage that was their marriage—their combined income could not nearly afford such a suburban structure. Nina and I were still in the dating stage in which I simply lingered within the entryway when I picked her up and dropped her off: a tacit sign of good faith on my part, though my presence was certainly still under suspicion. I did not blame the family for that.

Thinking Nina would want the happy-ending safety of her home, I'd fully prepared for her to offer a polite good night before fleeing, seeking security within the confines of her diminutive mansion.

"Will you walk me up?" said Nina.

Distantly relieved that she'd adhered to this part of our date-night routine, I stepped out of the car and tailed her around to the front door.

After unlocking the door, she said, "Wait here a sec," before pushing through to the shadowed interior. A few moments passed, her slender arm emerged, extended toward me; she whispered, "Come in for a minute."

I stepped through the threshold, into their foyer (where I'd done most of my waiting over the past few months). I was almost more nervous than I had been during the filthy cop's impromptu interrogation.

Nina led me past the antechamber of their entryway to where the hall gave into the living room. It was dark, save for the television displaying something on low volume. It took me a moment to register the figure sitting in the recliner.

Mark Lacefield initially appeared to be sleeping, but as his sister and I entered the room, he tilted his head in our direction. Nina whispered, "Mom and Dad asleep?"

Mark gave a drowsy response, but then grew more alert as he looked past Nina, registering the guy behind her.

With a routine cadence, Nina said, "Mark, this is Spencer—Spencer, this is my brother, Mark."

I raised a hand. "Hey, man."

Now clearly awake but equally uninterested, he said flatly, "What's up?"

Then to Mark, Nina said, "I'll be right back." She canted her head and began walking away, indicating that I should follow her further into the house. With clueless reluctance, I smiled and shrugged at Mark, who remained impassive, clearly trying to put something together.

Nina led the way through a corridor that led to the main staircase, and we were somehow climbing those stairs to the second floor. She steered us down the hall, veering around a corner before slipping her hand into the dark rectangle of a room—her room, of course.

She pressed her hand on my chest there at that boundary. Reflecting on this strange procedure, it was as if Nina, whether aware of it or not, were defying some sort of rule—yes, certainly a literal one, but possibly something tacit, superstitious—penetrating deeper within the house under her parents' noses. It was not then, but only now as I write, that I think about that passé axiom offered by some of the more notably baroque Victorian writers: that Stoker's unnatural night creatures had yet to obey some of nature's laws . . . that they could not enter a household unless one living there has offered invitation.

The appearance of Nina's room was not unusual. Like everything in the Lacefield's home, it was tidy and cleverly decorated. Lots of photos, several swimming and soccer trophies, along with awards from uncountable competitions.

Nina went to a desk drawer and began rooting through clutter while, like a nervy lookout, I appraised the dark hallway, anticipating her father to emerge from one of the many closed doors along the passage, surely marking a second authoritative confrontation for me that evening.

She returned, clasping something in her hand. Without warning, she strode forward and gave me a lingering kiss. In her way, she was penetrating some sort of custom—a self-imposed violation, subjectively innocent as it may have been for her, but a violation nonetheless.

She pulled away then and hissed. "Let's go . . . I'll walk you out."

Mark was still in the recliner as we passed back through the living room, the television radiating its pale coruscation. He was evidently more alert now, his posture rigid.

"Be back in a sec," she said. Mark did not respond. Rather,

he merely looked at me.

In a low voice that I hoped was imbued with reverence, faux or otherwise, I said, "Nice to finally meet you."

Again Mark said nothing, but simply fixed me with a bland stare. That glare, along with the scene at Dillinger's about seven months later, is still very sharp in my mind. And, as I passed, averting that unblinking, partially uninterested gaze, the transmitted sentiment was clear: *Don't even think about fucking around with my sister . . . don't even think about fucking around with* me.

And then we were back at our accustomed spot on the front porch. I tried to shake off the sour sensation not only of her brother's staredown, his overall demeanor, but of the humiliation that the cop had attempted to inflict less than an hour earlier.

"Thanks for being so cool back there," she said, understanding that she meant the Foundry and not her older brother. She gave a small laugh—the first true sign of relief she'd exhibited since the close-call with the cop. "I just about wet my pants when I saw those flashing lights."

It took me a second. *Flashing lights?* Never once did the cop turn on any sort of colored lights. My grin wavered a bit, wondering what she meant. "You saw red and blue lights?"

Nina giggled. "Well, yeah . . . you were practically bathed in them while that guy was talking to you." I convulsed a troubled look, but Nina cut me off by raising a palm, her hand cupping a tiny silver key. My frown wore away as I looked down at the key then to Nina. "My grandpa was a sheriff, and he used to have this great big old house over on the other side of town—and he had this storage office upstairs filled with equipment and supplies. I don't remember it ever being locked, but it was off limits to everybody, especially the grandkids. Sometimes he'd chaperone Mark to let him have a look around. But everything in there was sort of important and dangerous—just a bunch of cop stuff, really.

"Anyway, once when we were visiting, having a cookout or something, and everyone was outside, I snuck into his office. I poked around a bit, just sort of tiptoeing and touching. And then the door swung shut. I ran to check it and the handle wouldn't twist. I thought it might be Mark playing a joke, but as I started struggling with the handle, I could tell no one was coming. I started looking around the room—just panicking. Over on top of a filing cabinet, I found this ashtray full of keys—most of them looked like nothing special; but I tried to find one that looked old, like the house. I grabbed one, frantic that I was running out of time. Grandpa was sweet, but he could also be a cranky asshole." She lowered her voice for a sidebar. "That's why I was relieved the cop back at the Foundry was so nice to us."

Again, and aside from letting us off the hook, I was trying to recall an instance when kindness had entered the picture. *What had she seen that I hadn't?*

"So I took this old key—a key that has no business in a regular door—and tried it on the lock." She shook her head, giving a wry sigh as she twirled the brass device in her slender fingers. "I know it sounds totally crazy, but the key went right in. I twisted the knob and the door popped open. The hallway and the house as quiet, everyone was still outside. I started calming down, jiggling the key out of the keyhole. I was about to put it back in the ashtray but, curious, tried it on the door one last time. No matter what, it wouldn't fit—and why would it? I mean, it was like a handcuff key, for God's sake. Anyway, I sort of dismissed it but thought it was . . . I don't know—not magic, but special at the same time, you know?"

I was still thinking about the "cop" back at the Foundry. An imposter, some sort of pervert, I decided. I smiled, nodded. "Yeah, I do."

"Yeah. Well. So I kept it, like a good luck charm." Nina offered it to me. "I thought since we got lucky tonight . . ." She laughed at inverted meaning and started fresh. "I thought since we shared such a narrow escape together tonight . . . that you could keep it."

Absent of kneeling, it was like a reverse proposal. I grinned, slightly embarrassed—for her adolescent innocence, for my own adolescent intentions with her. "That's very sweet," I said, accepting the key.

Almost in a rush, as though mind-reading my mental sentiment, Nina added in a whisper, "And I know you really want us to"—she blinked, tilting her head, shifting the weight on her legs—"to move *faster*." I was already wagging my head in sheepish protest, though I knew it was futile to appear chivalrous at this point. Nina reached out and touched my forearm. "No, I understand. But I just need more time. It's just that—" She bit her lower lip and made an awkward gesture. What her expression conveyed was what she could not bring herself to say: *I've never done that before.* "Do you know what I mean?"

Back then, I did not. Sex, being a natural impulse, seemed like the natural, progressive step. This would not be the first time that I would have confused the primitive with the redemptive. More than ever, I was certain this had something to do with an ingrained flaw within me rather than a dignified decision within her. "I understand, I totally understand."

Uneasy about the possibility of her father or big brother eyeing us through one of the dark windows, I gave a cautious, conscientious kiss. The remaining goodbye was brief. Then I was back in the car, my headlights coning a tunnel as I exited the Lacefield's moneyed subdivision.

It would only come into articulated clarity years later (not long before dabbling with the messy missive that you are now reading), but that night I'd stumbled onto some form of inadvertent alchemy: something about the complex trinity of physical animus, the "charge" of intangible emotion, and the implementation of Nina's keepsake key hypostatizing (for lack of a better description) a malignant, supernatural intrusion.

As main roads gave to backroads—backroads giving to the country (I happened to be living with my dad at this time)—a low wave of regret began lapping over me. Why was it so fucking important anyway—this "conquest"? Validation, I concluded. Validation that I could integrate myself with the likes of the Lacefields. Needling me was the thought of that goddamn condom spilling out—my presumptuous agenda spilling out into plain view.

The cop-imposter came back to mind. My anger and bewilderment—some sort of unsteady, perhaps even psychotic, individual out there skulking around the Foundry robbing kids (or worse)—mellowed when I thought of Nina's innocent offering: the slender, antique key in my front pocket. *Robbing kids,* I thought. *Cash*. Then another thought. He'd taken my *entire* wallet. *Why?* I bucked up, digging for the leather billfold in my back pocket. The light cast by my dashboard diffused the interior with a dim, weak-tea-tinted glow. Still driving, one hand on the wheel, my free hand pried open the main fold, my fingertips touching the contents.

I flung the wallet on the passenger seat and hit the brakes, controlling a swerve and coming to a stop along a sideroad ditch. I flicked on the light, and its anemic burn made the discovery even more inconceivable—as subsequently inconceivable that the Thing we'd encountered was both fixed to the place and had sought me out.

I slowly picked up the wallet, and there within the black-mouthed pocket was not my meager money and the sealed condom, but rather the withered, alabaster length of a common, molted snakeskin.

*

Background noise from the trendy pub came careening back. I'd only been distracted for a few seconds, my mental descent into the past had stuttered by in an instant. These scenes I've described had supplied enough confusion and regret, they'd become distilled in my mind.

I encouraged Nina to continue telling me about the life she'd created for herself, and she did a deft job of seamlessly slipping and shifting from one subject to another, making my task of playing soothing interlocutor more functional. We talked about her job mostly, anecdotes about the children and families she assisted. I tried to pivot the conversation away from myself as much as possible.

At some point, we meandered onto the topic of her brief marriage. Though curious, I did not pursue the details. We continued ordering drinks. She said, "For years, everything in town has seemed the same, and I've kind of enjoyed that. But now everything just seems . . . distorted, you know." I did. As an interloper from some many miles away, I did understand. I nodded. "What's it like up in Gallaudet?" she said. "What will you end up doing there?"

I honestly did not know how to answer. Before I could polish a more impressive response, I smiled. "Move somewhere else and start over."

Nina nodded and tilted her head up, scouring the ceiling, her smooth cheekbone catching the glow from an overhead lamp. "God, if only we could." Of course, in invoking "we" she was speaking generally, not referring to the two of *us*. She'd evidently drifted inwardly for a moment, slipping as I'd done a short time before. After a moment she smiled and shivered. "It's a nice idea," she said, finishing off her drink. (I was, at that moment, growing intrigued—concerned, of course, with the fluidity with which she was consuming her drinks.) Without looking at me, she said, "Just to go somewhere . . . just to be anonymous." The bar had filled up a bit since we'd began our chat, and now the agreeable music and noise filled the silent space between us. Nina was gently twisting the rim of her tumbler left and right.

After a time I said, "Do you live near your parents?"

She blinked a few times. "My place is on the other side of town. But I've been staying with them off-and-on for the last few days. Told them I'd stay as long as they needed me. And work's been really decent about time off." She trailed away.

Our server returned. I declined another drink, but Nina ordered one more.

Filtering any semblance of sanctimony, I said, "You sure you're okay to drive?"

She flitted her hand. "I'm fine. Really. Just feel like"—she did something with her fingers, as if she were tracing the lines of an invisible Möbius strip, gesturing at the bar patrons, at me— "I'm in a time warp or something." She may have heard, as I did, the implication in her statement. She made a sympathetic pout. "Not you, really." I supplied a sheepish laugh, hoping she understood I took no offense. "It's just this place . . ." She trailed off with a sigh, shifting her gaze again, looking through the window along the front of the building. It was dark now. The snow had returned and shone in falling flecks against the mild light of sconces along the sidewalk.

Something came back to me then. A few years ago I was routinely driving my mother to the city for rounds of chemo treatment, accompanying myself with a pulpy paperback or '80s- era horror novel while I waited. As I listened to Nina here at the bar, a line from Charles L. Grant asserted itself: *Life in places like this is static, and patient, waiting for the right person to feed it, and to let it grow.*

I adjusted my position and cleared my throat. I didn't know a way to agree with her (which I did) about the town's ostensible staleness while also not elaborating with derogatory comments of my own. I said, "I think I'm going to get one—can I order you a coffee?" She shook her head, returned her gaze to the window. Only just then did it occur to me that she'd had something to drink before she'd arrived. I didn't know another way of saying it: "I'm going to follow you home," almost adding, *The last thing you need to deal with is getting a DUI . . . or worse.* But I omitted that last part for obvious reasons.

Nina did not protest. Rather, she looked down into her empty glass for a stretch before looking directly at me. Her tone was low, sobering and startling. "I'd like you to come in for a few minutes when we get there." To clarify, she added: "To finish talking." She blinked and let out a small, nerve-shaky breath. "Please."

I recall being unable to speak. Instead I nodded, motioned for the server, paid the bill.

*

I realize I'm asking you to invest this puerile chronicle from my youth with something more than its inchoate insignificance. This was my life, and I don't know how to dismiss it.

But I know now that this is really about the unintentional assembly of action that essentially converges to elicit an emanation—but an emanation of what? I don't know. I still do not have a name for It, Them, these supernatural species. Ghosts and Phantoms are heavy-handed terms. Spirit is too vague and somehow bypasses the sense of malevolence that these beings possess. I think I like "Nolongers" the best. These boundary-breakers are not aimless apparitions. They are, quite simply, dead things—dead things with sentience, anchored to *place*.

I am not making a profound statement when I propose that these Nolongers are layered on our own reality. What I am saying is that they come into sharper focus during moments when profound pivot points emerge—during times when the fulcrum of choice is most pronounced: when the branches diverge toward our most redemptive decisions or depraved impulses. I am still unsure whether these phantoms, which linger on the liminal fringes, exist to help or hinder. I understand now that they exist somewhere near the junction of these critical confluences. Particular activity reactivates their awareness. And they are everywhere.

You've come this far, and you've endured some backstory that, to the metropolitan eye, is certainly a bucolic bore. So I won't flirt with losing your attention now. I really don't know another way to put it: what happened at the Foundry that night with Nina, and the thing I found in my wallet as I was driving home, was real, and reconciling it all has been a trying task these past years.

Though the encounter was incidental, relaying the digression is necessary to the momentum of this story. The Foundry still exists. Some of the outbuildings have been torn down, but—where the visitor (read: trespasser) can glimpse through the ivy-and-weed-threaded security fences—the main facility still stands in its decrepit, stone glory.

I will begin this short segment with a name: Brandy. I don't believe that most high-school-aged kids (back when I went to school, at least) have the sophistication to adhere to long-term, malignant strategies when it comes to hurting people. They're impatient and they're sloppy. I do believe, however, in their tremendous capability for casual cruelty. And that includes cruelty of the tacit variety—the flagrant abortion of culpability.

So let me start with the simplest of scenarios for a kid of that age: I was at work—work being my typical after-school shift at Waterman's Hardware on the town's main drag. The job, as usual and by tedious design, required me to stock shelves, wander and tidy the aisles, and make small talk with the locals who drifted in looking for implements for their residential projects.

One day in early February, I noted the presence of Brandy Vansickle. I'd been distantly acquainted with her since our elementary days. By high school, Brandy (vis-à-vis small-town standards) had carved out an illicit reputation for herself. I'd had scant interaction with her growing up, and I could piece together her indecent hobbies by the stories other guys shared. Back then, I wouldn't have been able to compose the description, but now the only classification I can succinctly associate with her is viciously disobedient. Not that that denomination is necessarily a bad thing; it's just that Brandy Vansickle had evidently never given a fuck about anything: rules, morals. She attended school, sure, but I think that was more to maintain her bucket in the well, as it were.

It was a cold weekday afternoon after school, which sometimes brought in folks trying to kill some time. Initially I merely noted that she and a girlfriend had come into the store, meandering a giggling route from aisle to aisle.

At some point she noticed me surreptitiously snatching glances (though I'd caught her doing the same), and I did my best to recover from my obvious ogling by moving on to another stocking project. Now truly trying to ignore them, I could hear them a few aisles over, whispering, sloppily rummaging through products that I'd have to clean up and reorganize after they left.

And then Brandy was walking down the aisle toward me.

As if this meeting had been prearranged, Brandy quite simply said, "Hey, Spencer."

I was cradling a box of door hinges under my forearm, almost blurting the store's stock-rehearsed greeting. "Hey," I smiled, trying to scoop up some semblance of social tact. "What's happening?" I noted that her friend continued drifting farther away among the nearby aisles, leaving the two of us essentially alone.

Brandy wavered, picking something up off the shelf and examining it for a second before replacing it. "Oh, you know. Usual shit."

I didn't really know, though was desperate to act as if I did know what "usual shit" Brandy Vansickle was getting into.

Fingers touching things on the shelf, she teetered toward me. I could smell a sheet of perfume unfurling toward me. Most of the time, if my peers arrived in the hardware store after school, they were loitering contemplatively over by the plumbing section, attempting to cobble together a homemade bong from PVC or crude pipe from the brass fittings; so I was used to helping stoners piece together their projects. "You need help finding something?"

She shrugged. "I don't know. Maybe. You guys carry railroad spikes?"

I twitched a frown. "Um, well, something close, but I don't think actual spikes." Trying to be more at ease than I actually was, I said, "What are you using them for?"

She looked at me directly, grinned. "None of your business."

Smirking, I said, "Fair enough," and continued removing stock from a box.

Done with me, I thought she might simply pirouette and track down her friend. Instead, she leaned an elbow against the shelf and canted her head. "You go out with that girl, right—what's her name?" After a moment she snapped her fingers—her *aha* expression a little overdone . . . as though it had just dawned on her. "Nina—Nina Lacefield. Mark's little sister."

Still stacking boxes of nails, I was already nodding. "Yeah."

"That's right. I've seen you guys together." Brandy gave a quick claw at her hair. "Yeah. Mark's all right. We hung out a few times last year." Noting Mark's social standing back when he was in school, and being aware with Brandy's dossier, I thought their union unlikely, or at least exaggerated. Still. She said, "But he sort of got, I don't know . . . too fucking fussy, you know?"

In the six months that I'd been dating his sister, Mark and I had interacted perhaps six or seven times, and he had probably spared a dozen words on me. I couldn't restrain a laugh. "For sure." And though I possessed no loyalty to him, I still felt a pang of unease at discussing him like some object of gossip. Even so, Brandy had my blood up. "It's like trying to talk to a minister from the Salem witch trials."

Brandy's eyes brightened as she gave what I thought was a genuine laugh. "Oh my God . . . that's perfect! I swear that guy thinks he knows just about every goddamn thing. And"—she lowered her voice to a conspirator's measure and slunk closer to me—"do you think he's . . . I don't know . . . a little *off?*"

Though ignorant of what she might be referring to, I sensed I was moving into territory that was, as Brandy had put it a minute earlier, none of my business. "I don't know. He just seems . . . like he has better things to do most of the time."

Brandy did a single, slow up-down nod, evidently reappraising our conversation. "So, how's all that working out?"

"What?"

"You and Nina. How's that going?"

I cleared my throat, aborting most of my integrity for the sake of appearance. "Fine. Really cool."

She sighed. "That's nice. But if she's anything like her brother, dates must be a drag."

I crimped the corner of my mouth. "No. It's not like that."

"You guys serious?"

"Sure. Yeah."

"Is she fun?"

Following our run-in with the Nolonger-thing mimicking a cop, Nina and I had never returned to the Foundry, though I had continued to pursue what I felt was a normal rhythm of physical interaction. And though Nina was a good sport, she—patient, principled—made it clear that the perimeter of sex continued to be prohibited. What fueled my frustration was that, when asked if it had something to do with me, her responses would grow murky. It was personal, or spiritual. Or both. But yes, my interpretation was that she was suspicious of me, which I simultaneously accepted and resented. Laughing, though unable to make much eye contact, I said, "Yeah, of course, she's a lot of fun."

Closing in tighter, what I'd initially mistook for chintzy perfume was now clearly the light aroma of alcohol coming off of her. She lowered her voice to an off-the-record level: "Bet you she's not as fun as me."

Just as I was about to get my mouth moving in an attempt to bring clarity into what, precisely, Brandy was doing here, she reached out and gave one stroke against my forearm. "Take me out this weekend."

The physical contact shivered a sliver of my pathetic compunction. I said, "I really can't." I continued stocking. "Wouldn't be cool if Nina found out."

She was fast: "Yeah, but you guys aren't even really going *out*, going out . . . right?"

Translation: *Nina's maintaining her well-known vestal reputation.* This is the part where decency would otherwise prevail—where Brandy's blatant disregard for boundaries would be repelled by principle. I exhaled a laugh. "Seriously, Brandy. Why are you even talking to me?"

"Because you and me've known each other since we were little kids." Partly true, I thought. *More like I've known of you*. We'd barely exchanged a glance in high school, let alone words. "It's our senior year, Spence. You're a good guy. I watch how you treat her. Don't you want to commemorate how far we've come together?" Again, I was certain that I was missing some crucial piece to this puzzling proposal. And again, silence—the near absence of integrity—set the course. Brandy took over. "Listen, no one would have to know. It'd just be you and me." I was shaking my head. Brandy, with tomboy flare, shoved my shoulder with aggressive affection. "Come on . . . live a little." In my hesitation she added, "If you haven't outgrown her by now, I swear to God you will."

I looked at Brandy—really *looked* at her: all that gorgeous damage that had been distilled in those tawny features. There was a radiance in her small-town lawlessness.

Yes: this all has something to do with regional isolation and our culture's paltry standards for what we consider rites of passage. Yet I would find out later it had more to do with Mark Lacefield.

Four nights later, I drove Brandy out to the Foundry.

*

With me tailing her, Nina, slow and steady, made it to her house on the far side of town.

She lived in an older neighborhood (with which I was only vaguely familiar from my youth), mostly houses built in the wake of the G.I. Bill. Quiet. Lots of trees whose limbs provided shard-crooked shadows along the car-lined sidewalks.

I parked down the street, uneasy about occupying the driveway. And again, as I'd done so many years before, I was accepting an invitation into Nina Lacefield's house. *The night creature*.

The predatory impulses I'd been attempting to defend grew

diffuse in Nina's house. Underpinned by a low-level shame, there were moments when I almost became confused as to why I was here. She turned on a few lamps, providing honey-colored light to the dim living room, and made a cursory comment about the place being a mess (which it was not). Without another word, Nina wandered into the kitchen and poured two glasses of wine.

Her house was comfortable. Files and other work materials were piled neatly on the floor at the foot of her couch. I spotted a stack of old yearbooks on the kitchen table, thinking that she'd had to pull together some photos of Mark or something. The mouth of her fireplace was charred from a recent fire. A few frames on the walls here and there, almost all depicting her brother and her parents. Most of the doors along the hallway corridor were closed.

Nina returned, handed me a glass. "Want to sit?"

*

Dillinger's.

Maybe this was Brandy's existential nailbomb—her variety of a senior prank wherein she gets to make her mark by literally fucking things up for the vox populi. I don't know. What I know is that I'd assisted with that instrument's assembly, and that the sex—though incredible in its self-seeking, almost ferocious disorder—wasn't worth it.

This was a few months later. It would waste time to explain that, after our surreptitious encounters (two, to be precise) at the Foundry, Brandy Vansickle returned to the mode of simply disregarding me at school. Not that it was that big of an adjustment. But in truth, I did feel as though something had been altered—not necessarily between us; but that having crossed a pronounced physical boundary with her resulted in some sort of transference. While thinking that Brandy had simply added me to some illicit checklist, I was grateful for the tradeoff of deviant discretion.

As I'd grown accustomed to it, a Friday in April found most of us meeting at Dillinger's. Dillinger's was this barnish, family-friendly restaurant-cum-tavern where kids loitered in the parking lot and made pleasant asses of themselves as they overran the booths inside—imagine a more rough-around-the-edges Arnold's from *Happy Days*. The woodsy decrepitude of the old restaurant perhaps added to the attraction for most of the kids, whose parents may have come here when *they* were in school, but whose social standing now compelled them to dine at more fashionable outlets. Anyway, going to Dillinger's and occupying space for a few hours had become a tradition for commoners and social elites alike.

With Nina assisting my integration into the Crooke's Chapel establishment, I'd taken to joining this popular throng of upper-echelon peers. Not that it was a comfortable transition, but I harbored the Saturday-night dalliances with Brandy a few months before (absent of intervention by phantom cops or No-longer entities, by the way), so that my socialization was a kind of penance for my impropriety. Looking at it another way, I did have some investment in the effort. I wanted to know how this *worked*: talking to people, having friends—communicating without a sense of agenda. Interactive normality, in other words.

We pulled into the crowded parking lot at dusk, waving to a few acquaintances as we passed. Nina and I milled around for a while before heading inside; but as we walked, she stopped me, pulled me aside. "Hey," she said—mischief tinging her expression. "I want to tell you something."

I gave a cursory glance to my left and right. "Sure."

She too cast a quick look to either side before leaning toward me. "I can't stand most of these people either." I smirked, opened my mouth to object, but she kept going. "And," she inhaled, exhaled, "I know you want things to be different with us. I'm just nervous—for a lot of reasons. Some reasons I think you'd understand, some I think would be impossible to share." She waited. "But I think I know who you are. I think I know what we are, at least." I thought about the things I'd done—not necessarily to her but affecting her all the same.

See, I now think of secrets as these tangible *things,* which never deteriorate, residing behind closed doors in a stretching hallway, the corridor darkening by degrees toward a shadowed terminus; and each time I passed by the events in my mind, I had the notion that one of the doors would crack open just a bit—small at first, almost imperceptible. But then, noticeable within, came the strip of pale skin. A dull eye emerging in the slowly opening aperture. The wrinkles of a snarl. Until such time as my own secrets became part of Nina's consciousness, I reckoned I'd not done anything *to* her—sort of like Schrödinger's cat, with those rooms along my mental hallway standing in for that customary black box.

She tangled her hands up by her sternum, her voice dropping. "I don't know what's going to happen after graduation, but I want things to change before—well, things *change.*" Nina jutted her chin, indicating the rowdy restaurant. "I know what it's like to be surrounded by—I don't know—sameness or conformity, or whatever. I've seen all that with my mom and dad and I don't want that, trust me. They can't stand each other. Changing things is going to make leaving this place possible, you know?" I suppose I did, but my expression must have reflected the opposite. "All I'm saying is that I want us to stay together after you leave. I know that the two of us being together . . . *that* way . . . is important to you."

We'd been over this topic several times before. "Nina, seriously, you don't have to explain anything. And I'm not saying that"—I pulled a face—"*that's* important either."

A car pulled in and the headlights momentarily lit one side of Nina's face white, and as it passed the glowing taillights touched the opposite side of her face with a haze of red. She said, "I want to." I looked at her, my jaw unclasped slightly. She smiled, shivered a bit. "Really, I do. I'm ready." Nina laughed. "And even if I'm not, I want it to be with you, Spence."

As difficult as it may be to bear: whether you recall them or not, variations of these conversations do indeed take place—or at least they took place between two kids in the spring of 1992. All I could muster was a few contemplative-quaky *okays*. And whether you acknowledge it or not, you'll not change my thinking on this: there is something elusively tectonic about vocalized consent. It is like a numeric segment of an equation—a variable in a system of constants, ultimately altering the expression. I could feel something fundamental altered between us. Just an idea, maybe, but still: a change. She extended her hand to clasp my forearm.

Nina had got me thinking about not just the next layer of our little relationship, but the shadow-ribbed curtains that divided the murky months ahead. The *years* ahead. And then I was the one shivering on our way inside Dillinger's. I felt an unaccustomed happiness. I felt like trash.

*

I am unprepared by Nina's aggressive directness in the bedroom. Her urgent fervency.

Moments before, sitting on the couch, sipping the wine she'd poured, nothing had been said to segue the shift. During a tranquil moment in the conversation, she simply settles her drink on the coffee table and we move toward each other with nearly rehearsed fluidity. We stumble down the hall, bumping against closed doors, plucking at pieces of clothing. The mingling of both alcoholic and erotic intoxication tinges her bedroom with a dark blue lambency. A forceful move from Nina sends us crashing to the bed.

I'm almost reluctant at the absence of her self-consciousness—the modesty I'd expected replaced by a jarring self-possession. The Nina I'd ventured to reunite with has disappeared—the girl existing in my marred, mental nostalgia has been substituted by a very adult and very human woman.

We fall into an almost precognitive rhythm. She asks me to do things that nearly obliterate my decades-long reverence of her. Still, we settle into a serene collaboration, crossing over physical perimeter after physical perimeter.

*

To the worldly, cosmopolitan eye, I had certainly committed a juvenile injustice to a decent, unassuming individual, resulting in ignominy and forfeiting ties to that segment of our small society. In later years, though, I had to ask myself: at what point does transgression transition to transubstantiation?

Like most Friday nights, the inside of Dillinger's was packed. On the far side of the restaurant, a group of previous-years' graduates—now college kids—congregated, with Mark Lacefield holding court with some of his usual retinue; Patrick Asher, of course, in among them, the inner circle ringed by a band of local, princely sycophants.

Nina clung to me (tighter than usual) as we moved deeper into the restaurant. Typically, with her brother in the vicinity, Nina would maintain a conservative distance. Not tonight. After a time, though, she indicated that she had to break away. A knot of her friends were waving, trying to get her attention. She leaned up on tiptoes and whispered, "I'll be right back, okay?"

I smiled, nodded, wanting to say something clever and considerate, lacking the supernatural awareness that the next time I'd be near to her—within reaching distance of her—would be twelve years later at her brother's funeral.

I shuffled around for a while, making small talk with the local lords. Blink-scanning the room, from face to face, I halted. Stared.

Brandy. She was carving through the crowd like a grinning shark, several of her cosmetically garish friends trailing in her wake. For a number of reasons I was startled to see her here. Typically, the too-clean-cut Dillinger's was dismissed by hoods and edgier cliques. But I had the sense, from the determination with which she moved, that she'd been here for a while, and that she was now making her penultimate exit.

As she made her way toward the door, it appeared, by the set of her shoulders and head, that she was trying to make eye contact with someone over on the far side of the restaurant. *Did this really have something to do with Mark?* She passed through the door and, with a twirl of bleached hair, spun, shooting me a look. For that instant her features were jarringly predatory, satiated.

As I had done—and would sadly continue to do, to real people—I had made rather assumptive judgments about Brandy's affective capability, creating a stock-like stereotype of her. While I watched her leave, a slim stalactite of ice elongated along my spine. I had underestimated Brandy and whatever story she had to tell, meanwhile overestimating my own scheming intelligence. Later I would discover my suspicions confirmed: that Brandy and her band had been there a while before Nina and I had arrived, inelegantly publicizing (among other anecdotes) our cheap collaboration. All that was required was for me to arrive: a hastily arranged staging of *habeas corpus*. To this day—after all this self-indulgent, self-loathing rumination—I still do not know precisely *who* it was that Brandy had been aiming to injure. Maybe all three of us.

Truth had a mitotic effect—clearly catalyzed by the unusual appearance of Miss Vansickle followed by the arrival of Nina and me. Slowly, clusters of people began to gravitate toward Nina. I was still on the opposite side of the restaurant, attempting to fend off an errant question or two from some classmates.

Eventually the regurgitated gossip reached critical mass. Nina—her friends cocooning her in a hissing spool—made her way over to Mark and his friends. It was all eyes and noise from where I stood, my heart trotting under my ribcage—my pulse a whir. The noise was slowly smothered as Nina leveled her eyes with mine, her expression as sufficient as a verbalized question: *Is it true? Is what that girl said true?* I recall swallowing sharply and hesitating, opening my mouth and beginning to move forward. But the complicated clique near Mark's booth shifted to inhibit momentum, and I found myself struggling to politely push my way toward her.

The group began exiting through the side door, Nina and her girls ushering her away with a wave of disgusted glances. Mark and his sneering friends were to pull up the rear, as it were.

From across the room, Mark Lacefield's gaze was like an awl boring into me, and as the small mass lumbered toward the exit Mark punctuated the incident with prominence. *"Hey,"* he shouted from a few tables away, his rich voice silencing the disparate snippets of lingering conversation throughout the restaurant. His upper lip curled and he thrust out his forearm, bringing a jolly, fuck-you finger up between us. *"I hope you're happy, asshole."* He shoved through the door—the sound was like a wood-slatted trapdoor crashing open on a hangman's gallows. And then they were gone. They were all gone.

Giving the group a few minutes to split, I didn't hesitate in making my way to the exit. People enjoy theater, particularly in small towns, yet I left Dillinger's unmolested. People tended to give a wide berth to the variety of reprehensible radiation I'd acquired.

*

It's not until you begin the exercise of reflective exorcism that the ritual pursuit of sex seems pitifully shallow.

Nina and I lay on our backs, shoulder to shoulder, panting. I stared at the ceiling, trying to rein in some sense of sobriety, more drunk by what'd just physically transpired than what I'd consumed hours earlier at the bar. Nina slipped her hand into mine and gave it a squeeze. "Hey," she said, "you alive over there?"

I smiled. *How could I not be?* "Yeah . . . beyond perfect."

The sheets beneath the discarded comforter were light-colored, and she snagged a tangle of them and pulled them across her chest as she came up on one elbow, lazily crooking an

arm and resting the side of her head on a hand. Between bobbing eyelids, she was appraising me. Finally she murmured, "It's
been so long."

I couldn't tell if she was referring to us simply being together
or the act of making love. Something in her delivery made me
think she was confessing the latter. I thought about what she'd
said at the bar, about her short-lived marriage and subsequent
divorce. I considered the experiences that had matured her: experiences—both good and bad—that involved other people. For
my own part, I squalidly cobbled together a list of my own experiences, each tacitly understood to negate commitment.

I nodded, hoping it was enough. I thought—*hoped*—then
that, perhaps, this was not just an instance of me taking advantage of Nina's emotional state, but rather just a case of two
lonely people taking advantage of a tragedy to anesthetize their
own emptiness; though I was aware, even more so now in front
of the keyboard, that there were varying degrees and gravities of
emptiness. I can write to convince a would-be reader until my
fingers fracture, but my intentions that day of the funeral were
simply to reconnect with Nina and in doing so happen upon
some antidote that might heal what had happened. What had
transpired in the past few hours, though, had been a surprise
even to me.

Her hand moved to my chest, to where the brass key was
threaded through a chain. Her fingers traced the small device, a
teenage token that had been a sentimental link between us. "My
God," she whispered. "I'd forgotten all about this." Time sluiced
by. I stared at the meager light on the ceiling, the webwork of
shadows in the corners. Outside, somewhere in her neighborhood, a dog gave up a volley of barks. I don't remember what I
was going to say, but as I opened my mouth, Nina, in a breathy
exhale, said, "I love you."

She may as well have shouted, its effect was that apprehend-
ing. I froze, eyes wide on her. I took in a breath and managed
precisely one *I* before swallowing hard and licking my lips, try-

ing to discern what my tactical starting point might be. I'd been so preoccupied by the physical that I'd entirely neglected the transformative effect of the conceptually abstract. I smiled, letting out a sharp breath.

Not to respond reciprocally would be irretrievably damaging. To make an articulated pledge bore an equal amount of uncertainty. And that's what it was about: it didn't have to do with rote behavior or proper preconceptions or platitudes about timing. Nina Lacefield had always had a certainty about *things* that she did not so much embrace as she embodied. Whether or not she believed it to be true—whether it was just post-coital banter—there was a guilelessness in what she'd said that made me shudder. What would the consequence be of responding in kind—of simply saying, *I love you too?* It would at least provide a temporary assent; and, as I was wont to do, I would cope with the ramifications later. I had flashbulb bursts of what crossing that verbal barrier meant. *What was next?* I tried to push past the present. Following our conversation at the bar, I knew nearly nothing about the circumstances of her brief marriage and its ensuring dissolution. Her friends, her family—ah, well, her family certainly knew me, and the challenge of repairing that union would come at the cost of encountering her mother and father, adding a tangible dread to my mediation. I'd not forgotten what I'd done to their daughter's innocent sense of trust, and, I was certain, neither had they.

Yes: I'd intentionally come to the cemetery to encounter the Nina from my memory, to discern if there was anything that might connect us—if there was any decency that might exist within me, and which might be recognized by her. And yes: Nina Lacefield was, in many ways, the *old* Nina; and it was startlingly true when it came to her credulity.

The disparate narratives of my conscience began stammering. *I wish we could go back . . . I wish we weren't so different . . . I wish I hadn't hurt you . . . I wish I knew how to be* good. I'd come back to the same calculation: I cared for her deeply. If not for the reality of facing the object of my endeavor, I would have even ventured to tell myself that, yes, I loved her. But then, for the first time, I wondered about the difference between love and obsession. Had I really loved her all those years? Or had I loved the narrative that, for a slim segment of my life, someone like *her* loved someone like *me*? If she was genuinely confessing her feelings to a person like me, had she done it under similar circumstances?

Like a hidden, previously unnoticed pulse, I sensed a type of danger in not only offering that type of casual oath in the wake of our encounter, but in impulsively responding for the sole sake of appeasement. And though it felt like someone else speaking, I smiled and said, "I wish I knew what to say."

Nina, angled up on her elbow, still had her head propped against her hand. She was very still. But then she shifted a bit, the sheets making a *shush* sound. Her tone altered, though delicately. "I really mean it, Spencer."

I reached out and placed my fingers on her shoulder. "How can you know something like that?"

As if she were considering it, her head sagged, her hair dragging across the pillow. Finally she looked at me. "Why did you come to the funeral today?"

I blinked. "To see you."

She made an impatient noise. "Yeah, I know. But, like, *why* did you drive all the way down here?"

I knew she saw it, and I could see it too. The responses (and maybe there was really only one) that I could submit, that would even hold a glimmer of gallantry, were few, and my words were as good as applying my own black blindfold before an impassive firing squad. I said, "I wanted to say I was sorry."

She pulled away from me slightly. "For what?"

For causing damage. Blinking, I said, "For everything."

"For Mark?"

"For everything."

After a stretch of silence, Nina snorted softly. "So the confession—this whole day—was for *you*?" I'd honestly not thought of it that way. As a manifest confession—but yes: I suppose there was an element in me that was curious to know if I could traipse into hallowed ground—into the Crooke's Chapel lion's den—reveal myself, speak, and escape unscathed. Nina now gratuitously pulled away, preparing to slip from the bed. "I can't believe I said that."

I drew up to an elbow. "Nina—I know how I feel about you. Please don't—"

She tensed up, her neck and shoulders going rigid. "How *do* you feel about me, Spencer? Is it so hard to let go of whatever has a hold of you?" In the dark, her eyes were silver corkscrews. "You can't even say it, can you?"

It was like sitting next to a window on a jostling train, staring at a snapshot tableau ahead of a swiftly approaching tunnel. I caught the glimpse of something amid the landscape, movement in the distance . . . a figure . . . a hand extended in a wave—a serene scene where the proper words would allow an unknown, insecure reality to unfold. I faltered, missed it. The tunnel closed over my mind—my mental compartment went black.

As if reading some unfortunate missive, Nina shook her head. "I thought you were someone else when you showed up today." She spooled a sheet around her torso and was swiftly moving out of the bedroom. "You're still just a coward." In the soft, dim light, she looked like a sheet-clad apparition as she disappeared through the door, padding down the hallway. I clawed out of the bed, tripping over my boots as I heard a door in the hallway slam shut. Struggling, I tugged on my pants and pursued.

Along the corridor of closed doors, a slim, glowing band was present at the foot of what I presumed was a bathroom. I heard water running as I neared. Chalkdust had found its way onto my palate. With my face near the door, I said, "Nina?" Static was the hiss of water rushing in the sink. I cleared my throat. "Nina—can we talk, please?"

When she spoke, she sounded completely composed. "Go away, Spencer."

To my ear, the tone of her voice intimated the possibility of negotiation. Was it too late to salvage any semblance of dignity? I took a step closer to the door, my fingers raised as if to apply a tender touch. "Listen, I—"

Within her scream was a word or string of words, but they were lost under the sound of something striking the other side of the door with such velocity that I flinched and staggered backward, plunging against the closed door opposite the narrow corridor. As I lost my already unsteady footing, the door flung open as I crashed down, dropping onto my ass with an uncoordinated thud. Wincing, twisting up to a crouch, I appraised the room and froze.

The room was dim, shadows and threadbare moonlight creating a space that gave the web-like illusion of all objects being covered in navy-blue crepe. It was a child's bedroom, with a crib in a corner, stuffed animals sentineled here and there. In another corner was an empty rocking chair with a long, light quilt draped over its back. I recalled our conversation back to the bar, to the dead-end anecdote of her not having children. *We came close.* Only then did I understand my lack of depth at comprehending what Nina's life—what *anyone's* life—had been like. I began crawling out of the room when subtle movement interrupted, causing me to stop short.

The rocking chair had not budged, but something beneath the quilt began to move, slowly thrusting itself forward. As though drawing in a silent inhalation, a form was expanding, taking shape—some crooked, broken-limbed thing pushing its disfigured gourd into existence just under the fabric.

Scrambling, I spilled into the hallway, scrambled into the bedroom, grabbed my clothes, and slipped into them the best I could as I withdrew to the living room, to the front door. And then I was in the cold. The night was still and the snow had picked up. I turned and looked at Nina's little house, aware that each retreating step was causing further damage.

Approaching my car, I looked up and down the street. Several vehicles lined the sidewalks on either side. I sank into the driver's seat, still trying to figure out a way to make this work. And maybe it was as simple as saying *the words.*

Eventually, feeling vaguely nauseous, I started the car and initiated the long drive home. I'd considered getting a hotel room somewhere in Crooke's Chapel, but thought better of it.

There is no omniscience in it; I just simply know now that I was too preoccupied to notice the black car uncleave itself from its parking space down the street, keeping its lights off as it followed me down a dead stretch of road.

*

I didn't make it too far away from Nina's neighborhood before the highbeams of a swiftly approaching vehicle pierced the interior of my car. Seconds later came the single, spinning red light.

I wasn't quite out of town proper. Squinting, I eyed a bank branch and its empty, snow-covered lot, opting to steer in as opposed to stopping on the shoulder of the road. I notched the car into park and let my foot off the brake, allowing the engine to idle. Familiar with the routine, I was already stretching out to retrieve my registration and cracking my window a bit, a spill of icy air infiltrating my already frigid car. It took a long time for something to happen. The single red light—one of those portable dashboard varieties—twirled, alternating my interior between shadows and dull crimson. Finally I heard the cruiser's door open and close, heard too the footfalls, saw the slim, ambling silhouette. As I angled my body for a better look, the beam of a flashlight was in my face.

"Keep your goddamn hands where I can see them."

My face had been crimped against the light, but now went slack as the beam fell away.

A genuine right-hand man, this one.

Outside my driver's side door stood deputy Patrick Asher.

*

Patrick opened the passenger door of his black, unmarked cruiser, gallantly indicating that I should take a seat. He slammed the door on me only moments after I'd sat down. The aroma in here was comparable to the sour hide of some hibernating animal. Trash and debris littered the floor. The pungency of alcohol was pronounced. Patrick fell in behind the wheel, not taking his large, avid eyes off of me. "Just couldn't help yourself, could you?" I stared back. "No," he said. "No, guess not. About an hour ago, thought I'd drop by to see if Nina was holding up okay. And what do you know?—whose car do I find parked out front? Ran the plates and I'll be damned if it's not our old friend, Spencer Brimm." He snorted, his ensuing sentences connected by occasional chain-linked slurs. "You know, the minute I saw you at the cemetery yesterday morning I knew you'd try something stupid. Shit . . . nothing changes, does it?" When I didn't answer, he repeated with vicious emphasis. *"Does it?"*

"No," I said; cleared my throat. "Nothing really changes."

After a period of quiet, Patrick, who'd been passing the silent seconds nibbling on his nails, finally chuckled. "Buckle up, champ. You and I," he said, "we're going for a little ride." He drove, the cruiser's headlights slashing across a circuitous route through town, the beams obliging shadows to yawn and contract in a kaleidoscope of Crooke's Chapel's past—an unsettling carousel of my past. Some fragments had changed; others appeared not to have been manipulated by time. Patrick spent the ride conducting occasional monologues for which my responses were useless. Supplementing his disjointed soliloquy was the constant static issuing from the CB; from time to time, a partial voice or unintelligible whine would slip through, though by and large it was a monotonous sibilance, a seething white noise.

As time passed and the course became more coherent, suspicion transitioned to certainty as to my coachman's intended destination.

We eventually ended up on Wichita Avenue; but instead of proceeding directly to the front wrought-iron gate of Crooke's

Chapel Cemetery, Patrick wound around to the rear, steering us onto a narrow tree-lined service entrance on the far side of the property that was cordoned off by a tall chain-link fence. The car jounced over ruts as thin, low-hanging limbs and branches made scratch-screeches against the windows and doors, both of us teetering as we rolled up to a gate. No padlock, just a looped chain. Patrick stopped the car. "Don't budge, pal." I watched him get out, stroll into the headlights, and unloop the chain, tossing the tangled mass into the snow. He shoved open the service gate and was back in the car, killing the beams and opting to run the parking lights as we entered the cemetery.

After a minute or so, the trail snaked onto the main course, which circuited the cemetery proper. Eventually we came to the hill, the snowy ground still pocked from where mourners had trample-trekked to pay their respects the day before. Patrick toggled the gearshift into park, allowing the engine to idle.

I didn't want to ask the obvious question, so I offered a comparable facial expression: *What do you expect me to do now?*

"You and me," said Patrick, "we're going to end this shitty day on a happy note." Then his hand shot out at me. I flinched but saw that, instead of grabbing hold of me, he was fumbling with the glove compartment, the panel's lip popping open. He withdrew a small, nearly empty bottle, amber liquid sloshing, which he uncapped and took a pull from before sloppily offering it to me. I shook my head. "Come on, Spence. You should have a drink . . . a toast to Mark."

"No."

His lopsided grin slipped. The knuckles that were wrapped around the bottle suddenly pressed against my chest. "I could haul your ass to jail."

I waited, both of us locked in on each other. I finally summoned a response. "Not likely. Not in the shape you're in."

Patrick's lower lip immediately bowed thoughtfully. "No. No, maybe not. But man, it'd be a shame if you got tangled up in a nasty incident here in the dead hours."

I thought about that. "I don't think you would."

He made an exasperated noise, his face was creased with true pity. "Shit, man. In a town like *this*? And considering that you just slithered out of Nina's house"—he licked his lips, clearly considering something—"I could get creative."

The mention of Nina amplified the regret that had instantly ruptured in the wake of my hasty retreat from her house. It would take years for me to reconcile how I'd abandoned such a promising opportunity.

The vinyl upholstery yawned as Patrick inched over a bit, his knuckles drumming my sternum with each teeth-clenched word. *"Now have . . . a fucking . . . drink."*

Time ticked by—not much, but I eventually took the bottle, drawing in a placating sip.

Reclaiming the bottle, Patrick grinned, the facial animation pulling his skin tight over his bony, already rodent-sharp features. "Okay," he said, the liquor disappearing within his coat. "Looks like we're all set." The interior light snapped on as he opened his door and stepped out. With a shaky hand I went for the handle and followed suit.

Patrick led us to the main path where the snow had been mauled by mourners. Moonlight made the forest a towering hoard of corpses. I stayed close behind as we stalked up the hill, weaving between headstones, deftly trying to sidestep the plots of resident remains. With the ring of trees creating a sort of netted tarp of shadow on the ground, it was difficult to discern details; but the most obvious thing was that the tent had been dismantled, while the grave itself had been filled in, a skirt of dirt fringing the oblong space that covered Mark's casket.

Slowing then, as we drew up, Patrick cast a quick look over his shoulder, apparently checking on me. *Where the hell would I go, anyway?* On the ragged verge of where the dirt freckled the snow, Patrick stopped. I cautiously crept closer to the site, but remained just off and to the rear of Patrick, who had reverently clasped his hands behind his back.

We stood there for—I don't know how long. A while. Patrick's head was hanging down. I thought he might be praying. I was thinking about Nina.

I shuddered when Patrick said, "Hey, buddy, how you doing?" Assuming he was speaking to Mark, I remained silent. With the low-level winds, things creaked and cracked in the nearby woods. This was the first time I'd ever trespassed in a cemetery; and at night it was easy to imagine the active animals within the insulative band of woods—the creatures that might reside in a morose and otherwise subdued place like this. Again, the image of the Nolonger that had attempted to emerge from the child's-room rocking chair at Nina's house came to me. I could not piece it together then, but now I understand that that was the first moment I suspected that a number of elements were required to summon these things—to see that the Nolongers were all around us, behind these frail barriers.

With his back to me, Patrick said, "Why didn't you tell him goodbye?"

I narrowed my eyes and licked my cold lips. "What?"

"At the burial," he said, his head hanging down as if speaking into his clavicle. "You didn't even walk by the casket. Everyone walked by the casket."

My impulse was to provide something sharp, barbed with verbal thorns. My impulses, though, had caused much damage, and I recognized that I had grown exhausted of hurting people. In so many different degrees and in so many different time periods, my necrotic narcissism had inflicted wanton damage. I sucked in a chilly channel of air before expelling it. "I wanted to see Nina."

A moment passed before Patrick snorted. The soft diffusion of falling snow sounded similar to delicate sizzling. "Couldn't help yourself, could you? Not your style. Not for a guy like you. You had to wait and take advantage of her when she was at her weakest."

I was squinting against the wind. As though tattered pieces of varied vestments were being applied, I began to sense something like veracity weigh over me. My voice was little more than a hiss. "No."

The figure in front of me shook his head slowly. "Mark loved her. Loved her and protected her and wanted her to leave this place. To thrive." A long silence passed. "I loved Mark," he said, and then added, "like a brother . . . I loved him like a brother."

Patrick, though his voice had shifted with sorrow, continued his clumsy eulogy. I'd been staring at the ground, listening to Patrick as much as I was slowly tuning in to the realizations that were revealing themselves to me, many of them recorded in these preceding pages.

My eyes drifted over to where Patrick was standing. To his feet. More than a trick of shadow and light, I now noticed two furrow-strips of dirt just on the grave's perimeter, the miniature mounds terminating near Patrick's feet. I blinked several times, sharpening my focus as best I could to focus now on the other anomaly: a delicate pair of coiled tendrils, the lengths dark against the carpet of snow, fine as grapevines, the lengths leading from the black earth and extending toward Patrick's ankles. "Just admit it," said Patrick, though the voice sounded unnatural, boggy, filmed with phlegm.

At some point I'd removed my hands from my pockets and had clenched them, my fists hanging at my sides. Between my own inward revelations—eclipsing a periphery that had produced underwhelming results—I had reached an intolerant apex for confessions. For tonight, at least. "Admit what?"

As though stung by some low-volt current, Patrick—*not* Patrick, you understand—with a twitchy, unsteady reel, lurched and spun around, revealing one of the worst stages of what Mark Lacefield would become in corporeal form. Mark: in the advanced stages of decomposition, with all its attendant purple-and-black hallmarks; but making the thing, the actual thing, worse was not only the ragged gunshot wound near his temple (which had been worried over by surgeons and dabblers at the morgue alike), but also the mutilation of his empty, eyeless sockets. *Organ donation,* echoed that news conference at the hospital shortly after announcing Deputy Lacefield's passing. Even in death, Mark would still be giving.

When he, the Nolonger, spoke, his voice came as through a tin-can receiver, its taut wire composed of tendon. The black, writhing ring that was Mark Lacefield's lips moved: "Admit that you only showed up because you wanted to seduce an innocent girl . . . that you showed up to fuck your high-school sweetheart."

I staggered backward, just as much from the profane articulation of truth as from the physical visage. I could not say that, from my misguided youth to my wasted adulthood, all this was more complex than I could comprehend—that, despite my behavior, I would have never hurt Nina. All I could muster was a feeble, "I loved . . . I love . . ."

The empty sockets were aligned directly with my own eyes, and now the necrotic body took a seesaw step forward, a gray-knuckled, gavel-shaped hand rose. "Admit that you came back because there was no one left to protect her."

I was still sliding back, unable to take my sight away from the thing shuffling through the snow toward me. I managed, "She doesn't need protection."

Mark's expression changed then, going from cadaverous impassivity to cruel, corkscrew scrutiny. His ruined brow tugged down in a scowl and his black lips contorted in a sneer, causing his gray, decay-dappled skin to crack like the fractured enamel of rotted pottery. "She needs protection from men like *you.*"

And then the taproot-talons of his blunt, hook-fingered hands were springing for me, the frigid, black-nailed appendages falling on my upper arms, my neck. The liquid words came as bubbles bursting in muck. *"I hope . . . you're . . . happy . . ."*

Rigid and dexterous, the frozen fingers constricted like a blood-pressure cuff. It was only for a stretch of seconds, but the compression compelled a sensation not unlike breathlessness—a seemingly unending inhalation. Though still standing upright, in a way I fell backward: the cemetery cranked away like a carousel, and I was speedily assailed by a murky mental passage. My perception rushed through an ocular tunnel, until a murky curtain of jittery images emerged. I saw, then, a night-walled hallway before me—quite literally traveling along a home's corridor; and then a foyer, a front door edged on either side by narrow windows. A surreptitious swoop, and I was peering at the graceless visage of my teenage self, lingering on the Lacefield family's front porch. And then, from the host that housed this vision, a palpitating anger; yet, in the wash of that emotional convolution, I sensed a claustrophobia in Mark, in his awareness that the provincial margins of Crooke's Chapel's one-act play were closing in. He would lose Nina. He would lose Nina to this place's fundamental and painful predictability. And there were other things swimming, suppressed, in Mark's mental darkness. At that moment I thought I understood something of his resentment— for my adolescent caricature, and for the All-American caricature I sensed him playing as well. Through Mark's eyes, I watched Nina tenderly extend the brass key toward me, the keepsake I would, for years, wear on a chain around my neck. A penance.

I wriggled out of its grasp; but my retreat was hindered, seized by the low-lying vines I'd seen extended from the grave— those crawling capillaries an ivy-spool at my ankles. I had two choices (three, really, if you include allowing this ambulatory cop-corpse to embrace me fully). Temporarily dismissing the organic appendages that had coiled over my shins, in a synaptic spasm, I threw a graceless though vicious punch at the Mark/Patrick figure, connecting squarely with its jaw and following through to complete an awkward arc. The sound was grotesque—sinew-lined bone dislodging from insubstantial, flesh-hinged housing, causing the figure to reel backward several paces, enough space for me grapple with the veins at my legs.

I tore at them, ripping and tugging. Almost immediately, a

wailing erupted—in a way, it emerged from the oblong black shape that was the Nolonger's yawning mouth, but worked like a suspended mist: the atmosphere quivering with agony. I winced at a cochlea-piercing scream. And still I tore.

I slithered out of the vessel-like vines, pivoted, and scrambled, picking up speed, sweeping over the snow, dodging headstones as I sprinted down the hill.

My hasty escape lasted merely a few seconds. With the momentum of my slick descent carrying me too quickly, I pitched forward. Realizing I was going to hit hard, my reflex was to break my fall. I brought my arm up in front of me, crossing my sternum, landing squarely against the upper edge of a granite headstone, the impact raggedly fracturing my forearm with a mulchy, meat-muffled *snap*.

You've just imagined my face become a thousand creases of pain, but you may not have yet imagined the howl that pealed from my mouth, the wail as I sailed to the ground, sliding on my side and skidding to a stop. Still screaming, I scrambled, rolling over onto my back. I glanced down at my crooked arm, a broken branch—no: a deserter cradling a crippled rifle. As seconds passed, I grew quieter, and soon it was just my ragged respiration along with the stratus of visible breath it produced above my face.

There came snow-squelching footfalls. Mark's pale face and surgically scooped sockets came up on me. "Shit, man," he said—the words gilded with gravelly giggles. "How in the hell did you manage to do that, champ?" When a hand came down toward me, I closed my eyes. And then the frigid fingers were at my throat, scrabbling at my collarbone. Soon there was a tug as the hand clasped hold of the brass key and yanked the chain off my neck. And then the rigid fingers were withdrawing. I opened my eyes.

Patrick Asher's rodent-esque but wholly living-human face was there, studying me with taunting fascination. In his hand he clutched the key—Nina's key that, somehow, a long time ago, had possessed so much figurative power for Nina and me. I do not have an answer, even here in this written medium, for how he *knew* I'd carried it with me.

Slipping the key into his own pocket, he said, "You know, Spence, I sort of like this story I've been thinking about—the one about the anonymous phone call . . . a no-name drunk injured in the cemetery." Patrick produced the bottle of liquor and slid it into my coat, patting my shoulder tenderly. "See you around, prick."

Footfalls faded. The cruiser's door slammed, the engine wheezed, the tires were crunching snow. And then all the sounds were fading. Cemetery stillness settled in.

I lay there, my dead hand and disfigured arm crossed over my chest as if preparing to make a pledge. Snow fell, landing on my eyelashes and lips before melting. I made an effort to wrench up, slipping my functional hand into my pocket to retrieve my cell phone. I shakily thumbed in Nina's number. The phone rang almost a dozen times before her cheerful voicemail clicked on announcing that she was sorry she'd missed the call. *I'll get back to you as soon as possible . . .*

I tried again. This time there was no ringing as the call skipped directly to the recording. I disconnected the call, but the vapor of Nina's voice hung in the air. *I thought you were someone else*. I heard something then, a furtive shuffling up by the wooded hill near Mark's grave. My heart continued drumming under my ribs but I listened, not with self-seeking sentience, but with the voluntary ear of an initiate. I concentrated on the soft susurration of falling snow—a hissing sibilance that filled the vacant cemetery. And then I was certain that, even in the stillness, the sprawling emptiness was beginning to whisper.

Acknowledgments

"Animalhouse," first published in *Nightscript I*, edited by C. M. Muller (Chthonic Matter Press, 2015).

"By Goats Be Guided," first published in *GNU Journal* (2016).

"Details That Would Otherwise Be Lost to Shadow," first published in *Twice-Told: A Collection of Doubles*, edited by C. M. Muller (Chthonic Matter Press, 2019).

"The Fall of Tomlinson Hall; or, The Ballad of the Butcher's Cart," first published in *Mythic Indy*, edited by Corey Michael Dalton (Punchnel's Publishing, 2015).

"Fiending Apophenia," first published in *Phantasm/Chimera: An Anthology of Strange and Troubling Dreams*, edited by Scott Dwyer (Plutonian Press, 2017).

"Fingers Laced, as Though in Prayer," previously unpublished.

"Haunt Me Still," previously unpublished.

"Her Laugh," first published in *I'll Never Go Away*, edited by Lyle Perez-Tinics and Charlotte Emma Gledson (Rainstorm Press, 2013).

"Knot the Noose," first published in *DM du Jour* (2017).

"Lisa's Pieces," first published in *Apostles of the Weird*, edited by S. T. Joshi (PS Publishing, 2020).

"The Pecking Order," first published in *Weird Fiction Review* No. 8 (2018).

"The Rive," first published in *Xnoybis* No. 1 (Summer 2015).

"The Undertow, and They That Dwell Therein," first published in *Nightscript III*, edited by C. M. Muller (Chthonic Matter Press, 2017).

CPSIA information can be obtained
at www.ICGtesting.com
Printed in the USA
LVHW051512251120
672679LV00016B/1438

9 781614 982869